ONLY THE DEAD

OTHER BOOKS BY BEN SANDERS

The Fallen

By Any Means

BEN SANDERS

ONLY THE DEAD

HarperCollins*Publishers*

HarperCollins*Publishers*

This edition published in 2013
by HarperCollins*Publishers (New Zealand) Limited*
PO Box 1, Shortland Street, Auckland 1140

Copyright © Ben Sanders 2013

Ben Sanders asserts the moral right to be identified as the author of this work.

All rights reserved. No part of this publication may be reproduced, stored
in a retrieval system or transmitted in any form or by any means, electronic,
mechanical, photocopying, recording or otherwise, without the prior written
permission of the publishers.

HarperCollins*Publishers*
Unit D, 63 Apollo Drive, Rosedale, Auckland 0632, New Zealand
Level 13, 201 Elizabeth Street, Sydney, NSW 2000, Australia
A 53, Sector 57, Noida, UP, India
77–85 Fulham Palace Road, London W6 8JB, United Kingdom
2 Bloor Street East, 20th floor, Toronto, Ontario M4W 1A8, Canada
195 Broadway, New York, NY 10007, USA

National Library of New Zealand Cataloguing-in-Publication Data

Sanders, Ben, 1989-
Only the dead / Ben Sanders.
ISBN 978-1-77554-005-2
I. Title.
NZ823.3—dc 23

ISBN: 978 1 77554 005 2

Cover design by Jane Waterhouse, HarperCollins Design Studio
Handcuffs by Yasuhide Fumoto/Getty Images; all other images by
shutterstock.com
Typesetting by Springfield West

Printed in Australia by McPhersons Printing Group

The papers used by HarperCollins in the manufacture of this book are a
natural, recyclable product made from wood grown in sustainable plantation
forests. The fibre source and manufacturing processes meet recognised
international environmental standards, and carry certification.

*Dedicated to my grandmother,
Ray McKitterick —
one of Sean's first and finest friends.*

'Death solves all problems. No man, no problem.'

— Stalin

▪ Prologue

MONDAY, 30 JANUARY, 6.00 A.M.

Sunrise and a nil body count: maybe they'd dodged a bad ending.

The officer leaned the rifle against the doorframe and stepped outside to the porch. A seam of orange traced the eastern horizon; the west in stark two-tone where a jigsaw edge of rooflines met pale sky. He pulled the door behind him and squeaked across tired boards to the front yard. Summer, but firearm concealment necessitated heavy clothing. A sweater hid a Glock 17 and a full backup clip.

West Auckland, a cul-de-sac south of Swanson Road. Single-level weatherboard shoulder to shoulder behind gap-toothed timber fencing. A light breeze, a chittered birdsong overture.

He moved out to the kerb and checked the road. A Toyota crewcab pickup sat a hundred and fifty metres west, a gold Nissan Maxima one-fifty east. A scatter of lit windows in an otherwise dark backdrop.

He walked east, towards the Nissan. He was fresh to this line of work. His first protection detail, his first shot at clearing a street. He was the subordinate half of a two-man team: guard duty for some shitbag armed robber turned police informant. This morning's briefing: keep the casualty tally at zero, and don't attract attention.

Fifty metres out from the Nissan. The sunrise backlit the interior: he could see a shape at the wheel, immobile, shawled by dark. He made an idle survey. All alone in those young hours. A ragged queue of wheelie bins clogged the kerb. He fingered the Glock. Thirty metres out. No mistaking it: there was a guy in the driver's seat of the Maxima. Potential threat, or dawn commuter? Maybe nothing at all. Maybe paranoia had a lot to answer for. He kept going. Turning back would be a giveaway. All he could do was continue past and loop back later.

Twenty metres from the Nissan, and he heard the Toyota's engine start, two hundred and eighty metres away, back along the street. He turned and saw the waft of exhaust, a faint stain high on that pale morning. The truck paused there at the kerb, then crawled towards him, eastbound, smoke at its heels.

He watched it for a second. It moved slowly, lights off. That alone felt wrong. Realisation hit with a dose of gut-chill: he hadn't heard the driver get in.

Don't attract attention.

Panic quashed the order. He drew the gun. A backwards glance at the Nissan, and then he was at full sprint towards the house, head pounding with the rush.

The truck didn't hurry. The officer made it to the porch by the time the Toyota swung in off the street and mounted the kerb into the yard. He snatched a glimpse across his shoulder — two guys hunched side by side, open windows, a shotgun peeping above the passenger wing mirror.

He took brief aim and fired. The Glock's mechanism jammed. He tripped and scrambled for the door, hands and knees, heard the roar as the passenger's first round hit him: the shotgun, one barrel, a half-load of buckshot to the shoulder blade. The impact tossed him prone and sent the gun skittering.

He gasped and made a one-arm stretch for safety. The truck

lurched short against its brake. Doors slamming as the two guys jumped clear, the noise amplified and terrifying. The door of the house opened before he reached it, the second officer framed in the open space. A pause, and then the passenger triggered his second round. Woodwork exploded, mute beneath the blast. Blood spray fanned wide. The second officer collapsed back inside, over the threshold. The first officer made a lunge for the entry and got an arm around the rifle propped against the frame. An awkward one-hand grip, a desperate twist, a squeeze of the trigger.

The round went high and left. It hit the windscreen of the Toyota. Crack scribbles splayed wide. The guys from the truck were metres away: he saw dark denim, balaclavas, a shotgun apiece. The driver's weapon butt to shoulder: a second's glimpse of those twin black barrels, and then the flash.

One hundred and fifty metres east, the man in the Nissan started his engine and began a slow approach. An Ithaca 10-gauge shotgun stood propped in the passenger footwell, a fresh box of shells agape and aromatic on the seat beside him.

Birdsong silent now, sparrows long since flown. Cordite stench, random flits of yellow as windows lit in random sequence. Gunshots keeping the curious indoors. The Nissan driver watched the men from the Toyota enter the house, the dead policemen in crimson repose on the threshold. More gunshots: assault rifle chatter, a deadened crash of another shotgun round.

The Nissan reached the house. The driver ripped the brake and climbed out, gun in hand. He wore a tan leather jacket zipped chin-high, ski goggles over a black balaclava. He entered the yard: tidy frontage turned scarlet homicide tableau. Spent shells here and there: bright twisted husks of plastic smoking faintly. He stooped and gathered them, collected the dropped

Glock and freed the jammed round. He checked his watch. Time elapsed: two minutes since first shot fired. The Toyota's rough diesel idle lonely in the brutal quiet.

He jogged back to the Nissan and slid in, cut a hard U-turn to get the car facing back east. People were watching now. Curtains twitching, panicked calls being placed. He dropped his window to pick up siren noise, reached across and popped the rear door. The shotgun was across his knees, the dead cop's Glock on the seat adjacent.

Another minute. He kept his eyes with his watch, split seconds accruing at breakneck pace. The two guys exited the house: full sprint, it's all go, police response imminent. They jumped in, shaky and breathless with the post-murder rush. A light blood mist flecked their jackets. Across the street, a woman risked a glance above a kitchen windowsill. The driver saw her. He made a gun from a gloved hand and finger-shot her as they pulled away.

■ ONE

Monday, 13 February, 11.58 a.m.

Tennis and iced water. He could think of worse ways to start the week.

John Hale sat in a deckchair beneath an umbrella and watched a heated backyard match unfold: prospective client Alan Rowe versus a woman Hale thought might be a girlfriend. The girlfriend could play. Rowe couldn't. He wasn't happy about it — hence the 'heated'.

The water was purportedly Evian, but he didn't know about the ice. Hale took a sip and watched another point. Rowe countered crisp groundstrokes with awkward lobs. He scrambled for a shot down the left tramline and swiped desperately. A big slow return peaked enticingly over centre court. The woman scuttled in under it and arched back. She threw up an index finger to track the drop and cracked a massive forehand smash. The ball skipped off the backline and lodged in the mesh of the rear fence with a chime like dropped keys.

Rowe swore on expelled breath. He wasn't a tennis build. He wasn't a tennis age, either. Five-six and stocky, pushing sixty. Midday heat and a sound thrashing had soaked his shirt see-through.

Rowe looked at her and hooked a grin. 'Jesus, love.'

He got a teasing giggle back. 'Don't be such a fart.'

Hale said, 'I hope you didn't get me out here just to watch you get thumped.'

The jibe stung: Rowe dropped his racquet and kicked it tumbling. He walked over and plucked the trapped ball free. The fence clicked him with a jolt of static when he touched it. 'You can toddle off home if you want,' he said. 'Otherwise suck it up and I might have some work for you.'

A retort formed, but Hale kept it tethered. It was a Remuera address, money and big trees aplenty. The fenced-off court paralleled a breeze-dimpled lap pool. A two-metre stone wall marked the boundary. The house was white, 'fifties vintage and two-storey, one corner overshadowed by a thick elm. A heavy suit-clad minder lurked hands in pockets behind French doors. Behind him, a massive flat screen TV reeled sports highlights. Remuera: old money, modern comforts.

The Evian was in a sweating pitcher on a low table beside Hale's chair. The sun umbrella cast a big oval of shade. Rowe pocketed the freed ball and scuffed his way over. He levelled up a wide tumbler, killed three quarters of it in one hit, flicked the dregs in a deft slash across the court.

He said, 'I know a couple of guys like you.'

'Like me how?'

He put the glass down. His opponent was nailing fake serves to stay warm. He admired a few before replying. 'Cops and ex-cops. I was told you were a good sort of guy to talk to.'

Hale smiled. 'I feel like we're kind of dodging the point here.'

Rowe thumbed a streak in the pitcher sweat. 'She's just about closed the set. Why don't you give it a couple more minutes, then we can take this indoors maybe.'

'Sooner rather than later would be great.'

'You have another appointment?'

'Not to hurry you along.'

Rowe shrugged. He looked across the court towards the pool. 'There're some people I'd like you to find.'

Progress. 'What sort of people?'

'You keep up with the news?'

Hale didn't answer.

'It's tied up with this heist shit,' Rowe said.

Heist shit: an ongoing armed robbery spate, dating back to October. The scorecard thus far: a bank hold-up that had left a teller dead and netted forty thousand dollars; an armoured van takedown that had profited another fifteen or twenty grand; a robbery of an amateur fight club premises — tiny takings, but seven people assaulted.

'The police are still involved,' Hale said. 'You need to talk to them.'

'That's why I got in touch with you.'

'I quit, though, so I'm not that useful.'

Rowe didn't answer. He walked away and picked up his spurned racquet. He raised it face level and spread his hand across the strings, clicked them back into alignment with clawed fingertips. The woman swung through on another serve. A gleaming sweat sheen shook free in sprinkle form.

'What's your interest in it?' Hale said.

'What do you mean?'

'Why do you want to find who's responsible?'

'Someone's dead. Do you need a better excuse?'

'This is an active police investigation. As much as they like me, they won't want me treading on their toes.'

'Can't you work *with* them?'

'That's not really their policy.'

'They can make exceptions.'

'Not really. We play on different sides of the court, if you will.'

'What does that mean?'

'Some of my practices are unique.'

'I can live with that.'

'The police can't. And that's speaking from experience.'

Rowe didn't answer. He turned away and loaded a serve of his own. The build-up looked good. He hunched into a strangle on the racquet and rocked back and forth a couple of times, prepping the release. He tossed up the ball and swung through and skied it off the frame. The racquet hummed with the reverb: he raised it up and slammed it against the ground. The bounce carried it head-high.

'Sweetie, you've got to toss it forward more.'

Rowe shushed her with a hand-flap. He looked at Hale.

'I didn't say you had to piggyback on their work. Either you're interested, or you're not.'

Hale smiled. He felt the carefully researched Alan Rowe back story becoming increasingly pertinent.

Hale said, 'You're a criminal defence lawyer.'

'Was. Not for a while, though.'

'Head Hunters gang had you on retainer for eight years.'

Rowe said nothing.

'That was the rumour, anyway,' Hale said.

'Who'd you get that from?'

Hale shrugged. 'Doesn't matter. They're not the sort of clients that endear you to law enforcement.'

'I don't think my past associations should be any of your business,' Rowe said. 'Alleged or otherwise.'

Hale reached over and topped up his water. Nice and slow, to keep the ice in the jug. 'I'd just like to know why you want to find these people.'

'Think of it as my gift to society.'

'Gang lawyer turned Good Samaritan doesn't really ring true.'

Rowe laughed. He folded his arms and propped his hip against the net post. He pulled one foot to tiptoe and crossed his legs. 'Look,' he said. 'I had you checked out, you seem okay.'

'Well, good.'

'But maybe you should just tell me exactly what it is you're uncomfortable about, before we take this any further.'

'All due respect, I don't think we're going to take this any further.'

'Humour me.'

Hale downed his drink, cradled the empty glass in his lap. He said, 'There's good money out and about and unaccounted for. Either you're after it because you're dead keen to get it back to where it came from, or you've got some other angle going.'

'Like Good Samaritan turned plain arsehole.'

'I was thinking more criminal defence lawyer turned criminal.'

A heavy stare. Hale held it for a solid four-count. Rowe broke it first. 'Maybe watch your mouth next time you go visiting,' he said. He let a smile flicker. 'You see the guy in there?'

Hale glanced towards the French doors. The man in the suit was still lurking.

'Used to be a boxer. He fought pro for a while. Got invited to go up against Sugar Ray Leonard.'

'What does he fight now? Other than prostate trouble?'

Rowe didn't answer. He pushed off the post and walked away. The woman was spot-jogging near the far fence. Hale stood up and brushed creases out of his shirtfront.

'Thank you for the offer, Mr Rowe, but I think I'm going to have to decline. If you've got any further details you'd like to give me, you've got my number.'

He let himself out via a gate in the fence. The French doors opened, and the minder stepped aside to let him pass.

■ TWO

MONDAY, 13 FEBRUARY, 4.29 P.M.

Sean Devereaux in the back of an unmarked patrol car, two uniformed officers up front, framing a windscreen view.

South Auckland, a quiet street east of Clendon Park. They were serving as light backup for nearby surveillance work, heavy backup a five-man Armed Offenders Squad a little further up the block. The target was high value hence the heavy support, hence the terse pre-op briefing, courtesy of Detective Inspector Alan Nielsen: 'Do it fast, and don't fuck it up.'

The radio unit on the dash chirped status codes from the two-man tactical team doing the real work. It was a two-phase operation: phase one a covert garage entry at the target address, phase two installation of a GPS unit on the suspect's vehicle. In and out, no fuss. The danger lay in the fact that if the car was home, the owner could be too.

Devereaux squirmed. Lookout duty wasn't his forte. Sit-about stints numbed him. Normally, he could avoid them, but his involvement in the bank and armoured van investigations had secured him a ride-along. He'd tried to opt out, tested his luck with an eloquent excuse: 'I think it would be a more effective allocation of labour if I were to continue with my regular investigative duties.' Nielsen's reply: 'Put it in writing, sergeant. Right now, suck it up and get going.'

He tried to focus on the radio commentary. It was hard work; the young guns up front were trading arrest stories: '... stopped this douche bag up on Weymouth. He was ten k's over the limit, so we pulled up behind and I'm all like, "You were speeding," and he totally flipped out and got out of his car, and I told him to back off, but the stupid prick didn't, wasn't even talking English at me, he was like yammering in Asian or something, so we ended up pepper spraying him. He went totally mental, ended up in ER. Fucking hilarious.'

They sat and laughed. Devereaux reached over and cracked a window. Across the street a woman was assembling a planter box out of timber.

Driver to passenger: 'What do you reckon she's up to?'

'Making a garden thing, probably.'

'Looks like a coffin.'

'Yeah, kind of. She's made it family-sized.'

'You reckon she's topped her family?'

'Maybe. Folks get up to all sorts down here, I tell you.'

Devereaux eyed the back of the guy's head. The passenger seemed to feel the weight of the attention on his skull. He spun the mirror so he and Devereaux were eye to eye.

'Do you like being a detective?' the kid said.

'Excuse me?'

The guy looked confused. Devereaux twirled an index finger. The penny dropped: 'Do you like being a detective, *sir*?'

'Yes. Sorry, what was your name?'

'O'Neil.'

'Yes, Constable O'Neil, I do enjoy being a detective. Also I notice we were fifteen over the limit the whole way here, so if you could grab me the pepper spray it would be much appreciated.'

They fell quiet. Devereaux leaned forward and plucked wet

shirt off his back. He needed a cigarette. The pack in his pocket was fully loaded and ready for consumption: Marlboros, tight against the pocket lining, like a kid's face on the shop glass.

The two guys in the front exchanged glances.

'Sorry,' the driver said. 'Some guys just kinda, you know. We're not that formal with them.'

'We'll call it even. I didn't know you guys were arseholes.'

No reply. They faced forward and shut up. He spread his arms full-wingspan across the top of the seats and watched the street. It was grime-smeared residential, light wind presiding, gangly tree shadows listless in the heat. The radio blipped in with nothing-updates: the target vehicle was parked in the driveway, not the garage; there was nobody around; it looked all clear; they were under the vehicle; they'd begun installing the device—

The transmission cut. They lost the guy mid-sentence. Dead air stretched out.

Devereaux leaned forward. 'Radio them back and see what's happening.'

The driver thumbed his shoulder mic, ducked his chin and requested a repeat on the last transmission. No response. More unacknowledged chatter as the Armed Offenders Squad sent out a similar request.

'Keep trying until they come back on line,' Devereaux said.

The driver keyed his shoulder mic again and requested a situation report. No reply, nothing on the dashboard unit. He repeated the message, got an identical result. The passenger propped his elbow on the sill and thumbed his lip.

'Head along up the street,' Devereaux said. 'We'll see what's up. Tell AOS to hold, we don't need a scene.'

The driver did as directed. Planter box woman's gaze panned with them as they passed. The target address was less than a minute away, a two-storey weatherboard shielded by one right turn. Up the street, the driver of the AOS truck flicked a peace sign out his window. They swung into the street just as the radio cut back in: 'Ten-ten, repeat, we are ten-ten.'

Urgent assistance required. Come bail us out.

'Ah, shit.' The kid's eyes in the mirror, before Devereaux was yelling at him to hit it, and he nailed the gas pedal.

The car lurched under the dose of throttle, the guys up front ducked to dash level to gauge progress, Devereaux braced door to door against the cornering forces. The passenger radioing the AOS team to roll.

The driver overshot his mark and stomped the brake. They thumped to a standstill. Devereaux snapped forward, lap belt cinching deep. They were skewed across the centre of the street, rubber smoking in thin twists. A dull pop as the boot released, ragged door slams as the guys up front beelined for the gun safe in back. Devereaux unclicked and slid out, saw the house twenty metres back along the street, the car in the driveway, blood daubs on the concrete.

'Oh, shit, someone's bleeding.'

The driver who'd spoken. The two uniforms had formed up in the street, shaky assault rifles to shoulder, sighted in on the house. A screech as the AOS team pulled up behind them. Devereaux rounded the rear of the car. The gun safe had been pillaged: one measly Glock the price for being third. Shaky fingers liberated it from its foam recess. A full clip: he drew a bead on the pavement to check the sights, jacked a round into the chamber.

The house was off-white, a garage adjacent spilling a strip of driveway to the kerb. The front door hung wide. He led with the gun and approached at a sprint, dizzy under the adrenaline hit. The two kids tailing him either side. AOS way back, the sergeant screaming for them to let his team in first to clear the premises. Devereaux had no hope of hearing: adrenaline rush swamped all.

The car's bonnet was up, he dropped to a duck-walk and checked beneath the chassis. A loose bundle of limp leads, a huge arcing slash of blood leading away from it towards the house. The downslope edge beaded with a thin wave. A wail from the house, frantic ten-ten pleadings from the shoulder mics of the two guys riding his heels.

Across the open yard and straight in the front door. Glock first, muzzle twitchy, trigger finger tight. One surveillance guy crumpled foetal in the entry, a mangled bicep leaking scarlet through clawed fingers. A whimper, and then crinkled eye contact. Devereaux stormed through. Stairs branched left and up, bloodstains on the treads like pursed lips, beckoning come hither. He jumped them two at a time and made the upstairs hallway, fanned the Glock in a shaky one-eighty to cover each direction. To the right: an open bathroom door, the second surveillance officer propped against mildewed tilework. Torso slumped, legs askew. The floor a bloody hand-smear collage. A deep leg gash leaking steady.

He heard Devereaux. A pummelled head raised from an exhausted slouch, a mumble on shiny lips as Devereaux entered the room, gun raised. A heavy sideways pan of the guy's gaze stopped him dead, right there on the threshold. A pause within that frantic, frantic moment. He tracked the fallen officer's line of sight.

Just do it.

He whipped left, a sharp ninety-degree turn, fired three times point blank through the door, wrist snapping back under the force. Dead shells arced and flipped, tinkling. Woodchips rode the cordite bloom and bit his cheeks. A man with a machete fell sideways from his position behind the door, two bullet holes through his stomach. He clutched himself, gasping, and thumped against the wall. A scream, a broken slash of red against the paintwork as he slid to the floor.

More backup arrived: another AOS team diverted off a nearby callout, and a roving patrol unit that had caught the ten-ten. Ample support to cover first aid. He sat on the landing and fought dizziness as the tension backed off, gun still in hand. He racked the slide to clear the chambered round. It rolled clear and toddled its way down the stairs. He watched its escape, gentle brushes of passing thighs against his shoulder preventing a total daze. Paramedics arrived, clipped directives in the face of carnage. Clatters and dull thumps as stretchers and first-aid kits ascended the stairs.

Someone tapped his shoulder. He spun and saw a female constable looking down at him.

'Sergeant, maybe you should give me your gun.'

He handed it over. She took it gingerly. Two fingers only, like something tainted. He caught a glimpse back through the bathroom door: the cop's blood everywhere, the cop himself looking well south of normal. An ambulance guy trying to raise a vein to put in an IV line. Machete man, prone on his back, getting oxygen via a mask.

A sudden, whispered prayer: *Please don't die.*

They sealed the street and took preliminary statements. Witness accounts came replete with big hand gestures and hyperbole. Wild-eyed bystanders drank in sordid hearsay. Devereaux watched it all from the back seat of a patrol car. The wounded officers were gone — stabilised, then whisked to hospital, good health pending.

Staying calm was proving hard. His victim had left the scene in full crisis regalia: mask, stretcher and IV. The cigarette box was biting his thigh — he'd shoot the guy again for just one puff. He freed the pack from his pocket and tossed it on the seat beside him. A taunt from arm's length, dog pulled up short before the bone.

He tipped his head against the glass to catch a glimpse of what was happening inside. No luck. Plastic evidence markers picked out driveway blood spatter. Reporters were clustered at the cordon. Stoic uniforms fended questions with stern replies of 'No comment'. He fidgeted. This was a fresh perspective for him. He was death's inside man. Prior homicide experience was from the other side of the glass. He kept his gaze on the front door and saw the senior on-scene detective walk out towards the street, phone raised to his face, mouth rigid. The receiving end of a one-sided chat. Devereaux didn't want to look concerned, leaned back in his seat to evince calm.

The guy came around the rear of the car and slid in next to Devereaux. The phone snapped closed in sync with his door slam.

'Sorry we've kept you so long.'

'How is he?'

'Which one?'

'The one I shot.'

The guy tapped the phone against his thigh. 'You got him twice. He lost some blood.'

'So did one of our guys.'

'Yeah. I know.'

'What's damaged?'

'Tilework, plaster.'

'No. Like, what happened to the guy I gave two rounds to?'

'I don't know. I guess they'll find out.'

'But he's breathing?'

'Yeah.'

'So then what's the deal? Let me—'

'We've got to take you in, do it all properly.' He paused. 'Nothing to worry about yet but, you know. We've got to do it formally. Maybe get a lawyer on the phone.'

Not bad advice. But, shit, it sounded bad. Worry oozed afresh: suspension, dismissal, manslaughter charge, in ascending degree of severity.

'Is anyone dead?'

A placating smile. 'No. Nobody's dead.'

He sighed — a held breath he didn't know he had.

'Are you okay?' the guy said.

'I never hurt anyone that badly.'

'I wouldn't worry. It'll probably be fine.'

'I hope so. "Not fine" is definitely worth worrying about.'

'He had a record, if it makes it any better.'

'It doesn't. It shouldn't. In fact, I think it'll probably make things worse.'

The guy didn't seem to understand. Devereaux looked away. The window was discoloured in a ring where his forehead had stamped it. Sweaty whorls cast by frown lines. 'Get out,' he said. 'You're sitting on my cigarettes.'

■ THREE

Monday, 13 February, 5.16 p.m.

Mitch Duvall met Don McCarthy at a café on High Street, just south of Vulcan Lane, and sat him down with takeaway coffee at a metal table outside. The street at that point was a narrow channel of masonry façades, random human eddies as people dodged glacial one-way traffic.

The Don wasn't a talker. Not much on offer other than a 'Hi' and a handshake.

Duvall tabled a soft icebreaker. 'I probably could have found something closer to the station for you, save you coming all the way down here.'

He was all nerves: a stutter doubled up his S's. McCarthy pretended not to notice, and shrugged it off. He sat sideways in his seat, his back to the wall. 'What can I do for you?'

Duvall took a breath to find even keel. 'I just wanted to follow up our conversation from last week.'

No reply. The Don was renowned as a consummate hard-arse. Grey crew cut, grey suit, and a grey disposition to match. Mitch had done some research. He'd unearthed some great Don-related rumours: he was reputed to carry brass knuckles and a .380 ankle gun; he'd faced an assault charge after beating a rape suspect; his torso bore embedded bullet fragments.

'You'll have to jog my memory,' McCarthy said.

Duvall read it as a lie. Legend held that nothing slipped past The Don. He observed the world with an outwardly flat disinterest that captured all.

'The robbery stuff,' Duvall said.

The Don sampled his coffee. A small mouthful, swallowed on a grimace. 'My position hasn't changed since we last spoke. I'm not prepared to grant you access to active police files.'

'I used to be a detective.'

'I prefer to deal with people who still are.'

'I just want to look at the files.'

McCarthy's cup made a click as he placed it on the table. He spun it with two fingers so that the label faced him square. He said, 'How old are you?'

'I'm fifty-two.'

He smiled. 'Year younger than me. Do you get offended easily?'

'I'm sorry?'

'I said, do you get offended easily?'

'I don't see what that has to do with anything.'

'I have thirty people younger and better than you, younger and better than me maybe, working this.'

Duvall drank coffee while he schemed a comeback. He could see a gridlocked slice of rush-hour Queen Street a block over, the foreground a clutter of Vulcan Lane restaurant patrons, taking in wine and late sun. He gambled, and went in strong: 'Why didn't you release a statement confirming the thing on January thirty was related to the robberies?'

The Don smiled: an expo of perfect dentistry. 'The "thing on January thirty"? We're talking multiple homicide.'

No denial. Duvall kept momentum. 'Multiple homicide nobody can attribute to anything because the police haven't issued any details.'

'That's not uncommon.'

'It leaves people free to speculate.'

'Not uncommon either.'

'Media reports said both officers and civilians were killed.'

'I don't want to comment on the issue.'

'That's okay. I just want to run something past you.'

'Please do.'

'All this robbery stuff dates back months. The Auckland Savings and Loan was back in October, the armoured van thing November, that fight club in January. Everything's gone quiet, makes people think you're getting nowhere.'

The Don said nothing. His legs were crossed ankle-on-ankle, stretched towards the kerb.

Duvall leaned in for a glimpse of the fabled .380. No luck. He said, 'January thirtieth, you've got a multiple homicide out West Auckland, neighbours are phoning in reports of what sounds like a shotgun.'

'So you read the paper.'

'I read between the lines.'

'Oh, yes?'

'Dead cops plus a dead civilian sounds a lot to me like botched witness protection.'

The Don linked his fingers in his lap. He was causing a pedestrian snarl-up, a bottleneck where people were forced to queue single file to get past his feet.

Duvall ploughed on. Toe-to-toe with McCarthy wasn't easy. He felt his shirt clinging. He leaned in across the table to boost emphasis. 'The homicides on January thirtieth are tied up with the robbery jobs.'

The Don said, 'And?'

'And it's not the sort of thing you want newspapers getting hold of.'

McCarthy laughed. 'They're not stupid. They'll have that theory already.'

'They haven't printed it. They might feel more inclined to if they have someone like me endorsing it.'

An eyebrow jerk: 'Someone like you?'

'A former police officer.'

McCarthy took his second mouthful of coffee. 'I'm glad you got me down here,' he said. 'Even if it was just for the latte.' He swilled his cup with fingertip pressure and mused. 'How long were you in for?' he said.

'Seventeen years.'

'Why did you leave?'

'I wanted to go private.'

He rocked sideways in his seat and pulled his investigator's ID from his hip pocket, like confirming he'd made good on his plan. McCarthy leaned in across the table and took it from him, perused it at arm's length, thumb propping the leather holder. He let it fall closed with a gentle clap and tossed it back across the table.

He said, 'Was it worth it?'

Duvall pocketed the holder. 'Going private?'

'Yeah.'

'I thought I might make more money.'

'And did you?'

'No.'

The Don's mouth dropped at the edges, like he'd banked on hearing something else. Another sip of coffee. He twisted in his seat and looked up at the wall behind him, maybe checking shadow height. A kid on a skateboard ran his mouth and told him to shift his feet. The Don gave him the finger: point and shoot without even thinking. He said, 'How long are we going to keep this little dance up?'

'What do you mean?'

'You ringing me. Me talking to you. You asking for access. Me denying.'

'Don't know. I kind of figured you would have relented by now.'

McCarthy laughed. 'If that's the case you should have done some better research.'

Duvall didn't answer. McCarthy's jacket hummed dully. He removed a cellphone and scanned a text message. Jaw flex hinted at bad news. He stood up. Duvall gauged his coffee as half full.

'You can come see me tomorrow. Nine a.m. If you don't make it, don't bother trying to set up another meeting. Pray I don't manage to dig up any shit on you, or you won't make it past the front desk. And don't go running your mouth to anyone you shouldn't.'

Duvall smiled. 'What sort of people should I not be running my mouth to?'

The Don looked out across the street. 'Put it this way: before you say anything to anybody, just ask yourself, what would my friend Don think, if he knew what I was up to? Okay?'

He dipped a hand in a jacket pocket. 'That was good coffee. Have a business card.' He flipped it off his thumb like a coin, dropped it fluttering in Duvall's lap.

'I appreciate it.'

McCarthy didn't answer.

Duvall said, 'Can I ask you a question?'

'Go.'

'I was told you've got bullet fragments in you.'

The Don said nothing. He walked away down Vulcan Lane, swallowed whole by traffic.

■ FOUR

Monday, 13 February, 6.00 p.m.

They drove him to Manukau Police HQ up on Wiri Station Road. A uniform served as chauffeur. He had more sense than to try to chat. Devereaux made calls on the way. He dialled John Hale and left a message, dialled his girlfriend but hung up when her voicemail kicked in. There was no way to sugar-coat 'I shot a guy'.

He called a Police Association representative and explained the situation. He was told someone would be there to meet him when he reached the station. He arrived at six-ten. He was feeling better. The drive time had let his nerves cool. Rationale and self-confidence were curing the initial fear.

The uniform found a park in the on-site lot and escorted him through to the Criminal Investigation Branch. A desk sergeant misread nicotine deprivation as anxiety: don't worry/ everything's fine/sit down and make yourself comfortable.

They led him through to an interview room. Two chairs and a table, walls within spitting distance. A female uniformed sergeant occupied one of the chairs, a binder and a sheaf of paper in front of her. She looked up and smiled. His Police Association rep.

'That was quick. I only called twenty minutes ago.'

She smiled. 'I was in the building.'

They shook hands and swapped intro lines. Her name was Charlotte Greer. She said she'd been a barrister with Crown Law. She was older than him, maybe forty. She looked nervous. Not a good look for a lawyer, flustered and laden with documents. He preferred calm with minimal paperwork, salient details memorised.

He pulled out the second chair and sat down across from her.

'Sorry,' she said. 'I haven't done this before. Well, post-shooting stuff.'

Hence the baggage.

'Don't worry. I have.'

Her eyebrows rose. 'You've had a firearms incident before?'

'I shot a guy a couple of years back. Not this bad, though.'

'Did he make it?'

'Yeah. I think he wished he hadn't.'

She didn't know what to say to that. She glanced down at her notes. 'Run me through what happened.'

He gave her a ten-minute rehash of the afternoon. She jotted in pencil.

'Did you give verbal warning?'

'Excuse me?'

'Before you opened fire. Did you give verbal warning?'

'No, I didn't.'

'It might be a problem. If you've got a history of this sort of thing, they might try to argue it was premeditated.'

'It can't be premeditated. I had two seconds' notice.'

'I mean they might argue you approached the situation with an intention to shoot.'

He didn't answer. The desk sergeant rapped on the door and asked Devereaux to step outside. He stood up. Greer gathered notes.

'I don't want you in the interview,' he said.

'Sorry?'

'You said you haven't done this before. It's a shooting. No offence, I don't want to be your guinea pig.'

'You don't want help?'

'Not right now. Don't worry. Like I said, I've done this before.'

The interview room was a dour-looking set-up. Men in dark suits, three-across behind a boardroom table. Ties and top buttons, present and correct. Pens poised over blank pads. Devereaux took a seat opposite and eyed the panel. Left to right: Detective Inspector Lloyd Bowen, the new Auckland Central Serious Crimes Squad boss and Devereaux's immediate superior; Detective Inspector Don 'The Don' McCarthy, Manukau CIB; one of The Don's lackeys, Detective Sergeant Frank Briar, a longtime staunch proponent of McCarthyism.

The Don looked pissed off. He said, 'You stuffed that up pretty neatly.'

'Are we on record?'

'Yes, we are.'

'With all due respect, I don't feel it's appropriate that this investigation should be conducted by officers I've had regular contact with.'

Bowen said, 'Sergeant, this isn't an investigation. We're merely trying to establish the details of what occurred this afternoon.'

The guy had a faint Afrikaans inflection, a soft rolling of the r's. He was early forties, younger than McCarthy, probably five years shy of Briar. Clipped and square: a real hard edge of a man.

'It just concerns me that Inspector McCarthy would offer such a prejudicial remark.'

Glances bounced back and forth. Bowen said, 'Inspector McCarthy will endeavour not to interject in such a fashion.'

Devereaux didn't answer. The room was windowless. A whiteboard occupied the wall behind them, ceiling lights watery inside the gloss.

Bowen said, 'Tell us what happened.'

He did. He laid out the key events: 4.29 in the afternoon until whatever time the constable had taken his gun off him on the stairs. They listened silently, gazes shifting to track scribbled notes.

Bowen said, 'What was the purpose of the operation?'

'I thought you'd been kept in the loop?'

'Just for the record.'

'I thought this was off the record?'

'Sergeant, humour me.'

'We were providing backup for a surveillance team.'

'Who was the target?'

'Someone wanted in relation to the armoured van robbery back in November.'

He recited the file number for Bowen's reference.

'Why was this operation being conducted at four in the afternoon and not four in the morning?'

'Because I wasn't the officer in charge.'

'Alan Nielsen was coordinating. Is that correct?'

'In theory.'

Bowen glanced across at The Don. McCarthy said, 'You had a specialist Armed Offenders Squad team providing additional support. Why were they not first on scene?'

'Because I beat them there.'

'You didn't wait for them to clear the house first?'

'No.'

'Why not?'

'I felt it imprudent to dilly-dally.'

Nobody replied.

Bowen paused and skimmed his notes. 'So your understanding of the situation is that while installing a GPS unit on the suspect's vehicle, your surveillance team was confronted by the suspect, who then assaulted them with a machete?'

'That's right.'

'But you felt you were capable of handling the situation better than your specialist armed backup.'

'Given my position I felt I could do it quicker. Not necessarily to a higher standard.'

Bowen looked at him. Devereaux sensed a set-piece being schemed. 'Okay,' Bowen said, 'Run us through it again. When you entered the house, you followed the stairs up to the second level, entered the bathroom, and discharged your weapon three times, blind, through a partially open door.'

'That's correct.'

'And as a result the suspect was struck twice in the torso?'

'I believe so.'

'Do you believe that in this situation you acted in an appropriate manner, with regard to the guidelines stipulated by Police Standard Operating Procedure?'

'Yes, I do.'

Bowen flicked through some papers, looked up like something had just occurred to him. 'Sergeant, just a side note: am I correct in saying you're currently considering leaving the police?'

'Where did you hear that from?'

'I don't recall. But is that the case?'

Don't recall. He'd voiced it calmly, but there wasn't a flake of truth to it. Devereaux said, 'No, that's not correct.'

'You have no intention of ending your employment?'

'That's correct.'

Bowen showed no reaction. A brief quiet settled gently as he reviewed his notes. He looked up and said, 'Can you outline the basis of your reasoning in choosing to discharge a firearm with neither verbal warning nor a visual fix?'

'My reasoning was that if I didn't shoot, someone could end up dead.'

Frank Briar said, 'That might still be the case.'

Devereaux didn't answer. He knew a bit about the man: the divorces, the four excessive force accusations, the liquor issues, the cardiac trouble. Whether by design or intention, his job had walled out every other element of his life. Twenty years of drugs and homicide didn't leave room for much else. He was bloodshot and unshaven, curled hair mussed. He looked worse than his own back story.

Briar said, 'There a problem?'

Devereaux let the question hang a second. He said, 'I was just trying to think why you might be in here. But I can't think of a single reason.'

Briar smiled. 'How about the fact I've never fucked anything up as badly as you just did?'

Devereaux didn't answer. Bowen and McCarthy pretended they hadn't heard, wrote in silence. Devereaux stood up. He dropped his hands in his pockets, trying to look unfazed.

'I didn't realise we were done,' Bowen said.

Devereaux tucked his chair in. 'If I don't have a cigarette I'm going to shoot someone else,' he said.

None of them smiled. The Don's stare burrowed straight to the marrow. Bowen clicked his pen closed and gave him the magic words: 'Don't leave town, sergeant. And answer your phone. We'll pick this up later.'

■ FIVE

Monday, 13 February, 6.58 p.m.

Smokeless for nearly three hours. Devereaux lit a cigarette on the way out the front door. He drew some glances, sensed people wanting to stop and chat. A look of stern preoccupation let him pass unhindered.

Charlotte Greer had gone by the time the meeting finished, probably put out by his decision to decline assistance. He checked his messages when he reached his car: one missed call, courtesy of John Hale. He dialled the number as he turned out onto Wiri Station Road.

'I got your message,' Hale said. 'You didn't answer my call-back.'

'I was in debriefing.'

'How was it?'

'Nobody told me I did the right thing.'

'What did you expect?'

Devereaux didn't answer.

'Is he okay?'

'Not really. I shot him twice.'

'Do you want a beer?'

'Yeah. Where are you?'

'The office.'

'Put a couple in the fridge for me.'

Hale rented office space in a unit on High Street, central city. Devereaux found a kerb slot and took the stairs up. The door was unlocked. He went in and found Hale feet up behind his desk, stereo on soft.

The fridge sat below the deep, west-facing window, the day in vast orange exodus beyond, the street below quiet and blue-shadowed.

Bottles chimed gently as he opened the door. He took two beers and de-capped them with an opener waiting on the sill. The motion in silhouette against the patch of late sun on the floor behind.

Hale said, 'I like it that you greet the fridge first.'

'It never gives me any lip.'

He placed a bottle on the desk for Hale and pulled up a chair. Hale took the beer and dropped his feet off the desk. He stretched forward and palmed the moisture ring.

Devereaux said, 'What are we listening to?'

'A nice nocturnal nocturne.'

'Hah.'

'Bob Dylan, "Love Sick".' He had some beer. 'I shouldn't have to tell you these things.'

'I knew it was Bob.'

'But forgot it was his romance malady melody.'

'Very clever.'

Devereaux sat down.

Hale said, 'What happened?'

Devereaux gave him the full story. Hale watched the window as he listened. He said, 'What are his chances?'

'Of living?'

'Or dying. Whichever way you want to look at it.'

'I don't know. He wasn't in good shape.'

Quiet between them. Hale's desk phone rang. He ignored it.

'Prognosis?'

'I don't know. Probably not brilliant.'

A nod, a small sip. 'Did he deserve it?'

'Depends whether or not he makes it.'

Hale's feet reclaimed desk space. They touched down in neat tandem, beside the phone. A small shelf held *The Satanic Verses* by Salman Rushdie, and an anthology of Kipling's poetry. 'Hindsight's irrelevant. You either deserve it at the time, or you don't.'

'I don't know about that.'

Hale ceiling-gazed for a spell. Down the corridor, the elevator chimed politely. He said, 'Forthcoming luck shouldn't sway whether you're deserving of something in the here and now.'

'Meaning?'

'Meaning, whichever way it turns out doesn't change the fact he needed to be shot when he was.'

'Maybe he didn't need shooting.'

Hale had another sip. He said, 'If he had a machete, I'd say he probably needed shooting.'

Devereaux didn't respond.

'Who was he?' Hale said.

'*Is*. He's still alive. In theory.'

'Who is he then?'

'Just a suspect. I never met him.'

'Robbery-related stuff?'

Devereaux nodded.

'You feel bad, even though you know nothing about him?'

He nodded again. 'I'd say that's the normal response.'

Hale nestled the beer in his lap and tilted it so he could look straight down its throat. 'I only feel guilty about the people I know.'

'Is that good or bad?'

'I don't know. Other way around, I'd be feeling pretty guilty.'

Devereaux didn't answer.

Hale said, 'How was debriefing?'

'I don't think they're too impressed.'

'Did you follow standard procedure?'

'Not really.'

'Who questioned you?'

'Guy called Lloyd Bowen. You ever meet him?'

Hale nodded. He thought for a moment. 'Sharp as a paper cut,' he said. 'And just as unpleasant.'

'Yeah. That's Lloyd. Frank Briar was there too.'

'Frankie. Everyone's most reviled human.'

Devereaux said, 'Bowen asked if I was planning on quitting.'

'What did you tell him?'

'I said I wasn't.'

'But you are.'

'Yeah. I don't want them to try to nudge me out the door, though.'

'That old "depart on your own terms" lark.'

'Yeah. That.'

'So who told him you're thinking of packing it in?'

'I don't know. That's the other thing. I need to be around long enough to find out who leaked, so I can kick their arse.'

Hale smiled, looked at the window. 'I wouldn't worry about anything just yet.'

'Yet.'

'He's still alive. Wait until he clocks out before you panic.'

'Thanks.'

They sipped in silence. Devereaux scored a crucifix through his beer label.

Hale said, 'Would you quit something, even if it was the one thing you were good at?'

'I'm good at more than one thing.'

'I know. But would you?'

'You mean, would I rather be unhappy doing something I'm good at, or happy doing something I'm shit at?'

He shook his head. 'That wasn't really my question, but it would certainly merit some pondering.'

'It would.'

Hale said, 'I turned down some work today.'

'What was it?'

'Check-up duty on your robbery job.' He toed the Kipling so its spine sat flush with the Rushdie. 'This ex-lawyer wanted me to find who did the bank and armoured van thing.'

'Why'd you turn it down?'

'He couldn't really give a decent reason why I shouldn't.'

'What's his name?'

'Alan Rowe. He did criminal defence.'

'Why didn't you take it?'

He flicked the neck of his bottle with a fingernail. 'You know how sometimes you get that feeling that something's a little off kilter.'

'Uh-huh.'

'Yeah, I got that feeling.' He sipped. 'Pity, though. He looked full of loot.'

Devereaux reached across and cycled the stereo back to 'Love Sick'. 'The shooting on January thirty is tied in with the heist stuff,' he said.

'That a guess, or did someone tell you?'

'It's a guess. Nobody's telling me anything.'

Hale closed his eyes and nodded the opening bars. 'They've kept it pretty quiet,' he said.

'Yeah.'

'So what happened?'

'I think someone in the know on the robberies went into witness protection, and his friends got wind of it.'

Hale's eyes opened. 'And shot everyone.'

'Yeah — and shot everyone.'

'Who's running the enquiry?'

'Not me. Lloyd Bowen, and McCarthy. You remember Don McCarthy?'

Hale nodded. 'He's not the sort of character one forgets in a hurry.'

'He'd probably say the same about you.'

Hale nodded. He had another sip. 'Yes,' he said, 'he probably would. How is old Don these days?'

'Driven and grey-tinted. He's based out of Auckland Central at the moment.'

'So you get the pleasure of seeing him on a daily basis.'

'I do.'

Quiet for a moment. Hale said, 'Are you going to tell Ellen?'

'About the guy I shot?'

'Mmm.'

'I couldn't get hold of her.'

Hale said nothing.

'How would you do it?' Devereaux said.

Hale thought about it. 'I probably wouldn't. But I guess that's why you have an Ellen, and I don't.'

Devereaux said nothing. Hale looked at the ceiling. He said, 'Would you rather die young and happy at the hand of someone you didn't know, or old and miserable at the hand of God?'

'I don't believe in God. You don't either.'

'I know.' He held his bottle up and watched the foam tilt back and forth. 'Still makes me wonder, though.'

They had another beer. Darkness settling gently, sky quilt-soft behind the glass. Devereaux didn't depart until after eight. The stereo was off. He left Hale alone in the office. The doorway framed a nice shot of quiet musing: feet on the desk, ankles crossed, toes swaying to some remembered tune.

He sat in the car and smoked a cigarette, window cracked to vent fumes. To his left a narrow alleyway formed a cut between buildings, restaurant patrons seated at a scatter of outdoor tables. Laughter and the smell of high-priced food. That weird juxtaposition of his own dark dilemmas against the merry good life. He found his cellphone and called Lloyd Bowen.

'Sergeant. Be brief, I'm on a tight schedule.'

'How is he?'

Bowen caught the meaning: *is my victim still alive?* 'He's still got breath in his lungs, but he's not in great shape. He's had surgery to remove the bullets, but he's still unconscious.'

'I want to see him.'

'I'm sorry?'

'I want to see him.'

'Out of the question, sergeant. It's too apologetic. It's an admission of liability. We can't have people thinking you did something wrong.'

'So you think I acted appropriately?'

He heard a door slam: maybe Bowen dodging eavesdroppers. 'No, I think this whole thing has been one major fuck-up. But we can't have the general public knowing that.'

Devereaux didn't answer.

Bowen said, 'I don't want you near the guy, so do yourself a favour and stay at home. We'll be seeing you tomorrow.' He paused. 'Have your story straight.'

■ SIX

MONDAY, 13 FEBRUARY, 8.24 P.M.

The Mitch Duvall bachelor pad was light on comfort: the living room boasted a single chair and a television. The kitchen had a fridge and a lot of vacant cupboard space. Neighbours were a mere wall's width away. Cheap baffling facilitated easy eavesdropping.

Mustering affection was a struggle. It was a narrow slice of a long two-storey complex that backed a busy arterial feeding the Northern Motorway. He'd only been in three weeks. The bulk of his possessions were still boxed, relegated to spare room status until he had the time to place them permanently. The master bedroom doubled as sleeping quarters and study. He was trialling an integrated bed/workstation layout: his laptop and paperwork littered across the mattress.

He downed a pre-dinner beer, then showered. Ten minutes in the ring with McCarthy had left him shaky. He alternated hard doses of hot and cold to shock himself back to even keel.

The bathroom wasn't ideal. The low mirror left his six-foot-three figure headless. He leaned on the sink and ducked to eye level with his reflection. It wasn't what it used to be. Age had chamfered off the hard edges. He preferred his younger version. Time had softened him to a 2XL shadow of his former self.

He dressed and did a once-over of still-empty cupboards,

drifted through to the spare bedroom. A wall to wall span of sealed boxes reached head-high. His no-stove contingency was to resort to canned food. He had peaches, fruit salad, creamed corn, spaghetti, beans, soup, all neatly packaged. He chose peaches. A fork and a can opener from the next box, and dinner was under way.

He sat in the living room and ate in front of a muted television. His story to The Don had been slightly embellished. He'd done five months with CIB, all of them as a probationary tag-along as opposed to full detective. He'd joined the police in 'eighty-one. It was poor timing. The Springbok tour had kicked off. The decision of whether or not to host a rugby team from a state blighted by apartheid had divided society. Liberals said send them home. Racists and rugby fans said let them stay. Violence and mass protests ensued, and one of the blackest marks on the nation's modern history served as Mitchell Duvall's law enforcement induction.

He was twenty-one years old, five months clear of a rough break-up, wedding plans burned. The tour was a perfect cure for a miserable split. He was dropped straight onto the front lines, posted to Eden Park for the third test on twelve September. Protestors turned out in full force. The politics of it was lost on him, and he couldn't have cared less. He couldn't even spell apartheid, and who knew where Soweto was? He left all opinions on the matter unformed, and used his tattered relationship as fuel to lash out uninhibited.

It was paradise.

Near-frenzied cops baton-whipped peaceful marchers with manic devotion. He joined in wholeheartedly: a pissed-off twenty-one-year-old in full riot gear versus unarmed protestors. The odds were favourable. He wasn't worried about consequences. He left two guys prone and bloodied on Sandringham Road. Pulped strangers the corollary of his own repressed frustration. It felt good. He'd needed it. He felt empowered. It purged baggage he'd wanted to ditch for a long time.

It was a rush, but it didn't last long. His conscience surfaced and labelled him a disgrace. Sandringham Road flashbacks kept him sleepless. He sank into depression. He felt his thoughts growing increasingly irrational. It was a bizarre experience, an onset he was aware of, but one he could do nothing to prevent. A forced bystander to his own state of mind.

Paranoia took hold.

Cancer was the main concern. He began checking his skin for lesions, up to sixty times a day when he wasn't on patrol, as often as he could when he was. He feared the toilet. Every piss meant a ball-check for lumps. He worried about bowel cancer, started holding in his shits in case he spotted a blood clot.

He confessed all to a doctor and won himself three months' stress leave. He was back at work by February 'eighty-three, minus the cancer obsession, still unhappy. He wanted to be a detective, but his applications were rejected. He suspected his forced leave killed his eligibility.

His parents died in 'ninety-five: father first, his mother eight months later. He organised the funerals: he had no siblings; it was his responsibility by default. He stayed on autopilot that whole year, numbly running through the motions. He couldn't hold down a relationship. Thoughts of 12 September 1981 pervaded his psyche, told him he wasn't worthy of other people. Some ingrained self-loathing worked to sabotage anything that matured beyond a casual fling. It didn't fade with time, either. He entered CIB as a probationary officer in 1997, loveless and unloved. It was a short-lived stay. Psychologically, it was too big a load. His first tag-along case was a woman named

Marie Langford, beaten to death by her husband. A traffic patrol pulled the guy over and found the body in the back of his van. She'd been dead two days. Duvall saw the confession. He watched through the one-way glass, ostensibly to glean interrogation techniques. But the triviality of the motive stunned him: *I'd just had enough of her lip.*

It was a turning point for him. He took a fiercer approach to his job. Restraint began to ebb away. Innocent until proven guilty began to carry less and less weight. His police career ended five months later, following an assault accusation: a burglary suspect claimed excessive use of force. Facial bruising helped reinforce the claim. Duvall denied it. Except a security camera had captured the moment. The evidence was still marginal. The suspect had been high on heroin at the time, and the footage was grainy monochrome. He offered his resignation in exchange for no criminal prosecution. They bought it, and he was out the door with a vehement 'good riddance'.

He went private. The clean record and police experience made him a shoo-in. He got his PI's licence. But work was thin on the ground. He did debt collection and bar security, pseudo-legal muscle work in place of plum investigative jobs. Rental income off his parents' house kept his nose above the breadline.

June 2002, he applied for work with a private military corporation headquartered in London. It was worth a shot. He bulked out his CV with falsified Armed Offenders Squad and Special Tactics Group experience. The gamble paid off, and he was posted to Iraq as part of a three-man team protecting a group of BBC journalists operating in Baghdad.

It was madness: 1981 replayed on a colossal scale. Private military corporations operated unpoliced. Baghdad was full of cowboy operatives doing whatever they wanted. He saw stuff that rendered the Springbok tour bland by comparison.

He pulled out in 2005, giddy with the mayhem. Back to repossession work that felt pedestrian by comparison.

He left his empty tin in the sink, bent lid gaping wide, and went through to the bedroom. Newspaper clippings and handwritten notes swamped the quilt in crisscrossed disarray, laptop tethered to the wall by its power cable. He stood in the doorway and beheld the clutter.

'Let this be my atonement,' he said.

■ SEVEN

MONDAY, 13 FEBRUARY, 9.12 P.M.

Repo work.
Hale had an evening appointment with an Epsom-based company executive a little tight on investor payments.

The guy's name was Paul Dryer. He part-owned a finance company, recently insolvent, leaving two thousand creditors one hundred and eighty million dollars out of pocket.

The client in this case was a highly pissed-off contingent of investors. The brief was simple: they'd financed hard-earned capital, said capital had been squandered, the company was being investigated for fraud, they wanted back the ninety-million-dollar dividend Mr Dryer had paid himself prior to collapse.

Hale took his Ford Escort. He was groomed for upscale evening work: Ray-Bans, a fresh haircut, a lustrous shoe shine. The address was a two-storey concrete tilt-slab in pearly whitewash, spared from liquidation by virtue of family trust ownership. A sixty-strong party was in full swing. Cars crowded both kerbs, jammed in sans breathing room. He did an idle cruise-past and parked around the corner. An open door had spilled the party into a front courtyard. He strode through calm, straight into the house. Smile in place, 'Excuse me's' in triplicate as he navigated the throng.

Rembrandt prints and white plaster adorned the entry. He hung a right through a closed door and entered a garage. Motion-triggered halogens draped a liquid gleam across a late-model Range Rover Sport, a Ferrari 360, an Aston Martin DB9.

He brushed past hallway-dawdlers and checked out the back. More boy's toys: a MacBook Pro fed music to a thousand-watt stereo system in a leathered living room. Through a ranch slider six people sprawled in a frothing spa pool, brimming wine glasses pinched aloft.

He found Dryer upstairs in a glass-fronted snooker room overlooking the spa. A game was under way. Dryer was lining up a shot. A handful of tipsy opponents used pool cues as props. Hale recognised some faces: Detective Sergeant Frank Briar, esteemed defence lawyer Ross Margrave QC. Margrave gave him a nod.

Briar stared, stepped in whisper-close. He was a tall man verging fifty. A rigorous alcohol regime had left his eyes bloodshot for the past ten years. Hale knew his divorce and heart attack count were at two apiece. Briar said, 'The fuck are you doing here?'

'Socialising.'

'You hear Mr Devereaux's got himself in trouble?'

'I wouldn't call it that.'

'He shot a suspect. It's what I call a shit result.'

'God knows I saw plenty of that, working for you.'

Briar offered no reaction. 'What are you doing here?'

'I told you. Socialising.'

'Yeah, and the pope's a Muslim. I know you. Don't make a scene. You and Devereaux in the same day would be too much for anyone.'

'I'll keep things cooled. I don't want to spark heart attack three.'

'Fuck you.'

Hale said, 'Are you on the clock?'

Briar raised a half-gone beer. 'What do you think?'

Hale nodded. 'You always seemed more suited to criminal perpetration than investigation.'

'You're a real hoot.'

'Yeah. Stay out of my way. It always takes a lot of self-control not to punch you in the face. Have a nice night.'

Briar laughed, and Hale stepped away. Dryer was prepping for another shot. He found his line and paused. His target wasn't evident: the baize still held a random scatter. He took his eye off the table as Hale moved towards him. He was a tall, fit-looking man in his early forties.

Dryer said, 'Have we met?' Party volume made him shout.

'Must have, if you invited me.'

Dryer looked confused.

Hale said, 'I'm kidding. You've never had the pleasure.'

He gave the room a once-over. Wall-mounted speakers did the downstairs MacBook's bidding. A side bar held a half-full bottle of Jack Daniel's, glass tumblers loaded with dregs-stained ice. Briar was at the window, making a call. Maybe a Devereaux-related shooting update. Margrave was with a trio in the corner.

Dryer said, 'You spoke to Frank when you came in; I assumed you work with him.'

'I've known Frank a long time. He was my patrol supervisor for a while.'

'You're a cop?'

Hale shook his head. 'Not any more. Right now, I'm kind of a repo man.'

Something clicked. Dryer laughed and found his line again. He jabbed a couple of short practices, sawed back and forth on the web of his thumb, drove through on his shot. He scored three glancing contacts that did little more than shake up the spacing. He leaned his cue against the side of the table.

'What are you repo-ing?' He sounded like he could guess if he had to.

'Ninety million dollars,' Hale said.

Dryer made a show of pocket-patting. He wasn't worried. 'I don't have it on me.'

Hale said, 'I understand your investors managed to claw back two cents in the dollar, so I'm glad you can still afford Dolby.'

'You can either leave now under your own steam, or security will give you a hand.'

'Don't get any misconceptions about what you can make me do.'

'Are you some sort of tough guy?'

'Yeah. I suppose that's what you'd call it.'

Hale turned and poured an inch of the Jack into a clean tumbler. Dryer followed.

'I love that you think you can just help yourself.'

'Could be worse. I could have stolen ninety million dollars.'

'What do you want?'

'I've got some photos to show you.'

'I'm not really interested.'

'Okay. Thanks for the whisky.'

'What are they?'

Hale put a hand in a jacket pocket, came out with a flash drive in two fingers. 'I thought we could go somewhere quiet.'

Dryer paused a moment. The flash drive triggered something: a suspicion this was real. He jerked his head, signalled Hale to follow. They went through to an adjacent office. A Mac computer waited patiently atop a glass desk. Dryer sat down behind it. Hale put his back to the door. Dense panelling all but blocked out party noise.

Dryer tried some drawers, found a pack of cigarettes. He lit one. The tip did a seismograph wiggle as he spoke: 'I've got cops in here, lawyers, the whole caboodle. Don't think you can walk in off the street and scare me.'

Hale said, 'You lost a hundred and eighty million dollars. I'm surprised you haven't scared yourself.'

Dryer blew some smoke. 'The market fucked out. Get over it.'

'It's the nice fat dividend you took that makes me a bit unhappy.'

'It was legal.'

'Legal and fair aren't necessarily the same thing. And I'm a bit of a stickler for the latter.'

He tossed the flash drive across the desk into Dryer's lap. 'Take a look.'

Dryer put the cigarette on the desk, plugged the flash drive into the Mac. The tint on his face changed as the pictures loaded. He mouse-clicked through a few images. His expression slackened.

'Fuck you. You had me followed?' He found the cigarette by touch and returned it to his mouth, kept clicking.

'No. I did it myself.'

'Jesus. There are hundreds of files in here. You piece of shit. Are these all me?'

'You'll see photographs of yourself in four different motor vehicles, none of which was listed on your Statement of Assets and Liabilities. Neither was the yacht you keep down at the Viaduct. I've got shots of that too.'

Dryer passed a sleeve across his mouth. 'You're disgusting. This is invasion of privacy. This is disgraceful.'

Hale said, 'It's the sort of thing that gets liquidators pissed off. Fraudsters being cagey about their possessions. It's another crime in itself.'

Dryer looked up. 'The hearing's pending, I haven't been found—'

'Yeah, but they don't investigate people they think are innocent. You know?'

Dryer said nothing. He put the cigarette back on the desk.

'So here's the deal,' Hale said. 'Pull your albeit legally acquired ninety-million-dollar dividend out of the trust account by close of business tomorrow, or Wednesday morning I'll lodge a notice with the Financial Markets Authority that you weren't entirely honest when it came to asset disclosure.'

'Photos can be doctored.'

'I'm a licensed private investigator and a former police officer. My professionalism is beyond reproach.'

'I can't move that much money that quickly.'

'Yeah, you can. Pull some favours.'

'It's not that simple.'

'Check images one ninety-eight and ninety-nine; might give you a hurry-up.'

Dryer did as directed. The file opened. Dryer paled. His mouth slackened. 'Oh, fuck. You bastard ... you bastard. This is blackmail.'

Image one ninety-eight: Dryer's Range Rover, kerbside on Karangahape Road, a young male prostitute bent to the window. Image one ninety-nine: Dryer and prostitute hand in hand, boarding Dryer's yacht.

'What would your wife think,' Hale said, 'if she got hold of those?'

'God, don't. You'll ruin me. Please. My children can't see this.'

'Move the money tomorrow.'

'I can't.'

'Open image two hundred.'

Dryer opened image two hundred. His hand went to his mouth. 'Oh, Jesus. No. How did you get that?'

'Return the money, or I swear to God I'll ruin you. I'll ruin you like you ruined all those poor people.'

Dryer didn't answer. He'd lost a lot of colour. Hale leaned in and put a business card face up on the desk, and walked out.

▪ EIGHT

Monday, 13 February, 9.58 p.m.

It was always going to be a shit night.
Shooting a guy was guaranteed to keep him sleepless. Devereaux sat in the living room and put The Smiths on the stereo. Morrissey sang to him about a light that never goes out. Thematically pertinent, if nothing else. He kept the volume low and tried to read. Nothing went in, words just toed the surface. He gave it up and just sat there. It was the downside of being alone: solitude left him torturously undistracted.

He dialled the cop who'd given him the backseat debriefing, but couldn't get through. He called Lloyd Bowen's office, but it rang to voicemail.

A saucer loaded with ash dunes sat on the floor beside his chair. He promoted it to an armrest perch, then stood and rearranged his bookcase. Anything to take the afternoon off mental replay. He grouped his vinyl collection on the bottom level, worked up shelf by shelf. Careful adjustments to get the spines flush. He thought about memorising the configuration. Six storeys high brought it to door level. He could spend days trying to rote-learn the line-up.

His cell rang. He hoped it was Bowen calling him back. It wasn't. It was a detective constable named Carl Grayson.

'I heard you had a rough afternoon,' Grayson said.

Devereaux lit a cigarette and thought about shifting Hemingway down a level. 'It wasn't one of my better ones.'

'Are you all right?'

He laughed. 'Don't go mushy on me, Carl.'

Quiet for a moment. Grayson said, 'People say you're going to quit.'

'Yeah, well, don't listen to them. And for God's sake, don't pass it on.'

No answer. He sensed the instruction was a bit belated. Devereaux said, 'So what's up?'

'They brought in that guy you wanted me to find.'

Devereaux sat down. 'You've lost me.'

'The bank job back on October eight. The Savings and Loan thing.'

The Savings and Loan. The armoured van. The fight club robbery. They ruled his life. They hogged his pre-sleep musings. They had his kill tally pencilled in at *one*. 'Uh-huh,' he said.

'You said you had an informant you'd used a couple of times but you couldn't track him down. Guy's name was Howard Ford.'

'Yeah. You found him?'

'Someone did. He got brought in tonight on something unrelated. He's downstairs.'

'In lock-up?'

'Yeah. In lock-up.'

'What was the unrelated charge?'

'Well, I don't know the exact details. Apparently, he was urinating in public, got brought in for the night. I don't think he's in good shape. He resisted arrest, and they came on pretty hard. He was bleeding when they brought him in.'

'Ah, shit. Have you spoken to him?'

'No. Well, I tried. I went down to see him, but Bowen won't

let anyone in. Don McCarthy's supposed to be talking to the guy tomorrow.'

'Okay. So you haven't spoken to him at all?'

'No. The custody sarge wouldn't let me past the gate. There were some other patrol guys down there at the time. Apparently, this guy Ford got roughed up pretty bad.'

'What's Bowen doing?'

'I don't know. He's in his office.'

'I just called his line, he didn't answer.'

'He never picks up.'

'Has anyone else been in to see Ford?'

'Bowen left his office for about half an hour, but I don't know what for.'

'Where are you?'

'At my desk.'

'Until when?'

'I'm off shift at twenty-three thirty.'

'Okay.' The cigarette was still young, but he stabbed it out. He missed saucer and got chair.

'Are you going to try to see him tomorrow?' Grayson said.

'No. I'm going to see him now.'

He shut off the stereo and left. His home was in Mission Bay, east of town, separated from the central city by a fifteen-minute journey along the harbour's southern lip. Bright restaurant windows invited patronage. He blanked them out and looked over at the Gulf. All sullen and without end. He liked his little nocturnal excursions. The quiet appealed to him. He lived in anti-phase with urban clutter.

Auckland Central Police is up on the corner of Cook and Vincent streets. It was closing in on eleven p.m. by the time he got there. The vehicle entry was choked with patrol cars, roving officers returning early to clear paperwork before clock-out. He stayed clear and parked in the Civic parking building under Aotea Square, walked back across the street to the station and entered through the Hobson Street garage.

Two officers manhandled a handcuffed youth out of the back of a patrol car. A teenage girl collapsed hands-and-knees from another vehicle, arched, and spilled a wide vomit pool. He queue-cut the wait at the booking window and rapped the glass. A custody sergeant called Eric Blake sat at a desk behind a sheet of Perspex. He was late forties, hair thin and mussed, like plughole trappings. Teeth crowding for centre stage. A constable typed at a computer on a table against the opposite wall, back to the window. A phone handset crushed between ear and shoulder.

'Sean Devereaux,' Blake said.

'Got a Howard Ford in tonight? He was bleeding a lot, you wouldn't miss him.'

Blake checked his screen. A thin white tracer of scar tissue marred a thick forearm. Worn knuckles hinted at a hands-on approach to prisoner custody. 'Drunk and disorderly,' he said. 'Resisting arrest.'

'I need to see him.'

'You can't. And you cut the queue.' He smiled, mouth only, corners of his eyes unchanged.

'Don't dick about with me. Let me through.'

The guy propped his elbows on the desk, linked his fingers to form a fleshy arch. All the time in the world. He leaned in towards the glass. A straining gut swaddled the desk edge.

'Bowen's got him off limits,' he said. 'So unless you're his lawyer, you need to fuck off.'

'Why's he off limits?'

'I don't know.'

'You don't know, or you don't want to tell me?'

'I wouldn't worry about it too much. Either way, you're not getting in.'

'I just want to check he's okay.'

'He's fine. Trust me.'

A fitting interjection: dulled screams and the frantic staccato slap of fist on steel. Blake smiled again. Lord and gamekeeper of his obscure little domain. The queue was building. Devereaux was causing a snarl-up. He checked the set-up. Left of the glass, sequential steel gates corralled the entry to the cell block. On the desk, two side-by-side red slam-buttons released the locks electronically. In the office: Blake and his backup constable, two phone lines, two chirping digital radio units.

'Go and have a cigarette,' Blake said.

'Open the gate.'

'Get out of my face.'

He gave it up. He shot Blake the finger and walked away.

Howard, I hope you're all right.

Another vomit launch served as exit music. He rode the elevator up to CIB. It was shift changeover, occupancy had hit a lull. He went through to the incident room for the October bank robbery. Grayson was at a desk reading paperwork, fingers skewering his hair.

Grayson glanced up. 'Shit. I didn't mean for you to come in tonight.'

'Doesn't matter. I need to see the guy.'

'I don't think you've got a chance.'

'We'll see. You get anywhere today?'

'Not really.'

Devereaux checked his watch. Eleven-twenty. 'Go home,' he said.

'What are you going to do?'

'Chat to Lloyd Bowen. You might want to avoid the fallout.'

Bowen's office was in a nearby corridor. Devereaux opened the door and walked in unannounced. Bowen looked up, closed the binder in front of him. A lamp held his desktop in fierce clarity.

'Don't you know how to knock?'

Devereaux pulled up a chair. The office was tiny. Table and filing cabinets made breathing space tight. Lack of windows left a ceiling fan struggling to stir up airflow.

'I was just down at custody,' Devereaux said. 'They've got an informant of mine.'

'Howard Ford.'

'They wouldn't let me in to see him.'

Bowen knuckled fatigue out of one eye. 'I don't want anyone seeing him until Don McCarthy gets in tomorrow.'

'He's my contact.'

'You can't see him. We're tightening things up.'

'What does that mean?'

'It means McCarthy's the officer in charge, he'll run the interview.'

'Right. He was bleeding when he came in. You might want to look at tightening up arrest protocol, too.'

A long silence, tripwire-tight. Bowen rolled his chair back and linked his hands behind his head. He said, 'Watch your mouth when you're sitting in this office.'

'I'm concerned that a detainee in this station has been assaulted, and I want to ensure that he doesn't require medical attention.'

Bowen smiled: Blake-brand emotion, mouth only. 'Remember you shot a guy today.'

'So?'

'So don't try to pull the "concern for others" card on me.'

Devereaux didn't answer.

Bowen centred his tie. 'He doesn't require medical attention,' he said.

'I'm still suspicious he's been mistreated. He's got an intellectual disability, he needs to be handled carefully.'

'I wasn't aware of that.'

'That still doesn't resolve the issue.'

'If you want to make a complaint, this is the wrong way to do it.'

'So outline the right way for me.'

Bowen didn't answer.

'He's my contact,' Devereaux said. 'I've dealt with him before. He'll talk to me. If he has any information, he'll give it to me. I can guarantee he won't give anything to Don McCarthy, and he won't give anything to you.'

'I disagree. And, unfortunately, I'm in charge.'

'You're making a mistake. And, unfortunately, I tend to be right.'

'Sergeant, I'm new to this job. Bear in mind first impressions last a long time.'

'I will if you will.'

'Part of the reason my predecessor was asked to move on was because you, among others, were given too much slack.'

'You're planning on keeping me on a tight leash, are you?'

He shrugged, swivelled his chair back and forth. 'Either that, or find a new job.'

Tempting.

Devereaux kept the retort private, scanned the desk: the binder, miscellaneous printed paperwork. He skimmed for the name Howard Ford. He said, 'Has his lawyer called?'

'Whose lawyer?'

'Ford's.'

'No. I suggest you go home and forget about it.' He made a

show of checking his watch. 'You've got bigger things to worry about.'

Devereaux gave it up. He walked out and went back to his desk. His in-tray was loaded: everything robbery related. He shunted clear space and cupped his face in his hands and thought about what to do. A phone was ringing. On and on, like some panicked bleating for him alone. He tried to block it out. Tactics began to cohere. A plan took shape. He stayed seated a minute longer. Committing fully was difficult: everything proactive had high risk attached. The phone finally cut out.

Just do it.

Devereaux put a cigarette in his mouth but didn't light it, got up and walked back through to the incident room. Grayson was about to head out the door, jacket slung behind him off a hooked finger.

Devereaux blocked the door. 'Need you to do me a favour.'

A smile. 'Could it wait until nine o'clock tomorrow?'

'It'll only take a minute.'

Grayson checked his watch. A curse on sighed breath. He turned back to the room and dropped his jacket across the back of a chair. 'What is it?'

'I just need you to tell Bowen you've got a call come in for him on one of the lines in here.'

'Why?'

'I just need thirty seconds in his office.'

'Ah, shit.' He raked his hair back, one-handed. 'Don't tell me that.' He spun the chair round and sat down again. His computer was still running, he shook the mouse to clear the screen. A wife and baby daughter snapshot adorned the background. Maybe subliminal guilt messaging: *look what you're keeping me from.*

Devereaux said, 'I need to go down and see this guy Ford.'

'Yeah, but he's hardly going anywhere.'

'Look, if you're right and he got the shit beaten out of him, I need to check he's okay, and if he knows stuff about October eight, I want to get it out of him before he sees McCarthy and decides to hold his tongue.'

Grayson chewed his lip and thought about it. 'What are you going to do in his office?'

'Just use his phone.'

'That's all?'

'That's all.'

'Who should I say is calling?'

'Nobody. Just go into his office and tell him he's got a call.'

'He'll wonder why I didn't just transfer it.'

'Maybe you don't remember his extension.'

'I transfer shit through to him all the time.'

'Look. Please just do it.'

'Man. It's dishonest. It's probably misconduct.'

'You told me yourself this guy Ford had been roughed up. Nobody seems to care. But he's my guy, my contact. I had his name on a list, and that's why they've got him, and I need to get in and check that he's doing okay.'

'Ah, Jesus.' He flapped his hand. 'Yeah. Okay. Get out of here before I chicken out.'

'Just wait until I've got back to my desk, and go and tell him.'

'Yeah, yeah, I know.'

He left the room and went back to his desk. He still had the cigarette in his mouth, sodden and flaccid from talking. Grayson didn't leave him much of a cushion: he'd barely sat down and the younger man was heading across the room, Bowen-bound. A second later and the pair of them were walking back across the room: Grayson's half-speed stymieing the inspector's quick-march.

Devereaux stood up. Perfect timing: shift changeover had left the room half full. Risk of being witnessed was appreciably low. He selected an unused desk phone and dialled custody and left the handset face up off the cradle, dial tone trilling faintly. Bowen's door was agape. He walked in and leaned across the desk for the phone and punched custody's second extension. Upside down from the visitor's side, cord stretched taut. Lamp heat warm on his cheek. He wanted the young backup constable, not Blake. He figured the first extension would ring and Blake would take it, the backup guy would pick up the second call. Held breath ramped his heart up to full hammer.

'Yes, Inspector?'

Not Blake. The young guy. Caller ID made him think he had Lloyd on the line. Devereaux gave his best Bowen: 'Yah, Devereaux's coming down to see Ford, you can let him in.'

Short and sweet. The guy bought it: 'Yes, sir.'

He hung up and strode out, headed for the stairs.

The short walk pulled his pulse back in line. The queue at the booking window was gone.

Blake was still at the glass. Footfall noise drew his gaze. He said, 'Wouldn't want to have to deal with you every evening.'

'Likewise. Open the gate.'

The constable from the phone was at the opposite desk, still at his computer. He glanced back over his shoulder and yawned against the back of his hand.

Blake said, 'I'd be careful who you give the finger to in future. I'm tempted to call old Lloydy back and tell him how much of a prick you were earlier.'

The threat chilled him, but he kept composure. He glanced around. People were looking at them. Concrete and steel construction, the acoustics were shocking: no spat went uneavesdropped. He mustered calm: 'Give it a try. See how he responds to "old Lloydy".'

Blake laughed. 'Yeah. Up yours, Devereaux.' He leaned and hit the first lock release: a short snapping impact, a grudging concession.

Devereaux stepped across and opened the first cell block door. A buzzer sounded until it was closed again behind him. A moment of imprisonment, and then the second door was freed and he entered the corridor. The constable from the phone stepped through from the office and beckoned him to follow. Hollers and the rattling smash of fists on doors tracked their motion. That standard lock-up symphony. Ford had a cell near the back of the block. Devereaux cupped the spy-grille and glanced in. Ford had a suite to himself. He was on his back on the bed, crook of his arm shielding his face. One leg pulled double, knee cocked.

'You want to go in?' the kid said.

Devereaux nodded, smothered a cough. The place stank: a potent urine/booze cocktail. The kid picked a master key out of a fat clinking bunch. He freed the lock and pulled the gate wide. Devereaux stepped inside. The constable's farewell was a door slam and a 'knock if you need me'.

Devereaux waited until the sound of footfalls died. 'Remember me, Howard?'

Ford removed his arm and turned to face him. One eye was swollen, both nostrils were ringed crimson. A heavy nosebleed had given him a red median strip. He was a tall man in his midtwenties. His jaw was bearded, his hair ponytailed.

'Sean Devereaux. Oh, help. They hurt me.' He whimpered and the arm went back in place. He smeared tears. 'Please let me out. I don't know what they want. I don't know what they want, man.'

He pulled the other leg up and wrapped his arms around his knees and rolled over to face the wall. Devereaux stepped across the room and dropped to his haunches beside the bed. The Howard Ford back story made for sad reading. He'd been in and out of correctional facilities for the better part of fifteen years, intellectual disability and lack of support keeping him off the straight and narrow.

'What happened, Howard? What did they do to you?'

'I, I ... I was just out having a drink, you know? I took a leak, and next thing I know these two cops are chasing me, so I tried to run away. But they caught me and took me here.'

'Where were you taking a leak?'

'I don't know.'

'Try to think.'

'Just outside this bar.'

'Where was the bar?'

'I don't know. I don't really know what streets are called.'

'But you were outside.'

'Yeah. And they got me and took me back here. I had to wait in here, and then they took me out and put me somewhere else. They kept asking me questions, Sean. They kept asking, October eight, October eight, October eight.' He snivelled. 'What's October eight? I don't know anything about October eight.'

'Okay. Who hurt your nose, Howard?'

A protracted whimper. 'The man at the desk.'

'Which man? There are two men at the desk.'

'It was the big man.'

'Blake.'

'Yes. He hit me. They put me in a room away from this one, and they kept saying, "October eight, October eight, tell us about October eight". And I said I didn't know anything about

October eight, and that man just bent right in my face and he was shaking a can, and he was like "do you want to get sprayed, do you want to get sprayed?" and I was telling him no, and I pushed him away and that's when he hit me.'

'How many times did he hit you?'

'One time. It hurt.'

'Okay. Who else was there when it happened?'

'Two men wearing suits. I didn't know them.'

'Did they hurt you as well?'

'No. One of them was asking me the questions. When I said I didn't know the answers, the big guy got in my face. The other guy in the suit wasn't even watching. He was just standing in the doorway with his hands in his pockets, and he was leaning there, facing the wrong way.'

It sounded like a Don McCarthy-sanctioned tactic. Or maybe he'd sent Frank Briar down. Maybe even Bowen.

'What did the men in suits look like?'

'I don't know. Normal guys, I s'pose.'

'How old were they?'

'I don't know.'

'Were they older or younger than me?'

'Older. A little bit. Maybe.'

Devereaux fell quiet. A shout/clang overlap from the corridor. Disinfectant odour hung ripe, the cool scorch of it deep in his airways. The head of the mattress was tear-stained: random dark lesions on the sheet. Ford was still facing the wall.

'Roll over, Howard. Let me see your nose.'

Ford rolled over. Devereaux leaned in for a close-up consult.

Ford said, 'Is it broken?'

'No, it's not broken.'

He placed his arm across his face again. 'Why are they asking me these things, Sean?'

'Because they knew I wanted to find you. And they thought because I wanted to find you, that you might know something that could help them.'

'So this is your fault. They wouldn't have done this if it wasn't for you.' Tears speckled the mattress in neat succession. 'Why did you want to find me?'

'To ask you about October eight.'

He raised his arm and slapped the wall to punctuate each word: 'I. Don't. Know. About. October. Eight.'

'Calm down. That's not going to get you anywhere. You need to chill out.'

Ford gave a long sigh and rolled away from him again. 'You fucking chill out. Jeez!'

Devereaux said, 'October eight was the bank robbery last year. Do you remember?'

'No.'

'You must remember. It was in the news.'

Ford hugged his knees. 'The one where someone was killed?'

'Yes. The one where someone was killed.'

'I wasn't the person who robbed it.'

'I know you weren't. But you've been in trouble before for robbery, haven't you?'

He squirmed on the bed. 'Little bit.'

'Yes. That's why I wanted to talk to you. Because even though you mightn't have done this one—'

'I didn't!'

'Even though you *didn't* do this one, I thought you could know someone who has information about it.'

'I don't know anyone who has information. About anything.'

'You've got lots of friends, though, haven't you, Howard?'

'Uh-huh.'

'And lots of them have also been in trouble with the police, haven't they? Some of them have been in similar sorts of trouble to you.'

He was still facing the wall. 'Yeah. I s'pose.'

'So do you think maybe you might have heard them talking about the bank robbery in October? Maybe just a small mention. Maybe after it happened. Do you think you might have overheard anything like that, from any of your friends?'

'I don't know. They talk about lots of stuff.'

'Yes, I'm sure they do. But remember, there's nothing wrong about overhearing something. You're not going to get in trouble by listening to something and then telling me about it.'

'I'm already in trouble, though. It's what I don't say that gets me in trouble.'

'Answer the question, Howard.'

'Which question?'

Devereaux rested his nose between steepled fingers. 'Have you heard anyone talking about the bank job on the eighth of October last year?'

'No. I don't know anything about it. Nobody I know does.'

'Okay. If you did want to know something about it—'

'But I don't.'

'I know, but for the sake of argument, pretend you did, pretend you *did* want to know something about it, which one of your friends would you ask for information?'

'I don't know.'

'Yes, you do. Think carefully, pretend you really, really want to know what happened with this thing, who would you go to and ask about it?'

He rolled onto his back and released his legs full stretch. He blinked. Dammed tears formed a thick bright film. 'I'd probably go and ask Leroy,' he said.

'Okay. Good. Who's Leroy?'

'He's just this friend I've got. He knows stuff about things.'

Devereaux's crouch was burning him. A stutter of joint pops as he stood.

'Where does Leroy live?'

'I don't know.'

'You must do.'

'I know how to get there. But I don't know what his address is.'

'Okay. Has Leroy been arrested before?'

'Uh-huh. Loads of times. Probably more than me.'

Devereaux dipped his hands in his pockets, felt the damp and tortured body of the chewed cigarette. He dropped it in the toilet.

'Sean, I don't want to stay in here tonight.'

'I know you don't. But you're going to have to. There's nothing I can do about that.'

'I don't want to get hurt again.'

'You won't.'

'What's gonna happen to the guys who hurt me?'

'I don't know yet. Nothing they'll be pleased about.'

He stepped to the grille and called to be let out.

The constable escorted him back down the corridor, prisoner choir prevailing. He was buzzed out through the booking window gates. Blake was still at the glass, elbows on the desk, watching his departure across netted fingers.

Devereaux said, 'You're lucky you didn't break his nose.'

'I'm lucky, or he's lucky?'

'I'm lodging a complaint. You threatened to spray him.'

Blake laughed. 'You should know better than to trust what comes out of the mouths of these people.'

Devereaux stepped to the screen. 'It was the blood coming

out of his nose that was most persuasive.' The glass fogged with his words.

'I've got two witnesses who'll say the force used was necessary. Ford took a swing at me. He was out of control, I responded appropriately.'

'Suffice to say he tells it a little differently.'

Blake creaked back in his chair. Departing headlights strafed a yellow blaze across them. Devereaux's shadow leapt ahead of him into the office.

Blake said, 'Everyone's tough from the other side of the glass.' He smiled. 'You and the fucking miscreants they drag in here.'

'Come out here and talk to me, if you like. I'll wait.'

Blake said nothing.

Devereaux said, 'Another day, maybe.'

Blake said, 'If you've got a complaint, go and fucking make it. But otherwise I don't want to have to deal with you.'

Devereaux didn't respond. He turned away and headed for the stairs.

■ NINE

MONDAY, 13 FEBRUARY, 11.13 P.M.

The arrival woke him.

Crunch of tyres on gravel, the broken ceiling-flicker as headlights panned the frontage. Hale slid out of bed. He felt his way to the front of the house, a strip of moonlight bent between hallway floor and wall. He checked the kitchen window. A silver sedan was idling at his garage, reflected headlamp blaze pooled around it. He backtracked to the bedroom, unseen edges nudging him in the gloom. A Remington 12 gauge lay loaded within snatch distance in the space beneath his mattress. Devereaux called it paranoid. Hale called it 'sensible': fourteen years' law enforcement had accrued a thick catalogue of people worth fearing. All firearm-based security measures were acutely necessary.

He kept the gun close as he dressed, awkward and unbalanced in the semi-dark. He made the front door in a crouch, fumbled to free the deadbolts. Two doors slamming. He stepped outside. The gun grips were sweating up already: he gathered a shirt hem and dried them, trotted down the stairs that led to the front left corner of the house.

His property was steep, the garage set in against the slope beneath the main floor. The car was parked nose in to the house, kissing distance to the garage door. Alan Rowe and his minder stood hands in pockets beside it, shoulders hunched against the evening chill, ankle deep in bright light.

Rowe heard the squeak of the stairs and glanced at him. He nodded at the gun. 'Expecting somebody else?'

Hale placed the Remington on the bottom step and leaned it against the house. 'You brought backup.'

'We were out and about.'

'This is a long way from most places.'

'I was told you were hard to get hold of.'

'Not if you ring.'

Rowe shrugged. 'Can we come in?'

'No, thanks.'

'It's cold.'

'I haven't tidied up.'

Rowe smiled. 'I don't mind seeing newspapers on the table.'

'We'll talk out here.'

Rowe didn't answer. He was dressed in a suit, breeze keeping his tie dancing. The property was west of Auckland Central, surrounded by dense bush. The smell of it hung heavy, clean and organic. Hale eyed the escort man: tall, mid-forties, grim and buzz-cut. Mental neon flashed 'ex-cop' in bold. His nose was kicked off-plumb, brow thickened with scar tissue.

Hale said, 'Looks like Sugar Ray landed a few.'

'Didn't fight him,' the guy said. 'Got invited to.'

'Maybe it was lucky you turned him down.'

The guy smiled. It wasn't a kind look. 'Fuck you.'

Rowe ignored him. He said, 'I was hoping you might reconsider your earlier decision.'

'I didn't realise I hadn't made myself clear.'

'I didn't give you the full story.'

'That's not a great way to win me over.'

'Just hear me out.'

'It's after eleven.'

'All I'm after is two minutes of your time.'

Wind caught the front door and ticked it against the latch. Hale said, 'I'll need a name.'

'Sorry?'

'Visit my house and I need to know who you are. It's like roll call.'

Rowe laughed, gestured vaguely. 'This is Wayne Beck. My chief of security.'

'Beck the boxer. Nice to meet you.'

Beck didn't answer.

Hale said, 'Turning up at this hour, I thought maybe you were planning on being unfriendly.'

Rowe laughed again, but with dampened gusto. 'No. Nothing like that.'

'Shall we get to it then? My bed's getting cold.'

Rowe placed his hands in his pockets. Wind put a ripple through his trouser shadow. He said, 'The fight club break-in on January third's linked in with the bank thing on October eight last year. Auckland Savings and Loan. Same guys did both jobs.'

'I'm aware of that.'

'My daughter was a victim at the fight club on January third.'

'Explain.'

'She was in the way of the getaway. She was hit on the side of the head with a hammer. It broke her jaw and left her unconscious. She bit off the end of her tongue.'

'How old is she?'

'Nineteen.'

'I didn't see her when I visited.'

'She doesn't live with me. And she's still in hospital.'

'I didn't realise fight nights were the sorts of things nineteen-year-old girls were interested in.'

'Yeah. Neither did I.'

'You could have told me this earlier.'

'I'd banked on you saying yes without needing the full details.'

Hale didn't answer.

Rowe smiled. 'She probably wouldn't want me to pursue anything anyway. Heaven forbid someone else gets hurt, even if they did hit her in the head with a hammer.' He nodded in the direction of the shotgun. 'You're not a violent man, are you, Mr Hale?'

'Lapsed pacifist.'

He nodded slowly and appraised the front of the house. 'I can live with that.'

'So what do you want me to do?'

'The brief's the same. Find who did it. And then tell me.'

'And then you'll send Wayne after them.'

Rowe laughed. 'I don't know. Perhaps something similarly effective.'

'Will she make it?'

'My daughter? She'll need a lot of rehabilitation.'

'Has she spoken to the police?'

'No. She's in and out of consciousness.'

'I'm sorry to hear that.'

'Yeah. Don't bother doling out watered-down sympathy. No offence. You don't know what it's like.'

Hale didn't answer.

Rowe turned away and stood facing down the driveway towards the street. 'Give him the file,' he said.

Beck circled the rear of the car and opened the passenger door. He palmed his tie flat and leaned in and removed a blue plastic folder from the footwell. He passed it across the bonnet to Rowe, who handed it to Hale. It was thick, bulked by documents in plastic page-protectors. Hale thumb-fanned it front to back. He checked the first page, angled it to catch headlight gleam. A digital photograph of a woman's face lay inside a plastic sleeve, the right side of her face abraded and swollen. Eye a narrow slit amid a purpled socket.

Rowe said, 'She lost teeth on that side, too. Nearer the back, so they reckon her smile will still be okay.'

'What's her name?'

'Charlotte Rowe. I've got the police shit in there too for you. Their reports and some witness info.'

Hale skimmed pages, file propped atop a cocked thigh. Photocopied pages of codified cop-speak, semi-legible.

'I'll take a look at it.'

'Does that mean "job accepted"?'

Hale closed the file. 'I'll call you tomorrow.'

Rowe tipped his head at the car. Beck slid in the driver's seat.

'I guess it's progress,' Rowe said. 'If you're as hard-nosed as you make out, I reckon we might strike pay dirt.'

Hale moved back to the steps and picked up the shotgun. Rowe opened his door. He paused there, half in and half out of the car, one elbow propped on the window. 'There was a guy they interviewed,' he said. 'Name was Leland Earle. He's in prison so they're probably not looking to pin it on him, but I think maybe they reckoned he might know something about it.'

'Did they get anything out of him?'

'I don't know. But I guess if there'd been an arrest we would have heard. You know?'

Hale nodded.

Rowe said, 'This isn't my area of know-how, but maybe you could have a chat to this guy Earle. If you can get to him ...' He slid into the car and pulled his door, buzzed his window down. 'Worst-case scenario, you'll just retrace their steps.'

'I'll call you tomorrow.'

Rowe nodded at the shotgun. 'Don't forget to unload.'

Hale didn't reply. The car rolled back off its brake and crunched down the hill towards the road. He watched the ghost of headlights dwindle between the trees, and then he went back inside.

■ TEN

TUESDAY, 14 FEBRUARY, 12.48 A.M.

Bowen had left. Devereaux passed his darkened office and used Grayson's computer in the incident room to access Howard Ford's details. Leroy James Turner, DOB 19 July 1985, was listed as a known associate. Offence code flags formed a résumé: 1510/6120 denoted serious assault and burglary. He was currently paroled to an Avondale address, pursuant to the assault charge.

Devereaux took the stairs down and crossed Vincent Street to his car. He cruised up town to K' Road and stopped at the lights. The grimed and weary frontages, the stencilled signage in paled pastel. A prostitute made a slow strut across the intersection, gloss-slicked lips pouted to entice, heading west. Devereaux stayed straight ahead and worked his way down to New North Road, southbound.

He got across onto Georges Road fifteen minutes later. Beer-toting teens lined the kerb beneath the Hollywood Cinema's brick façade. Gazes tracking in perfect sync as he passed. A homeless man draped a bench in the reserve opposite, arms crossed as if arranged for burial.

Leroy Turner's address was a minute's drive further south, a single-storey weatherboard unit backing the railway line. A grey Fiat Punto sat beneath an open-end carport. A mail-choked letterbox bookended a limp wire fence across the yard. Devereaux parked behind the Punto and climbed out. His door slam set a curtain rippling. The front entry was recessed in a little alcove above a concrete step, spotlit by a single bulb. He walked over and knocked twice.

A voice called through the door: 'Who is it?'

'Police, Leroy.'

'What do you want?'

'A chat about Howard Ford.'

'I'm not Leroy.'

'Then get him.' The request harsh and echoic in the little alcove.

'Leroy isn't here.'

'He'd better be. His parole conditions say if he's somewhere else at this time, he's in trouble.'

'Well, whatever. I don't know where he is.'

'Well, either he's here, and he needs to let me in, or he's not here, and you need to let me in so I can find out where he is.'

No reply.

Devereaux said, 'So which is it?'

'Ah, Jesus. Yeah, I'm Leroy.'

'Right. So open up, now.'

'What's your name?'

'Sean Devereaux.'

'You're the cop Howard knows.'

'I am.'

The handle turned and the door eased back an inch off the catch. Devereaux leaned forward and straight-armed it the whole way open. A man he recognised from the file photograph as Leroy Turner tripped back a step. 'Whoa, man.'

'Whoa, man, what?'

'You can't just come barging in like this.'

'You lied to a police officer. It waived your rights.'

'That's not in my parole rules.'

'It's in everyone's parole rules. It's called not breaking the law.'

Turner didn't reply. He was a short, slight man in his late twenties. A string of pink scar tissue arced from cheek to hairline. Devereaux knocked the door closed behind him with his heel. The serious assault record dictated eyes forward at all times.

'Have you got, like, ID or something?'

Devereaux took his badge and ID from his coat pocket. He flipped them open, eye level.

Turner leaned in: a squint to check face and photo were in agreement. He took a step back and pocketed his hands. He wore a grey hooded jumper above jeans that slippered his feet. Toes protruding past frayed edges. An open door to the left framed a muted television, DVD cases on the floor scattered agape. 'What do you want?' he said.

'Just a sit-down and a chat.'

'About Howard?'

'Mostly.'

'I might have been in bed, man.'

'You weren't, though. You were up drinking, which is a parole violation.'

'You can't prove—'

'Leroy. I'm not an idiot. I could smell your breath through the door. Do not try to sell me bullshit. Have you got any cigarettes in the house?'

'Yeah, I'm allowed to.'

'I know. All I'm after is a cigarette and a bit of a talk, and then I'll get out of your hair. Okay?'

He leaned against the wall. He had dark hair, glazed with a

thick waxen coating. Narrow frame, weak lumps of shoulder pressing his jumper as he folded his arms.

'Howard reckons you're an okay dude,' he said. 'For a cop.'

'Yeah, I am an okay dude. Where can we sit down?'

'I dunno. Kitchen.'

'Good. Let's go.'

The kitchen was at the rear of the unit. Turner swiped a switch. A neon light tube hummed and found full wattage on the third flicker. A bench and fake wooden cupboards wrapped two walls. A frosted glass door accessed the back yard. A cat flap whistled softly through its teeth.

Folded newspaper chocked the fridge level. The seal broke with a wet sigh as Devereaux pulled the door.

'Dude. You can't just raid the fridge.'

'I'm not. Just wondering what you've got all this beer for, given you're not allowed to drink it.'

Turner didn't answer. Devereaux closed the fridge. He took a seat at the small table.

'I don't normally just let pigs in for a chinwag. But Howard said you've been all right to him.'

'I'm touched.'

The cat flap clacked. A grey tabby slunk in, hugging the baseboard. Devereaux leaned down and waggled a finger at nose level.

'You like cats?' Turner said.

'No. But it's his house, I'd better be polite.'

'It's a girl. She's called Millie.'

Devereaux stroked the animal's head. It closed its eyes, pushed up against his hand.

Turner said, 'So what are we talking about?'

'October eight.'

'What's happening on October eight?'

Devereaux took his hand back. 'Don't know. It's October eight last year I'm interested in.'

'The Savings and Loan job?'

'Yeah. Well done.'

'I didn't do it. Who told you I did it?'

'Nobody. I've got it on good info that you might know something about it.'

'"Got it on good info." What's that meant to mean?'

'Howard thought you might know something.'

Turner grinned. He propped himself against the doorframe. 'You won't get far if you're just asking for gossip.' He checked his watch. 'At half past one in the morning.'

'That doesn't answer my question.'

'The fuck should I know anything?'

'Because you've pulled robberies before.'

'So?'

'So you've got connections. People keep you in the loop.'

'Connections. How would you know?'

'I read your file and extrapolated.'

'Extrapolated. Whatever.' He laughed. 'October eight last year, I was in prison.'

Devereaux didn't reply. The cat traced a figure eight around his ankles.

'You said you wanted to talk about Howard or something,' Turner said.

'Howard's been brought in because they think he might know something about October eight. And he doesn't, so now I've got to ask you.'

'Is he okay?'

'Yeah, he's okay.'

'He doesn't know anything about October eight, though.'

'I know. So I'm asking if you know anything about it.'

A smirk. 'Yeah, well, it's all bad news, man.'

'How?'

'What, you want to hear the rumours?'

'Lay them on me.'

'I heard cops did it, and the reason you're making fuck-all progress is because the guys who did the job are the ones in the investigation. Shit's just getting stalled and obscured and stuff. Like, I bet you've got all kinds of dead ends and stuff that just goes nowhere.'

Devereaux said nothing.

'That's why that shooting that happened has been so hush-hush. The one where those cops got cooled out, you know? Like, people got killed, but we hear almost nothing about it in the news because they're keeping it super, super tight. And you want to know why?'

'Why?'

'Because cops did it. Because cops robbed that bank. Because cops robbed that fight club thing. Cops thought someone was going to snitch them, and killed those people in that shooting a couple of weeks back.'

'Who told you this?'

He shrugged. 'I dunno. It's just info that people know. You know?'

A train passed: a laboured seismic rumble. Different regions of the room rattled faintly in loose sequence. A shiver beneath his fingertips as the table trembled.

Devereaux said, 'So who should I be talking to?'

'I don't know. Not me. I've already been talked to anyway.'

'By who?'

'I don't know. Cops. Maybe even the cops that did the job. They thought they were hardcase.'

'What did they do?'

'There were two of them. They just came to the door, like you did, and one of them gave me this big-as grin and flicked his head and was like, "Why don't you come for a bit of a drive with us, Leroy?" And what choice have you got when a cop says something like that to you?'

Devereaux didn't answer.

'So I got in the car with them. In the back. One of them was in the back with me, one was driving, obviously. They took me for a drive just around the block. They'd had me on what they called "rolling recon" or some shit, where they'd just had a dude following me for a few days. They'd got this long-shot photo of me buying half a gram of speed. They showed me that, like it could be some sort of leverage to get me to say whatever. But the guy in the back with me was playing it super-cool. He had one arm stretched out along the back of the seat, holding up the photo in front of my face. And he said something like, "Boy, Leroy, if this ever got out, you'd be going straight back to prison." You seen much of what prison's like?'

Devereaux nodded.

'Yeah. Me, too. And I didn't like any of it. And I was telling this guy I didn't know jack shit about what had happened with this bank job thing, but he just said, you know, "Don't believe you." He had this lighter that he whipped out and he held it next to my head, under my ear, and said he was going to start sizzling my earlobe if I didn't give. Man, I'm not a bad guy. I drive getaway cars. I'm not in there telling people to get on the ground. I've never shot anyone.'

The cat mewed. Devereaux leaned down again and ran a hand along its back. 'When was this?'

'I don't know. Good few weeks back. Early January, I guess.'

'They tell you their names?'

'No.' He folded his arms and hunched into them. Features vacant, eyes with the floor.

'What did they look like?'

He shrugged. 'Medium-sized guys, maybe forty or so. They laid into me.'

'What do you mean?'

His tongue traced his top lip. 'I mean they laid into me. Or the guy in the back did. He was fucking quick. He'd just reach across and hit me upside the head; I'd knock straight into the window. The window hurt more than his hand. But I didn't give them anything; I didn't know what they were after. They drove me back here and parked, and the driver got out and opened the door for me, like a chauffeur or something, but the guy in the back with me just reached up with his foot and gave me a couple of kicks to get me out the door. Hurt like shit. Glad Millie didn't see, or she'd be off.'

He pulled his shirt and twisted sideways. The skin above his hip wrinkled. A U-shaped bruise stamped his lower ribcage. 'See. I'm not even bullshitting.'

A car turned in off the road. A thump and a suspension squeak as it crossed the kerb. Turner dropped his shirt and hit the light switch. The room darkened. The cat slipped beneath the table.

'I'm near paranoid now. Every time someone comes round, I gotta kill all the lights and check the peephole first, you know? Jittery as hell.'

He left the room: light footsteps towards the front of the house. Darkness deepening as he killed the lights in the front room. Devereaux pushed his chair back, palmed his way around the edge of the table. He followed Turner down the hallway: direction obscured, weaving wall to wall as he moved. Right into the television room, plastic disc cases cracking under blind feet. Turner was at the window: a cupped gaze to a gapped curtain. Everything a faint sketch under weak light.

'Oh, shit. It's another cop.' He pulled away from the window, face ashen. 'This your backup or something, what's going on?'

Devereaux pulled him back and looked outside: one unmarked police car behind his own, Don McCarthy silhouetted mid-exit.

'I didn't call him.'

'So what's going on?'

'I don't know.'

'So, then, what the hell? Man, cops are the last people I want round here. Last time cops came here I got the shit beaten out of me. I tell you. Vicious as hell.'

He exhaled and linked his hands behind his neck. Leroy Turner, assault and burglary record, almost frantic.

Devereaux stepped away from the curtain and moved through to the entry.

Leroy's hissed whisper: 'Don't let him in. Please. You've gotta make him leave. I don't want anything to do with this.'

Devereaux ignored him. He opened the front door and set the lock. Then he stepped outside and closed the door behind him.

■ ELEVEN

Tuesday, 14 February, 1.42 a.m.

The Don was dressed suave: a gleam of shoeshine as he crossed the headlamp glare. He smoothed his tie and buttoned his jacket, a neat one-handed pinch.

'Thought I might find you here,' he said.

Devereaux stayed on the step, back to the locked door. The Don's high beams swamped the yard, blades of grass etched in stark monochrome.

'Didn't realise I needed a minder,' Devereaux said.

McCarthy shrugged. 'Thought you might need backup.'

'I'm fine. I appreciate the concern.'

'What are you doing here?'

'I could ask you the same thing.'

The Don smiled. He pocketed his hands and propped a foot up on the edge of the step. Loafer: black leather, laceless, a deep heel. 'You first.'

'Howard Ford told me the occupant of this address might know something about October eight.'

'And does he?'

'I don't know. He isn't in.'

'His car's here.'

'But he definitely isn't.'

The Don's gaze roved: Devereaux's eyes, the window, back

to the eyes. Lie detection with an ice-blue tint. He said, 'The lights were on a moment ago.'

'That was me.'

'You entered the house uninvited?'

'I knocked and nobody answered. The door was unlocked. I went in and found the house empty, turned the light off and locked the outside door.'

The Don smiled thinly. 'A good faith entry, then.'

'Yeah.'

'You have no idea where he is?'

'No.'

'That's a worry. If he's got information about an active investigation, it would be good to get hold of him.'

'Won't be able to now. I locked the door.'

McCarthy came up onto the step. Half a metre between them. 'You know how to pick locks?' he said.

'I do.'

'Now might be a good time to get some field practice in.'

'I don't think so.'

McCarthy didn't reply.

Devereaux said, 'I can't justify re-entering the house. I checked it a moment ago and found nothing suspicious. There's no reason to go in a second time.'

McCarthy scanned the eaves. 'How did you come to be talking to Howard Ford,' he said. 'Given you had strict instructions not to interview him?'

'Custody sergeant let me in.'

'Clearly.'

'I was concerned Ford was being mistreated. I didn't want to wait until morning to find out.'

'And was he?'

'He'd been punched in the face. So, yes, I'd say so.'

'And in the process of assessing his health, you somehow elicited the name Leroy Turner.'

'That's right.'

The Don nodded and mulled it over.

Devereaux said, 'What are you doing here?'

McCarthy raised his hands and jiggled his jacket by the lapels. 'One of the privileges of rank,' he said, 'is that you get to ask questions, but you're not obliged to answer them. How's that?'

Devereaux didn't reply. He felt his pulse ticking at high revs.

McCarthy said, 'Am I going to have problems working with you, sergeant?'

'Let's hope not.'

McCarthy took a step back. 'You shot a guy yesterday. That in mind, I think it would pay to be doing exactly what you're told until everything is ironed out. And carrying out an investigation by yourself at quarter to two in the morning is not what you have been told to do.' He half turned and scanned the street, keeping a tab on his blind spot. 'Don't do anything,' he said, 'unless so instructed by these very lips.' He turned and walked away.

Devereaux didn't answer. He pictured Turner, eye to the split curtain. The Don clicked his tongue and jerked his head, a slight wink of incisor, beckoning him towards the road. Devereaux followed as he walked back towards the drive. McCarthy drew his keys and blipped his locks. He pulled his door and slid in. His lights stuttered as he started the motor. The driver's window dropped.

Parting scorn: 'Remember, sergeant: from these very lips.'

He propped an arm atop the sill, raised a cocked thumb and first finger and shot him once in the chest. Devereaux waited until the car had disappeared from sight, and then he climbed into his Commodore and drove home.

Sean Devereaux is ten years old, and through the wall he can hear the officer fighting with the new wife.

The officer's name is Derren. He's British, ex-air force, clipped and square. Sean's been with him close to six months, only since his mother went into hospital, and each week he hopes it's the last.

The wife is a relatively new pickup. The relationship has freight-trained from just met to just married in the space of three months. Sean thinks the wife probably regrets it, because these late-evening face-offs are beginning to be a nightly occurrence.

Sean doesn't like the wife. She swears a lot. She doesn't have a job. She has a yen for daytime TV. She ignores Sean when he's around her, and criticises him when she thinks he can't hear. Her favourite rhetoric, laden with contempt: 'Why would you want to look after a kid that's not even yours? He never says anything. I don't even know if he can speak. He's probably retarded or something. Why would you even want to look after a kid like that?'

Sean doesn't know the answer to that last question. He doesn't know why Derren would want to look after him. He also doesn't know why the wife's wellbeing worries him. Certainly, there's no reciprocal concern. Regardless, he's upstairs in his bedroom so he can hear what's happening and make sure everything turns out okay. He doesn't even know what they're arguing about. He thinks maybe they don't either. But this is the third night of shouting. The second night the wife's been driven to tears and retreated to the bedroom. Derren isn't one to offer any slack, though: he follows her in and slams the door and stays on the front foot. He cracks a fist on something hard to emphasise his position on the matter at hand.

Sean sits on his bed and listens. There's a pattern to the conflict. Snivelling mumbles followed by shouts, in quick, predictable rhythm. He hugs his knees and looks out his window. The house is a big old weatherboard place on a rectangular lot. A wooden fence borders the back yard. Derren keeps things air-force neat: the lawn's mowed in precise alternating bands. All yard clutter is contained in a shed in the back corner. The bench and barbell Derren uses every day from six-thirty p.m. to seven prior to his run has been stowed indoors. The only sign anything was ever there is two parallel indentations stamped in the grass. Derren takes care to put the bench in a slightly different position every day, so the lawn has a chance to recover.

The view from Sean's window is a grid of side-by-side boundary fences, none of the yards as tidy as Derren's, none of the indoor conversations as heated. Next door, a guy's dumping a plastic bin liner in a metal trash can, ignorant of the nearby conflict. Sean wonders whether people really are clueless to others' lives. Maybe the bin liner man is only pretending to know nothing of nearby troubles. Derren makes a hell of a racket, and the guy has actually visited a couple of times. He's sat in the kitchen with Derren and drunk beer, legs stretched and crossed beneath the table, Lion Red perched atop his gut, laughing with the sudden harshness pull-tabs make when you rip them back suddenly. Sean knows the bin liner man likes to complain about his wife. He doubts Derren cares what the bin liner man does to his own wife, and in this respect it's probably a two-way street. Beer and bloke-chat have forged the bond. Derren will get a free ride from the bin liner man.

Sean gets off the bed and steps to the door. Acoustics are better here. The wife's tears have ceased. Her volume's built. Derren's has, too. Everything overlaps: verbal white noise. Sean's worried. He knows when Derren gets wound up he can hit people. Sean found out the hard way when Derren found him snooping in his cupboard. Sean hadn't found much. Some shoe boxes and some clothes, a light blue uniform on a hanger at one end. He'd thought Derren had been outside, mowing the lawn. He hadn't noticed the motor stop. He hadn't noticed Derren come up the stairs either. Derren grabbed him from behind by the neck, and he got a jolt that stole his breath. And Derren spun him round and got him face to face, and Sean could smell the rank, hot sweat on him, and see the dust and grime trapped in the perspiration on his neck. And Derren was so pissed off his lips curled inwards on his teeth, mouth just a tight horizontal gash. He pulled Sean close and whispered, 'If I catch you in here again, you are going to be so sorry.' His voice whistled softly on the S's. And then he'd spun Sean round by the collar of his shirt and shoved him out through the door and gut-punched him hard enough to leave him breathless and aching. Then he'd dropped down on his haunches beside him and run a big palm over his chin stubble, said that if Sean ever breathed a word that he'd been hit, Derren was going to use the mower to chop off his little finger. So Sean swore it would be their little secret. And when Carole, the foster lady, came by to check up on him, he stayed true to his word.

Sean remembers it. He remembers Carole, who he quite liked, and he remembers wanting to explain himself to Derren at the time he'd been caught. But innocent curiosity hadn't seemed much of an excuse to defuse that kind of outrage. He imagines the wife is probably experiencing much the same issue right now. He hears a slap and a thud and the wife's crying again. Their bedroom door has come off the latch, open about two inches, a thin band of lamplight escaping, but the thought of sneaking a peep makes his bladder feel limp.

He could use the phone. The only telephone is in Derren's study, but Sean knows how to use it. It's a rotary dial, big as a cinderblock, colour of old bone. He knows 111 is about the quickest number you could hope to dial. He thinks that's why 111 was chosen to report emergencies because it's quick to ring on that sort of phone. A neat consolation prize in the sort of situation that would justify dialling it.

He hears the slap-thud again. He makes up his mind. Derren's study is at the end of the corridor. He'll have to pass the bedroom to get there. The phone's on a desk. He can picture it sitting there, a gleaming and untended portal to a place where people are calm and caring. It's a quick sprint down a short corridor. It's a dash across a small room. It's a scramble across a desk. It's seconds' worth of finger work. Nothing.

Do it.

He runs. He passes Derren's bedroom door. He senses his own shadow blot the stripe of light across the carpet. He's in the study. He's at the desk. The handset's heavier than it looks. He cranks the dial, and it purrs back home. He turns it a second time.

The handset clatters on the desktop as he's grabbed from behind. He's lifted and dropped from a great height. The weightless rush of momentary freefall, before he strikes the ground with a crash, and the impact leaves him motionless. He sees Derren step across him, weird and gangly from this low angle, and reach across the desk. He dabs the cradle a couple of times before replacing the handset. He doesn't say anything. He reaches down and grips Sean by the ankle and pulls him out of the room, and Sean knows he's in trouble.

■ TWELVE

TUESDAY, 14 FEBRUARY, 6.18 A.M.

Hale had ignored advice and left the gun loaded, propped against the wall beside the headboard. Rowe's evening visit had put him on edge. He wanted backup close by.

He showered and dressed and went through to the living room. The ceiling fan was still spinning from the day before. Outside on the deck a pigeon toddled, then rose in a snapping flurry. About him the detritus of a lonely evening: a single unwashed plate, an inside-out *Economist*. A congregation of empty beer bottles atop a side table. The cardboard LP sleeve of Patti Smith's *Horses*.

He sat down on the couch. Alan Rowe's file awaited him, fat and well thumbed. Charlotte Rowe's pulped face greeted him at page one. He slipped it free and left it face down on the seat beside him. He flicked through. Paperclipped news articles gave general detail: January third, two armed men robbed an amateur South Auckland cage fighting ring. The club was in a boxing gym off Everitt Road, Otara. Ten dollar entry, the ticket office a caravan parked beside the front door.

The area was low socioeconomic. Crime stats flourished and wealth didn't. Cage fight fans were secured by word-of-mouth advertising: a promise of cheap liquor and edge-of-seat entertainment. The main event was scheduled for eight p.m.

Doors opened at quarter to, closed at eight sharp. Total turnout was two hundred-plus. The ticket caravan was still on the premises at eight twenty-five when two men wearing balaclavas and carrying cut-down shotguns arrived.

Hale document-skimmed: attending officers' incident forms, CIB progress reports. Blurred photocopies and hieroglyphic cop scrawl. The two guys had axed the lock of the caravan door to gain access and forced the man and woman inside to the ground. Takings for the night were secured inside a floor-bolted office safe. Punches were thrown until the correct code was ascertained. The safe held an estimated twenty-two hundred dollars. The two men bagged it. They were on the way out the door when the woman got brave and made a lunge for one of the guns. A brief scuffle ensued. A shotgun round was discharged through the roof of the caravan before a blow to the back of the head from the axe handle put her back on the floor.

But firearm action drew a crowd. A gym side door broke and seeped onlookers. Matter of seconds, and a throng of forty people choked the parking lot between the caravan and the road. A second shotgun round from the door of the caravan thinned things out. People scattered for cover. A red '92 Ford Falcon parked kerbside served as a getaway vehicle. The two guys bludgeoned an escape path across the parking lot towards it: the axe, a hammer, chopped-down shotgun stocks to keep onlookers at bay.

The first emergency calls came in at twenty-nine minutes to nine. Collateral damage totalled the man and woman in the caravan, plus five people caught in the exit panic as the two guys fled across the parking lot. Seven people. A four ambulance roll-out, a frantic police Armed Offenders Squad dispatch.

The Falcon had long since disappeared by the time the first

sirens were audible. Paramedics gave on-site aid. Among the victims: a young woman, presumably Charlotte Rowe, left unconscious from hammer-inflicted head injuries.

Hale browsed. The assumption was that the break-in was linked to the bank and armoured van robberies the previous year. He checked the back half of the file. October eight, two masked men with shotguns had robbed the Mangere branch of the Auckland Savings and Loan. They hit just after nine a.m., four tellers on just-filled cash drawers, three customers. They went in heavy: shoving, screaming, shotguns to shoulder. They put the customers on the floor and promised fatalities if demands weren't met. The bank staff paid up *tout de suite*: two minutes, and almost thirty-eight and a half thousand dollars. Twelve hundred from the teller drawer floats, a little over thirty-seven thousand from the safe. It could have ended cleanly: forty grand profit and no injuries, but they shot a teller. Her name was Janee Tyler. Fifty-six years old, a bank employee for the past seven. The security glass above her counter wasn't bulletproof. She took most of a shell's worth of buckshot to the chest. She died within seconds, just as the heist team departed in a gold Ford Laser.

The 16 November robbery had occurred on the Mount Wellington Highway, eleven a.m. An Armourguard security van was stopped at a traffic light. A white Toyota Land Cruiser SUV that had been tailing it since Ellerslie pulled out and blocked the road ahead. Two masked men packing sawn-off shotguns got out and commanded the driver of the van and the front seat passenger to remain in their seats and keep their hands on the dash. They used a circular saw to cut the lock on the van's side door, and transferred cash bags from the rear load space to the back of the SUV. They gunned all four of the van's tyres, then escaped southbound. Crime scene photographs of buckshot-scarred tarseal were attached. Sixteen thousand, eight hundred dollars of unmarked non-consecutive bills, gone.

Hale checked the reports. They'd picked a good location. It was a straight, flat section of highway. The driver of the Toyota had an uninterrupted view southbound. The guy guarding the officers in the van would have had a clear line of sight northbound. A two-minute robbery, an easy five-minute run down to State Highway 1, heading away from police deployments out of Panmure and Mount Wellington stations.

All three getaway cars had been found abandoned and torched on rural roads south of Auckland. Heat-stripped to the panelling, windows blown, wheels sunk in claggy whorls of rubber residue. The grand scorecard: one death, seven serious assaults, three burned-out stolen cars, nearly sixty thousand dollars AWOL. Arrests pending.

He got up and set the stereo going: another rendition of *Horses*. He gathered the beer bottles together on the plate and washed everything in the sink and sat down in the living room again with the file. The Rowe girl's headshot was still face down on the armrest. He pinched a corner and raised it high, held it to the light from the ranch slider, like X-ray inspection. She must have been pretty. Bad luck has no qualms about where it lands.

His cellphone was on the side table beside the couch. He put the photograph down and called a detective he knew at Manukau CIB.

'Pollard.'

'It's John Hale.'

'Hale. Jesus, how are you?'

'Moderate.'

'You're early. Haven't even got my toast in.'

'Sorry.'

'Nah. I'm messing with you. I'm straight cereal these days.'
'What do you know about these robberies?'
A yawn. 'Which ones?'
'October eight, November sixteen, the fight club.'
'Oh. The big three.'
'Yeah, the big three.'

Pollard said, 'Screwy jobs. I haven't been in the middle of them for a while.'

'I'll pick your brain anyway.'
'Yeah. Go on.'
Hale said, 'How did they link them?'
'What do you mean?'
'How did you conclude it was the same guys on all three?'
'I didn't conclude anything. Someone else did.'
'And what was the logic?'
'I don't know. MOs are similar. Two or three guys, shotguns, balaclavas, no mucking about.'

'That's a bit of a loose connection.'

'Maybe. It's the sort of crime where if you're getting three of them in three months it's going to be the same people. I don't know. There's some other stuff too. Apparently, a couple of bars have been hit, but it was clean in and out. No real details. Talk to Sean D about it.'

'I have. Sean D doesn't know anything about bars being hit.'
'How do you know?'
'Because he didn't mention anything.'

'Oh. Shit.' Pollard spoke through another yawn: 'The intel sharing's been shitty. We've had some stuff that hasn't even been forwarded to the task force because nobody thought to pass it on. Fucking useless. I've given up on it. I'm slowly but surely backing out.'

Hale didn't answer.

Pollard said, 'Lot of blood and trouble for not a lot of money, you know what I mean? Not that more money would justify it. I don't know. What's your interest in it?'

'Someone wants me to do some digging.'

Pollard laughed. 'Good luck with that. Hey, I heard Sean D shot a guy.'

'He did.'

'Sean all right?'

Hale thought about it. 'I don't know.'

'Mmm. Yeah, I need to give him a ring. Hey, you got time for a story?'

'Not really.'

'It's quick.'

'Right. Go on then.'

'You'll love this. Arrested this guy day before yesterday, Class A drug possession, fairly unpleasant sort of bloke. Anyway, he reckoned his favourite activity was to smoke speed and then hop on a bus, get off at a random stop, and then try to sense where murders had happened. Apparently, the speed gives him psychic powers or something, I don't know. He reckoned he wasn't having a lot of success so the other day, before he went out on one of his sessions, he Googled this murder out in Henderson. Some guy called Brent had been axed, something like that. So he smokes his speed, hops on the bus, gets off out in Henderson, and he's wandering round calling "Brent, Brent, what happened, Brent?" And he's getting absolutely nowhere, no answer from the ghost of Brent. So he goes home, can't understand why he's made no progress, fires up Google again, and this is classic, he finds, oh shit, it's not Brent it's *Bret*.'

'You're killing me.'

'I know, right?'

Hale ended the call, then dialled Rowe's landline.

'Rowe residence.'

Not Alan: probably Beck stuck on morning duty.

Hale said, 'Morning, Wayne.'

'Is that Hale?'

'It is.'

'Mr Rowe isn't up yet.'

'Wake him for me.'

Beck put him on hold. The dial tone claimed the line for a moment, and then Rowe picked up. 'It's not even seven o'clock,' he said.

'My apologies.'

'I hope you're not calling to back out on me.'

'I'm calling to tell you I'll take the work.'

Rowe paused. An alarm chirruped and then cut out. 'You said you'd call today.'

'I did. This is the call.'

'All right. Well, thank you.'

Hale didn't answer. He picked up the photograph again and looked at it.

Rowe said, 'What's that you've got on in the background?'

'Patti Smith.'

'In person or CD?'

'Vinyl.' He set the photograph down. 'I'm sorry about your daughter.'

'You told me that already.'

'I only just had a proper look at the photograph.'

Rowe went quiet. 'You ever had something like that happen to someone you know?'

'No. But I can understand what it's like.'

'Yeah.' He paused, and Hale caught his breath on the line: soft aborted syllables, like he was struggling to phrase something. He cleared his throat. 'I'll take your word for it. You going to check out this guy Earle?'

The name came up blank for a moment, before he recalled Rowe's claim from that night: inmate Leland Earle, questioned for robbery leads.

'You still there?' Rowe said.

'Where are they keeping him?' Hale said.

'Mount Eden Prison.'

Hale didn't reply.

'Can you get to him?' Rowe said.

'Maybe … I'll see.'

'I appreciate it.'

'Yeah. I'll be in touch.'

▪ THIRTEEN

TUESDAY, 14 FEBRUARY, 7.13 A.M.

Devereaux woke to bad news: a voicemail message, with Lloyd Bowen's name attached. The timestamp showed the call had come in at 4.37 a.m. Nothing at that hour was ever going to be cheery. He almost couldn't bring himself to check it. Something foreboding in that neat glowing text. He could guess the gist of what lay in store.

He dialled his mailbox number and put the thing on speakerphone. Bowen's clipped tone: 'Sergeant, Lloyd Bowen. Unfortunately, I have to inform you that as of thirty minutes ago, Michael Porter has passed away—'

Devereaux deleted the message.

Michael Porter: his surveillance target from yesterday. His *victim*.

He dropped the phone on the nightstand and pushed the covers aside, sat on the edge of the bed. The floor yawed. He felt faint.

My victim.

He repeated it a few times. Maybe the first time he'd coupled those two words aloud. He ran a hand through his hair. The guy was dead. He tried not to think: an influx of pessimism might spark something rash. Let's not be stupid.

The one thought he couldn't suppress: marvel at this weirdly novel horror. *So this is what it's like.* A vision hit: a brief preview of the remaining forty-odd years he'd have to bear this new hard truth. He considered calling John Hale, but decided not to. He'd killed the guy unaided; he'd endure the guilt of it alone, too.

The phone rang, and he saw Bowen's name light up again. Devereaux ignored it. He sat there a while, and then he went to take a shower.

The McCarthy meeting was scheduled for nine. Duvall arrived early, combed and squared away in dark attire: his funeral suit, replete with tie.

A constable met him and led him through to a meeting room. It was a small cubicle, equipped with a table and three chairs. A window gave out onto the Cook/Vincent streets intersection. Duvall claimed a chair and sat. The constable promised DI McCarthy's arrival was imminent. Duvall shifted his chair back and tried for casual: stretched legs and crossed ankles, reminiscent of The Don on High Street.

It was a seventeen-minute wait. The door opened at a minute before nine and McCarthy walked in. He had another, slightly younger, guy in tow. Duvall stood and traded handshakes. The younger guy was a cop called Frank Briar. They had takeaway coffee but no paperwork, which meant they probably had nothing to give him, which meant no file access. Which meant the following tête-à-tête might not be all that useful.

The Don drew his chair close and hunched in over the table. He was a very big guy: a one-hand coffee cup grip took his fingers full circle. He nudged the table a fraction, shunted it towards Duvall, forced him closer to the wall.

'I honestly didn't think I was going to be able to find any dirt on you,' McCarthy said. 'But I did.'

Duvall didn't answer.

'You assaulted a suspect back in 'ninety-seven,' McCarthy said. 'You want to tell me about that?'

No notepad, no recorder. He wasn't that interested in the finer points. Or maybe he already had them.

'I allegedly assaulted a suspect.'

'You resigned shortly after. Makes me think it was a reasonably credible accusation.'

Duvall kept his arms unfolded for fear of looking cagey. He was backed up in the corner of the room, table inches from his abdomen, forcing him upright. He said, 'I was at a point in my career where I was ready to move on. I didn't want to stain my record, so I walked away from it.'

McCarthy said nothing. Briar thumbed his chin stubble. The silence grew. Tried and true cop tactics: wait for the interviewee to fill the silence. Duvall didn't bow to it.

McCarthy checked his watch, like timing the pause. He said, 'You'd had enough of everything?'

'Yeah, I was sick of it.'

'The people or the work?'

'The people are the work.'

'So who was worse: the cops or the criminals?'

'I'm not sure. Some of them were both.'

McCarthy smiled, stiletto-thin. He said, 'Ironic you say that, given the circumstances of your resignation.'

'Not like you to be accused of misconduct, though, is it Don?'

McCarthy laughed. He said, 'I'm glad we're on first-name terms.' He had some coffee. Duvall drank in his body language: relaxed posture, no telltale arterial tick as he tipped the cup back. Morgue-drawer cool. Briar crossed one leg and rocked back in his chair, cup cradled in his lap.

The Don said, 'Here's the thing, though, Mitchell. I've still got my job, but you don't. I'm just trying to get a handle on why that might be.'

Duvall smiled. He shunted the desk away a fraction and regained nominal comfort. 'You told me yesterday if you managed to dig anything up on me, I wouldn't make it past the front desk. And yet I have. I'm just trying to get a handle on why that might be.'

McCarthy had some coffee, and his gaze came back to Duvall. Sharp enough to pierce lead. He smiled. 'My tolerance for lip runs pretty low,' he said. 'You're going to have to work to endear yourself to me now.'

'I'm just worried that this meeting is a waste of time.'

'How could it be a waste of time?'

'Because you've brought me in here just to tell me you're not prepared to offer up any of the information I've been asking for.'

McCarthy shrugged. He prised one edge of his plastic coffee lid, then resealed it. 'Divulging the contents of official files is a decision we take very seriously,' he said. 'Especially when the requester has been accused of assault.'

'Okay. I understand. Maybe you could stop wasting time and tell me whether you're going to grant access.'

Nobody spoke. Duvall read it as a 'no'. Briar and McCarthy settled into an easy stare. He figured if they weren't going to give him access, they'd either brought him in for a scaring, or to gauge how much he knew.

Duvall took a breath and theorised, off the cuff. He said, 'October eight was an inside job.'

McCarthy clicked out of his flat gaze. 'Why?'

'It was neat, in and out, which means they knew what they were doing, but for some reason they didn't do a prior stakeout.'

'What makes you think that?'

'The area around the bank is commercial, it's under camera surveillance. If you'd found anything, you would have made an arrest. But we're four months down the track and there's been nothing. So there was no visible preparation on their part.'

McCarthy said, 'Maybe they did slick recon.'

'Nobody's that good.'

'A bank's a bank; you know what you're getting in to. You don't need that much preparation.'

'They hit at a time when it was quiet and the safe was loaded.'

'You can make an educated guess about when it's quiet. And the safe could have just been luck.'

Duvall said, 'They used different getaway cars each time; the bank and the armoured van jobs were three minutes, maximum.'

'So?'

'So they're smart, they've worked with each other before; there's some sort of strong past association, they're comfortable with using force.'

'But they burned the cars. That strike you as a smart move?'

'Depends.'

'On what?'

'Maybe there was no way of making certain they could eradicate forensic evidence. Which suggests they'd had the vehicles a while, or used them a number of times, something like that.'

'So then, who are we looking for?'

'Three, moderately clued-up guys between the ages of twenty-five and forty, either with prison, military or police backgrounds.'

'Prison, military or police. That's quite a moral swing.'

'Maybe. They knew what they were doing.'

'Albeit only moderately clued-up.'

'At least two of them. The driver isn't necessarily a bright spark.'

'Maybe they rotate roles; three jobs, they all get a turn driving.'

'I doubt it. Well-oiled machine; they go with a proven system.'

Nobody replied. Briar finished his coffee, set it down and adjusted the edge flush with the side of the table.

Duvall said, 'At least one of them has ties with the Otara community. The fight club thing in January was publicised word of mouth, so that was the only way they could have known about it.'

Nobody replied. The Don had some coffee and let the pause drag on. At length he said, 'Coming back to your original question, no, we're not actually prepared to grant you access to police information.'

'Right. So this was a waste of time.'

The Don laughed. Mercury fillings nesting way back. 'It's not a waste of time,' he said. 'By no means a waste of time.'

He leaned in over the table again. The hunch hiked his shoulders to ear level. 'Here's the official line,' he said. 'Nobody's letting you anywhere near this thing. Nobody's answering questions; nobody's granting you file access. Nobody gives a shit about what you've dreamed up from reading the *Herald* online.'

Duvall didn't answer. The Don spread his hands on the table. 'There's a point,' he said, 'when offers for help sort of drift into time-wasting. I'm sorry to say we are well past that point. We passed it a while back. Think of this morning as a sort of 'eye for an eye' type thing: you wasted my time, I just wasted yours.' He saw a reply coming and raised a finger to cut it off. 'I've got filing cabinets' worth of opened, unsolved serious crime,' he said. 'There's nothing to stop me from taking your assault case from back whenever it was and paying it some real close attention. You know? I don't give a shit what sort of arrangement you came to that let you resign with a clean slate; if you keep getting in my face, I'm going to go digging. All right? You wouldn't believe the sort of stuff I can dredge up. I'm a bit of a magician really. I can make credible evidence and witness testimony just spring up out of thin air.'

He clucked his tongue and sat straight and glanced down at Briar's coffee cup. 'You finished with that, Frank?'

'Yes, thank you, Don.'

McCarthy stacked the two cups neatly in front of him. He smiled. 'I'm glad we managed to clear that up,' he said. 'Frank will show you out.'

▪ FOURTEEN

TUESDAY, 14 FEBRUARY, 9.31 A.M.

An Auckland Central interview room, the official post-shooting debriefing. A boardroom table separated Devereaux from a line-up of Lloyd Bowen, Frank Briar and a Police Conduct Authority investigator named Thomas Rhys. Rhys was a heavy, flushed man in his sixties, face like a bee sting.

Devereaux had skipped breakfast for fear it wouldn't stay down. He was running on four hours' sleep, coffee and half a cigarette. The glass of chilled water in front of him had worked up a full sweat, almost as nervous as he was. He'd shined his shoes, faint tang of polish lingering. Tie so tight he could feel his neck pulsing. He fingered the knot and tried to work up a bit of slack. Fainting wouldn't look good.

A digital camera stood atop a tripod to one side. Briar stood up and set it running, sat down again and stated the date and time, those present and the purpose of the meeting. He spoke leaning forward on folded arms, tie spilled across a forearm, head bent to read from a printed memorandum. His right hand fanned a ballpoint absently.

He said, 'I just want to get a bit of context to begin with. Sergeant, could you explain the background to yesterday's operation?'

Devereaux breathed out, dredged up what he'd rehearsed during the drive over. 'The occupant of the target address was suspected of involvement in the Auckland Savings and Loan robbery on October eight last year.'

'Okay. When you say occupant, you're referring to the man that you opened fire on and shot yesterday afternoon. Is that correct? Michael Porter.'

'That's correct.'

'In what capacity was this man suspected of being involved in the October eight robbery?'

'That was what we were attempting to determine.'

'Okay. So what was the basis of the warrant application that enabled you to focus on this particular individual?'

'Maybe you should pull the paperwork.'

Briar exhaled. He spread his hands and glanced up at the ceiling, appealing to some unseen audience. Bowen checked his watch, stated the time, and announced the interview was being suspended. He stood up and stopped the recorder, sat down again.

'Sergeant,' Bowen said. 'You need to answer the questions, or we're not going to get anywhere.' His pen tapped in rhythm with his instruction. Briar smiled, mock warm.

Devereaux looked at him. He remembered Leroy Turner's story from only hours earlier, imagined Frank Briar in the back seat of an unmarked car, threatening to burn an earlobe if questions weren't answered.

Devereaux said, 'This is essentially the prelim for an excessive force investigation.'

Briar said, 'And?'

'And don't you find it a little ironic that you're the one asking the questions?'

It was a weak jibe. Rhys didn't get it. Bowen caught the

meaning but said nothing. Briar took it on the chin, held his gaze.

At length Bowen said, 'Sergeant, I don't want to have to interrupt this interview a second time. Just answer the questions.'

He set the camera going again, stated the time and that the meeting was being resumed. Briar cleared his throat, repeated the question: 'What was the basis of the warrant application that enabled you to focus on this particular individual?'

Devereaux said, 'The getaway vehicle used on October eight was a red '92 Ford Falcon that was stolen specifically for the robbery. The suspect was seen loitering in the vicinity of the vehicle shortly before it was taken.'

'And that fact alone provided evidence enough for a warrant?'

'That fact combined with the suspect's offending history of armed robbery.'

Such purity in the pause between answer and question: scratch of pen nibs, the clock ticking faintly.

'Okay. And what was the specific purpose of the operation?'

'It was intended to install a GPS tracking device on the suspect's vehicle in order to map his movements and identify potential associates.'

'How many personnel were involved?'

'Me and two other uniformed staff, a five-man Armed Offenders Squad team, two additional undercover tactical officers who were to install the device.'

They nodded and jotted intermittently. Bowen kept a frown in place.

Briar said, 'Why was it that this operation was conducted in broad daylight at ...' He licked a digit and finger-walked through a stack of paper. 'Four-thirty in the afternoon, rather than after dark?' His eyes lifted, eager for a faltering reply.

Devereaux said, 'I didn't make that decision. You'd need to

refer that question to the officer in charge.'

'But, to the best of your knowledge, why was the operation undertaken when it was?'

'The suspect worked nights; best access to his vehicle was during the day.'

Briar said, 'Describe for us the events leading up to the shooting.'

Devereaux watched the clock, massaged his tie knot for extra breathing space. 'Just after sixteen-thirty hours, our radio cut out—'

'Sorry. When you say "our"?'

'I mean me and the two uniformed officers who were with me in an unmarked vehicle. The AOS team was in a second car further up the street.'

'Right. So your radio communication failed?'

'We lost contact midway through a broadcast. A moment later we received a request for emergency support.' He downed some water. 'We moved in, and when we reached the target address, there was a large quantity of blood on the driveway. I entered the house and found one of the tactical officers injured just inside the front door. I went upstairs, and discovered the second tactical officer, injured, in a bathroom, together with the suspect.'

Briar flipped through his paperwork. 'It was at this point that you fired on the suspect?'

'That's correct.'

His notes rustled faintly as he palmed them. 'Explain why you felt it necessary to discharge your weapon.'

'I could see the second tactical officer on the bathroom floor, injured, against the far wall. As I approached the door, he indicated that the suspect was also in the room, concealed behind the door. At this point I opened fire.'

'You fired through the door?'

'That's correct.'

'Three times?'

'Yes.'

'How did the injured officer indicate to you that the suspect was in the room?'

'Eye contact. He indicated with his line of sight that somebody was concealed behind the door.'

'And this provided you with a comprehensive description of the situation?'

'I'm not sure what you mean.'

'Well. From what he conveyed to you by the direction of his gaze only, was it evident whether the suspect had a hostage?'

'No, it was not.'

'So, in effect, you fired blind through a door with no definitive indication of whether or not it was safe to do so.'

'I knew from Habitation Index records that the house had only one occupant.'

'But you had no way of being certain.'

'I was certain that if I didn't shoot him, someone else would be hurt instead.'

Briar let the comment hang unchallenged. His tie had pooled atop his wrist again. He nudged it free and smoothed it against his shirt. 'Did you offer a verbal warning before opening fire?'

'No, I didn't.'

'And given the fact the suspect was behind the door, as you say, it would have been impossible to get a visual fix?'

Devereaux paused, pictured the set-up: the open door, the blood on the floor, bright and irregular. He tried to think whether the hinge side was wide enough to allow a view through.

'Sergeant?' Briar said. 'Did you have a visual—'

'No, I did not.'

'So what was your reasoning in choosing to fire as you did,

as opposed to challenging the suspect to surrender?'

Devereaux had another swallow of water. Rhys had racked up a page of notes, Briar and Bowen at a half-page apiece. He hoped the words 'followed procedure' were in there somewhere.

'My appraisal of the injured officer in the bathroom was that he was critically hurt. His colleague downstairs was bleeding severely. From this I concluded that the suspect was both violent and equipped with a dangerous weapon.' He paused. 'In light of this assessment, I didn't want to act in a manner that could lead to anyone else being injured. We were in a confined space with a clearly volatile offender. I felt that any action short of engaging the suspect as I did could result in further casualties.'

Briar and Bowen absorbed it blank-faced. Rhys appended another line to his notes. He was yet to utter a word.

Briar said, 'So would you say that your ensuing actions were well considered?'

'With regard to the context, I'd say they were.'

'Explain what you mean.'

'I didn't have time to do anything but pick a course of action and follow through on it.'

'You didn't act impulsively?'

'Two men were badly injured. I think a certain amount of impulsiveness would have been appropriate, irrespective of whether or not I displayed any.'

Briar raised his stack of notes, cut the deck with a thumbnail. He skimmed for a moment then looked back at Devereaux.

'Sergeant, this is not the first time you've been involved in a violent incident, is it?'

Devereaux didn't answer.

'Sergeant?'

'You read the answer straight out of my file; I assumed the question was rhetorical.'

Bowen sighed and shook his head, twirled his forefinger for Briar to continue.

Briar said, 'August 2011, you were involved in an arrest during which you discharged a taser at a suspect, before ramming another suspect with your vehicle.'

'I'd been threatened with a sledgehammer.'

'But it's true the incident occurred?'

'Correct.'

'And also a year prior to that, July 2010, you shot a suspect in the leg with a handgun.'

'I'm struggling to see the relevance of this.'

'I'm merely trying to establish a pattern of behaviour.'

'You mean you're attempting to introduce prejudicial material.'

Bowen said, 'Chrissakes.' He got up and stopped the camera. 'Sergeant, I told you to answer the questions.'

Devereaux said, 'Unfortunately, this isn't just Q and A; you can't pull the plug every time I make a point you disagree with.'

Bowen sat down. 'Watch your tone with me.'

Devereaux didn't answer.

Briar said, 'All we're doing is trying to establish whether you've been involved in similar incidents.'

'Right. Why would you want to do that?'

Briar, with a cruel simper: 'To determine whether this pattern of events occurs because you premeditate violent actions.' He almost purred on the last three words.

Devereaux said, 'One minute I act impulsively, next I premeditate my shootings.' He stood up. 'Pick one, because I'm pretty sure I can't be guilty of both.'

He turned and walked towards the door. 'Let's take five minutes.'

▪ FIFTEEN

TUESDAY, 14 FEBRUARY, 10.43 A.M.

The interview lasted another hour. Devereaux found a bathroom and lit a cigarette: never better than after a sustained grilling, employment prospects shaky. He kept his eyes closed for the first lungful, head raised to vent smoke through a ceiling duct. He undid his tie and pocketed it. The top edge of his collar had stamped a ring in his neck. He ran the tap and finger-combed his hair with water, glanced up just as Briar himself walked in. The sight of Devereaux cued a pause, but he didn't leave. He stepped up on the urinal pedestal and unzipped himself. Gaze on a shallow upwards tilt, like he didn't want to bear witness to what was happening down there.

He ducked his chin and hiked one leg as he zipped himself up. He turned and made the hand basin at a slow amble, eyes on Devereaux's face in the mirror, like it was the only place to look. He began washing his hands. Devereaux's tie was spilling out of his coat pocket. He gathered it and stuffed it deeper, out of sight. Briar saw the movement and smiled, like he sensed the relief in being free of it. He held eye contact and found the soap dispenser by touch alone, worked up a thick lather.

Devereaux's mental clock notched twenty seconds. He kept the cigarette between his teeth and puffed idly. The water gurgled gently. The duct fan kicked in with a rush and tugged at the cigarette fumes. Briar shut off the tap and flicked his hands dry and pushed backwards through the door. He mouthed something on the way out that looked like 'Killer'.

Back at his desk. He took a five-minute pause to recoup, then called Don McCarthy. No answer. He tried Bowen's office line.

'Sergeant. So soon.'

'I was just wondering if there's been any news.'

'In regards to what?'

'The man shot yesterday.'

The man shot. Something made him skip the crucial pronoun. Something stopped him saying 'killed'.

Bowen said, 'He's dead. That's pretty much the end of the bulletin.'

'I'd like to attend the funeral.'

'Out of the question.'

'You say that a lot.'

'I seem to go round in circles with you sometimes. I don't want you near the man, even if he's dead. I don't want you near the family. I don't want you anywhere near the issue, and I don't want you to raise it with me again.'

He walked down to Queen Street. Late breakfast/early lunch was a kebab from a place on the corner of Wellesley, chased by a large serving of McDonald's fries. The footpath was choked. He kept close to the gutter, twisted litter tottering ahead in the breeze. His cellphone rang as he was walking back up Queen, but he let it go to voicemail. Newsagent's stands bore grim news: *Man Hospitalised in Police Shooting; Police Shooting Leaves Man Critical.* They hadn't been told 'critical' had been upgraded to 'dead'. No accusatory photographs, but he kept his head ducked anyway. A brisk march, like he could outpace his problems.

He stopped at a phone booth on the corner of Wellesley. The directories were tattered, but he managed to find Howard Ford's number. He stayed in the booth, used his cellphone to dial. Ford's mother answered.

'Mrs Ford, it's Sean Devereaux. I'm a police detective, I believe we've met—'

'You let them hurt Howard.'

'I understand he was arrested last night, I just wanted to check he's okay—'

'Well, he's not. He's not okay, goddamn you. He's got a bloody nose, and bruising, and he's absolutely goddamn terrified. I tell you. You know what he's like. Here I was thinking you're a decent man, but you let this happen to him.'

'Look, I had nothing to do with it; I just wanted to check he's been released, and that he's all right.'

She was crying. She shouted to cut him off. 'I told you he's not. I told you he's not all right. You lot, you're just pigs. You're a pig, and you're a disgrace. That you could stand by and let this happen to him. My God.' Her voice shivered. 'You're a disgrace, don't you dare call me again. Why would a boy like him know anything about the nonsense you were asking him?'

She hung up. He put his phone in his pocket and stood there a moment, shoulder against the glass. The light changed and pedestrians disgorged across the intersection. The earnest urban scurry. The phone handset was off the hook, swinging gently by its cord. He'd seen hangings match that same weak oscillation. His cell went again, but he ignored it.

Do I still really want to do this?

He got back to the station at eleven-twenty. Thirty-eight unread emails greeted him. Don McCarthy's name claimed first and second place: message one informing staff of a case progress meeting at eleven-fifteen, message two a terse instruction to attend said meeting.

Shit. He was already five minutes late, and The Don had a thing about punctuality. He left his tie in a desk drawer and went through to the robbery situation room. Desks were pushed aside to accommodate temporary rows of seating. Frank Briar and a felt-penned whiteboard occupied centre stage. The crowd was thirty-plus: tall, suit-clad men skewed sideways on plastic chairs, on tiptoe, and knees together. A Mexican wave of turned heads as they sensed his entry. A curled patchwork of paper on the walls. He took a seat in the back row beside Grayson. He saw Lloyd Bowen in the front row.

Grayson leaned in for a whisper. 'How did it go?'

Meaning the interview.

'I don't know. If I don't turn up next week, assume it went badly.'

A tap at his shoulder. He turned around, saw Don McCarthy bent forward and beckoning. They stepped outside.

The Don said, 'How was this morning?' A flat tone implied indifference.

'Peachy.'

McCarthy nodded at the door. 'The meeting's a waste of time; we're just going through the motions to keep the brass at Bullshit Castle happy.'

Devereaux didn't answer.

McCarthy said, 'Go home, you look like shit.'

Probably a fair assessment. He didn't feel that flash. Fast food probably hadn't helped. He thought of the files on his desk, the work he needed to do. Then again, in his current state he was unlikely to make much headway.

McCarthy said, 'I need you back here at nineteen hundred. We've got some work to do.'

Devereaux looked at him. He wanted to say no. He wanted to say he'd killed a man, that he felt wrung out, capable of nothing. But he sensed McCarthy could see this: nothing like a glimpse of weakness to make the bastard's day. So he said, 'What is it?'

McCarthy smiled, like he'd already seen the script. 'I wouldn't want to spoil the surprise.' He clapped him on the arm. 'Bring your A-game.'

■ SIXTEEN

TUESDAY, 14 FEBRUARY, 12.10 P.M.

Background checks.

Hale constructed a piecemeal Leland Earle history via Google. *Herald* archives yielded good information: Earle was doing time for robbery, and assault on a police officer. Six years, non-parole. He was no cub scout.

Hale called the prison direct and spoke to the senior Department of Corrections supervisor at general populace, and requested an interview. Ex-cop status won him leniency: fifteen minutes with Mr Earle, alone.

He arrived a little after one. He left his pocket contents in a locker at reception, and a corrections officer led him up to meet the guy he'd spoken to on the phone. The officer's name was Kenzie. He was heavy and fiftyish with wide, Irish-looking features. He hiked his belt with his thumbs as he stood up and came round his desk to shake hands. Judicious combing partially disguised a wide bald spot.

'Can't say he's awful happy about having to talk to you.'

'I'm not exactly thrilled either.'

'Normally we wouldn't be so snappy about setting this up for you. But I'm an ex-cop myself, matter of fact.'

He shot Hale a wink.

He was led to an interview room. A wire mesh window

showed a man he assumed to be Leland Earle seated at a small table. An empty chair sat opposite.

'You just holler if you need anything,' Kenzie said. 'There'll be a couple of fellas standing right out here.'

Hale thanked him. An officer unlocked the door, and he went in. Earle didn't seem to register the arrival. His gaze was static, head canted sideways, like a mannequin in storage. He was mid-thirties, shaven head branded with WHITEPOWER in harsh Gothic stencil, letters edged scarlet for emphasis. He wore a white singlet and an unzipped orange jumpsuit, the top half bunched at his lower back. Empty arms cast limp to the floor.

Hale scraped the spare chair back and sat down. Earle's gaze was somewhere beyond the far wall. Hale turned his chair sideways and stretched his legs out and crossed his ankles. He appraised Earle openly. The man had some bulk: long hours pumping exercise yard iron had left his chest and biceps looking barely contained. Purple slugs of vein lay fatly beneath taut skin. A thin arc of scar contoured his left cheek, rail ties of sutures still present.

The long-range stare drew in closer to home. 'The hell you looking at, gay boy?'

'What'd you do to your face?'

Earle smirked. 'How you think I might've got it?'

'Painfully.'

'Yeah, painfully.' He mimed a lasso. 'Padlock on the end of a bit of rope.'

Hale didn't answer.

The smirk again. 'What you after? You a cop or something?'

Hale didn't reply. He just sat and held eye contact.

Earle grew uneasy. 'Did you not hear my question?'

'I wanted to ask you about the fight club robbery on the third of January this year.'

The gaze zoned back to long distance. A gentle back-and-forth shuffle of his focus, like watching a far-off ballgame. 'It was down in Otara.'

'That's right.'

'You're not going to find anyone who tells you jack shit.'

'That's why I came to see you first.'

Earle spread his arms. 'Why would I know anything about fight clubs?'

'I don't know. The police interviewed you after it happened; I thought maybe you could just tell me what you told them.'

A triumphant look: 'So you're not a cop, then.'

'No.'

'So who are you?'

'I'm an ex-cop.'

'What's your name?'

'John Hale.'

Earle's head tilted back. 'Not the John Hale worked Manukau Patrol 'bout ten years ago?'

'That would be me.'

Earle nodded. 'Yeah. Got a couple of friends who crossed your line one time or another. Remember at New Year's drinks one year, someone said we'd all be better off if you were dead, and I toasted it at the time without knowing who you were, so I'm glad I can put a face to the name, you know?' He laughed.

'What did the police ask you?'

'Why should I tell you?'

'I can put in a good word for you.'

'You've got that sort of cred, do you?'

'You've got nothing to lose by finding out.'

Earle thought about it. Garbled prison noise reached them faintly. 'They were asking me about this guy I used to know called Glyn Giles.'

'Used to know?'

'Still know. I haven't seen him in a long time.'

'What did they want to know about him?'

Earle shrugged. 'Can't remember.'

'You have anything at all you'd like to tell me?'

The guy smiled, almost playfully. 'About what?'

'About the robberies.'

'I know whoever did it pissed off the wrong people. There's a ransom out, or a contract, whatever you want to call it.'

'For what?'

'Guess.'

'Tell me.'

'Money for finding the guys who did those robberies. A dead-or-alive type thing.'

'How much is it?'

Shrug.

Hale said, 'Who issued it?'

'Beats me.' He gave a little smile, like the reality was contrary.

'You look like you're lying.'

He shook his head. 'Everybody wants them found.'

'Who's everybody?'

'I don't know. Like a few different parties. I heard some guys in the chemical trade want to track them down.'

'The chemical trade.'

Earle smiled. 'Euphemism. They pissed off some drug dealer somehow, and now the dealer wants to know where they are. Don't ask me for more, that's just what I heard.'

'I'm sure you could elaborate a little more.'

'Not really. This is all just gossip. I'm passing it on out of the goodness of my heart.'

'Who's this dealer?'

No answer.

'Did this dealer issue the contract?'

'Dunno. Squeeze someone else.'

Hale said, 'A young girl was hit in the head with a hammer.'

'Yeah, yeah, I know. They showed me a photo. But at the end of the day, I don't know her. I don't really give a shit.'

'I'm disappointed that's your position.'

'Yeah, well, I'm disappointed that good guys I know have done hard time just because they met you.' The sanctimonious inmate look: incarcerated, but still privy to the truth of the world.

Hale smiled at him. He drew his chair in tight to the table and steepled his fingers in front of his face.

'What's so funny, dickweed?'

Hale shrugged. 'I never met a fascist I didn't want to suffocate.'

Earle shimmied himself closer. A brief flash of definition in his shoulders as he pulled his chair in. 'I'm going to send up a little prayer,' he said. 'Here goes: I pray that the next time you see my face, you'll be drawing your last breath at the same time.'

Hale smiled again. 'I look forward to it.'

Their faces were a foot apart. Earle snapped forward suddenly from the waist, lining up a head-butt. Hale leaned sideways in his chair and slipped outside the line. He popped Earle a single right-hand jab. Open fist, the heel of his hand. The blow caught Earle flush on the brow. He fell back in his chair, eyes shock-glazed.

Hale stood up. Earle flinched, stayed seated. Nothing like a darn good fright to keep them docile. Hale checked the door: no worried faces at the little window. Moral tuition was best unobserved.

'Good prison lesson for you,' Hale said. 'Watch your mouth.'

He resisted the urge to flex the impact out of his forearm. He slid his chair in then stepped to the door and knocked gently to be let out.

▪ SEVENTEEN

TUESDAY, 14 FEBRUARY, 1.29 P.M.

It was a West Auckland address: single level, brick, a gentle sag in the street-facing guttering. A low hedge fronted patchy lawn scarred by tyre swaths. Duvall was disappointed. Part of him thought she might have gone a little more high class. A central city suite, in preference to the suburbs.

Then again, he hadn't turned out any different.

The door was protected by a two-sided shelter of corrugated plastic on timber framing. He knocked. He'd drafted a greeting on the way over: an apologetic icebreaker that steered clear of full-blown pathetic. Ultimately, wasted rehearsal: the anxious doorstep wait obliterated recall.

A little boy answered. His little boy? Surely not. A tiptoe stretch for the handle, a one-eye peep around the edge of the door.

Duvall said, 'Hello.'

The kid said nothing. He took a step back and bit his bottom lip, hands clasped tightly in front of him. He must have been seven or eight years old.

'Is your mother home?'

The child nodded, disappeared with a pattering scurry, door left ajar.

She appeared a moment later, hair bloated in a loose tousle

as if she'd been sleeping. She had the door fully open before she recognised him.

'Shit. *Mitchell?*'

He smiled. 'Hi.'

She kept hold of the door, reached across herself to smooth her hair. 'What are you doing here?'

'I just wanted to see you.'

She stood there for a moment, palm turned in against her hip, elbow cocked, like she always used to. 'Jordan, you can play on the PlayStation for a wee while.'

She jerked her head to signal him to come inside. He ducked his chin to his chest and stepped in. She closed the door after him. The kitchen was left of the entry. She led the way through and stood leaning against the edge of the sink, fists propped knuckles-down either side. Her eyes hadn't left him, like he couldn't be trusted unwatched. He drew out a vinyl-covered chair and sat down at the table. The chair was metal tube. A bent leg left it jittery.

She said, 'I don't even know why I let you in.'

'Thanks anyway.'

She didn't answer. He noted a trio of beer bottles arranged beside the door.

'Is that your son?' he said.

She nodded.

'How old?'

'Seven.'

She saw his quiet arithmetic: 'Relax: he definitely isn't yours.'

Duvall tried for a laugh, saw her expression, sealed his mouth. He said, 'Were you asleep?'

'I've got a migraine coming on. So you can make it quick.'

Migraine. He restrained himself from a reflexive glance at the bottles.

'Did you call me earlier?' she said.

'Yeah. Wanted to check you were in.'

'And you hung up without saying anything. Big of you.'

'I'm sorry. I just wanted to check that you're doing okay.'

'First time you've ever had that thought.'

'No reason not to start.'

She bent and delved in a cupboard, came out with a silver blister pack of Nurofen. She cracked a tablet into her open palm and threw it back like a breath mint. A wincing, dry swallow.

'Might want to keep them a bit higher,' he said. 'Case the young fella finds them.'

She arched an eyebrow. Still looked great as she did it. 'Right. Anything else?'

He shrugged, like he meant nothing by it.

She shook her head, like marvelling at good luck. 'I thought maybe one day you'd come back.'

'Well. Ta-da!'

She ignored him. 'Probably spent half my time hoping I'd never see you again, and the other half hoping you'd come back so I could tell you some things I wanted to say.' She picked a cuticle. 'So I guess they sort of cancelled each other out, because here you are and I don't really know what to tell you.' She shrugged again and looked at the floor. 'Other than I got married and had a child and found someone who doesn't make me hate myself. Actually feels pretty good, if you know how that feels.'

'It must be great.'

She didn't answer. Electronic noise from the next room: the PlayStation in action. 'Why isn't he at school?' Duvall said.

'Behaviour problems. They're giving him a break for a couple of days.'

'Like, being stood down?'

'Yeah, I guess that's what it is.'

He took a breath and went for it. 'I came because I wanted to tell you I'm really sorry.'

She combed her hair with her fingers. 'You may as well not have bothered.'

He didn't answer.

She looked at the door. 'I think we're past that point where apologies actually mean anything. Just makes me feel sorry for you really because you've actually gone this long before it occurred to you that you'd done something you needed to fix.'

He didn't answer.

She smiled wryly. 'So what sparked this great guilt then? Did you find religion? I've had guys do that before. "Since I've found God I realised it was bad of me to abuse you."'

He shrugged. 'Just thought the scales were stacked one way and not the other.'

'Which means what?'

'I think I've done more bad things than good. I want to switch that around.'

She flicked the Nurofen sleeve idly, seemed to consider another helping. 'I don't think one "sorry" is going to tilt the scales back the other way very much.'

'Better than not at all.'

She returned the tablets to the cupboard and pulled out a chair and sat down opposite him. 'You're not a bad person. You're just an idiot.'

He avoided her gaze. 'I dream about the people I hurt during the tour. I used to dream about them virtually every night. On the nights that I didn't, I'd worry that they had dreamed about me.'

She didn't answer. He said, 'Sometimes I just lie awake in

the dark and I think about everything bad stacked up behind me, and I wonder if at some point something changed for the worse, or whether things were just never any good.'

'Is that meant to win some sort of sympathy vote?'

'No. I think that's just the truth of it. Don't do anything you think you'll regret. Hindsight will blow the dust off it one day.'

She palmed something unseen off the table. 'What did you hope I was going to say to you?'

'I don't know. I guess if I was hoping for something then it's probably a bad sign. I just wanted to get it off my chest.'

The noise from the television paused. She waited for it to resume before speaking. 'So. What are you doing with yourself?'

He smiled. 'Balancing the scales.'

'Don't. No one cares.'

'I care.'

'There's no point. Nobody's keeping score. People waste half their lives doing bad things. The dumb ones feel remorse and try to do something to fix it. The smart ones just move on and try not to waste any of the time they've got left.'

'And what do the good ones do?'

She didn't reply.

'I don't see this as time wasted,' he said.

'Depends whether you've got something to show for it. If you don't, then I'd say it's time wasted.'

She squinted one eye, like the headache was gaining ground.

He said, 'There were internal police investigations after the Springbok tour. We all just closed ranks and walled them out. Nobody cooperated. They made us do this run along Hobson Bay. They had some assault victims at various positions who were supposed to identify us as we went by.'

'And?'

He shrugged. 'And nothing happened. I did the run. I got

from one end to the other and nobody picked me out.'

'Which is a good thing.'

'I don't know. I spent a long time thinking that maybe I somehow sidestepped what was owed to me.'

She was quiet for a long time. He didn't know whether she agreed with him, or she'd run out of things to say. 'I'm training to be a nurse,' she said. 'End of this year, I'll have my degree.'

'Congratulations.'

'You need to do something, too.'

'I am doing something.'

'Whatever it is it's not doing you any good.'

'I thought maybe I could come back and see you.'

She shook her head. 'That isn't going to do any good either. I've boxed you away and forgotten about you. It isn't going to be any good for either of us if I start pulling stuff out of storage. I'm pleased you came today because I thought I hated you but having you sitting here I realise that I don't and that's a good thing. But you can't ever come back.'

He didn't reply.

She said, 'Forget about everything that happened up to now and try to make everything that happens after it worthwhile. I'll see you around, Mitch. Or, maybe not.'

■ EIGHTEEN

They're at it again.

The same old ritual. They're in the bedroom. She's crying. He's shouting. She's firing accusations between snivels. Sean's downstairs. The television's on. It's early evening. The Goodnight Kiwi has just come on, telling him it's time to go to bed. Sean thinks it's too early for bed, and he won't get any sleep with the noise going on.

He climbs the stairs. It's not an easy process. He's still hurting from where Derren struck him with the belt three days before. Derren's study and the phone within it are sacred. They're strictly off limits, and failure to adhere to this brings savage penalties. The penalties had remained nameless until three nights earlier when Sean tried to ring 111 on the desk phone. Retribution was swift. Derren dealt punishment with a calm and wordless determination: a faint smile, a small showing of tongue at the corner of his mouth. Derren took his sweet time. Derren beat him raw.

Sean reaches the landing. The door to the master bedroom's shut this time — no gap. He puts his ear to the door. The shouting's all one-way traffic: Derren only. The wife's crying. Sean hears slaps in rapid succession.

He pauses at the door. Conflict lulls. He can hear snivelling. Sometimes when the wife's been put in her place, Derren leaves her be and goes downstairs and drinks a beer, or pumps some iron in the back yard. Sean hurries along the hallway to his own bedroom, fearful Derren's on the way out. He's just reached his doorway when the wife crashes out of the master bedroom in a stumble and disappears into the adjacent bathroom. Derren's not far behind, and he drops his full weight into a shoulder-slam against the bathroom door, but somehow she manages to get it closed and throw the catch across.

Derren steps back. He's in a singlet, fresh from lawns duty. His shoulders are rising and falling with exertion. Maybe the new wife is more than he's bargained for. He stands there, hands on hips, facing the bathroom door, in profile against the entry to the study, maybe weighing up the pros and cons of busting the lock. A mirror shatters.

'Bitch,' he says. 'If you bust up my bathroom, you're going to be so fucking sorry. I tell you.'

He sees Sean hovering in his periphery, and turns to him. 'Piss off, you little shit.'

He takes a step towards him, palms him in the centre of the chest and sends him sprawling on his back into his bedroom. Sean's head whips back and cracks the floor. He sees stars, like a handful of crushed glass tossed beneath a bright light. Derren slams closed the bedroom door. Sean hears him move back down the hallway. Shouts back and forth through the bathroom door. A tap is running full on.

It takes Derren a minute to put two and two together and work out what's going on. When it all clicks he's hammering on the door with his fist, hollering to be let in. No luck. He decides on a break-in. He's a big guy: two kicks and he's through. Sean hears the panelling crack like dry bone.

'Oh, shit. Shit. Shit. No.'

Sean picks himself up off the floor and steps into the

corridor. The bathroom door's in tatters. It's creased lengthways at midpoint, twisted backwards and clinging by its fingertips to the bottom hinge. Sean steals a glance around the frame. The tap's still running. The bath's half full and rising, the water deep scarlet. The wife's draped limp as old bedding across one edge of the tub, one pale arm trailing gashed and blood-red in the water. Her head's sideways, hair lank atop the water's surface like some stringy weed. The frame and winking detritus of the trashed mirror are all around her. She's got a wide pointed shard in one hand. She's torn her forearm bone-deep, wrist to elbow.

Derren's on his knees, but his hands are in his hair, not helping her. He's realised the time to stop her was maybe twenty or thirty minutes back. He's a military man. Maybe he's seen this before. He knows she's on the verge of a flat line.

Sean lingers there a second longer, and then he's away down the stairs, full sprint. This time around, Derren doesn't even bother to chase.

He followed advice.

He went home and slept: catch-up on hours owed from last night, plus preparation for his outing with The Don. He woke at two-thirty p.m. and brought himself round with a shower and a cup of coffee. His phone was loaded with missed calls. He hit redial without checking the number, waited to see who picked up. He figured it could only be bad news. Call it Russian roulette, all chambers loaded.

Ellen picked up: 'Are you okay? I've been trying to call you but you haven't—'

'Yeah ... sorry.'

'So are you okay?'

'Yeah, I'm fine.'

'You shot someone.'

'It's under control.'

'Christ.' She sounded strung out.

'Are you at work?' he said.

'Yeah. I mean no. I'm at home.'

'Should I come round?'

'Yeah, come round. We need to talk.'

He didn't reply. The 'need to talk' line stalled him.

'Not *that* talk. Just come round.'

He washed his coffee mug and left. Across-town traffic was light, mid-afternoon. She was house-sitting at her parents' place in Herne Bay, just west of the CBD. It was an old two-storey villa, well maintained. A Marine Parade locale afforded panoramic harbour views. He left the Commodore at the kerb and walked down. The front door was open, he made a clatter of removing his shoes in preference to calling out. It was a routine he didn't know why he'd adopted. She came through from the kitchen: a concerned bustle, threading hair behind an ear as she moved.

She kissed him and hugged him close. Her hair smelled so good he wondered why he hadn't visited sooner.

'I'm sorry I didn't call.'

She hung on to him. He realised he was just standing there blankly. He put his arms around her.

'I hate having to find out from other people that you shot someone.'

'I shoot anyone else I'll tell you right away. I promise.'

She laughed.

'God. I'm glad you're okay. I thought you might have been hurt or something.'

'They would have told you if I was dead.'

She pulled away and led him through to the front of the

house. The dining room's bay window framed picturesque still life: pohutukawa trees below a two-tone block of blues where the harbour met horizon.

They sat at the table, adjacent corner seats, her knee against his thigh. She looked out at the view.

He tried for idle chat: 'How long are your parents away?'

'You can't ever do that.'

'What?'

'Not tell me stuff. You didn't ring to tell me anything. It scared the shit out of me.'

'I didn't know what to say.'

'I'm sure you would have thought of something.'

'I tried. Nothing came to mind.'

'You could have just started with "I shot someone" and we could have worked from there.'

'I think I'm just used to dealing with things myself.'

'Yeah, but I'm not. And that's the whole thing about a relationship. You kind of work together.'

He didn't answer.

'You can't just internalise everything. You've got to tell me about these things.' She smiled. 'Otherwise I just worry, and I'm sure it can't be good for you.'

'I told John Hale.'

'Yeah, but he's not a normal human.'

'Just because he drives a Ford Escort.'

'Mmm ... hilarious.'

Devereaux didn't reply.

'So what happened?' she said.

'I was light backup for a surveillance job. They were putting a GPS thing on a guy's car. But the guy caught them at it, went at them with a machete. I had to shoot him.'

'Was it ...' she searched for the word, "proper"?'

'Could be touch and go.'

'Why?'

'I shot him through a door.'

'So there could be trouble.'

'I think there is trouble.'

'Are you going to lose your job?'

'Probably not.'

It didn't seem to reassure her. She released a breath, touched a thumbnail to a cut in the edge of the table. 'Is he still alive?'

'No. He died this morning.'

'Oh, God. Sean, I'm sorry.'

He didn't answer.

'Why didn't you tell me?'

'I was building up to it.'

She blinked, wiped tears with the heel of her hand.

He said, 'It'll be all right.'

'I'm meant to be the one saying that.'

He almost laughed, but bit down on it. 'You shouldn't chew your mouth. Makes you look slightly less pretty.'

She smiled and took his hand in both of hers, then leaned and kissed him on the mouth. He kissed her back, conscious of the fact he probably tasted like cigarettes and fast food. Maybe she liked it. Something about the mix had appealed to him. Her hand went to his collar, ran out along his shoulder.

'Let's go upstairs,' she said. A whisper, an inch from his lips. He felt the heat of it in his mouth. She took his hand again and she led him.

The cop's name is O'Dwyer. He's a tall fat man in a suit. Sean can tell he's had a long day. His jacket's creased, and his tie's spilling out one pocket. His hair's rooster-tailed at the front like he's been running a greasy palm past it for the last eight or ten hours. He puts Sean in the back of a police car and smiles and tells him he'll be along in a minute. He offers a piece of chewing gum, but Sean tells him no thank you.

The street's choked out with patrol cars, all of them parked crooked, doors wide, light bars flaring, dashboard radio units cranked to high volume so the cops on the footpath won't miss an urgent callout.

O'Dwyer and another, younger, cop in a suit rendezvous by the letterbox. They're relaxed. They've seen suicides before. O'Dwyer's checking his watch, like he's late for dinner. Sean scoots across the back seat and drops the window a crack so he can catch what's said.

The younger cop says, 'She's got facial injuries that look ante-mortem.'

'Okay.'

'She bled out a long way, and the water makes it look even more than it is.'

'Has the husband said anything?'

'No.'

'Be real fucking tiptoe if you question him. I don't want him confessing something good, and then some shit-hot lawyer claiming he thought he was being questioned about an assault and not a homicide. You know?'

'Yeah. I'm with you. Are you going to chat to the boy?'

'Yeah. I'd better see the scene first.'

O'Dwyer goes to look in the house, and he's gone about thirty minutes. When he reappears he walks back to the car, and climbs into the back seat next to Sean. He turns sideways on the seat and pulls one knee under him and props an arm up on his headrest. He wasn't chewing gum earlier, but he is now. Sean thinks maybe he always has a piece before he checks a crime scene, to take the edge off the smell.

O'Dwyer says, 'How are you doing?'

'Good.'

'Do Mum and Dad fight very often?'

'They're not my mum and dad.'

O'Dwyer says nothing. He chews slowly and waits for Sean to volunteer the details.

'I got sent here to live with Derren,' Sean says. 'He looks after foster kids. I'm just staying with him while my real mum's in hospital, but when she gets better I'm going back to live with her.'

'Okay.' O'Dwyer nods to himself. 'I understand. So how long have you been staying with Derren?'

'Six months. About.'

'Okay.' He dips a beak of thick fingers in the breast pocket of his shirt and finds his gum. He pops another piece in his mouth. 'Sure you don't want some?' he says.

Sean shakes his head.

'Is there anything that you want to tell me?' O'Dwyer says.

Sean's quiet a second. 'About what?'

O'Dwyer shrugs. 'About anything really. Maybe about what was happening this evening, if you happened to see anything.'

'I don't think I saw anything,' Sean says.

'You don't think you saw anything?' But he's smiling, and there's nothing aggressive in the question.

Sean doesn't answer.

O'Dwyer says, 'I saw that poster of R.E.M. on the wall in your room. You like R.E.M?'

'Yeah. They're cool.'

'They are pretty cool. What's your favourite song?'

Sean gives the question careful thought. '"It's the End of the World As We Know It",' he says.

O'Dwyer nods slowly to himself, eyes narrowed, like that's what he'd been expecting to hear. 'That's my favourite song, too,' he says.

Sean says nothing.

O'Dwyer's big arm is draped along the back of the seats, hand the size of a lampshade hanging next to Sean. O'Dwyer nudges him gently on the shoulder with his fingertips. 'Do you reckon you might be able to tell me a bit about what happened tonight?' he says.

Sean thinks about it a long time. Cops are milling about on the footpath, eyes downcast, swiping footpath grit with their soles. O'Dwyer has a friendly look on his face. He likes R.E.M. 'I was downstairs watching TV,' Sean says. 'I turned it off when Goodnight Kiwi came on.'

'Did you? Good man.' O'Dwyer smiles. 'My little boy's meant to turn off the telly and go to bed when Goodnight Kiwi comes on, but sometimes he doesn't.' O'Dwyer shakes his head, and looks a little disappointed. 'So what was going on when you were watching TV?'

'They were upstairs fighting.'

'Where were they upstairs? Do you know?'

'In Derren's bedroom.'

'In Derren's bedroom. Okay. So what did you do after you'd turned off the TV?'

'I went upstairs, too.'

'Where did you go upstairs?'

'To my room.'

'Okay,' O'Dwyer says. 'So you're in your room. And the others are in Derren's room, fighting.'

Sean nods.

'What happened after that?'

'She ran out of the bedroom,' he says. He knows the wife's

proper name, but for some reason he can't bring himself to use it. 'She locked herself in the bathroom.'

He hasn't told O'Dwyer about the sound of the mirror breaking, or the bath running, but that's okay. He would have seen them and figured it out for himself.

'What happened after that?' O'Dwyer says.

'Derren stood at the bathroom and told her to let him in. But she didn't. He saw me standing at my bedroom door, and he pushed me over and slammed the door shut.'

'Did he hurt you?'

'A little bit. I hit my head on the floor.'

'Is your head okay?'

'Yes.'

O'Dwyer feigns concern: 'Is the floor okay?'

Sean smiles shyly and nods. 'The floor's okay.'

'All right. So then what happened?'

'Derren broke down the bathroom door. Well, that's what I heard.'

O'Dwyer waited for more.

'After that, I went and looked in the bathroom. She was lying in the tub, all bleeding. Derren was crouching next to her, with his hands on his head.'

O'Dwyer sucks a tooth and patters his fingers against the seat. 'Do you think you might have seen anything else after Derren broke down the door?'

Sean says nothing.

O'Dwyer looks at him. 'Like maybe you saw Derren cut the lady's arm,' he says slowly.

Sean says nothing.

O'Dwyer shrugs. 'I don't know. Maybe you didn't see anything like that. I just thought this chap Derren's not a very nice guy, maybe you saw him hurting the lady in the bathroom.'

Sean doesn't reply. O'Dwyer's nailed it, though: Derren isn't a nice guy. He remembers being grabbed from behind when he was looking through the cupboard. He remembers being dropped when he tried to use the phone. He doesn't need to remember the belt; he can still feel the injuries. He thinks if he tells O'Dwyer he heard the mirror break and the tap running before Derren was even in the bathroom, then things might play out a little easier for Derren. Sean definitely didn't see Derren cut the wife, and he gets the feeling O'Dwyer's trying to put words in his mouth.

Not a very nice guy.

O'Dwyer leans across and claps him gently on the knee. 'Have a careful think about it,' he says. 'We'll get one of the ambulance people to check you out, and then we'll have another little chat. Okay?'

Sean nods. The suspension wriggles as O'Dwyer climbs out, and the radio noise from outside spikes loud before he slams the door.

Afterwards they lay in bed and he told her about the morning: the post-shooting inquisition, his talk with The Don.

'You're scared of him,' she said.

'Who?'

'McCarthy.'

He thought about it. Wind caught the drapes and threw fluid shadows on the roof. 'Honestly, yeah, I think I am.'

'Why?'

'I interviewed two suspects last night, both had been assaulted.'

'And it was McCarthy?'

'No. But he keeps in the loop. He knows what's going on.'

She didn't reply. She had hold of his hand under the sheet.

'We left the front door open,' he said.

She didn't reply, tented the sheet with a raised knee. 'What did you think when you first met me?' she said.

'I can't remember.'

She fell quiet, like she was waiting for him to add something. She said, 'I remember you struck me as a nice guy.'

'So?'

She rolled over and looked at him in profile. 'So someone else will have figured that out as well. They won't get rid of you.'

'I killed a man.'

'You had to.'

He didn't answer. The more he considered it, the more he doubted it. He took a shower in the bedroom en suite, dressed and sat on the end of the bed. He could see her body through the sheet, vague lines of a graceful design.

'My parents are back tomorrow,' she said. 'They're having evening drinks here.'

'That's nice for them.'

'You're coming, too.' She nudged his thigh with her foot.

'I don't think they like me.'

'All the more reason to try to create a better impression.'

He fell quiet. He'd wanted a reply that allayed suspicion.

'They might not be too happy if they knew what we were up to in their bed,' he said.

She laughed. 'This isn't their bed.'

He turned where he was seated and looked at the closed bathroom door. 'I had a dream,' he said.

Her forearm was across her face; she let it fall to the pillow above her head and looked at him. 'About what?'

'When I was a kid.'

She waited for more.

'When I was about ten, I stayed with this ex-air force officer.'

'The English guy?'

'Yeah. He didn't get on with his wife.'

'You've told me this.'

'Do you want the full version?'

She was silent a long moment. 'Yeah, you can tell me.'

He leaned forward, elbows on knees. Hunched form headless from where she lay.

'They had a fight one day; she ran into the bathroom and killed herself.'

'You told me that bit.'

'She used a mirror and a hot bath.'

Silence for a short spell. She said, 'I guessed it was something like that.'

'I saw it.'

'You watched her actually do it?'

'Well, I saw her afterwards. Dead, or heading that way.' He adjusted his sleeves, pushed ragged blossoms of cuff to his elbow. 'I saw her lying there, bleeding.'

She waited. The drape folds shuffled for position.

He ran his hands through his hair. 'I think she'd just had enough. He'd abused her before. There were old ante-mortem injuries. Bruising and stuff. She'd called the police on him a couple of times.'

She drew her legs in and sat upright. 'Did he ever abuse you?'

'I got off pretty lightly. He beat me up, but not as bad as the wife. I hadn't been with him very long when it happened. Few months. But they moved me to somewhere else.' She sensed him smile. 'And I never went back.'

'I wouldn't dwell on it.' She nudged him again. 'Although you look like you've done a fair bit already.'

He smiled. 'I just think about all the time people have lost. All those years stacked up. It's got to be attributable to someone.'

'Not you.'

'Maybe.'

'What was the dream?'

'That was the dream. I woke up one day thinking about that guy I used to live with, and all those people robbed of their lives. It was just there in my head when I came awake, and I figured it must have been on my mind in my sleep. But I didn't remember it.'

'You think about him often?'

'Sometimes. I managed to block him out for a few years. They gave me therapy after it happened. I'd tried to call the police another time when they were fighting, but he'd stopped me. If I'd succeeded I could have saved her. She'd be a completely different person. She'd be alive. I'd have rewritten history, better or worse.'

She didn't reply. They sat together on the bed for a long time. After a while he picked his jacket up off the floor and left without looking at her.

▪ NINETEEN

TUESDAY, 14 FEBRUARY, 3.12 P.M.

Prison visits. Paperwork for major crimes riding on his passenger seat. It was like being back on the beat.

Hale drove south. The female ticket attendant during the January third fight club robbery was named Leanne Blair. Rowe's file gave a South Auckland address. He got down there a little before four in the afternoon. It was grim viewing, even under summer sunshine. Low socioeconomics made for drab real estate. Grey weatherboard abounded. Youths draped on sofas and loaded on premixed drinks watched him flatly from an open garage. He'd encroached on Crips gang territory: a trio of teens in blue bandannas posed raised middle fingers and masturbatory gestures for his rear view. Overlapping blue and red fence graffiti implied a Crips/Bloods turf war.

Blair worked a day shift at a liquor store on Everitt Road. He figured it was worth a check on the way through. He parked in the bay out front and went in. Shop-front sandwich boards boasted bargain whisky. Left of the door, boxed grog was pillared floor to ceiling. A guy in his forties manned the register, folded forearms a thick black-haired stack across his stomach. A hockey stick stood propped against cupboards behind him, two kids about six or seven kicking a ball in a metal shelving aisle.

Hale found her stocking twelve-pack boxes of Bud in the

walk-in cooler out the back. She was a medium-built woman in her late thirties. Her nose was kinked fractionally, ghost of a bruise hanging from one eye.

She shelved her last box and flicked her eyebrows at him. 'Help you?'

'Leanne Blair?'

'Uh-huh.'

'Wondering if you had a moment to speak with me about the incident back on third of January.'

'Incident?'

He stood and waited for a firm reply. The chill had tensed him up, faint metallic odour to the air. She realised he wasn't going to move until she answered.

'You police or something?' Rounded fricatives: something was 'somefing'.

'Private investigator.'

'Got, like, a badge or something?'

He showed his ID.

'What's the time?' she said.

'Almost four.'

'All right. Well, how's this: give me a ride home, and along the way, you can ask me all the questions you like. How's that?'

'That sounds fine.'

'Give us a couple of minutes, and I'll see you out front. You got a car or something?'

'Black Ford Escort.'

'Shit. Don't see many of them round nowadays.'

He left the store and waited for her in the car. A concrete-block wall had been freshly whited over: paled tags beneath like veins through pallid skin. She emerged a minute later, imitation white leather handbag over one shoulder. From a distance he could see she was pregnant: a slight bulge gapped a sliver of clothing along her waistline. She pulled the passenger door and sat down heavily, twisted and dumped her feet in the footwell. She closed the door.

'I'm not too far from here,' she said. 'So if you like, you can run me home and just come in and talk or whatever.'

'Okay. We'll do that.'

They made a right out of Everitt, passed one of the Crips kids a moment later. He stopped on the footpath and jutted his pelvis and shot the finger, one thumb hooked through the front of his belt.

They reached her house a moment later. It was a single-level weatherboard box in lime green. The fence boasted newly minted blue graffiti.

'Just leave the car here. Safe as.'

He parked at the kerb. They got out, and he followed her to the open front door. He could hear children's voices, backed by a video game console cranked to high volume.

'The fuck …' she said.

The entry gave straight into the living room. Six boys, aged maybe four to ten, were crowded around a television set.

'Isaac,' she screeched. 'Fuck's sake, turn it down.' She paused in the middle of the room and looked around. 'Actually, fuck off, all of you. Look at this mess. Shit.'

She kicked a grounded pillow and twirled to take in the mayhem. The kids scattered and disappeared. No doubt a well-rehearsed dispersal. The screen was paused on a still-frame: a digital cop's head cross-haired by a sniper's scope. She stepped to the television and killed the power, kicked a plastic controller aside. A sofa faced the television. She sank into it, head back and legs spread.

'Long day. Shit.' She looked up. 'Right. You can just ask whatever.'

'I appreciate you taking the time to do this. I realise it's probably not that easy to talk about.'

'Yeah, well.' She clucked her tongue softly and checked the ceiling.

'I understand you witnessed a robbery back on January third.'

'Yeah, victim more than witness.' She pointed with a hooked finger. Vague, like a deathbed directive. 'Feel free to sit down or something, if you want.'

He claimed a plastic deck chair next to the television. Static crackle as his arm brushed the screen. 'Can you describe what happened?'

'When the robbery happened?'

'Yes. When the robbery happened.'

She pulled her legs up on the sofa, squeak of squabs. 'Yeah. We were selling tickets to the fight out of this caravan we had parked up there beside the front door. Have you had a look at the place?'

'No, I haven't.'

'Yeah, well, anyways it was a caravan. We pulled in two, maybe three grand, something like that.'

'You were inside when the theft occurred?'

'Uh-huh. Yeah, in the caravan.'

'Cashing up?'

'Yeah. Counting and bagging everything up, and I just glanced at the window, and saw this dude standing there pointing a shotgun at me.'

'And you let him in?'

'Didn't have to be a brain scientist to work out what would happen if I didn't. You know? So I let them in, and, I ain't joking, soon as it's unlocked, they hit the door with an axe or something to knock it back, and they came in.'

'Did anyone else see this?'

'Don't think so. Just us in the caravan and the fellas outside.'

'What did they do once they were in?'

'Am I getting paid for this?'

'No. Sorry.'

She nodded and thought about it. Carpet had pulled back off the skirting like a snarl. 'How long do you think this'll take then?'

'Not very long.'

'Not very long. Sweet as.'

'What did they do once they were inside?'

Her mouth downturned as she thought about it: 'They just came straight in the door, and one of the guys just punched Doug straight in the face.'

A flash to Rowe's file: Douglas Haines, the second ticket attendant that night.

She said, 'You think you break into somewhere with guns and shit, you don't really need to do any hitting. Anyway. They did.'

'What size guys were they?'

'Dunno. Same size as you maybe.'

'Big then.'

'Yeah. Pretty big.'

'Nationality?'

'Dunno. They had masks on, and sunglasses over their eyes, and gloves on. Didn't say too much, either.'

'Did you notice an accent?'

'No. But I'm not good with how people talk. I just hear words; all pretty much sounds the same.' She looked at the dead TV. 'They knew what they were doing, though, eh. Shit. They kept everything covered with those guns. My old lady used to say it's better to be good at nothin' at all than to be good at sin. I quite like that one.'

'They give you that black eye?'

'Oh, yeah. Shit.'

She touched a fingertip to her lid, glanced at it like she might have picked up a smudge.

'Got beat up pretty bad.' She patted her stomach. 'Kept the baby, though.'

'That's good.'

'Yeah. Fuckin' good.'

'How did you get the job?'

'Guy I know offered it to me. He used to be a church minister. Now he runs fight clubs.' She laughed. 'Reckon they'll let him into heaven?'

'I'll keep him company if they don't.'

She nodded slowly. 'You believe me, though?'

'Yes. I believe you.'

'Good. Just, normally when I tell the story, people look a bit more impressed.'

'I guess I knew what to expect.'

'You're like the cop I spoke to. Gave him what I gave you and it didn't rattle him too much one way or the other. Like he'd heard all kinds of stuff in his day and there ain't none of it that surprised him all that much.'

He rolled in his seat and slipped his wallet from his pocket. He removed a copy of the Charlotte Rowe headshot and offered it in two fingers. She leaned in to take it, grinning with the stretch.

'Who's this?'

'She was hurt during the robbery.'

'Looks like she got hit with a hammer or something.'

'She was.'

She drew her legs up on the cushions again.

'Yeah. Some folks heard all the commotion or whatever,

came outside to see what was happening. They had to just sort of smash their way through to get away.'

'Have you seen her before?'

'Maybe.' She held the photo nails-only at one corner, waved it like airing a Polaroid. 'I dunno. Doesn't really ring any bells.'

Hale waited, in case of clearer recollection.

'You want this back?' she said.

'Please.'

She passed it back.

'How do I find this guy Doug?'

'Don't know.'

'So who's this friend of yours that got you the job?'

'I call him Pastor Drinnan.'

'Where can I find him?'

'At home. He's pretty much retired.' She gave him the street name. 'It's a yellow place with a house bus-thing parked next to it. You'll know the one.'

■ TWENTY

TUESDAY, 14 FEBRUARY, 4.25 P.M.

Devereaux didn't think going home was a good idea. He was a recidivist over-analyser. Solitude implied an afternoon of dwelling on things best forgotten.

His former boss was a woman named Claire Bennett. She owned an old villa in Grey Lynn, just south of the central city. Her block was a line-up of houses of the same 'twenties vintage, pressed close to low front fences, footpaths cracked by root upheaval. He saw her car in the driveway and pulled in behind. She must have heard his arrival: barely a pause between his knock and the door opening.

'Still not above cold calls,' she said.

'You free?'

She stood aside. A stern, heavy woman, nearing sixty. Face lined with sharp precision, as if aged by intention. 'Yeah … in you come.'

She had a combined kitchen and living area in an addition at the rear of the house. A floating counter split the space lengthways. French doors opened onto a low deck and square back yard corralled by brush fence. A rug took the afternoon gleam off the timber flooring.

'You had some drama,' she said.

'News finds you fast.'

'I heard a cop had shot someone; you topped my list of likely candidates.'

He didn't reply. She saw something in his expression and waved the comment off. 'No. I've still got my contacts.'

'I'm sure you do,' he said.

'Are you all right?'

'People keep asking me that.'

'And what do you keep telling them?'

He ignored the question. He stood at the French doors and looked at the yard. 'Got any coffee?' he said.

'No. I can do tea, or hot water.'

'Tea will do.'

He stayed at the window. She bustled in his periphery, filling a jug, gathering mugs. The reasons behind her resignation varied. The official line was she wanted to be at home to care for her daughter: the girl was autistic and recently expelled from high school. But gossiped conjecture held that Bennett had been asked to move on. Devereaux attributed the exit to a measure of both. The former, helped along by the latter. He turned away from the window and saw her watching him.

'It's giving you grief,' she said.

'Sorry?'

The jug built to a roar. She took teabags from a ceramic jar in a cupboard and allocated one per mug.

'It's on your mind.' She smiled. 'Made me think you popped round so you can hear me say, "Don't worry about it."'

He laughed. 'Alternative was I could just go home and listen to myself say it.'

She pulled a drawer and rummaged for a teaspoon. 'But you wanted to share the load?'

'Something like that.'

She looked at him a moment. 'Jesus, cheer up.'

Devereaux said, 'He's dead.'

She was quiet a long time. In his periphery he saw her lean against the counter and fold her arms. 'Oh, God, Sean. I'm sorry.' Ellen's words exactly.

He stood facing the window. He couldn't look at her, sensed her desire for further details. The jug clicked. He said, 'Milk, two sugars.'

He heard the scrape of mugs on bench top. Bennett said, 'We'll go on the deck. Got some good sun at the moment.' Contrived levity in her tone.

He shouldered the door against a snug frame and stepped outside and took a seat on the step down to the lawn. Bennett joined him a moment later and passed him a mug. She sat down beside him. She'd read him instantly. He'd conned himself into thinking his visit held no strict purpose, but she'd burned that: *You popped round so you could hear me say, 'Don't worry about it.'*

He dropped the mental ruse. Let's get her verdict.

Right on cue: she leaned forward and placed her mug on the step between her feet. 'So tell me about it.'

Devereaux said, 'I shot him, and now he's dead.'

'I know. Tell me about before that.'

'I thought you'd heard the story.'

'Not from you.'

He took a slow swallow. 'I feel like I'm guilty of something.'

'You mean you feel guilt, or you're worried someone will decide you did something wrong?'

He thought about it a moment. 'Both, I guess.'

She nodded slowly, like she'd guessed the answer. 'It's a big deal,' she said. 'Whether it was needed or not.'

'It was needed.'

'So we'd better hear all the details then.'

He gave her the rundown. She listened quietly and nodded once when he was done.

'What did the Merry Prankster think?' she said.

'Who?'

'John Hale.'

'He said it sounds like the guy needed shooting.'

'Never did fluff around when he had something to say, did he?' She looked at him sideways, lids low. Her lips stayed almost static as she spoke. 'Reality is, every so often you're in a situation where you have to shoot someone. And that's pretty much the long and the short of it.' She had some tea. She held the mouthful, as if second-guessing the swallow, then eased it down gently. 'And I've known you long enough to know I'm sure you wouldn't cancel anyone's flight unless they really needed to get off the plane.'

'Thanks, Claire.'

She gave his knee a pat.

'You ever have to do it?' he said.

She shook her head. 'No.'

Devereaux didn't answer.

'Got any of those cancer sticks?' she said.

'Excuse me?'

'Those things you smoke. Cigarettes.'

'Why? You want one?'

She propped her elbows on her knees and nodded to herself. 'Yeah. Why not?'

He leaned back on one elbow and pinched two cigarettes free from a flattened pack in his jacket. Kinked, but still serviceable. He passed one to Bennett. She put it in her mouth and leaned in for him to light it.

He said, 'I thought you quit.'

Smoke leaked through a smile. 'It's a work in progress.'

He lit up his own. 'Where's Hannah?'

'My sister's got her today.'

'How is she?'

She shook her head and made a face. She cupped a hand across her neck and rubbed her throat. 'Not brilliant.'

'She going to go back to school?'

She leaned across herself and tapped ash off the edge of the deck. 'I don't know. Nobody's lining up to take her. She needs a dedicated teacher aide, and nobody's prepared to fund it. So it's not looking good really.'

Devereaux didn't answer.

'Major behaviour problems suddenly; she's into breaking things. Plates, walls.' She bit her lower lip lightly and watched the steam off her tea. 'So much for an easy retirement, eh?'

'You're more than welcome to send her for a visit with me, if you ever need it.'

'Yeah, thanks. You're a honey.' She stretched crossed ankles out in front of her. 'Anyway. Mustn't gasbag on.' She glanced at him. 'Have you been missing me?'

'I have actually.'

'Aw, Seany. You're too much.' She removed the cigarette to make room for a sip of tea.

'You could always come back.'

She tilted her head back and laughed. It struck him as out of character: he'd known her ten years, she'd always kept amusement pinned down. Maybe quitting had agreed with her. 'Don't think they'd eat that one too easy,' she said. 'Jesus.' She took a swallow. 'I think I'm happier out than in, if I'm being honest.'

'Why's that?'

She cupped her mug in two hands and looked left, away from him. Her cigarette bled a lazy curlicue. 'I'm not a man. And it's definitely a man's world.' She tilted her head slightly, narrowed one eye as if testing a theory. 'I don't think I ever drank enough, or was offensive enough. Think people would have been a lot happier if I had a penis. You know?'

'You could just come back anyway. Be an improvement on the current arrangement.'

She took a sip. 'So I hear. Yeah, I think you're right.'

They sat and puffed. 'Seeing anyone at the moment?' she said.

He nodded. 'Forensic tech named Ellen Stipe. I met her on that bus shooting last year.'

'She nice?'

'She's growing on me.'

She laughed. 'Bet she'd be thrilled to hear that.'

'No. She's very nice. I like her.'

'What does she think about this whole business?'

'The shooting?'

She nodded.

'I think she'd prefer it if I hadn't killed anyone.'

She took a last pull: a fierce drag that corded her neck and dropped her eyelids. She stabbed out the cigarette in the bottom of her mug and stood up. 'Come and have a look at my veges,' she said.

There was a small garden by the rear fence. He followed her over. A thatch of bamboo stakes supported a dense bloom of leaves.

'I specialise in peas,' she said.

She bent and picked a half-dozen pods.

'Here. Nutritious. You want some to give to John?'

'I don't think he's much of a pea man.'

He cracked a husk lengthways, ate the peas one by one. Quiet and methodical as she watched.

'Making progress with this bank robbery stuff?'

'Probably shouldn't tell you.'

'I'm good with secrets.'

He shook his head. 'No. There's not a lot of progress. There's no internal transparency. I'm sure there's a tie-in with these shootings back in January, but it's hush-hush.'

'So make it un-hush-hush.'

'I can't. It's locked down.'

She thumbed peas off a split pod and tossed the remains back into the planter box.

'Shouldn't stop a resourceful young lad like you.'

He turned away and headed for the house.

'Even people you liked couldn't make you do as you were told,' she said. 'Let alone people you didn't.'

He paused on the step. 'I'm sorry if I ever caused you any grief,' he said.

'Been and gone now. All you can do is pay it forward. Dish out some grief to someone who needs it.'

'I'll do my best.'

'Make sure you talk to someone about everything. Won't you?'

'I talked to John Hale.'

'Talk to someone who isn't a psychopath.'

He didn't answer.

Bennett said, 'You want to stay for a bit of dinner?'

'No thanks. I'm going to go and visit the Merry Prankster.'

'Good for you. Can you find your way out?'

'I'll holler if I get into trouble.'

She laughed. 'Take care, Sean.'

Hale found the house easily enough. The bus in the yard made it an easy find. Pastor Drinnan's wife was waiting for him when he arrived. She opened the front door and spoke to him through the fly screen. A short, heavy woman sketched in silhouette on grey mesh.

'Leanne called to say you were coming round. He's not in at present.'

'You mind telling me where I could find him?'

'He's taken the dog to the park. So that'd be your best bet.'

The park was a small council reserve just along the road. A guy in his late sixties and a black Labrador sat side by side on a bench atop a low rise, overlooking a playground. They were a neat pair: same hunched posture, same slackness of jowl. The guy hitched one elbow up on the backrest, glanced over his shoulder as Hale approached.

'Pastor Drinnan?' Hale said.

He smiled. A worn grey fedora kept his eyes in shadow. 'More like Mr Drinnan, these days.'

'You mind if I have a word?'

'Regarding?'

'Regarding a fight club robbery on the third of January of this year.'

Drinnan placed his hands in his lap, looked out over the playground. 'Well. You'd best take a seat then.' He glanced at the dog. 'Scoot over, Gerry.'

The dog licked its lips and shuffled over to free up bench space. Hale sat down beside it. A hatchback was parked out on the street, a cardboard placard behind the windscreen. A request in bold marker pen: *Please stop braking into my car. I am a single mum with no money.*

'Gerry's leaving home today,' Drinnan said.

'Leaving the nest at last.'

The guy sighed. It sounded like closure of deep musing. 'Something like that. No, he and the wife don't really get on.'

'Irreconcilable differences.'

The dog gazed down at its front paws. Drinnan smiled. 'Yes. Exactly.'

Hale said, 'Better the dog than you.'

'I think the exact phrasing was "Either the dog or you". Anyway.' He watched a young mother pushing a little girl on a swing, placed a hand on the back of the dog's neck. 'He loves the park. He used to love coming here. I wanted to give him a last visit.'

The animal leaned its head against Drinnan's shoulder.

'I'll miss you, Gerry. I'll miss you, mate.'

He looked over at Hale. 'I don't think I caught a name.'

'John Hale.'

He touched the brim of his hat. 'Pleasure. Arthur Drinnan.'

'I'm sorry to intrude like this. Your wife only told me I could find you here.'

Drinnan nodded slowly. 'That's okay. Margaret wouldn't have worried about interrupting Gerry's last visit.' He smiled slightly, whistled faintly through his teeth. 'Don't you go worrying about it though, Ger.'

He reached across himself and stroked the dog's ear, a thumb and index finger massage, eyes still with the swings.

'You got a dog, Mr Hale?'

'I used to. It died, I never got another one.'

He nodded slowly. 'Must be an interesting life, don't you think? No conscious recollection, no conscious expectation of what's around the corner.' He smoothed a palm over the dog's head, animal's eyelids lifting as he did so. 'Must give things a certain kind of purity, even on the brink of the Big Exit.'

'Is he dying?'

'Probably not. Although he's a lot less sprightly than he was once upon a time.'

Hale didn't answer.

'Are you a police officer?'

'Private investigator.' He handed his ID along the bench. Drinnan took it and glanced at it, passed it back. The dog oversaw the transfer: a slow swing of head as Hale's wallet was accepted and returned.

'There you go, Gerry. Your first and last private investigator.' His laugh caught in his throat. He nudged his hat back with his forearm. 'What did you want to ask me?'

'Did you organise the fight on the third of January this year?'

He shook his head. 'No. Well. Sort of.'

'How sort of?'

He shifted in his seat and crossed his legs. Grey cotton trousers, cleanly creased. Tan and wizened boat shoes. 'It's a community hall. I had an evening slot booked, I used it to run an AA meeting. People stopped turning up. Someone requested I run a boxing session during that time. It turned into more like bare-knuckle fighting. But anyway. Ten dollar entry … was going to give the money to the church.'

'You have any idea who robbed you?'

'Wasn't me that got robbed. Physically or financially. I'd like to make that clear as I can to you.'

'I wasn't meaning to cause offence.'

'No, I'm sure you weren't. I just don't want you getting the wrong idea about the kind of arrangements I had in place.'

'But do you have any idea who's responsible?'

'If I did I wouldn't have waited this long to tell someone.'

'Who would have known the money was stored on the premises as it was?'

He shrugged. 'I don't know.'

'You don't seem too worried about it.'

'Don't get me wrong, it's a tragedy. But everybody pays. This side of the grave or the other.'

The dog dipped its head, as if to concur.

'How did you advertise it?' Hale said.

'The fight?'

'Yes.'

'Word of mouth. Ghastly how quick it spreads. Couldn't get good news to move that fast, I tell you.' He was wearing a green work shirt, unbuttoned to the chest, a scrunched plastic bag blooming from a breast pocket. He leaned forward, elbows on knees and watched the swings. 'You ever seen a cage fight, Mr Hale?'

'No, I haven't.'

'It's fairly self-explanatory. They brought in a steel cage off the back of a truck and put two guys in there and watched them beat each other half to death. Or that's what I imagined. Pretty bleak social commentary, wouldn't you reckon? That's what constitutes evening entertainment.'

'But you needed the money.'

He nodded. 'Well. The church did.' He smiled. 'Guess my morals aren't that hard to sway.' He thought about it a moment. 'Or maybe they aren't morals, if you can sway them.'

'I'm looking for a man named Douglas Haines.'

'Ah, Douglas. He was doing the money.'

'Do you know where I can find him?'

'No. But a phone book might prove useful.'

'I appreciate your time.'

'May I ask who you're working for?'

'A man whose daughter was injured during the robbery.'

'What's her name? Might know her.'

'Charlotte Rowe.'

He pouted and shook his head. 'Doesn't ring any bells.'

The dog commiserated with a sloppy tonguing of jowls.

Drinnan looked down at it. 'Taking him down to the SPCA

this evening,' he said. 'I don't know what's worse. Having him here but needing to say goodbye, or not having him at all.' He clicked his teeth together gently. 'I know which one Marg would pick. No questions there, m'boy. None at all.'

The little girl dismounted the swing. A shrill refusal for assistance, a clumsy hands-and-feet impact as she dropped to the ground. A swift whirling of arms as she regained balance. Drinnan observed the little manoeuvre, unfurled a coiled lead from the bench beside him. The dog heard the clasp's telltale tinkle and its tail gave a quiver. 'I really do hope you make some progress,' he said. 'Let me know if you do.'

He clipped the lead to a hoop on the dog's collar. 'We're well overdue for some good luck.'

Hale thanked him and stood up, then walked back to the car. The pair of them were still seated on the bench as he'd found them, even as he drove away.

■ TWENTY-ONE

TUESDAY, 14 FEBRUARY, 6.00 P.M.

Devereaux's Commodore was waiting for Hale when he arrived home. He parked and went inside, found the man himself stretched out on the couch in the living room: one leg hiked, an arm draped across his forehead. His eyes stayed closed, even as Hale entered the room.

'I can leave out a spare key, if you want.'

Devereaux said, 'I like to keep my skills honed.'

'How long have you been here?'

'Don't know. Twenty minutes.'

'Lucky I wasn't home. Might have shot you.'

Devereaux sat up, hair fuzzed from the cushion. 'I always knock before I pick.'

Hale didn't answer.

Devereaux glanced up. 'He's dead.'

'Your friend from Monday?'

'Yeah. Him.'

'Since when?'

A wry smile. 'It's too late to bring him back.'

Hale said, 'Maybe we should have a beer.'

'Yeah, I think maybe we should.'

Hale visited the fridge. Supplies were dwindling: four Heinekens and a solitary Corona. He brought the Heinekens back to the living room, placed them two by two on a side table. Devereaux leaned across for a bottle and flipped it lip to lip against another and popped the cap. Hale took the second bottle and cracked the top with an opener off his key ring. They sat, side by side, on the couch.

'Have you seen Ellen?'

'Uh-huh.'

'Did you tell her about it?'

'Yeah. She already knew.'

'Telling her and her already knowing aren't the same thing.'

Devereaux palmed his hair flat, shrugged a concession. He stood up and found the wall dial for the ceiling fan and set it running. 'Whatever. She knows about it.'

'How is she?'

'Okay. Probably equal parts worried and angry.'

'Why angry?'

He sat down. 'Apparently, I don't communicate.'

'You communicate with me.'

'I told her that.'

'Not good enough?'

'No. I have to communicate with her, too.'

Devereaux stretched his feet out in front of him. The bottle took up roost in his lap. He propped his elbow on the rest and leaned his head against his hand. 'I always thought I was pretty black and white,' he said.

'Like how?'

'Like I thought I'd be okay if I had to do something like this one day.'

'Kill someone.'

He arched one foot and tapped the heel against the ground. The fan wound up and settled into a light rhythmic click. 'Yeah.'

Hale didn't answer. Late afternoon gave the light through the ranch slider a molten tint.

Devereaux said, 'I always had the sense I was given an inside line on how the world works. Now I don't feel like I do.'

'Shooting people isn't easy.'

'No. It isn't.'

'So what did you think it would be like?'

'I don't know. Something clear-cut. Acceptance, if he deserved it, regret if he didn't.'

'Regret tends to spread itself fairly wide.'

He nodded. 'Question is whether it's better to regret something you did or something you didn't.'

Hale didn't reply. They had some beer: neat fluked symmetry as bottles tipped in unison.

'You tell Ellen this?' Hale said.

'Sort of.' He paused. His cellphone caught a text: a muffled triple buzz left unanswered. Outside on the deck, a neat slatted shadow pattern courtesy of the handrail. 'I told her about Derren and his wife.'

'What did she have to say about it?'

He shrugged. He cleared his throat gently against his fist. 'Nothing really. She probably would have been happier if I'd kept it to myself.'

Hale didn't reply. They sat there in silence, eyes forward, this strange couch confessional.

Hale said, 'You ever wonder if there's a parallel universe in which you're slightly better off?'

'No.'

'I do. If you graphed the misfortune corresponding to every separate John Hale in the cosmos, you'd get some sort of bell curve, and I'd be closer to either one end or the other.'

'Maybe you are one end or the other. Maybe you're one of

two possible extremes.'

Hale didn't answer.

'They interviewed me this morning about the shooting,' Devereaux said.

'And?'

'I think they want to get rid of me.'

'What makes you think that?'

He was quiet a moment. 'Actually, I don't know. They could if they wanted to. I didn't follow procedure.'

'You've done that before.'

'Yeah. At some point they'll get sick of it.'

'Could always come and work for me.'

Devereaux leaned back and watched the fan, ran a hand across the stubble on this throat. 'For or with?'

Hale took a drink. The bottle had stamped a ring of moisture on his thigh. 'We could negotiate on that point,' he said. 'Should the need arise.'

Devereaux tipped his bottle vertical and downed the last of it. He set the empty back on the side table, cracked his second off another bottle: his neat little flip-trick. He took a quick pull to clean a swill of foam that rose above the lip.

Hale said, 'Are you going to quit?'

'I don't know.'

'Really?'

'Yes. I honestly don't know.'

'You know you'd be more than welcome to work for me. If you wanted to.'

'I know. You're a first-rate human.'

They had some more beer.

'I met two suspects last night that said they'd been assaulted,' Devereaux said.

'Badly?'

'They were still walking around.'

'Maybe it's just normal wear and tear. Folks get arrested, stuff can happen.'

'This wasn't normal wear and tear.'

'Stuff happens. I caused a few bloody noses in my day. So did you.'

'When necessary. We never crossed the line.'

Hale didn't answer. His arm was outstretched beside him, elbow propped, neck of the bottle snagged through two fingers.

Hale said, 'How was my old friend Don McCarthy today?'

Devereaux laughed drily. 'You know how some people you instinctively trust and some people you don't?'

'Uh-huh.'

'Yeah. I don't trust him. He's got me lined up for something this evening.'

'Doing what?'

'I don't know.'

Hale placed his bottle on the floor. He said, 'I took that Alan Rowe job I told you about.'

'So you caved then.'

'I caved.'

'What does he want you to do?'

'His daughter was hurt in the fight club robbery. He wants me to find who did it.'

'Solve a crime there's been no progress on for weeks.'

'Essentially.'

'Have you made any progress?'

'I accrued some good hearsay.'

'Hearsay.'

'Apparently, there's a contract out on whoever did the robberies.'

'Who issued it?'

'I don't know.'

'How much is it?'

'I don't know. Evidently, they got some drug dealer fired up as well, and now he's looking for them too.'

'Where'd you get all this from?'

'Just some caustic sleazeball.'

'Right. Try not to get under anyone's feet.'

'You can save me if I do happen to.'

'I think my clout is pretty well shot, so to speak.'

Devereaux downed the rest of the bottle in one swallow. He stood up: a slow unfolding, creased clothes and a symphony of joint clicks. 'Let me know if you turn up anything good,' he said.

'Yeah. You staying for some dinner?'

'No.' Devereaux paused in the middle of the room, facing the window. A wince into dying light as he rolled his shoulders.

Hale said, 'I wouldn't worry about it.'

Devereaux didn't answer. He turned and headed for the door, flicked a loose salute as he went out.

■ TWENTY-TWO

Tuesday, 14 February, 7.00 p.m.

The trip back to the city was easy against the rush-hour flow. Devereaux left the car in the basement garage and rode the lift up to CIB. McCarthy's office was locked, peep glass blocked by a sheet of newspaper taped behind it. A Post-it note blamed his absence on a case meeting due for wrap-up at seven-thirty.

He walked through to the situation room. Productivity had lulled: screensavers, the smell of fast food. Stretched phone handsets and whispers as overtime was justified to those at home. He saw Grayson at a desk, and pulled a chair up opposite. He looked strung out: hair awry, workspace a Stonehenge of empty coffee mugs.

'Progress?'

He looked up. 'No. I'm working on something else. Everything's piling up.'

Devereaux said, 'Can you do me a favour?'

Grayson smiled but his eyes stayed flat. Mouth parted, tongue probing one molar. 'What is it?' he said.

'Lookout duty.'

'Breaking and entering again?'

'Sort of.'

He laughed drily. 'No thanks. I mean, no offence.'

'I'll owe you.'

'You already do. People aren't stupid.' He leaned forward. 'Bowen's not an idiot. He knew I was up to something last night when I got him out of his office.'

'I don't need you to—'

'Okay. What I hope you're going to say is, "Actually, I don't need you to do anything at all." Because, to be honest, I've got enough on my plate.'

His voice had risen as he built steam. People looked across at them. Devereaux walked away from it, feeling like an idiot. He felt eyes riding his back all the way to the door. He checked his watch. Seven minutes after seven. McCarthy would be back in about twenty-five minutes.

He went back to his desk. His tie was still in the top drawer. He popped his collar and slipped it on and knotted it. Might as well do things dapper. He took a torsion wrench and a rake pick from his bottom drawer. The Don's door was a standard keyed deadbolt. Reasonably robust, but he'd done office work before. He was fairly sure he could crack it.

The office itself was in a short corridor off the main suite. He jiggled the handle again and knocked. Still empty. He checked Bowen's office next door, but it bore the same Post-it note: estimated time of return, 19:30.

Make it quick.

He'd chosen a good time. Shift change wouldn't start for another three hours. Meal time had thinned office occupancy. The corridor saw through-traffic roughly every thirty seconds. Initial lock appraisal suggested a twenty-second pick time. He waited for a clear hallway, and then he went in hard with the torsion wrench. Good movement: he felt the barrel free up. Another anxious twelve seconds with the pick, and he was through the door.

Trapped office air: stagnant, and dog breath-hot. He couldn't afford to run the air-con. He moved around the desk. A dormant monitor. Three wife and daughter colour snapshots framed side by side, a World's Best Dad mug, still dregs-stained. A penned reminder to get milk, a framed MBA degree dated 1986. Human touches that jarred with the hard-arse demeanour. It was tidy, though: no case files left for prying eyes. A four-drawer steel filing cabinet stood adjacent. He rolled the chair in close and sat down, the lock at eye level. He tried the rake pick. Too fat.

Shit.

He couldn't risk going back to switch gear. He wished he'd had the balls to do this earlier when the office had been unlocked.

He checked his watch. Thirteen minutes after seven. Call it a fifteen-minute safe window. He wiped his forehead with his tie. Improvise: bent paperclips made ideal backup hardware. He rifled drawer contents, took one off a stack of blank 258 forms. His hairline trickled cold beads. Sweat fell and ticked against the desk top. He drew his hand inside his sleeve and palmed it clear, flicked the desk lamp on and angled it until the lock was spotlit. His hands shook as he lined up the insert. Thirty seconds, and he was in. The top drawer rolled out seamlessly, drew up short against the end stops. Devereaux paused. His pulse ran at a high patter.

Fifteen minutes after seven.

The cabinet was choked, bound documents crammed front to back, breath held. Everything in numeric sequence by file number. Neat printed spine labels: McCarthy-grade organisation.

He found the January thirtieth shooting file in the second-to-bottom drawer. It was an impressive item, maybe two hundred pages. He wasn't going to be able to get all of it.

Eighteen minutes after seven.

A compact printer-cum-photocopier/scanner was on the floor beside the desk. He powered it on and configured it for scan to email. There would be a record, for anyone who cared to check. But no one would check, because no one was going to know.

He thumbed the file. The front half was page protected in plastic sleeves, the back portion loose sheets hole-punched and bound. He removed the second half of the file and set it in the feeder tray, one hundred pages worth of A4. The scanner started in, sheet by sheet. How fast could they operate? Ten pages a minute? Fifteen? He had no idea.

Twenty-two minutes after seven.

He hoped they didn't wrap up early. It had been known to happen. He ran a quick search. There were more paperclips in another drawer. He matched one colour for colour with his stand-in pick, attached it to the stack of forms. He looked at the photographs: three shots, a stuttered time lapse that tracked about fifteen years. Their presence made him feel guilty, like he'd strayed inside the guy's sentiments. Lock-picked past the hard exterior to this place of things dear.

Twenty-seven minutes after seven. He moved around to the printer. It had managed about half the stack. He stopped it there and watched the scanned pages transmit through to his email, picked up the documents and tamped them square. Mistake: it skewed the original alignment. He couldn't get the binder hole to line up.

Twenty-eight minutes after seven. Feet in the corridor.

He braced the open folder across his knees and held the loose papers in two hands and ground them onto the steel binder.

Voices in the corridor. The filing cabinet drawer began to roll shut on its own accord. Murmur that sounded like McCarthy.

Key-chime, and then the door handle turning.

Devereaux just sat there blankly, the open folder across his knees. Sweet talking would be futile. He just waited for impact.

It never came.

The door cracked an inch. Hallway light slipped in, shy. Keys clacked and peeped around the edge of the frame. Bowen's voice further along the corridor — a question — McCarthy's reply from the other side of the door, terrifyingly clear. Footsteps as The Don moved away down the hallway to Bowen's office.

Devereaux let out held breath through ground teeth. He got the folder contents square and pulled the drawer back just before it closed, slotted the binder home. He realised he wouldn't be able to relock it: a key was needed whether you wanted to open or close. Leaving it as he'd found it would mean repicking the lock.

No time.

No choice either: a clean scene was paramount. He knelt close and worked the paperclip, clenched teeth, focus split between the lock and the door.

Six seconds. Seven. A frantic inverse break-in. McCarthy's voice faint in the corridor, filtering from Bowen's office.

Fifteen seconds. *This is madn—*

The pins aligned. The barrel twisted. He tried a drawer for certainty: locked.

He stood up and rolled the chair back behind the desk and shut the photocopier down. He stepped across the room, reached around and cupped the keys to stop them ringing, then pulled the door and slipped into the corridor. A neat escape: tiptoed, like some dance move, heart in mouth.

Canned food wasn't going to cut it.

Duvall ordered pizza for dinner, treated himself and had

the thing delivered. He paid cash. The transaction almost cleared his wallet. It was a fitting analogy for his net worth: combined savings from the Baghdad work, plus his parents' now-liquidated property, were fast declining. Bank statements didn't make for happy reading. Somehow he'd reached the point where he had only two grand to his name. Either he made some money or he'd have to sell the house.

He collected the laptop and his case folders and brought them through to the living room and sat cross-legged on the floor under a narrow tent of lamp-glow. A sitcom from a neighbouring unit reached him word-perfect. Ten years ago the intrusion might have pissed him off, but the Iraq work had reset his datum for tolerance: two or three times out of ten, Baghdad apartment noise meant an armed break-in. Regular exposure to danger had bolstered his lenience, tenfold. Any noise that didn't imply kidnap was imminent, he could live with. So he blocked out the blare and focused on his files. He had reams' worth of redacted witness testimony. Compiling it had been a nightmare. He interviewed bank employees after the October eight robbery. He assuaged suspicion with claims he was a police consultant. His PI licence made for enhanced veracity. People were very helpful. He ran a solid week's worth of questioning. He canvassed the street following the armoured van robbery, got vague descriptions of gunmen and hyperbolised robbery recountals. All a waste. He had nothing tangible to pursue. The cars used had been stolen. Nobody even glimpsed a skin tone, let alone facial attributes. He tried searching for related crimes going back five or ten years, but robberies were too numerous and imprecisely documented. It was impossible to establish correlations. And Google only got you so far.

He switched his attention to January thirty: his hypothesised botched witness protection job. His background on it ran light. He had three newspaper items, single-column pieces, a cumulative twelve inches of reportage. Details were scarce. He guessed a media block was in place — he'd worked a mid-'eighties kidnapping under similar circumstances. The exposition was bare bones, fleshed out with bold supposition: drugs/gang activity/organised crime. None of the victims was named, although all three pieces noted that both civilians and police staff had been killed. How hard would it be to fill in the blanks? He'd done doorman work at joints frequented by cops, he could probably gain some ground by questioning them directly. Bit of luck, he could even unearth some of his old contacts. 'Eighties policing had been a different flavour. Criminals and detectives had frequent social contact. Friday afternoon bar visits facilitated easy hobnobbing: he'd built a thick portfolio of people privy to unsavoury happenings. But that was twenty-five years ago. By now they'd be either dead or eaten by the system. Same was probably true for the other side of the equation. He stared at the computer screen. He had database subscriptions to births, deaths and marriages; credit ratings; vehicle ownership; but all they were doing was steadily draining his net worth.

He rubbed his eyes. The print was ghosting double. He squinted in favour of finding his reading glasses in the box clutter.

Maybe he was yet to exhaust Google. He fired up the search engine. He tried variations of '30 January shooting' and '30 January murder' and '30 January multiple homicide'. The system returned a page worth of hits. Most were regurgitations of what he had: verbatim reprints under a *Guardian* or *New York Times* or *Weekend Australian* header. He trawled the archive sites of the local publications that had filed the original pieces. He skimmed and sparked on a name: Robert Davis.

He'd authored a three-inch *Herald* piece. He couldn't think why it had tripped his recall. He checked his original hard copy, but his scissoring had excised the author's name.

He ran a search on Robert Davis. Links to archived news articles unfurled. He skimmed headlines. Pages one through five, nothing triggered. Memory flared halfway down page six: *In retrospect: the Marie Langford murder, fifteen years on. Robert Davis investigates.*

Marie Langford, the body in the van. His first CIB case, vintage 'ninety-seven.

Had he met Davis? He must have, otherwise why the recollection?

He navigated back to the paper's web page, found a general enquiries contact number. He stretched his mobile tight against the charger cable and dialled. A courteous female tone informed him his balance had dropped below the five-dollar mark. Shit. So let's make it quick.

An automated system answered his call and launched a flavourless welcome. He button-pushed his way through the proffered options until reception picked up. He crossed his fingers and asked for Davis.

'He's out of the office until Monday.'

He asked to be put through anyway, hoping the answer machine message included a cell number. Reception complied. Alas, he got a stock-standard speak-after-beep instruction. No mobile.

He persevered. He brought up the digital archives and found Davis's piece on the January thirty shootings. His name and email address were footnoted. Duvall opened a blank email and sent it to Davis's listed address. He got an automated out-of-office reply in seconds. It was more informative than the answer machine: a mobile number was conveniently listed for after-hours contact. He called it. Davis picked up. Duvall took a breath and went for it, reeled off a haughty announcement that they'd met during the Langford case back in 'ninety-seven.

Davis met it with a long pause. He said the name rang a bell.

Duvall stayed on the front foot: 'I saw your retrospective piece earlier this year; it was very well done.'

'Thanks. What can I do for you?'

No small talk: the guy didn't remember him.

Duvall said, 'I'm looking at these shootings in West Auckland, back on January thirtieth.'

'In what sense?'

'I'm investigating them.'

'You're still with the police?'

'No, I'm not.'

'Then I don't think I'm going to be of much use to you.'

'If you could just bear with me a moment I could run some questions past you anyway.'

'Unless you've still got a badge in your pocket, I don't think it's appropriate for us to be discussing this.'

'We haven't discussed anything yet.'

'What did you say your name was?'

'Mitchell Duvall. I worked the Langford case.'

'Yeah, to be honest, it's not triggering anything.'

'I don't know what else to tell you.'

'You were CIB back in 'ninety-seven?'

'Probationary. I was a uniformed tag-along.'

'You remember the case well?'

'I guess.'

'So what was the first thing the husband said, during confession?'

'I could just look it up.'

'You could. But I want an answer right now.'

'He said, "I saw things going differently".'

The phone went quiet. Duvall pictured his phone credit slowly bleeding out. Asking Davis to call him back probably wouldn't be tactful. Davis said, 'All right. What can I do for you?'

'What do you know about January thirtieth?'

'Not a lot. Read my article?'

'I have. You didn't give many details.'

'Wasn't a lot of choice.'

'I guessed that. I'm just trying to work out whether it's because you don't have any info, or you've been told to pretend you don't.'

'What do you think?'

'I think you're experienced enough you know what's going on, but you're operating under a media block.'

'That's lavish praise.'

'Am I right?'

'Yes, I'm very experienced.'

'No, is there a block on information?'

Davis hesitated. 'Yes, there is.'

'Who requested it?'

'The police.'

'But who specifically?'

'It came through a guy called Don McCarthy.'

McCarthy, hellbent on containment.

Davis said, 'You still there?'

'Yeah. You must know who's involved, surely?'

'Depends what you mean by involved.'

'Victim names.'

'Look, what's your interest in this?'

'I'm trying to solve it.'

'Thought you said you'd retired.'

'I've crossed the line. I'm a private investigator.'

'Leaking info isn't going to win me any favours.'

'It will with me.'

'Look, I'm sorry.'

The phone gave a soft beep: credit critical. 'Please. I just need to know if you have a name.'

'It's covered by the block. I can't divulge anything.'

'I'm not looking to publicise anything.'

Maybe that was the wrong thing to say, might set the guy's imagination working on the possibility of rival stories.

Duvall went for terse: 'Come on. Just give it to me.'

Davis took a breath. He relented. Just like that.

Constable Ian Riley, dead by gunshot, morning of January thirtieth.

Duvall thanked him. His credit hit nil, and he lost the line.

Hale drove into town and found a bar on Ponsonby Road. It was a heritage area, hundred-year-old buildings fronting the street. Road slashed narrowly by fingers of late sun, taxis dawdling in hope of a pickup. Sidewalk tables and chairs let patronage spill outside. He saw huddled trios, a tent of hunches over tall dew-glazed glasses. Sudden hard laughter and the slow, white unfurling of smoke from laden ashtrays.

The bar was a narrow place on a corner site. An outdoor couch beneath a silver gas heater spanned the front wall. Inside, a bar along one side reached half the depth of the room, a small band podium in the back. Tuesdays must have been a slow night: patronage was him, and two guys at a table near the rear.

It was a familiar environment. He'd been exposed to it his whole life. His father had been a factory foreman, forced to pull night shifts at the local bar to make ends meet. He remembered watching from a stool behind the counter: taste of cold Coke through a straw, acrid waft of cigarette smoke that hung like grey cloth below the ceiling. The line-up of big men crammed elbow to elbow along the counter, lined faces cut by thick wedges of gap-toothed smile. Rolled sleeves above worn forearms. The shift of atmosphere as the night progressed: rowdy blare of a packed room, to the dark quietude of the small hours. The downturned faces, the soft click of fingers as refills were summoned. The overlapped moisture rings across the counter, across the tables. The frustration at that ubiquitous chainmail print.

His phone rang. He eased himself off the stool and checked the screen. Unfamiliar number: he walked to the door and took the call outside.

'Any luck with Mr Dryer?'

Dryer: his finance company friend from Monday night.

'I spoke to him yesterday,' Hale said.

'"Spoke" doesn't sound that persuasive.'

'It was a firm discussion.'

'And what did he say?'

'Nothing concrete.' He took a seat on the couch. Supple leather creased and caved. 'I told him I knew he had undeclared assets.'

'And that rattled him, did it?'

'Maybe. Either way, if I'm right he can go down for perjury.'

'I don't care if he does time. I just want my money back.'

Hale didn't reply. He sipped his drink and watched traffic crisscross his vision.

'So what exactly did he say?' the guy said.

'Not very much,' Hale said. 'But he didn't look very well.'

'I was hoping for a bit of guilt.'

'I don't think that's a feeling he's familiar with.'

'So this was a waste of time then.'

'Not necessarily. It's fear that'll get your money back.'
'And is he scared?'
'He was initially. Question is how fast it'll wear off.'
'You don't exactly fill me with confidence.'
'I can't force him to do anything. I've got no legal backing.'
'People have lost their life savings.'
'It's devastating. I understand.'
'No offence, but unless you've lost forty years' worth of careful investment, you've really got no idea.' He went quiet before continuing: 'Some people here'd really like to snip his line, if you know what I mean.'

'Best I can do is apply pressure and hope for the best,' Hale said. 'Which is what I've done.'

'I hired you on the basis you get a quick result.'
'Depends how hard I push.'
'I get the feeling you could have pushed harder.'
'Maybe. People with money and lawyers need special finesse.'

The guy laughed drily. 'I'll bear it in mind. You've sent an invoice, have you?'

Hale thought about it. 'I want to try a new system,' he said.
'Does the new system benefit you, or benefit me?'
'Both of us. We'll give him to the end of the week. My payment is one per cent of whatever goes into your account by five p.m. Friday.'

'One per cent of ninety million is nine hundred thousand dollars.'

'And one per cent of zero is zero dollars. The risk cuts both ways. I've spent three weeks full-time on this. But if Friday comes along and nothing's happened, I won't charge you.'

'Performance-based payment sort of thing.'

He felt the gentle warmth of the heater on the nape of his neck. 'Exactly.'

'And in the event we get to the end of the week and our account's still empty?'

'Then you'll need to approach this from another direction.'

'You're not going to go back for round two?'

'There's no point. All I can do is scare him. If it didn't work once, it's going to work even less the second time around. Much as I sympathise, it would be a waste of time. Mine and yours.'

'I'll be in touch,' the guy said.

Devereaux went back to his desk, used a double espresso to caffeinate himself back to even keel. At seven-forty he went through to McCarthy's office. The break-in was running a constant mental loop: he couldn't lose the feeling he'd forgotten something. An open drawer, an errant staple — had he nudged one of the photographs?

The door was ajar an inch, just as he'd left it. He knocked once and walked in. McCarthy didn't even look up. 'You're late,' he said.

'I've been here since seven.'

No response. The computer had McCarthy's attention. He'd changed since this morning: a navy blue suit in preference to his trademark grey.

'What are we doing?' Devereaux said.

McCarthy took his eyes off the screen and looked at him. 'Interview work. Maybe something, probably nothing.' He paused a moment. He grinned. 'Promise not to shoot anyone.'

Devereaux didn't reply. He ran a quick appraisal, eyes only: the desk, the cabinet, the printer. They seemed okay.

The Don flicked paperwork on his desk, fingertips only, like brushing off lint. 'Go and book us out an unmarked,' he said. 'I'll be down in a minute.' He yawned and linked his hands behind his head. Elbows cocked, he had a massive wingspan.

'And for Christ's sake, lose that tie,' he said.

The tie stayed on, just to spite him. Devereaux rode the lift down to the garage and signed out a CIB pool vehicle. He parked up just inside the exit and waited, window down, the garage beyond cool and exhaust-laced. McCarthy joined him a moment later. He walked over and braced one forearm against the edge of the roof, leaned in like a roadside stop.

'Rule one: I always drive.'

He stood straight and gestured him out of the car with a flick of chin. Devereaux slid out. He kept his face empty: unperturbed, and averse to small talk. He circled the back of the car and climbed in the passenger side. The Don got in beside him. He slammed his door, belted up with a flourish.

'Holy shit,' he said. 'You kept the tie.'

He drove the car out onto Hobson and hit traffic lights. The Don exposited: 'We're not going far,' he said. 'Keep your fingers crossed, this might actually be worthwhile.'

They worked north, down towards the harbour. Evening traffic was easy. McCarthy racked his seat back. 'I've got an informant in an apartment down on the Viaduct. He's been missing calls; I want to see what's happening.'

'And I'm your backup.'

He adjusted the mirror. 'Yeah … nice inference.'

'Could be a lot of fuss just to find his phone's off the hook.'

The sarcasm slipped past him. He shook his head. 'Guy's a shitbag. Can be a handful, time to time.'

'What does he inform on?'

'Everything. He's got his ear to the scum current. He knows about all kinds of things normal people wouldn't dream of.'

'Such as?'

'Such as a certain series of robberies over the past couple of months. But we'll see.' He pulled sunglasses from his inside jacket pocket, dipped his wrist to pop them open. He slipped them on. 'When they go to ground, you know they're hiding something. Strong correlation. People start dodging more than one call, you know you've found a gold mine.'

Devereaux didn't reply.

McCarthy said, 'So. You've killed a man.' Falsely casual.

'I don't want to discuss it.'

'You'll have to eventually. It's not the sort of thing you cart around by yourself. Or you can, but you'll end up swinging by your neck in your wardrobe. Might even use that tie.'

Devereaux didn't answer.

McCarthy looked at him. A long glance, amid fast-flowing traffic. He said, 'I thought you'd be more of a talker.'

Devereaux turned and looked at him. 'How far would you push me to make me say something?'

Northbound on Nelson Street. They pulled up at another light. McCarthy squared his glasses, two-handed. 'That some sort of underhanded accusation?'

'I'm sure you must have had to work pretty hard to get Howard Ford to open his mouth.'

McCarthy laughed. 'Don't push your luck with me, boyo,' he said. 'Don't sit there thinking you're tough.'

Devereaux held his tongue.

'What? Nothing to say.' He smiled to himself. 'That's the great thing. I've heard about you; I saw your interview transcript from this morning. Never short of a word, always got the right reply. So here we are, on the one hand you're itching to hit me with something slick; on the other you're remembering the fact your job's on the line, and at some point you've got to stop pissing people off, or you're going to end up unemployed.' He turned. The glasses slipped on his nose. 'It's the beauty of the world. If you've got leverage, people shut up and stay in line. Conversely, if you want something from them, and they think you hold something over them, you won't be able to shut them up.'

They turned left on Fanshawe. The Don picked a gap in the traffic and U-turned back the opposite way. He maintained commentary. Devereaux didn't know whether the aim was to educate, or whether he just liked the sound of his own voice.

'Good thing about this sort of crime,' he said, 'is that nothing ever stays a secret. Too many angles to pin down. You've got to make sure your getaway driver doesn't say anything. You've got to make sure your backup shooter doesn't say anything. *You* have to make sure you don't say anything. And it's hard, I tell you. There's a crack somewhere, you can guarantee it; someone's bragged to a friend, someone's told a spouse, someone's mentioned something stupid to a guy in a bar. And it spreads, and it gets away on you, and as long as you're persistent enough, as long as you push hard enough …' He paused. 'Long as you've got the right leverage, you can find out what's been going on.'

They turned off Fanshawe and made another right into the narrow streets fronting the Viaduct. It was high-class, high-rise living: modern apartment buildings overlooking the water, strolling distance from the marina and restaurants lining the harbour. They stopped out front of a building down the western end of Customs Street. It was a corner site a block back from the water, ground floor restaurant verandas forming a skirt along two sides. The Don slowed to idle for a second and ducked low to see the upper-floor windows, then turned into an alleyway adjacent. Deep, sheer walls and low sun left the space in grey shadow. McCarthy turned off the engine.

'Our guy's name is Shane Stanton,' he said. 'This is actually his girlfriend's place, but it seems this is where he spends most of his time. He knows me so he shouldn't be too much of a handful, but just bear in mind he's done time for grievous bodily harm, so eyes forward. We'll do it quick and no-nonsense, lean on him hard.' He opened his door and put a foot outside. 'Steer clear of his bodily fluids, too. He's HIV positive.'

McCarthy got out of the car and walked to the rear. He popped the lid with the key. Devereaux got out and followed. McCarthy unlocked the gun safe and prised a Glock 17 from the foam.

Devereaux said, 'Didn't realise you were planning on clipping him.'

'Contingency,' he said. 'In the event he decides to clip us.'

He holstered the weapon above his right hip. He relocked the safe, slammed the lid.

'I'd offer you one as well, but I understand you're prone to premature discharge.'

They rounded into the street. The elevator core and emergency stairwell accessing the upper levels were tucked next to the restaurant, on the alley side of the building. The street-front door was open, tiled foyer empty. The elevators required swipe-card entry. McCarthy took a multi-tool from his pocket and crowded close to the fire escape door. He kept his eyes on the exit and jiggle-picked the lock one-handed, touch only. A deft, ten-second job, and they were in. The Don led the way up, jacket pinched closed with one hand. They stopped outside a door on level four. McCarthy tried the handle: feather-light, fingertips only. Locked.

The corridor was empty. McCarthy let his jacket gape and knocked hard. He turned square to the door and stepped close, filling the frame.

A woman's voice from inside: 'Who is it?'

McCarthy said, 'Use the peephole.'

'Is that Don?'

'Good guess, Monique. Open the door.'
'What do you want?'
'I just told you. I want you to open the door, please.'
'Shane's not here.'
'Open the door anyway.'
'Aw, now's really not a good time. Can I just come out and talk?'
'Monique, either you open it or I bust it. You choose.'
'You can't bust it.'
'Five. Four. Three.'
'Okay, okay, okay. Don't break anything.'

The door eased back; a wary ten mils only. The Don braced one outsized palm at mid-height and pushed it wide. He strode in: a swarm of blue suit that filled the little entry hall. Devereaux chased his wake, nudged the door closed with his heel.

The entry hall expanded into the living area. A picture window neighboured by a strip of metal louvre gave a view of the harbour. Cardboard boxes were stacked chest-high. The woman named Monique fingered long hair behind one ear and propped an elbow up on a stack. It wobbled, but she held the pose and took her weight on her feet. Feigned insouciance. She might have been thirty. Stonewashed jeans lined with thin white rips. A grey sweatshirt with the cuffs rolled, thin taut limbs protruding. A ticking neck pulse betrayed anxiety. Her eyes stayed with McCarthy as he did a loop of the room.

'Who's this?' she said.
'My plus-one. He's making sure I don't get too out of hand. Nice view.'
'What do you want?' she said.
'I need to know where Shane is.'
'Told you I don't know where he is.'
McCarthy said, 'We'll see.'

The kitchen was left of the entry, a long counter segregating it from the living area. McCarthy wove a casual route through the boxes and raised a cordless phone from a cradle and hit redial. He saw the number displayed and set the phone down again.

'You called his number,' he said.

'Yeah. So?'

'Don't wind me up, Monique. I've got a gun.' He pinned his jacket back on his hip, showed off the Glock and a Big Bad Wolf grin.

Nobody spoke. Devereaux was still in the entry. He eyed up the boxes: computer units, DVD players, GPS systems. A dusty cardboard odour hung light. Monique's eyes skittered between the pair of them, unsure how to read the play.

'Where'd you get all this stuff?' McCarthy said. He'd barely paused, maintaining aimless loops of the room, gaze in constant motion.

'None of your business.'

'What's your drug use like these days?'

'Nothing to do with you.'

He broke stride and sidestepped in front of her, caught her jaw in two fingers and angled her face towards him. 'How'd those pupils get so dilated? It's not even that bright in here.'

Devereaux said, 'Let her go, Don.'

Two sets of eyes on him: the girl's, desperate, above a horribly pinched mouth, McCarthy's, faintly surprised over his shoulder.

'First name terms,' he said. 'That's good.'

But he let her go. She was still leaning against the stack of boxes, pretence of calm undermined by the tears in her eyes. She worked her jaw and roamed her tongue behind her cheeks. Panelbeating out The Don's pinch.

'Gotta say,' McCarthy said, 'in light of the fact you've been convicted of receiving stolen goods, all these boxes seem a bit suspicious.'

He looked at Devereaux. A long, narrow gaze that told him to get in line. Devereaux dealt deadpan calm in return, pulse hammering with the knowledge that if McCarthy touched the girl again, he was going to have to do something.

Monique blinked. She traced her bottom lids with the tip of a cocked pinkie. Precision tear eradication. She began to follow him around the room. 'It's none of your business.' Dangerous waver in her tone. Terseness yielding to tears.

McCarthy, still traipsing round, ramrod rigid: 'Monique, Monique, Monique. I pulled the property details for this address. I know your father owns the apartment.' The threat struck a chord: she started to say something and caught herself, lips parted in heightened fear. He turned and faced her. She met his gaze. The height differential tilted her gaze back.

'What would Daddy say, if he knew you were harbouring stolen electrical equipment—'

'It's not.'

'—and doing drugs—'

'I'm not. I swear I'm not.' Wringing her hands, panic building.

'—and keeping a shitbag like Shane Stanton around for company?'

'I'm not, I'm not. I swear.'

'Where's that phone? Maybe I'll give Daddy a buzz right now.'

She jostled in front of him. 'No. Don't.'

'Why not? You said you're not up to any mischief.'

'I'm not but—'

'But what?'

She didn't answer.

McCarthy dipped his knees, aligned himself face to face. 'So then: Tell. Me. Where. He. Is.'

'I told you.' She choked, glanced at Devereaux, pleading. 'I don't know.'

McCarthy shrugged. 'Okay, Monique. Okay. We can do it that way.'

He pushed past her, a solid shoulder-on-shoulder nudge that spun her in a half-turn. He stepped back into the entry hall, into the bathroom, the girl at his heels.

'You can't just search my place. You can't do that, what are you doing?'

'Nothing, nothing. Just having a casual poke around. You know how it is.'

Devereaux backed up to the front door. Part of him berating his own failure to step in more decisively, part of him knowing if he intervened and helped the girl he'd be unemployed by sun-up. McCarthy caught his eye again through the door: a sharp sneer as he rifled the woman's medicine cabinet, testing how far he could push before something dropped. The girl was beside him, clawing at his arm, pleading for him to stop. Band-Aid boxes toppled, scissors clattered to the floor. She crouched and scrabbled for them, tear drops bright on the tile. The Don trapped them with a foot, caught her finger in the process. She shrieked and crawled away and sat against the edge of the bath, legs hugged to her chest.

Devereaux watched from the bathroom door, fists clenched so tight his nails had drawn blood. McCarthy was still at the cupboard, nosing idly. His back was turned, arms raised. His torso was exposed. One kick would do it. Hard enough and with a bit of luck, he might rupture a kidney and kill the bastard.

Do it. Take him down.

The girl looked up at him from the floor, tear-stained and

defeated, misery an instant sanction for what had crossed his mind. He waited.

Do it. He's way, way out of line.

The cupboard door closed a fraction. The exterior was mirrored and McCarthy caught his face in the glass. Such confidence in that quick glance, resolute certainty of continued inaction: *don't kid yourself you'd actually do something.*

The moment passed. He stayed in the door. McCarthy reached up and felt above the cabinet.

'Whoa. This feels promising.'

He removed a worn and faded toilet bag. He unzipped it and peeped inside, expression faux eagerness.

'Heavens. What's this?'

The girl didn't answer, near catatonic on the floor. McCarthy inverted the bag. Half a dozen three-mil hypoderms dropped and ticked gently into a wide scatter across the tilework. Cotton wads, a tourniquet, three zip-lock bags of white powder followed suit. McCarthy stepped back from the mess, lined up a big kick, and swung through. A zip-lock bag went airborne and hit the girl in the forehead and fell in her lap.

McCarthy dropped to his haunches. His cuffs hiked: white socks, rolled over a half-inch. 'Don't push me,' he said. 'You pathetic little shit.'

No reply.

McCarthy pouted. 'Who do you want me to call first,' he said. 'Daddy, or the Drug Squad?'

'Please. Just leave me alone.'

'Please won't cut it, sweetheart. Where's Shane-o?'

She wiped tears. She bit her lower lip.

McCarthy took his phone from his pocket. He waggled it in two fingers. 'Daddy or Drug Squad. Daddy or Drug Squad?'

He thumbed a key. Close walls amplified the tone.

'Okay, okay. Don't. He's gone to Pit. He's gone up to Pit.'
'When?'
'Earlier.'
'Give me numbers, Monique.' He waved the phone in her face. 'Specificity keeps the hounds off your heels.'
'I dunno. Around six.'
McCarthy thought for a moment. 'Pit the bar?' he said.
She snorted hard. 'Good guess, you fuck-head.'
McCarthy tipped his head back and laughed. 'What a charmer.' He stood straight, shook his hands in his pockets to get his trouser cuffs settled right. He looked at Devereaux and jerked his head. 'Let's go, hotshot.'
The girl was huddled in the corner as they went out the door.

■ TWENTY-THREE

Tuesday, 14 February, 8.33 p.m.

Devereaux led the way back down the stairs. He kept a quick trot, but The Don slipped ahead on the second floor landing and boxed him in tight against a corner. Whiskers in close-up, a soft hiss of breath through a small smile. McCarthy spread both arms and placed his hands flat against the two adjacent walls. Devereaux's eye line reached the cleft in his chin.

'What was that all about?' McCarthy said.

'What?'

No response. The stairwell was a tall concrete chamber. The question's echo lingered. Devereaux assessed options. The John Hale conflict doctrine stipulated 'Take him down hard'. Tempting: The Don's solar plexus was a short straight-right away. Both his knees were in heel-jab range. A head-butt would break his front teeth, both storeys.

Devereaux took a breath, went for it. 'You were out of line,' he said.

A long, long pause. The Don's gaze was deliberately above his head, highlighting the height advantage. Devereaux could see a slow pulse ticking: barely one per second. Coma-calm. McCarthy's weight shifted from one foot to the other. Devereaux braced for a knee in the balls.

'That's troubling,' McCarthy said. He flexed his hands slightly against the walls. 'What are you going to do about it?'

'Probably less than I should have.'

The Don let out a long breath. Devereaux felt it on his forehead.

'Here's the great thing, Sonny Jim,' McCarthy said. 'I've been around such a long time, what I say tends to matter. If I say that Sean Devereaux shouldn't have killed that guy like he did, and needs to be gotten rid of, you can bet your back teeth someone's going to take it as gospel.'

Devereaux smiled. 'If I spread the word about what just happened in there, you can bet your back teeth someone's going to take it as gospel.'

McCarthy smirked it off. 'I'll put it in binary terms for you: either shut up and maybe keep your job, or blab and definitely lose it.'

He squared up Devereaux's tie knot for him. 'You didn't do her any favours. In her eyes, you're passively responsible. She only hates you slightly less than she hates me.'

He stepped away and put his hands in his pockets, started back down the stairs. 'Don't try to take me on, Skippy. I'm The Don.'

Pit was uptown, a ground floor unit in the back of a long, low-rise stretch that fronted onto Queen Street. The bar itself was below street level, at the base of a wide pool of carpark that dipped down from the road behind the building. Age and weak light did no favours: the place looked like a black eye.

The Don turned in off the street and parked in the lot. It was near capacity. A crowd had spilled out onto the entry stairs. Two bouncers just inside the entry, facing the room. The Don approached, badge raised, Devereaux on his coat-tails. The crowd pulled back in a fat vacant wedge. The bouncers turned as McCarthy reached them. Their gazes did a neat two-step, Devereaux to The Don. They were big men in their thirties. Peppery buzz cuts hugged bald crowns. The Don had two inches and ten kilos on both of them.

'Gentlemen,' McCarthy said. Ambient bar chatter made him shout.

The guy on the left tilted from the waist and read the ID details. 'Inspector. What can we do for you?'

McCarthy flashed a Shane Stanton mug. 'Seen this man tonight?'

Two 'No's', in unison.

McCarthy looked between them a couple of times. The two guys maintained far-off stares, palace guard-style. 'We'll have a look around anyway,' McCarthy said.

'We haven't seen him.'

'We'll have a look around anyway.'

'What's that you're packing on your hip?'

McCarthy smiled, fastened a jacket button to keep the Glock obscured. 'Contingency,' he said. 'In the event things get uncivilised.'

Guy on the right said, 'Take it easy. Got a good vibe going at the moment.'

McCarthy looked at him and nodded. 'What's with the crowd?' he said.

'Got a gig starting up later.'

McCarthy smiled at him. Devereaux didn't think he was the sort of guy who'd had any trouble, two on one, with bar security. 'We'll be sure to let you know if it changes,' he said.

He took a step and then paused, nodded at their haircuts. 'I've had a few close shaves in my day, too.' He winked.

They nudged through. The bar was to the right of the door,

people thick around it. They turned sideways to cut through the crowd. Devereaux spotted pseudo-celebrities: a musician, a novelist, a radio broadcaster. They reached the middle of the room. A door marked *Private* led off to the left. McCarthy turned. He cupped Devereaux's ear.

'I've found him in here a couple of times so we could get lucky.' He paused. 'I'll go lead. If you call me out again, I'm going to bust your front teeth.'

Devereaux looked up at him, nothing in his face. 'Good luck,' he said.

The Don laughed and stepped away, clapped Devereaux on the side of the head, hard enough to set his ear chiming.

The Don pushed for the side door, shoulder-nudging oblivious drinkers. He reached the door and pushed it open, Devereaux trailing close. Space was tight. Three guys reclined on couches, boxing in a low cluttered coffee table. The guy facing the door was Shane Stanton. Their arrival zipped him out of a drowse. He recognised The Don before he was half through the door, twitched forward and cleared the coffee table, faster than a stomped rat's nest. His reaction panicked the others, but McCarthy's proximity kept them seated: one stride from the door, and he practically loomed above them.

'Sign on the door says private,' Stanton said.

He had mid-length blond hair cut curtain-straight, a beard strengthening a weak jaw.

'I didn't want to do this in public,' McCarthy said. 'I take it that was icing sugar you cleared off the table?'

The two others' faces went slack, jail time scenarios parading the mind's eye. Stanton's eyes ran back and forth. He shrugged. 'Wouldn't be able to do anything, if it wasn't,' he said. 'You'd have needed a warrant to get through that door.'

'Why you been missing my calls, Shane?'

He shrugged. 'Probably wouldn't have if I knew you'd get this uppity.'

'Probably wouldn't have either, if you knew how much stuff I conned Drug Squad into ignoring.'

The two others shared a glance, dabbed brow sweat.

Stanton said, 'What do you want, Donald?'

'Just a moment of your precious time, run some questions by you.'

Stanton pouted, weaved his head back and forth. 'Or I could get the bouncers to chuck you out.'

McCarthy laughed. 'I'm good for four on one with bar security. They might need to call some friends.'

Stanton thought about it. He looked like he believed it. 'Where do you want to go?'

'Will here not do?'

Stanton shook his head. 'Here will not do.'

'Outside then.'

He shook his head. 'There's a queue. I'll never get back in.'

'Can the bathroom take three people?'

Stanton sucked a tooth audibly, mulled it over. His eyes drifted wide, and he smiled at some private memory. 'Yeah,' he said. 'It can take three.'

It was cosy. Stanton stood backed up against the bowl, The Don next to him, back to the wall, almost too broad to stand square. The door was locked, Devereaux hemmed in beside it. The cistern hissed faintly, trying to keep to itself. A frosted glass window high on the wall was open a crack, smell still sharp enough to trigger a puke.

McCarthy said, 'Don't think I'm an idiot. I know you were either buying or selling something in there.'

'Whatever. Either cuff me or piss off.'

'Look, dipshit. I keep all kinds of people off your back, just so you can give me info when I need it. So when you stop keeping me in the loop and missing calls, I start having a serious think about talking to the lads at Drugs. Or Burglary.'

Stanton held his gaze, but licked his lips. 'What do you want?'

'What do you know about these robberies? And don't say, "What robberies?"'

'Robbery isn't my field any more.'

'You've diversified. Congratulations.'

'No, like, I'm not privy to the inside goss.'

McCarthy paused. He sniffed, nodded at the toilet. 'Anything in there?'

Stanton checked over his shoulder. 'Nah. Empty.'

'Maybe give it a flush anyway.'

Stanton thumbed the lever. The S-bend recycled with a roar. McCarthy waited for quiet before continuing. 'Here's the deal: we've got half a dozen guys we're currently looking at, many of whom have files as thick as Dickens, and many of whom have you listed as a known associate.'

'Associate. Associate. *Associate*. Doesn't mean I did anything.'

'Yeah, but people brag, people talk. And you're a nosy little shit: don't tell me you heard about what happened on October eight, and November sixteen, and January third, but it never occurred to you to ask around about what might have happened.'

Stanton said, 'Don, Don, Don, Don, Don. I don't like your tone.'

McCarthy smiled. 'We popped in to see Monique just before. She was chirpy enough when we arrived, but she looked fairly miserable by the time we were on our way.'

Someone knocked on the door. Devereaux felt the shock of it

through the back of his head. McCarthy called out 'Occupied'. He freed his jacket button, let the Glock show.

'What, you're going to shoot me?'

'You going to give me a reason?'

'This is why I hate talking to you; you're always on the front foot.'

'I'm *always* on the front foot because you *always* piss me off. Don't push it, Shane. Your missus is a bit of a repeat customer in court.'

'What's that supposed to mean?'

'Means if I take her in for possession again, chances are they're going to lock her up for a while.'

Stanton shrugged. He shook his head. 'Man. I really don't have time for this. You want a sit-down heart to heart, you get me in formally, but right now I need another drink.'

'Give me something good, I'll shout you.'

'I don't know anything good. If I knew something good, I would have rung and told you about it.'

McCarthy laughed. 'You've never called anyone with good news in your life.'

Stanton looked offended.

'Don't hold back on me, Shane. The smell's killing me.'

Stanton said, 'Look, I don't have any names.'

McCarthy smoothed a palm down his tie. 'Why don't we start with what you do have, and we'll work from there.'

'It's all just whispers.'

'That's okay. Whispers are good. I'm partial to a good whisper.'

Stanton bunched a fist, cracked his knuckles. His shirt front bore coke residue. He said, 'Some drug guys I know are after them.'

'That sounds better than a whisper, if they're people you know.'

Stanton, hand raised. 'No. That's not what I said—'

'Yes, it is. You said you know them.'

'No. Well. What I meant was, I *know* them, but I heard this stuff through some other people I know. I didn't get it direct, you know? It was just info from a friend, about another friend.'

'And all you have to do is repeat it. So easy, Shane. So easy.'

Stanton scratched his head. He looked uncomfortable. He looked set to capitulate. He said, 'Okay, look. I know a few guys in the business.'

'What's "the business"? I'm old, Shane. I need this shit in plain English.'

Stanton, defensive, shoulders hiked: 'I know guys who deal drugs, okay. There it is.'

McCarthy laughed. 'Is that meant to be some sort of revelation?'

'I don't know. I don't give a shit.'

McCarthy wheeled a finger. 'All right. Keep it rolling.'

'There's nothing to roll. I heard some guys in the biz are after the crew that did those robberies.'

McCarthy smiled. 'We'll take this in baby steps: who are the guys in the biz?'

'There's a dealer after them. Don't ask me why, that's all I've got.'

A dealer after them. Devereaux sensed links forming. He recalled what Hale had said earlier: *they got some drug dealer fired up as well, and now he's looking for them, too.* It was corroboration. It was progress.

McCarthy said, 'Names, Shane. This is nothing to me without names.'

Stanton didn't answer. He patted for a cigarette, came up empty.

McCarthy said, 'Who's the dealer?'

'Name's Leonard.'

'That his first or last name?'

'I dunno. I think he's just got the one. Like that Ronaldo guy that plays soccer.'

'So who is he?'

'I dunno. Look him up in the phone book.'

McCarthy clicked his fingers, rapid fire. 'More names, Shane. Who's he after?'

'I don't know.'

'Yeah, you do. I know you. You love being in the loop. You always know more than you let on.'

Stanton said, 'Whatever, I'm done with this shit.'

McCarthy hit him a straight left: effortless, no build-up. Stanton never even picked it up. His arms were still at his sides when the blow caught him in the gut, high on the solar plexus. He doubled up, breathless, went down beside the toilet. The Don moved in and stomped him on the shoulder to get him sitting. A heavy impact: the polished loafer with the deep heel.

Stanton raised an arm. 'Stop. Please stop. Someone said the name Glyn Giles. I think they're after a guy called Giles. That's all I heard, I swear. Giles.'

McCarthy moved in for another kick. His back was to the door, he didn't see Devereaux move in. It was well-timed: Devereaux flipped the hem of McCarthy's jacket, exposed the butt of the Glock, grabbed it free of the holster. He jacked a round. The muzzle was aimed at McCarthy's face by the time he turned.

He froze, genuinely surprised. 'Holy shit. That's ballsy.'

Stanton looked up from the floor, a gash through his hairline from where his head had struck the bowl.

Devereaux looked down at him. 'Out.'

Stanton didn't need telling twice. He scrambled out from

beside the toilet, hands and knees. Shaky fingers freed the lock, and he was gone. Devereaux kicked the door closed behind him. McCarthy lowered the lid on the toilet and turned slowly and sat down. Shock had been short-lived, he was back in control.

'People go to prison for this sort of thing,' he said.

Devereaux said, 'Your word against mine. I fancy my chances.'

He opened the door, kept his back to it. He pulled the slide back and shook out the live round from the chamber, let it fall to the floor. A neat arc as it rolled outside. He freed the magazine and pocketed it, tossed the gun into McCarthy's lap.

Devereaux stepped out and pulled the door shut behind him, walked away through the crowd to the exit.

■ TWENTY-FOUR

TUESDAY, 14 FEBRUARY, 9.07 P.M.

At least the station was close.

Devereaux went in through the garage entrance. He felt calmer than he thought he would. Maybe courage of convictions had a steadying effect.

He logged his car out and drove back down to the waterfront. An idling taxi had claimed the alley beside Stanton's building, so he left the car on the kerb. The street door was still open. The fire escape was locked, as they'd left it. He considered a quick pick, but he'd had his share of breaking and entering for one night. He hit the intercom buzzer for Monique's unit.

'Who is it?'

'Sean Devereaux.'

She didn't reply. He remembered McCarthy had introduced him as his plus-one: the name meant nothing to her.

'One of the policemen that was here earlier,' he said.

'The one here with Don?'

'That's right.'

No answer. The speaker held a light hiss.

'Are you there?' he said.

No answer.

He stabbed the button a couple of times. 'Hey. Just listen a moment.'

'What do you want?'

'Just to come up and speak to you.'

'What for?'

'Just to talk. I can help you.'

'You weren't much help last time you were here.'

'I know. I'm sorry.'

'Who else is with you?'

He paused. A man entered the building. Eyes downcast as he key-carded the elevator, lest he see a plea for access.

'Who else is with you?' she said.

'Nobody.'

'You're by yourself.'

'I'm by myself.'

'So how did you get in last time?'

'McCarthy picked the lock.'

She was quiet a long time. He was watching the street door: pre-existing cautiousness, bolstered by the evening's events.

'I'll come down and let you in,' she said.

The elevator doors opened a minute later. She was leaning against one wall, arms folded, legs crossed.

'Is Shane home?' he said.

She shook her head. 'He's not back yet.'

He stepped inside the lift. The doors closed, and they rode up in silence. She used a key to unlock her door, held it for him as he stepped inside. The cardboard boxes hadn't moved, but she'd cleaned the mess off the bathroom floor.

'He shouldn't have done that,' Devereaux said.

The keys rang as she dropped them on the counter. 'Yeah, no shit. You could have said that a little louder and a little sooner. Like, an hour ago when you were here.'

'I know. I'm sorry.'

She smiled thinly. 'Whose side are you on anyway?'

'Not his.'

'Where is he?'

'Don? I don't know.'

'Where's Shane?'

'I'm not sure. He got roughed up a little.'

'What? Shit.' She looked panicked, hustled round in front of him. 'Is he okay?'

'Yeah. He's okay. He's fine. He took a fist in the gut, but he's okay.'

'Oh, my God.' She nudged a path through the boxes and stood at the window, arms folded, not looking at him. 'Where was this?'

'In Pit.'

'Oh, God. I knew I shouldn't have said where he was. Shit.'

'He's okay. I'm sure he's okay.'

'So why isn't he home yet?'

'He knew we'd visited earlier, he probably wanted to stay clear.'

'Does he need to go to hospital?'

'No, he doesn't need to go to hospital. I'm sure he's fine.'

He fished in his pockets for a business card. He found one in his jacket and offered it to her, but she ignored it. He set it face-up on the counter. 'I'm sure he's fine, but if he doesn't turn up in a couple of hours, you can give me a call. My mobile's on there.'

She didn't reply. Hopefully, he thought, because he was sounding rational. She gestured with one arm. 'This stuff isn't stolen,' she said. 'Case you were wondering.'

'I wasn't.'

'But Don thought it was.'

'I think he just wanted to scare you.'

She dipped her head, she touched away tears. 'Will he send

people round to go through the house?'

'I doubt it. He wanted information from you. He wasn't looking for an arrest.'

She looked at him. 'But could he arrest me, if he wanted to?'

'I don't know. You tell me.'

'Nothing here is stolen.'

'Well, okay then.'

Thin lips below a long stare. 'What about, like, the drugs?'

'I'd get rid of them, if I were you.'

'They're Shane's, not mine.'

'Whoever's they are, they're not the sort of thing you want around the house.'

'This isn't the sort of conversation I thought I'd be having with a cop.'

'No ... well, I think my continued employment's in jeopardy.'

'How come?'

'Don's got a lot of pull. And I pissed him off pretty bad.'

'How?'

'Thirty minutes ago I pointed a gun in his face. I don't think it went down well.'

She pondered it. 'You were helping Shane?'

'Hopefully, I stopped punch number two. Otherwise I just threw my job away for nothing.'

'So you've lost your job?'

'We'll see.'

She looked away. Awkward with the quiet, teeth gritted gently. One of the boxes was open at the top, like slack lips. She waved the flap idly, revealed squat plastic tubs packed side by side. 'Protein powder,' she said. 'I order it online, then on-sell. I used to have a couple of gyms I sold to, but I'm going to get a website-thing set up so people can just look me up and do orders. I've got to ring the guy next week.'

'Good for you.'

She flicked a nail on a plastic lid, smiled shyly. 'Thirty-four fifty if you're that way inclined. Just add milk. Although you don't look like you need it.'

He laughed. 'I'll take it as a compliment.'

Something boomed in the stairwell and she flinched, raked her hair one-handed to camouflage the motion. 'You sure Don won't send anyone to follow up?'

'I wouldn't worry about it.'

She didn't look convinced. She moved around to the counter and picked up his card, delicate and two-handed. She inspected closely.

'Let me know if he comes back,' Devereaux said.

'Who, Don?'

He nodded. 'Or anyone with a badge.'

She didn't reply. He let himself out and took the stairs down to ground.

He'd forgotten about the paperwork.

His pilfered files, courtesy of McCarthy's cabinet, sitting in his own inbox, untended.

Shit.

He should have moved them sooner. Unopened and un-deleted, they were a liability.

His phone rang. Caller ID told him it was Don McCarthy. Imagination offered a stern précis — he felt it wise not to pick up. He tossed the phone on the seat and sat quietly in the dark. Nobody had reason to check his computer. Unless The Don had already filed a complaint — in which case his computer contents rated low on the worry list. On the other hand, if he wanted to see what the documents contained, he might not get another chance.

Just do it.

Devereaux smiled. He'd given himself that same advice before, and it hadn't ended well. He started the car and cruised south uptown towards the station. He channel-hopped between patrol and CIB Comms frequencies. Just standard chatter: Sean Devereaux didn't make the Be On Lookout alerts. He played it safe anyway, and left the car in the Civic parking building in favour of the station basement. He walked across Mayoral Drive and went in the main entrance, rode the lift to CIB.

Still in the clear: his desk hadn't been red-taped. Nobody looked up as he arrived. Lloyd Bowen breezed straight past him, not even a nod. Devereaux claimed his seat, cleared his screensaver and brought up his emails. A page worth of unopened messages unfurled. He skimmed subject headings: nothing threatening. He found his illicit document cache, fifty-three pages all told. He couldn't afford the time to read anything. Printing was off limits too: fifty-plus pages of usurped paperwork, Murphy's Law guaranteed a computer breakdown followed by awkward questioning. Plus he couldn't risk Bowen stealing a look over his shoulder.

He brought up Hotmail. He didn't have an account, but surely it wasn't hard to register. It proved more difficult than anticipated: sean.devereaux@hotmail.com and sean_devereaux@hotmail.com were both taken. He scored third time lucky with sean_devereaux56@hotmail.com. The time it took to supply the required information, maybe he should have just risked a full print.

He forwarded the scanned document to his newly minted Hotmail. Sluggish progress: PDF conversion had bulked out the file size. The upload would take a while. He ran a search on the name Leonard while he waited. The National Crime Information database offered up screeds. A litany of misdeeds by people named Leonard unfurled: Male Assaults Female, theft, receiving stolen goods. He made a fast scroll-through. Nothing leapt out at him. Nobody stood out as likely to pursue stolen money. Or maybe they all did.

He picked up his phone and called Frank Briar. The purpose was two-fold: Briar had worked drugs, and might divulge Leonard-related info. More importantly, he wanted to know if Briar had heard about the gun incident. He needed to know how much time he had.

Briar let it ring a long time. He must have recognised the number: he answered and said, 'What is it?'

'That's not a nice way to answer the telephone.'

'It's late.'

'It's called police work. We keep tough hours.'

'What do you want?'

'You used to work drugs.'

'On and off. If you're wanting to score cheap smack, you'll have to grease someone else.'

'Hilarious.'

'What do you want?'

'What do you know about a guy called Leonard?'

Briar laughed. 'The drug guy?'

'Yeah. The drug guy.'

'It's a pseudonym. Nobody knows anything about him.'

'So how do you know it's a pseudonym?'

Briar didn't answer. Devereaux caught background TV noise. He said, 'An informant told me a dealer named Leonard's after the guys who did the bank and armoured van job.'

'Is your informant reliable?'

'I don't know. I only met him once.'

'Well. Whether he's reliable or not, saying Leonard the dealer's looking for someone means fuck-all, because nobody knows anything about him. People have name-dropped him, but nobody can say what he looks like.'

Devereaux went quiet. Briar ramped up his TV noise: canned laughter came through loud and clear. He seemed bored, eager to brush him off. Devereaux's gut feeling: Briar didn't know about what had happened between him and The Don. Maybe he had more time than he thought. Maybe McCarthy would anoint it their little secret.

He said, 'Thanks for your help.'

'Whatever. How've you been sleeping lately, now you've got a dead man sitting on your conscience?'

Devereaux put the handset down gently and stood up. The computer had finished. Devereaux erased the original email, then shut down the machine. He passed McCarthy's office on the way out: door closed, no light beneath. He was back across the street and in his car by ten o'clock.

Grayson's address was south of central city, off Gillies Avenue, in an upmarket area west of the Southern Motorway. His home was the right mirror-half of a two-unit building, close to the street behind a high ivy-draped wall. Plush living on a young cop's wage, especially given the young cop in question had a wife and two kids. Police station rumours spoke of a breathtaking mortgage.

Devereaux parked illegally on a yellow line, mindful of headlights waking sleeping children. He crossed the street and knocked on the front door. Grayson's wife answered. She was still made-up, dressed formal as if she'd just got in.

'Hello, Sean.'

'Sarah. Hi.'

'Sophie.' She smiled. 'Close.'

'Sophie. That's right. Is he in?'

He waited at the open door while she went to find her husband. Grayson himself appeared a moment later, noose of a tie round a stubbled throat.

'Shit. Are we on call?'

A sing-song instruction from beyond to mind his language around the kids.

'No. I just need to use your printer, if that's okay.'

The question took a moment to register. Devereaux got the feeling a 'no' was tempting. Light and dinner smells ebbed out around him. An excuse formed on Grayson's lips, but it never made it off the mark: 'Yeah. Sure. Just brush your feet on the mat.'

They had a small home office downstairs at the rear of the house. A desktop PC and a boxy laser printer huddled on an L-shaped desk in one corner. A window above showed a neat rubbish bin line-up on a narrow backyard path.

'You only just on your way home?' Grayson said.

'Yeah. Big day.'

'What do you need to run off?'

Devereaux sat down at the desk and told him.

Grayson propped himself in the doorframe. He looked at the floor and thumbed more slack in his tie. 'I thought that stuff was all off limits,' he said.

'It was. It is.'

'So where did you get it?'

'McCarthy's office.'

A pause. 'Was he in there at the time?'

'Guess.'

'Shit. You broke in?'

'I'll pay you back for the ink.'

A little girl about four or five wearing pink pyjamas appeared at the door. A bold T-shirt slogan proclaimed her *Miss Perfect*.

She reached up and tugged on Grayson's trouser pocket. He got a start and glanced down. 'Hey. You should have been in bed ages and *ages* ago, Miss N*aughty*.'

He got a shy giggle in reply. She eyed Devereaux, tilted her head back and cupped a stage whisper, one-handed, up at Grayson. 'You have to brush my teeth and tuck me in.'

'Mum already brushed them.'

'Yeah. But I drank juice.'

'You drank juice. Right. Well, go upstairs and hop into bed, and I'll be up in a minute. Did you say hello to Sean?'

'Hello, Sean.'

'Hello, Miss Perfect.'

She giggled behind clenched fists and scurried off back down the corridor. Devereaux smiled, wondered briefly whether his own home would ever hold that same cheerful patter.

Grayson stepped inside the room and pushed the door closed quietly. He slipped his hands in his pockets. 'I don't know about this,' he said.

'About what?'

'I'm struggling to reconcile this on a moral level.'

'Which part?'

He smiled weakly, shrugged. 'The breaking and entering. The theft.'

'McCarthy's a shitbag.'

'That's subjective. Stealing stuff isn't. There's no crime in being an arsehole.'

'Look. I went out on a job with him tonight. He used drugs uncovered in an illegal search to coerce information out of a witness. He physically assaulted a guy in the course of an interview.'

He shrugged again. 'It's happened before. It's happened worse.'

'I know it's happened worse because he's probably the one responsible.'

'So what did you do?'

'What do you mean?'

'You say he assaulted this guy during an interview. What did you do?'

'Pulled a gun on him.'

'On McCarthy?'

'Uh-huh.'

'Oh, Jesus.' He pushed hair off his brow. 'You're not serious.'

Devereaux nodded. 'You might be getting a new boss.'

Grayson was shaking his head, not listening. 'I can't deal with this. I can't deal with this. What if they track the files you stole here? You'll land me in a bunch of shit.'

'Nothing will be tracked here.'

Grayson opened the door, took a step out into the corridor. 'Look, I sympathise, I really do. If you say the guy's bent, you're probably right. But I just can't get involved. Like, I can't have anything to do with this.'

Devereaux didn't answer.

'I've got a family, man. I mean, far as I'm concerned, ignorance is bliss.'

He stood with his back to the door and pulled his tie up over his head. 'I'm going to draw a line under it there. I don't want to discuss it with you, I don't want to run decoys while you burgle offices, I don't want to do late-night printer runs.' He gestured at the screen. 'Do whatever you need, but that's the end of it.'

He moved away from the door and called from the end of the hallway. 'You can let yourself out.'

He did let himself out. The house was dark when he left. He drove home in the quiet, radio off, just thinking. The ghost of a dead man right there in the car with him. When he got home he sat on the couch under a reading light and started in on the paperwork. It was after eleven p.m. He could feel the weight of the day, but he knew he wouldn't sleep if he left the file for tomorrow.

He scanned photographs: street-perspective shots of a house off Swanson Road, close-in images of two men dead and bloodied by the entry. A crew cab truck abandoned in the yard, doors open, keys in. He read witness accounts and got a sense of chronology: six a.m., January thirtieth, two armed men had driven the truck onto the property. Shooting ensued, hence the bodies out front. The guys from the truck went inside the house. More shots were heard. They exited a minute or so later, whereupon a third man in a gold Nissan sedan collected them at the kerb and drove them away.

Police reports: the dead men out front were cops. Constable Ian Riley, Senior Sergeant Kyle Miller. A third murdered man found in the living room of the premises was identified as one William Rankin. Rankin had a criminal background: armed robbery, possession of stolen goods, assault. Scene examination notes: the attackers had used shotguns, and recovered all spent shells. A strange precaution, given they'd left a truck in the front yard.

He read until half past eleven that night. Then he turned the reading light off and sat there in the dark. He didn't know what time he went to sleep, but he stayed awake a long time.

■ TWENTY-FIVE

WEDNESDAY, 15 FEBRUARY, 6.58 A.M.

Witness work. Duvall rose early and donned the funeral suit, no tie. It struck him as a good look: sharp, not oppressively formal. He downed a canned peach breakfast, and packed a site-visit carry bag: business cards, the laptop, a cut-down version of his own case file. He left just after seven and drove south to town, turned west out towards Henderson, traffic still sluggish after waking up.

Newspaper coverage of the January thirtieth shooting had been scant, but he'd managed to glean the street name. Quarter to eight in the morning, he turned into the little cul-de-sac, just south of Swanson. It was nondescript housing. Only homicide could ever have found it fame. He slowed and checked frontages. The address hadn't been published: he ran mental comparisons against his paltry file photos to try to get a fix. The car engine held a low murmur. It was an old Commodore, 'nineties vintage, a typical CIB pool car circa his retirement. If nothing else, it made him feel authentic.

He found the place midway along the street. Single-storey, deep porch, twin grassed-over wheel ruts across the front lawn. He parked further up the street and walked back. It was full daylight, sun bright amid neat blue powder-coat surrounds. Cars passed, faces blanked by thoughts of yet another nine-to-five obligation. No other foot traffic: murder makes for good pedestrian management.

He stood at the kerb and surveyed the house. A few doors up across the street, an old guy in a mid thigh-length dressing gown claimed his morning paper, eased away hunched and bow-legged. Duvall stepped up onto the porch. Dry boards squeaked at his weight. He saw bloodstain shadow: dark irregularities implied seepage. He stepped to one side and tried to take it all in, identified two overlapping patterns.

He ran his hand over the woodwork. Dimples in the grain: maybe sunken nail heads, maybe shotgun pellets, extracted and plastered over. He stepped back. Too random for a nail pattern: odds on a half-load of buckshot.

He stepped onto the lawn and crouched over the wheel ruts. They were deep and harsh, grass growth a little balder towards the house, like a front-wheel skid had ripped down through the topsoil. Impossible to tell whether they'd been inflicted the morning of January thirtieth, but they looked recent enough. He stayed on his haunches and theorised. Pellet damage in the front of the house implied gunfire from the direction of the yard. Maybe a sudden lurch in off the street from a heavy vehicle, a shotgun round out a side window.

He looped the house on foot and found no further exterior damage. He checked the street again. The guy with the paper had wandered back out to his letterbox, front page snapped open waist-high, remaining sections rolled beneath his upper arm. His presence made front door entry too risky. The ranch slider at the rear was bolted solidly from inside. Which left the side door as the only real option. Frosted glass with a neat butterfly imprint: he smashed an elbow through and reached in to free the lock.

He set himself three minutes once he was inside. If the

old guy called him in for burglary he didn't want to hang about. He made a quick walk-through. Old indoor air with a faint chemical undercurrent. Stale, but sterile. The place was barren. No furniture. He checked the kitchen. Pale lino and empty shelves behind open cupboard doors; the whole room naked and slack-jawed.

He moved through to the entry. Polished timber floor: varnish would have repelled spilled fluids. The shotgun damage was visible in the wall, in perfect inverse to the exterior pattern. He moved through to what might have been a living room. The wallpaper had been torn back to the gypsum board. Light switches dangled from short lengths of electrical lead. Random stains of filler suggested gunshot damage repair. He leaned close and looked one-eyed along the plane of the wall. Hasty patch-up work had left subtle bullet-sized divots. He stepped through to the adjacent room. Rounds that missed framing timber had made it out the other side of the wall. He shuffled between rooms, gauging the line-up. A neat half-dozen row was stitched up high, near the ceiling architrave. Assuming living room discharge, the entry holes were smaller than the corresponding exit holes, meaning hollow point ammunition. The stitched line-up, maybe a police M4 on full automatic.

He stepped back to the living room. Massive bloodstain shadow on the carpet by one wall. Maybe one person's hard farewell, maybe several people's visit to an ICU. He struggled to make sense of it. Extensive bullet damage made trajectories seem non-coherent. He stood in the middle of the room. Pellet damage near the floor on one side, the neat stitch near the ceiling on the other. Maybe a shotgun round from the door, met by an assault rifle volley from the floor.

Carnage.

He went out the broken side door. The street was still quiet.

He hadn't gained any undue attention. No watchers behind split curtains. Maybe the suit made him look halfway kosher. He walked back to the car and made a flip-through of his file. Recountals of the January thirtieth shooting were imprecise: 'early morning' was as specific as it got. Maybe the neighbours would shed some light.

He crossed the street and started door-knocking. The file came with him. Paperwork imbued legitimacy. He figured post-shooting police canvassing would have been extensive: visitations by big men in suits would have been common. This shouldn't be too hard.

Nobody answered at the first house. He tried next door. The peephole darkened for a long moment before the door opened, tethered by doubled security chains. A woman's voice asked him if he was with the police. He told her he wasn't, but his investigator's licence was enough to make her open the door. She was young, dressed in hospital scrubs, looking exhausted. Probably fatigue from a regime of hyper-vigilance since the morning of January thirtieth.

Her recountal was from a principally aural perspective: gunshots woke her around six a.m. She'd grown up rural; she knew the difference between car backfire and a shotgun discharge. She guessed three or four shots in quick succession, another few several seconds later. It was maybe another minute before she risked a look out a front window. She saw some sort of pickup truck in the front yard of the house across the street, people lying hurt.

He pushed for details. She waved off the questions: he wasn't probing fond memories. She licked her lips and swallowed. 'Look, I only risked a glance, I'm sorry I can't be more helpful.'

'No, it's okay. I understand.'

She said she was running short of time and started to close

the door on him: apologetic smile, knees bent. He managed to get a business card through the gap before she shut him out.

He lucked out on the next two houses: nobody home. A young guy at the next place he tried gave him a variation on the first woman's story. Shots around six a.m., maybe four followed by a pause, then a volley of another ten or so a few seconds later. Duvall asked him if he knew who owned the house across the street. The guy said he didn't. The previous owner had died six months back and the place had just come off the market. Best guess was that it had been sold.

'You don't know who the new owner is?'

'Nuh-uh.'

Duvall said, 'Do you know how many people were in the house when the shooting happened?'

'No idea.'

'You see anyone coming or going on January twenty-ninth?'

The guy thought about it. 'That was the day before the shooting?'

Duvall nodded.

'Don't think so. Not that I recall.'

'Did you see anything during the shooting?'

'Not during. I hit the deck. All I saw was carpet.'

'You take a look outside afterwards?'

'I had a little look through the curtains.'

Duvall said nothing.

The guy made a shape with his mouth as he remembered. 'Crew cab truck in the front yard,' he said. 'All shot up. Two guys in the yard, on their backs, blood in the yard, you can imagine. This big cloud of gun smoke just sort of drifting.'

'You sure about the number of shots?'

'Why?'

'People sometimes overestimate things under stress.'

The guy shrugged. He made to close the door. 'Can't see that it matters,' he said. 'People still got killed.'

Duvall thanked him through the closed door and walked away. He got no answer with the next three places he visited. He jumped a couple of doors and tried the home of the guy in the dressing gown.

'I saw you peepin' round there across the road,' the guy said when he answered. He had a glass mug of tea in one hand, tortoiseshell glasses anchored on a thick nose rife with capillaries. The dressing gown was knotted around a bulbous paunch.

'I wasn't peeping.' Duvall showed his licence.

'That print's too small for me,' the guy said. He frowned and took a cautious sip. Gentle, like he didn't want to ripple the surface. 'But it looks mighty official.'

'Do you have a spare moment to answer a few questions?'

'About that ruckus the other week?'

'Yes. The ruckus.'

The guy nodded slowly. He stepped back and let his gaze circuit the doorframe. 'Yeah. I reckon we can slot you in. Better come indoors and sit down. The old knees don't much fancy doorstep chats these days.'

Duvall stepped in and closed the door. He followed the guy down a short corridor carpeted off-yellow, smell of tobacco smoke and buttered toast prevailing. They turned left into a small living room. Old furniture and packed bookshelves made for homely clutter. Faded novels stuffed floor to ceiling, thin yellowed ears of random papers peeping between. Everything warm and close and familiar. A wide armchair was set up in one corner beside a window. The open newspaper was draped on a footstool before it. A table adjacent held a magnifying glass and a pack of matches and a crinkled packet of tobacco trapped beneath a wooden pipe. High shelves displayed ancient trinkets: a globe on a rusted pedestal, a hand-painted Lancaster bomber, a line-up of brass ammunition shells.

The old guy bent awkwardly and lifted the paper before sitting down. He set the mug on the table and crossed swollen ankles on the footrest and smoothed the paper over his lap.

'I saw men shot,' he said. 'A long time ago.' He looked out the window. 'Never thought I'd see it again, in a suburban street, eating breakfast. Gordon Bennett.'

He grimaced and claimed a fibrous pinch of tobacco from the pouch, thumbed it into the pipe. He lit up with a match and eased the stem in one corner of a shivering lip. 'You can shift them things off the chair there if you want somewhere to sit.'

'I won't keep you long.'

He shrugged. 'Suit yourself. Your knees're probably better behaved than mine anyway.'

'You saw the shooting back on January thirtieth.'

'Bits and pieces. It ain't the shooting that's important; it's what's going on afterwards. And I tell you, it ain't easy looking. Shit.'

'You recall what time it all happened?'

'Well, I think so. Police came by a few times, and I've been telling them it all went down just after six a.m., and I don't know whether that was the actual time, or whether saying it enough has convinced me that's the truth.' He laughed softly, leaked a skein of smoke.

'Did the shots wake you, or were you up already?'

'I was up already. Fixing some tea.'

'How many shots did you hear?'

'What did the folks down the street say?'

'About what?'

'How many shots did they think they heard?'

Duvall looked at him. Detective Training 101: don't let witnesses compare notes. Fuck it. He'd never been a detective. 'Maybe four or five.'

The guy was shaking his head. 'People get stressed, things get overestimated.'

'How many shots did you hear?'

'No more than three to begin with.'

'And then more later on?'

The guy nodded. 'Handful of shots, a few seconds later I couldn't count. A big one over the top that sounded like a shotgun. But don't bet your kids on it. The old ears aren't what they used to be.'

'Did you take a look outside?' Duvall said.

The guy crossed his legs, knees stacked neatly. He sipped at his tea. The steam misted his glasses. He used a dressing gown hem to de-fog the lenses.

'Can't say I rushed out,' he said. 'Gunfire in your street, it's not quite the same as when you hear the ice-cream truck, is it?' He chuckled to himself, rubbed a thumb over a tobacco burn on the armrest.

'Did you see anything of the house while the shooting was happening?'

'Not while it was happening. I got a look out the front window when it was all over.'

'How soon after?'

'Don't know. 'Bout the time it takes an old fella to shuffle over to a window. Not too long.'

'Can you describe what you saw?' Duvall said.

He made a face. 'Pass me one of them coasters there, would you?'

Duvall shifted a stack of auto magazines and passed the guy a cork beer mat. He set it beneath his mug. 'Ta. No, I only had a quick peek. Just enough to get the gist of it without getting something I could do without. If you know what I mean.' He cleared his throat gently. 'There was a light sort of truck parked up at a funny angle on the front lawn.' He took a long hit off the pipe and looked out the window. 'Guy dead on the front step, sort of half on the lawn. Guy dead in the doorway.' He shrugged. 'Looked sideways along the street and there's this car pulling away.'

'You ever seen the car before?'

He shook his head. 'Don't think so. Didn't recognise the colour.'

'What colour was it?'

'Yellowish. Maybe gold or something. I dunno. Old eyes aren't so good. Time was maybe I could have picked out some details. Nowadays I probably couldn't even if it was parked in my lap.'

'Was it moving fast?'

'Not really. It's wasn't mucking about, but it didn't look in too much of a hurry.'

Duvall thought a moment. 'What did the truck on the front lawn look like?'

'It was white. Sort of old.'

'Was there anyone in it?'

'Not when I looked.' He mulled it over. 'Can't be dead certain on it, but I had a view straight through the back, and I'm pretty sure it was just seats and no heads, if that makes sense. Engine was still running, too. I told that to the police. And the doors were open.'

'The driver and passenger doors were both open.'

He clucked his tongue and nodded. 'That's what I said.'

'Okay. So after the car drove away what happened?'

'All quiet for a couple of minutes. I was still sort of peeping through my curtains, and I could see up and down the street, every man and his dog doing the exact same thing. I tell you, every place you looked, someone looking through a wrinkled curtain. Like some sort of dead man's peep show. I dunno. But I got hold of the phone and gave the police a ring, and nobody's going outside to check if these poor guys on the porch are actually okay because the guy on the phone at the police is telling people to stay inside and keep back from the windows. So I guess I scored fifty per cent on that.'

'How long did it take the police to arrive?'

'Not long. They did a pretty cautious job of it. There were a couple of cars parked way off down the street, blocking it off I s'pose. You could just kind of see the red-blue-red-blue of the lights going back and forth. Then some chaps in fatigues scooted over fences and started drawing in closer. Had one of them in here, aiming a gun out the window. Had it propped up against the back of the chair. Asked the fella if he wanted a cup of tea or something, and he said to me, fairly sharp too, "If I need anything, I'll let you know." Like it was a hotel or something. Tickled me pink. Susan wouldn't have had any of that lip, if she was still around, I tell you. Jesus.' He took a gentle hit off his pipe. 'Anyway, I found myself another window and laid up there. Big guy in a suit turned up maybe fifteen minutes later, I guess. Pulled up at the kerb and just walked into the yard, wary, but kind of nonplussed at the same time, you know? Checked the pulse of the guys sprawled out there, one then the other, and then he went into the house for a moment, but he came back out fairly smartly and stood out there on the kerb with his hands on his hips. And, damn me, if he wasn't thinking this was one hell of a mess. Damned if he wasn't right too.'

'What did he look like?' Duvall said.

The guy moved his tongue round his cheek, like searching

for taste more than memory. 'I ain't much good on the details from this range. But I'd say he'd be around your age. Great big guy, ramrod-straight.'

Don McCarthy, no question. Duvall ran some closing questions: Had the address seen any prior trouble? Did he know the owner of the house? Did he witness any arrivals at the house the day before the shooting occurred? He got three unhesitant No's.

Duvall smiled. 'Police ask you anything that I haven't?'

The guy chuckled. 'Maybe. But blow me if I can remember.'

'Thanks for your time.'

'Pleasure. Most horrific thing I ever seen while eating toast and marmalade, I tell you.'

He took another puff off his pipe, and Duvall let himself out.

He needed food, and thinking space.

He headed south and east and stopped at a Denny's in New Lynn. It was busy with the breakfast rush, but he claimed a table for four and fanned his file contents. The booth offered nominal privacy. With a bit of luck, paperwork would deter company. He found a pen and outlined the morning's progress: *six a.m. shots fired/truck in yard (panic skid?)/house owner unknown/gold car getaway post-shooting.*

He flagged a passing waitress and ordered coffee and a toasted sandwich. A mental red light told him his savings might not appreciate the hit, so he cancelled the sandwich. Caffeine would have to do.

He flipped through his file and appended another note: *Both doors on truck left open.* So what? He couldn't see the relevance at this stage. He re-read his news clippings. It had reached the point where he almost had them memorised verbatim.

He tried for a chronology. The lawn tread marks indicated

the truck had pulled in off the road and skidded to a stop. Both doors open, implying a driver and at least one other passenger. So did they come in off the street and just start shooting? The bullet damage to the front of the house seemed to indicate they did. But why fire before they were inside? It didn't make a lot of sense to shoot before they were through the door. Unless there was somebody standing outside on the porch.

Too many unknowns. He closed the file as the waitress brought his coffee. It had slopped over the rim and left a thin tan film in the saucer.

Gold car getaway post-shooting.

There was nothing definite linking the gold car to the mass homicide further up the street. Could have been an idle commuter's poor timing. But the guys from the truck had to have left somehow: it reeked of a last-minute exit.

He drank some coffee and thought about it. On Monday his theory to Don McCarthy had been the house was used for witness protection. Meaning the occupants of the address would have been maybe one witness, plus a team of either two or three cops. McCarthy hadn't denied it. He'd more or less told him to keep it to himself.

So what happened?

Say it's six a.m. The house is being staked out by the two guys in the truck. They see someone at the target address step outside, they decide to move in. They skid into the front yard and shoot whoever's standing out front on the porch. They gain entry through the front and take down whoever's inside. They spend a moment or two indoors, then leave the scene.

He sipped more coffee.

The truck wouldn't make a good getaway vehicle. So they'd ditched it, and presumably been picked up. Which was potentially where the gold car came into it.

He drained the cup and placed it on the seat beside him to free up space.

So it's a dual stakeout: the guys in the truck are watching from one angle, the guy in the gold car's got everything pinned down from another. The guys in the truck move in. The gold car driver holds his ground, collects the guys from the truck a moment later. Cue a clean getaway.

Duvall jotted *gold car driver* and boxed it in with a fierce border of ballpoint. It felt like progress. He gathered the file and paid for his coffee. He asked the girl at the counter for directions to the nearest payphone. He got a shy smile and a shrug. Public phones were nearing extinction.

He wandered the shopping centre. A shower had passed through during breakfast. The pavement radiated hot bitumen aroma. He found a booth one block over on Memorial Square. It had a copy of the Auckland residential White Pages, burn marks on one corner the only sign of abuse. Still serviceable. He propped his folder above the console and made a quick flip-through.

Constable Ian Riley, dead by gunshot, Monday January thirtieth.

His old journo contact Robert Davis had given him the name the night before. He hoped Riley wasn't too common a name. Ring-and-hope approaches were effective provided they didn't take all week. He flipped through to R. Auckland boasted a one-page column of Rileys. This could take a while.

He fed the phone his credit card and worked down the list. He had a concise greeting mentally rehearsed: introduce himself as a private investigator and ask if he was speaking to a relative of the late Ian Riley.

He got five 'No's' in a row. Monosyllabic answers made for quick phone work. He tried the next Riley on the list.

No answer. He got three more no-pickups. Admittedly, mid-morning on a weekday wasn't an ideal time to catch people at home. He persevered and got an alternating sequence of no's and no answers. The thought of the phone patiently nibbling his credit card balance kept things snappy. He tried the next Riley on the list. An elderly woman answered.

'Madam, I'm a licensed private investigator named Mitchell Duvall. I wonder whether I'm speaking with a relative of the late Constable Ian Riley?'

He got a long stretch of quiet on the line. It felt like progress. 'What is this about?' the woman said.

Duvall laid on the manners: 'Madam, I'm currently investigating a shooting that occurred back on the thirtieth of January, and I understand Constable Riley was a victim.'

'That's correct.'

'I'm sorry; you say you're a relative?'

'I'm his mother.'

'I see. Would you be available at all today to meet with me and perhaps answer some questions?'

'Yes, I think I would.'

'What time would suit you?'

'Well, I'm here all day, so whatever time suits you will suit me, I suppose.'

She put down the phone.

■ TWENTY-SIX

Wednesday, 15 February, 9.28 a.m.

Devereaux rang in and had his regular duties reassigned. He didn't cite a reason for absence. Nobody queried him. Maybe nobody cared. Or maybe news had already broken of his dust-up with Don McCarthy.

He dialled John Hale's office. Hale caught it on the first ring.
'That was quick.'
Hale said, 'I don't like to leave paying clients waiting.'
'You going to be in the office this morning?'
'Uh-huh.'
'I'm coming for a visit.'
'Good.'

It was a slow drive into town. February heat left traffic sluggish. Every passing car brought a windscreen flash of high sun. To his right a flat ocean nudged gently on the high-tide mark. Above it the inert bronzed forms of UV revellers, prone and gleaming in the heat.

He found a park on High Street and fed the parking meter, walked up to Hale's office. He had his stolen file with him. The door was unlocked, and he let himself in. The business had downsized. Three years back Hale had had an assistant and one junior investigator. Then the recession hit and left him with neither. The reception area boasted carpet and paint and little else. Hale was at his window, palms propped on the sill. Neck lost inside a deep hunch.

'You bring me breakfast?' he said.

'Maybe next time.'

'Jug's there if you're under-caffeinated.'

'You always use such good vocab.'

Hale nodded and looked at his view. 'It enlivens the quotidian drudgery,' he said.

The window was close to where Vulcan Lane ran between High Street and Queen. He stepped away from the view and moved behind his desk and sat down. The window was open a crack. Devereaux laid the file on the desk and leaned on the sill. He lit a cigarette and vented fumes outside.

'Don't get ash on my carpet.'

'It's grey anyway.'

Hale nodded at the file. 'What's this?'

'January thirty shooting.' He stood the lighter and the cigarette pack side by side on the sill.

'From who?'

'Don McCarthy.'

'The whole file?'

'Part of it.'

'How'd you get it?'

'I picked the lock on his office door. Then I picked the lock on his filing cabinet.'

Hale slid the file towards him but didn't open it. 'That's not a good way to keep your job.'

Devereaux looked out the window. Vulcan Lane traffic had peaked: wall to wall pedestrians, cutting across from Queen. He folded his arms and crossed his legs. 'I had a run-in with McCarthy yesterday,' he said.

'Verbal or physical?'

'I pulled a gun on him.'

Hale leaned forward on knitted fingers. 'That's not a good way to keep your job either.'

Devereaux didn't answer. Bright window light drew him in brooding silhouette.

Hale said, 'What happened?'

'He and I went out yesterday evening to interview some contact of his. McCarthy thinks the guy's holding back on him, and starts roughing him up.'

'So you pulled a gun on him?'

Devereaux didn't move. The cigarette wavered with the reply: 'It was McCarthy's gun. But, yeah, essentially.'

'Are you in trouble?'

'Probably.'

'Have you heard anything?'

'No.'

Hale leaned back and folded his arms. The movement strained his shirtsleeves. He put his feet up on the corner of his desk. 'You could lose your job.'

'Or he could.'

'I don't think the odds are quite even.'

Devereaux tapped ash out the window. 'Depends how he decides to play it. He might not want to run the risk of me telling my side of the story, in which case he might keep quiet.'

'And what are the chances of that?'

'I don't know. But I haven't heard anything yet.'

'Yet. That magic word.'

Devereaux didn't answer. He held the cigarette vertical in two fingers in front of his face. He looked at it a long time.

'You can come work for me,' Hale said.

'You told me that.'

'I'm reiterating the offer.'

Devereaux glanced at him. 'For or with?'

'We can work out the nitty-gritty later.'

'Do you even have the work?'

Hale creaked back gently in his chair. He looked at the ceiling. 'No, probably not.'

Devereaux looked down at the street. The cigarette leaned out one corner of his mouth. 'Were we ever that bad?' he said.

'In what way?'

'Did we ever lean on people too hard?'

Hale thought about it. 'I never lost sleep over anything,' he said.

'Neither does Don McCarthy.'

Hale was quiet. He opened the file cover, closed it again. He said, 'I think me and you and old Don are probably sewn from the same stuff. Difference is we know where the line is.'

'And he doesn't.'

'No. I think he just has a different line than you.'

'Just a question of which line's right.'

Hale shrugged. 'All the time I've known you, your line's held up pretty well.'

Devereaux nodded slowly. The movement caused a shiver in the thin rising smoke. He said, 'I think I'm going to quit.'

'Is that a definitely or a maybe?'

'I don't know. I think the only way I can stay is if a number of people end up dead.'

'Could be a big ask.'

'I just don't like the way things are heading.'

Hale said nothing.

Devereaux said, 'I just don't know whether I want to be a part of this side of things any more.'

'Too Orwellian?'

Devereaux didn't answer.

Hale said, 'So ride out the next couple of days and just see what happens.'

Devereaux nodded. He looked down and watched the street. The countless throng; no one with fears that matched his own. He said, 'If I don't make it, will you speak at my funeral?'

Hale said, 'Only if I'm not busy.'

Devereaux laughed. 'I have to go to a thing with Ellen tonight,' he said.

'What is it?'

'Her parents are back from overseas. It's some kind of party for them, I think.'

'What are they like?'

'I think I liked them best when they were overseas.'

'Would they like you best if you were overseas?'

'Probably.'

'Have you told her about all this?'

'What?'

'The Don business.'

'No. She'd just worry.'

'All that worrying you do by yourself, maybe it would be worth spreading it around.'

Devereaux didn't answer. Hale opened the file again and skimmed. He flicked through and selected a random page: '"Witness heard what she thought were shotgun rounds, soon after six a.m. Witness said a brief pause then preceded more shots. Witness looked through front — street-facing — window and observed two men prone in yard of target address."' He fanned pages and found another statement. '"Witness observed bullet damage to front of target address. Witness observed at least one man lying bleeding in front entry of target address." Jesus. It's a mess.'

Devereaux reached out through the open window. He

tapped ash and watched the breeze catch it. 'Yeah,' he said. 'It is.'

He hadn't caught an address. Duvall almost called the woman back, before he realised it was in the phone book, right in front of him.

It took him forty minutes to find the place. It was a Sunnynook location, across the Harbour Bridge on the North Shore. It was a small unit down a right of way, backing onto the motorway. He parked at the kerb and walked down. A German shepherd chained to a steel stake watched him from the lawn of the front house. Ears and tail perked, slow eyes and a slow licking of lips.

Another dog started barking when he knocked at the rear unit. The door was frosted glass. A woman appeared behind it, smudged and ghostlike. She pulled the door back against a chain. A wet canine nose claimed the gap.

'You the investigator I spoke to earlier?'

'That's right.'

'You give me just a tick and I'll do away with these darn animals.'

'Sure.'

He stood and waited. Beside him a single chicken toddled and flapped inside a wood and wire hutch. A three-wheeled Daihatsu hatchback nested in a thatch of long grass.

'Now, Henry, you sit and behave and let the man through. Goodness sake.'

The dog nose disappeared. He heard the chain squeal off the catch. The door opened. A short elderly woman with crutches stood in its absence. She offered her hand. The proffered forearm dangled the crutch and a thick sheaf of loose skin. They shook.

'Mr Duvall. Susan Riley. Come on in and we'll have a sit-down. Just ignore Henry. He needs to learn he's not the centre of attention.'

He stepped inside and closed the door behind him. A Dalmatian stared up at him, tail wagging stiffly, eager for an introduction. A cat brushed past one leg, fluid and eel-like. The entry was yellow linoleum, overlaid with a dog-hair patchwork. The air carried the stink of it. To the right, an internal door led to the garage. He saw a wall of mesh-fronted animal hutches, a camp stretcher on the floor below.

He followed the woman through to a living area at the rear of the house. A ranch slider framed a vista of tufted lawn edged with metal fencing. Through a door to the kitchen, he could see maybe ten or a dozen saucers heaped with jellymeat. Above them the sleek and hunched forms of as many cats, heads bent, tails upright and swaying.

In the corner, a boxy television set topped with rabbit ears sat mute. The woman wedged herself down in an armchair adjacent. She sighed and raised her feet a fraction, easing pressure on thickened ankles. She wore a salmon-coloured cotton jumper above a long lime-green skirt, slack and formless as a shower curtain. She leaned her crutches against an armrest. Duvall claimed a couch opposite her. The Dalmatian followed him in and took up post beside the armrest, tail working at mid-revs.

'Long as you don't pat him he'll leave you be,' she said.

The dog looked disappointed.

The woman said, 'So you're some sort of PI?'

'That's right. I used to be a police detective.'

'How long ago was that?'

'Fifteen years or so.'

She looked at the floor, trawling some mental back catalogue. 'Did you work with my Ian, back in the day?'

'No, ma'am. I didn't.'

She looked up. 'You can quit the ma'am business. Your ears won't fall off if you call me Susan.'

'Right. Susan.'

'And you've gone private now?'

'That's right.'

'So who are you detecting for?' A smile fought heavy cheeks. 'Or is that where the private part comes in?'

'Behalf of myself, I guess.'

'Yourself.' She nodded slowly. 'Hell of a pastime you got yourself.'

Duvall fell quiet. The ceiling was low. A wide lid of plaster trapping that stagnant feline odour.

He said, 'I just want to talk with you about the shooting on January thirtieth.'

She looked at him blankly a moment, jowly and bespectacled. 'When Ian was killed.'

'Yes.'

The meal in the kitchen concluded. Cats moved about the empty saucers like whorls in river water. A grey tabby slinked into the room, wide eyes on Duvall. It traced a path along the baseboard to the woman's chair, jumped atop her lap and balled itself tightly. The Dalmatian tired of sitting and sank to all fours, ears still attentive.

He said, 'I'm sorry, I'm sure it must be difficult to try to think about.'

'No, it's okay. Best approach with most things is to take a deep breath and look them in the eye.'

Duvall didn't answer.

Susan Riley said, 'What have they told you?' She was frowning. Maybe myopia, maybe a desire to catch and archive every word.

'Nothing. I've got news clippings, and that's it.'

'Well. I don't know whether I'll be able to enlighten you much beyond that.'

'Do you know why your son was even involved?'

The frown softened. She shook her head. 'I know he got a call late in the evening, January twenty-ninth. This is the day before it all happened. He got a call, and said he had to head out somewhere for work. I asked him where he was off to, of course, and he said it was some place out West Auckland way. And that was the last thing he said to me.' She looked down and stroked the cat. 'In this life anyway.'

'I take it he called you before he left?'

She looked confused. 'No, he spoke to me in person. He lived here. He lived with me.'

'Oh, okay. I wasn't aware of that.'

'It was just temporary. I had him on the little stretcher in the garage. I don't think he liked staying with all the cats, but it was better than nothing, I suppose. Ian's luck's been a bit crooked the last few years, I think it's fair to say.'

Duvall said nothing, waited for her to continue. The TV showed a glossy infomercial.

She said, 'His marriage broke up about five years ago now, I think. His wife ended up with everything; got the house and the kids. Obviously, every story you hear's got a second or a third side to it, but how he tells it his wife just sort of woke up one morning and said, "It's over, Ian, get out, I don't love you any more." He was devastated, I tell you. It's a miserable thing to have someone just stop feeling for you. But I suppose love's doled out at random and I guess something similar happens when you're talking about the reverse. But he struggled to get another place, and he's always had a problem with gambling, and, truth be told, drinking hasn't been on his side either, and all of that rolled in with the pressure he was under at work, he ended up just coming to live with me. He used to joke and say it was a disgrace, him being forty-eight and all and still living at home, and I used to just say, "Oh, Ian, it's not like you've been at home this whole time." You know. I liked having him at home. All that bad luck stacked on his ticket didn't stop him being a good man. I loved him so much. His father would have been so proud of him. You can do all kinds of things with your life, but it's being a decent person that counts for the most.'

'I'm sorry, I know nothing about him.'

'That's okay. Nobody does. Police clung on to all the information like it's going out of fashion.'

'I got his name from a journalist.'

'Journalist have anything else to say for himself?'

'No. He just gave me the name.'

'How did you find me?'

'I looked up Riley in the phone book and just started ringing.'

She made a little shape with her mouth like it struck her as sensible. 'Well. I don't know what to tell you other than he was forty-eight and he was a policeman, and there were fewer people than I'd have hoped for at his funeral.'

'Did they tell you how he died?'

She looked up. 'Quickly.'

Duvall didn't answer.

She glanced down and pinched something from the cat's fur. 'No, I'm sorry. I didn't mean to get sharp with you. They said he was shot.'

'Okay.'

She said, 'I'm not so sure on how quick that would actually be. Got a feeling you'd have time enough to suffer.'

Duvall left a pause to let that settle. He said, 'Do you know what division he was with?'

'I don't know what you mean.'

'With the police. Did he do patrol, or investigations?'

'Patrol. He wore a uniform and drove a car. He was based in the central city awhile, then, heaven knows why, he volunteered to do a bit of a stint down Manukau way. Why he wanted to drive all the way down there, I'll never know.'

'He was still based down there early last month?'

'Yes. He got seconded to a big investigation down there. Those bank robberies that started up back in November. You know the ones?'

'Yes.'

'He was assigned to do work on that.'

'What sort of work?'

'I don't really know. Talking to people, I think. Way I understand it is they had a whole list of people who could have done it, or might have done it, or might know something about it. And then they went out and talked to them, and people they knew, tried to squeeze out some gossip. Apparently, they reckoned if you stole as much money as these fellas did, you'd be driven to gloat about it at some stage. And so I think they spent a fair bit of time eavesdropping underworld tittle-tattle.' A soggy cough flared. She doused it on a sleeve.

'Did you see much of him, day to day?'

'Towards the end I didn't. He did a lot of night work. I think they liked to knock on people's doors after the sun's gone down. But I'm a day creature, so I suppose we lived in a different pattern. Often I'd be getting up just as he got in, and he'd bring me a cup of tea. Which was nice.'

The couch was too low. Duvall stretched his legs to ease a calf cramp. 'How did he seem during the last few weeks?'

'I haven't seen him the last few weeks. He's been dead.'

'I mean the weeks before he passed away.'

'I don't think he was all that good, to be honest.'

'Why's that?'

'Don't know, really. Although there wasn't much else in his life beyond work, so I'd say at a bit of a guess that something with his job was eating at him.'

'Was he okay, financially?'

'Casino ate his savings. But I'd say his income was probably okay.'

'Did he talk to you about why he might have been upset?'

'No. I just deduced it, I suppose.'

'Based on what?'

'The happy pills he kept in the bathroom. Prozac or what's it called.'

'Had he been on antidepressants before?'

'Not as far as I know. Can't hardly blame him for taking them when he did. Wife had gone, money had gone, and he was sharing his bedroom with a dozen cats. Lucky he wasn't allergic, or life really would have been a shambles.'

'Do you know of anyone else I can speak to who might be able to help me?'

The infomercial ended. The woman watched the transition to an *Oprah* re-run and then looked back at him.

'Not really,' she said. 'A lot of his friends were through his wife. I think he lost touch with them after the split.'

'What about people at work?'

'There's a guy called Charlie. The surname'll come to me in a minute.'

'Okay. Who's Charlie?'

'He knew Ian. They worked together a lot, I think. He's still with the police.'

'Have you met him?'

'I did actually. Many years ago. They graduated Police

College together. I met him then.'

'Do you have any way of contacting him?'

'Ian will probably have a number somewhere. It'll be with all his things.'

'You mind if I have a look?'

'No, I don't mind.'

She looked at him quietly. 'What's made you feel you got to dig through all this misery?'

'I just feel like I should.'

She didn't answer.

He said, 'I've done a lot of things in my life I regret. I just want to do something that I don't.'

She smiled. She said, 'You seem like a decent chap. I wish I could absolve you of whatever it is that makes you feel you've got to do what you're doing.'

Her eyes teared up. She removed her glasses and cleaned them on a sleeve and slipped them on again. She watched *Oprah* for a brief moment. 'I remember holding him at the hospital,' she said. 'Probably the happiest day of my life. But maybe I should have left him there for somebody else if I knew where he was going to wind up a little further up the street. I don't know.'

Duvall didn't know what to say to that. He stood up. The woman set the cat on the floor and gathered the crutches. She stood awkwardly: gulps and a grimace. A wide stance and hunched posture stabilised a shaky equilibrium. She nodded at the door. 'Head on through. It's in the garage. I'll bring up the rear.'

He walked through to the garage. Animal stench greeted him: dense and heated, like inhaling a used glove. Cats swirled and mewed at ankle height. Taped cardboard boxes were stacked against a metal vehicle door. He threw a switch and got weak single-bulb illumination. The camp stretcher was crisply made up. A small dresser stood adjacent, lamp and a couple of paperbacks atop it.

The woman clattered through behind him. A feline entourage rode her wake. 'All that boxed stuff is his. Police only just gave it back.'

He crouched and checked out the dresser. It was only three drawers deep. A broken tongue of masking tape ran lengthwise. He found a framed wedding photograph and a creased passport in a worn envelope. A wad of bank statements not much cheerier than his own. A Prozac prescription. Framed headshots of two young children. He tilted it under the light and picked out a smeared thumbprint collage. He imagined Ian Riley looking at it in the dim solitude, reliving better days.

The top drawer held a softback address book. He thumbed it, front to back. Entries were seldom. He found a Charles Easton. He showed it to the woman.

She raised her glasses, brought a harsh squint in close. 'Yes,' she said. 'That's the boy.'

The second drawer held a ballpoint pen. He transcribed the Easton details to a receipt stub in his wallet. She watched him, breath short, propped up in teetering stability. He thanked her for her time. He offered his condolences. She didn't reply. His sympathy hung out there unacknowledged. He made for the door.

She said, 'I'm not normally one to be asking favours of strangers, but if you get a hold of whoever did all this, you can look them in the eye and tell them perdition's waiting, and he's got a wry grin.'

She eased herself down onto the stretcher. The mattress sagged deep and met the floor. She looked at the bedside table.

The book and the lamp. Artefacts of life wasted, an unintended tribute in household clutter.

Duvall said he could let himself out. He nudged through eddies of roaming cats to the front door and left.

He walked down to the busway and found a public phone beside the platform. Thank God it took coins. He consulted his receipt stub and dialled Charles Easton's home number. The call rang unanswered. No message service. He dialled Manukau Police Headquarters from memory, and a patrol administrator put him through to Easton's desk. No answer there either. Duvall shook his pockets for change and heard a feeble jingle. He fed the slot and called the same number, got hold of Charles Easton's supervisor. The guy told him Easton was out on patrol. Duvall asked for a cellphone number, and the guy transferred him direct. Third time lucky: Easton picked up.

Duvall said, 'Mr Easton, my name's Mitchell Duvall. Susan Riley gave me your number.'

'I didn't realise I knew a Susan Riley.'

'Ian Riley's mother.'

Three seconds. 'Okay.'

'I was just wanting to ask you some questions about Ian.'

'Convince me you're not a journalist.'

'I'm a private investigator.'

'Who's your client?'

'I can't reveal that.'

Easton didn't answer.

Duvall decided not to lie: 'Look, I'm not working for anyone; I'm not looking for a story. I just want to know what happened.'

'That's some pretty intense curiosity.'

Duvall said, 'I'm not bullshitting you. I just met his mother; she said she was at your graduation.'

'What year was that?'

'She didn't tell me.'

'What's to say you weren't bullshitting her?'

'All I want is to meet and ask you some questions.'

'We're not meeting. I'll tell you that now.'

'Five minutes of your time.'

'Well, we've been talking for thirty seconds, so you've got four and a half minutes left.'

'She said you and Ian worked closely.'

'On and off.'

'So do you know why he was on antidepressants?'

'Ever had someone just ring up and start asking questions about a dead friend? It's a bit weird.'

'I'm sorry. I'm just trying to help; you didn't want a face to face.'

A brief stretch of quiet. 'No, I don't know why he was taking the pills.'

'His mother said he seemed withdrawn before his death. Do you know anything at all about that?'

'Have you got a pen?'

'No. Why?'

'I'll give you a number and you can call me back.'

'Just bear with me. Two minutes.'

'No. Listen to what I'm saying: I'm going to give you a different number, and you're going to call me back on it. Okay?'

'Okay.'

'You got that pen?'

A bus passed: he palmed his free ear to suppress the roar. 'Yeah. Give it to me.'

Easton recited another mobile number. 'I'm driving,' he said. 'Wait two minutes, and then call me back.'

'I'm at a payphone, and I'm running low on change.'

'Tough shit, you should have thought ahead.' He hung up.

Duvall emptied his pockets and topped up the phone, repeated the number continuously under his breath. The handset was dewed with palm sweat. He wiped it off, let his watch step around two minutes. He dialled, fingers timed to the spoken mantra.

Easton answered. 'Well done,' he said. 'Two minutes, bang on.'

'Look, as I said, I'm low on money here so it would be great to keep this brief.'

'Uh-huh. Well, shut up and listen carefully. I'm going to give you some info, and if it gets out that you got it from me, I'm going to break your spine. All right? If the sergeant or receptionist or whoever patched you through, asks you what we spoke about, you can tell them I was absolutely fuck-all use to you. Understand?'

'I don't really get where we're going with—'

'Do you or do you not understand?'

'Yes, yes, I understand. Okay.'

'Good. So here's some good tattle for you: back in January, Ian was assigned to this robbery investigation shit—'

'His mother told me.'

'Okay, right. Just temporary help-out work. He said he got allocated to run interviews with this detective — guy was called Frank Briar — remember the name. Anyway, they went out to this address in Avondale to talk to some guy Leroy Turner, this is last month, beginning of January, because someone thought he might have had an inside line on some of these robberies. Cut a long story short, turned out he didn't. But they knocked on this guy's door and got him outside and put him in the back of the car for an interview; Ian driving and Briar in the back running the questions. And as I said, the guy's got nothing to give, so he clams up, says nothing. So Briar punches him in the side of the head, threatens to burn his ear off with a lighter if he doesn't start spilling something. And the guy's freaking out, because obviously he's got nothing to say. Anyway, this keeps up; Briar's asking his questions, the guy's saying he knows nothing. Eventually, Briar clicks that the guy's none the wiser, so he packs it in, lets old Leroy out of the car, and gives him a kick in the guts to get him on his way. That's how Ian told it, anyway.'

'How long have you known this?'

'I don't know. Since after it happened, I guess. He was a good guy. Ian, I mean, he knew where the line was. If he was down, odds on it was something to do with what I just told you.'

'You think he felt guilty at not doing anything?'

'Yeah. Well, not doing anything to help.'

'Would you be prepared to testify to what you just told me?'

'No.'

'Why?'

'Because I wear a uniform and drive a patrol car. I can't afford to stand up and put my name to something like that and put my livelihood on the line. Simple as that.' He paused. 'Do with it whatever you want,' he said. 'But leave me out of it.'

■ TWENTY-SEVEN

WEDNESDAY, 15 FEBRUARY, 10.37 A.M.

He needed breathing room.

Devereaux left the file with Hale and went out for a walk. He headed north down to Quay Street and the waterfront. The whole atmosphere was a head-clearer. That salt-diesel maritime odour. A roadside doughnut trailer's hot grease aroma. The idle swill of pedestrians, the manic Stuka-style dive bombs of gulls seeking food scraps. He lit another cigarette and leaned on the railing past the Ferry Building, face to the harbour. A group of school kids passed behind him: a single-file parade of merry pastels and a whiff of sunblock. He wondered what they thought of him: this strange grey figure, propped on a rail. Smoke and furrowed brow. He looked at the water. A malformed fluid shadow gazed back, dimpled by ash. He couldn't recall past aspirations embodying this moment. He wondered if it was true for anyone.

He was geared towards response to aftermath. But he couldn't reconcile a wait-and-see approach when it came to Don McCarthy. He needed an indication of mindset: was the guy going to indict him, or was there too great a risk if the Devereaux side of the story went public? *He pulled a gun on me. But he was assaulting a suspect at the time; he's made a habit of it.* Vote now on the lesser of two evils.

Devereaux stabbed the cigarette dead on the rail and binned it. He walked across to the corner of Queen and Customs and browsed a music store. Finger-walking CD rows had a therapeutic effect. He bought some Ryan Adams. His phone rang. Caller ID said Lloyd Bowen. The pessimist in him ruled the call a dismissal announcement. He got mental audio snippets of potential phraseology. He blocked it out and answered.

Bowen said, 'Sergeant, when your phone rings, it's a good idea to pick up fast.'

'What can I do for you, inspector?'

'I want you in my office in ten minutes. We need to get this shit cleared up.'

Devereaux checked his watch. Ten-fifty. He said, 'What shit?'

The line went quiet. He thought Bowen almost laughed. 'You shot a man on Monday, sergeant. If your memory's going after two days, you need to rethink your chosen profession. Ten minutes.'

'I'm down the bottom of town.'

'So walk fast.'

Out of habit, he'd dressed for work: suited, but no tie. He needed a tie. He bought one on the way up High Street, knotted it on the run. Must have been the fastest purchase the place had seen: cash and keep-the-change. He'd barely broken step.

Devereaux checked his watch. Ten fifty-two. Eight minutes to get up to Cook Street. He wasn't much of a runner. Smoking ensured it. He tried for a jog. Lung capacity permitted a brisk walk. Footpath traffic was slow-moving. He kept to the gutter to dodge congestion. Wing mirrors made swipes for his elbow. He reached the station, dead on the hour. A uniformed officer met him outside Bowen's office.

'Where is he?'

'They're in a meeting room, I'll show you through.'

He was led to the same conference area they'd used for him on Tuesday morning. Lloyd Bowen, Frank Briar, and Thomas Rhys from Police Conduct sat dour-faced behind a long table. An empty straight-backed chair faced them. The room was hot. Bowen was sideways in his seat, legs crossed, an impatient toe tapping a table leg. A glass of water sweltered under his stare. Devereaux stepped inside. The uniform closed the door behind him. Three glances in neat unison.

Briar said, 'You're a minute late, but we decided to wait anyway.'

'You're a sweetheart.'

Briar didn't answer. He topped up his own glass from a communal jug. Rhys dropped his gaze and jotted something on a pad.

Bowen said, 'Sergeant, if you're ready, we'll begin the interview.' He nodded to his left: a camera and mic system ready and waiting on a tripod. Briar did the honours and got up and started the recording. He recited the standard litany: time, date, persons present. He said, 'Sergeant, you look a little flustered. Do you want a drink of water?'

'Clear the recording and start again,' Devereaux said.

'May I ask why?'

'You've inferred for the record that I'm somehow uncomfortable. You've prejudiced the interview before we're even under way.'

Rhys and Bowen said nothing. Briar shrugged, affected confusion, like he'd enquired in good faith. He stopped the recording and erased the brief exchange, recited the requisite preliminaries for the second time.

Devereaux slid low in his seat and got comfy. He poured

himself some water. Half full, to prevent a nervous slosh.

Briar leaned forward on his elbows and spun his wedding ring. 'Sergeant, the purpose of this interview today is to discuss some of the violent situations you've previously been involved with.'

'I thought we'd covered that in my first interview.'

'Only briefly.' Briar paused and took a small mouthful of water. 'You seemed reluctant to address the topic.'

'Only because I can't see how past events bear any relevance to the shooting I was involved in this week.'

'One of our aims is to determine whether there was any element of prejudice or recklessness on your behalf when these incidents occurred.'

'Well, don't worry. There wasn't.'

'If you could agree to bear with me and answer the questions, maybe we can determine that.'

'I can't think of better irony than you probing me on prejudice and recklessness.'

Bowen pinched the bridge of his nose, swore on expelled breath. He stood up and stopped the recording. 'Sergeant, I'll tell you now, we're not going to have the same bullshit we got last time. Get rid of the attitude and answer the questions.'

'You can't deny me right of reply.'

Bowen started to say something then clenched his jaw on it. His cheeks were colouring. 'Answer. The fucking. Questions.' Spoken like a dripping tap.

Devereaux took a sip of water.

Bowen hit Record and sat down. Briar said, 'August of two thousand eleven, you were involved in an arrest during which a suspect was fatally shot in the neck.'

'The suspect in question was a paedophile.'

'It doesn't alter the fact he was shot.' He checked his notes.

His gaze flicked back up. 'Name was Jon Edward. I take it the name's familiar?'

'Uh-huh.'

The room went quiet. Three seconds. Four.

Devereaux said, 'Was there another question there I'm supposed to be answering?'

Briar said, 'Can you describe what happened?'

Devereaux said, 'Me and a private investigator named John Hale had been kidnapped by Edward and a gang member named Clayton Cedric Moore. When Hale attempted to apprehend Moore, Moore's firearm discharged a round which hit Edward.'

'And that round proved fatal?'

'That's correct.'

'So how did the gun discharge?'

'Moore's finger was on the trigger at the time.'

'How do you know this?'

'John Hale told me.'

'Okay. Moore's testimony at the time was that you executed Edward, and subsequently modified the crime scene to reflect the scenario you just described.'

'That's a lie.'

Briar moved on. 'Do you typically involve private investigators in official police operations?'

'No, I don't.'

'So can you explain the circumstances that led both you and John Hale to be kidnapped?'

Devereaux took a breath. He had some water. 'It's all laid out in the report. Pull it and read it. But I'm not going to answer any more questions on it in the context of an interview relating to a completely separate event.'

He drained his glass and stood up. Bowen twirled his pen.

He said, 'Walkouts are never a good look.'

Devereaux slid his chair in.

Bowen said, 'Sergeant, you're here voluntarily, but I'd strongly recommend you sit down.'

Devereaux drew himself square. He centred his tie and said, 'In light of the fact Detective Sergeant Briar is the subject of a complaint regarding the assault of a suspect in custody, I don't feel it's appropriate for him to be conducting this interview.'

Briar didn't flinch. He glanced at the recorder, quashed the urge to turn it off. Bowen stalled a beat and then shook his head and said, 'I wasn't aware of such a complaint.'

'That's because I haven't filed it yet.'

Briar lost patience. He stood up suddenly, and his chair toppled. He stopped the recording. 'Fuck you, Devereaux,' he said.

Bowen raised a finger to cut him off. Devereaux didn't even bother replying. He stepped to the door. Bowen said, 'We'll let you know if we're going to charge you. Keep your phone close.' He dropped his pen on the desk. 'And keep your fingers crossed.'

Devereaux glanced back at them as he stepped out. Briar was staring at him, a real white-knuckle gaze. He mouthed something that looked like 'Toast'.

Devereaux checked McCarthy's office, but he wasn't in. He found his cellphone number and dialled it from his desk line. McCarthy caught it on ring three.

'Mr Devereaux. What's your current employment status?'

Devereaux said, 'We need to talk.'

The Don laughed. 'Will the phone not do?'

'I like being able to look people in the eye.'

'So where and when?'

'Where are you?'

'I'm at home. If you want you can look me in the eye in the comfort of my own living room.'

Devereaux thought about it. 'Okay,' he said.

McCarthy gave him directions, and hung up.

It was a Parnell address, five minutes south of Auckland Central. Upmarket, a couple of blocks back from the main drag. Streets were narrow, plush housing on small sections crowded tight to the footpath. The Don had a two-storey sandstone-coloured place on a corner site, sheer plaster walls on both street frontages. Devereaux left the car straddling the kerb, and knocked on the front door. McCarthy opened up and waved him in without a word. They went upstairs. An open-plan kitchen and living area shared polished timber floor space. A wide east-facing picture window was shielded by a wooden blind at one end. Couches formed two sides of a square in the ladder-grille of light that filtered through.

Devereaux took a seat on a couch. The adjacent wall boasted blow-ups of the family photographs he'd seen in McCarthy's office.

McCarthy said, 'I hope you haven't come here to bargain.'

Devereaux didn't answer. McCarthy sat down on the adjacent couch, in profile against the window.

Devereaux said, 'Normally, people offer me coffee.'

McCarthy grinned thinly. 'I would normally. I make an exception for people I don't like.' He leaned forward, elbows on knees. 'I think we can safely say the number of people who want you gone now outnumber the people who want you to stay.'

'And what camp are you in?'

McCarthy shrugged, rubbed cheek bristles. 'For a while

I probably would have voted to keep you. Now I guess I'd advocate for dismissal.'

'Because you think I'm a threat to you, not because you think I was out of line.'

'Yesterday evening you pointed a gun at me.' He laughed and looked at him again. 'How out of line do you want?'

'You assaulted a potential witness.'

McCarthy stretched his legs out and knitted his fingers behind his head. Eyes still on edge. He said, 'Don't make the mistake of thinking you hold something over me.' He licked his lips. 'Don't pretend you have clout, or that your testimony could someway outweigh what I have to say. I've got a distinguished thirty-year career behind me. Your CV boasts a handful of years and a fatal suspect shooting. Give it a while, it might read "fired" as well.'

'We'll see.'

McCarthy shook his head. 'Bad deeds have a scale. Up one end you've got sadist sociopathic shitbags like Jeffrey Dahmer; near the middle you've got the sorts of guys who dished out torture at Guantanamo Bay; then down the other end you've got the likes of me.'

'Putting things in relative terms doesn't change anything.'

McCarthy laughed. 'There are terror suspects in Middle East jails putting up with all kinds of shit. Sensory deprivation, waterboarding, probably electrocution. You get all sanctimonious over a coke addict in a bar getting a dig in the ribs. You're stupid.'

Devereaux didn't answer.

McCarthy smiled. A cloud shrouded the sun and the ladder-grille light pattern softened. 'Here's the difference between you and me: I never regret anything. I act decisively and have faith that I'm in the right. I know I'm in the right. Hindsight means jack shit to me. In contrast you do things that strike you as good at the time, but then fret about them afterwards.'

He looked at Devereaux hard. *Am I right?*

'I only regret action not taken,' Devereaux said. 'I regret not kicking your head in while you were going through that girl's medicine cabinet.'

McCarthy shrugged. The threat didn't faze him. 'Don't know about you, I think one messy bathroom and one mildly intimidated drug addict is okay collateral in the context of a major robbery investigation.'

'I think said drug addict had a different opinion.'

'Yeah, well.' He found a hangnail by touch and bit it clear. 'Maybe a few more loops of the block will work the bullshit out of you.'

Devereaux said, 'So what are you going to do?'

'What do you mean?'

'You claim I'm not a threat to you. So when are you going to tell someone I had you at gunpoint?'

'Maybe I already have.'

Devereaux shook his head. 'I saw Lloyd Bowen this morning. He didn't mention it.'

'Maybe I'll take my time. Make you sweat.' He leaned forward, slid along in his seat and turned so they were face to face. Contempt left his eyes hooded. 'You're already nervous enough you made the trip out here to try to talk me out of it.'

'You've talked yourself out of it already. If you were going to make a complaint, you would have done it.'

A shimmer of a smile. Devereaux caught his scent: caffeine and aftershave, riding heated breath. McCarthy said, 'So then why are you sitting in my living room, trying to feel me out?'

'If they sack me, I'll have nothing to lose.'

'So?'

'So there'll be nothing to stop me telling someone about what I've seen you do.'

'You'll be a disgraced former policeman. Your word won't be worth a lot.'

'Maybe. But you can just about guarantee others will step forward to back me up.'

'"Just about" doesn't seem that certain.'

'Take the risk then. I just wanted to lay it out for you. Keep your nose clean and I'll keep my stories private.'

McCarthy grinned. 'You'd do well in prison,' he said. 'They're always needing ex-cops to play pick up the soap.' He reached across and clapped Devereaux on the side of the knee.

'Where're your wife and daughter?' Devereaux said.

McCarthy's eye line tracked slowly. The photographs, then back to Devereaux. He clucked his tongue gently. 'It's none of your fucking business,' he said.

Devereaux shrugged. He stood up. 'Whatever,' he said. 'They must be ashamed of you.'

McCarthy said nothing. Devereaux headed back down the stairs to the door.

■ TWENTY-EIGHT

WEDNESDAY, 15 FEBRUARY, 12.26 P.M.

Hale took a drive south, Otara-bound.
A phone book check for Douglas Haines had yielded nothing. He'd delved deeper. Alas, nothing on the Securities Register, ditto for Land Information and the credit rating databases. He'd called Devereaux's desk line, but it rang through. He did a ring around, got hold of Pollard down in Manukau.

'Can you background-check a Douglas Haines for me?'

'I'm on lunch.'

'You could talk and chew.'

'Yeah … hang on, I'm not at my desk. I'm eating a lamb kebab.'

'Good.'

'Give us the spelling on "Haines".'

Hale spelled it. Keyboard noise as Pollard checked the system. A wet noise in his ear, like sauce kissed off a finger.

Pollard said, 'Nothing. Sorry.'

'Securities and Land Information was empty, too.'

'Then I think someone's passed you a fake name.'

Hale didn't answer.

'What's he done?' Pollard said.

'Nothing I know about. He's just a witness.'

'For what?'

'That fight club robbery back on January third.'

'Huh. Shit. I wonder if they've checked him out properly.'

'If you've got the witness lists, they might have got a driver's licence or an address.'

'I don't have the witness lists.'

'You can get them.'

'I've got mayonnaise on my fingers.'

'I'd appreciate it.'

Pollard said, 'Look. You might want to back off and just pass this on to someone.'

Hale said, 'Yeah. Maybe.'

He pulled up in front of Pastor Drinnan's house a little before one p.m. The man himself was on weed duty: crouched with shears in hand, tending to a parched tongue of lawn. Low hunch like a parody of prayer.

He stood when he heard Hale's door close. They shook hands across the low garden fence.

'Mr Hale. What can I do for you?'

'I'm having trouble finding this Douglas Haines.'

Drinnan stabbed the shears in the grass. He smiled. 'He's out there somewhere. Maybe you need to look harder.'

Hale smiled back. 'He wasn't in any of the usual places.'

'Well, that's funny.' He braced a palm on the small of his back, ironing out an ache.

'Do you have an address or phone number for him?' Hale said.

'No, I don't.'

Hale looked at him. Drinnan met the gaze calmly, unblinking and unperturbed. He said, 'Don't do me the discourtesy of thinking you're going to catch me in a lie. I don't know how to find the man.'

'So who does?'

He reached across himself and massaged a tender shoulder. Perspiration had moulded his shirt to his skin. 'I don't know. You're the detective. Ask Leanne. She got him the job.'

'Leanne Blair?'

'Yes. I think you spoke to her yesterday.'

'She told me she hadn't met him before.'

'Well. Maybe that was a mistruth.'

'You mean a lie.'

Drinnan didn't answer.

Hale said, 'You think it's wise to trust someone you know nothing about to be left in charge of money?'

A truck passed on the road behind them. Drinnan waved off the fumes. 'I trust Leanne's judgment of character. She's a good person, Mr Hale. You shouldn't assume everyone's out to deceive you.'

'It's safer than believing nobody is. Thanks for your time.'

Drinnan stood and watched him as he drove away, miniaturised by the rear view. Hale headed round to the liquor store on Everitt Road. Two cars were leaving just as he arrived. He parked nose-in beside the front door and walked in. Leanne Blair was behind the counter. The door buzzed and she glanced up and saw him. He checked the shop as he walked towards her: no customers, two kids from yesterday kicking a ball in the centre aisle.

Blair flicked her eyebrows at him when he reached her.

Hale said, 'Step outside with me for two minutes.'

'I've gotta watch the till.'

'Step outside with me for two minutes.'

'Someone might come.'

He aimed a cocked finger at his lips. 'Step outside. With me. For two minutes.'

He exited the store and sat on the hood of the car and waited. A moment later the door buzzed and she followed him out.

She stopped in front of him, ducked a cigarette to a cupped lighter. She looked at him over the flame. 'What?' she said.

'How do I find Douglas?'

'I don't know. Look in a fucking phone book.' She laughed.

He stood up, directly in front of her. She took a step back. The wall of the shop was behind her.

'You told me yesterday you hadn't met the guy before.'

'Yeah.' Her cheeks hollowed as she sucked smoke. 'I hadn't.'

'But you got him the job counting cash back on January third. So how does that work?'

'What?'

'I didn't realise you were hard of hearing.'

'Friggin' hell. What happened to Mr Polite from yesterday?'

Hale didn't answer.

'Who told you that?' she said.

'Who cares? It's the truth.'

She was backed up against the wall, cigarette in two fingers of an upturned hand.

'Where does he live, Leanne?'

'I don't know.'

Her gaze ran back and forth. There was a lie floating there somewhere, close to the surface. She brought the cigarette to her mouth. He reached out and took it from her. Fluid and precise, thumb and forefinger, somehow unrushed. The thing just left her grip. She stood there a second empty-handed, lips ajar: an accidental mime.

'Where's Douglas, Leanne?'

She held her tongue, ogling the cigarette snatch. He dropped it on the concrete and stomped it dead.

'Where's Douglas, Leanne?'

'Back off. Jeez. I barely even know him.'

'You're dodging the question. Where does he live?'

He stepped to within kissing distance. Her face was upturned. Hale turned and saw a patrol car idle through the intersection, a slow flare of sun sliding off its windscreen. He dropped back a half-pace.

She smiled slightly. 'Maybe I could start hollering. Then you'd be in trouble.'

He watched her face. An eyelid gave a subtle quiver. He gambled: 'Get them over here. We'll tell them about Doug.'

She didn't reply. They stood there face to face as the car slipped past. Crackle of grit beneath slow tyres. A skin-deep tingle as wary eyes roved. His guts cooled at the thought of it turning into the parking lot. But it didn't. It carried on past the intersection and vanished around a bend.

'Well,' he said. 'That was your chance.'

She didn't answer.

Hale said, 'Who is he, and where is he?'

He stepped forward again. He could smell the cigarette on her. The closeness had her rattled: she winced slightly, like anticipating a strike.

'Look, he's the kids' dad and he's not meant to be living near them but he is.'

'Is Douglas his real name?'

'Sort of.'

'Either it is or it isn't.' He hadn't blinked in a while. Her lip started to quiver.

She said, 'He's got some stuff in his past that he's kind of not that proud of. So he uses a different name than his real one to sort of try to keep it all out of the way. You know?'

'What's he not proud of?'

She shrugged. Her mouth opened and closed, like she'd

opted out of saying something glib. Hale's proximity encouraged good behaviour. 'Little stuff, I guess,' she said. 'He used to rough up the kids a bit. Cops told him he's got to stay clear of everyone. But I like to see him, now and then.'

'Where can I find him?'

'Well, he's not working, so at home probably.'

'Where's home?'

She paused.

Hale said, 'Either you can tell me now, or you can come in the car with me and point it out. You choose. But don't lie about anything.'

His tone had harshened. It brought a stuttered reply: 'I — I'm not lying.'

'Where does he live?'

She looked at the ground, gestured circularly, searching for words. 'I don't know the address, but I can tell you where the house is.'

'I'm all ears.'

He still hadn't backed off. Tears started to well. She laid out some local directions. 'It's sort of on a corner. Not the one on the corner, but the one next to it. It's a yellowy colour.'

'What's his real name?'

'Why are you asking me all this?'

He put a hand on her shoulder and pushed her hard against the wall. She gasped at the jolt, winced and shied away. 'Jesus, don't hurt me. He's Allen. Doug Allen. His name's Doug Allen. Please don't hurt me.'

He let her go and stepped back. She stayed against the wall, bent-kneed and tear-rimmed. Her vulnerability finally registered, and he backed off. The shove had been reflexive. She'd clammed up, and he'd transitioned to use of force, as per long practice.

'Get away from me, you pig. Jeez.'

The two kids were watching from inside, just out of buzzer range. Wide-eyed, like they'd been front row through the whole ordeal.

Hale moved away and got back into the car. Leanne Blair wiped tears from her eyes and gave him the finger as he pulled away.

Violence found him early.

'Eighty-four. Cancer had claimed his mother that April. It didn't muck about: three months, diagnosis to deathbed. The memories are discontinuous: he recalls the angst of the prognosis, the bedridden final weeks in wasted delirium. And then she was gone. She wasn't a smoker, she wasn't a drinker. The local pastor was stretched to justify the Lord's reasoning. Everybody was. He remembers them standing there as the hearse pulled away, petals scurrying in its wake, the downcast faces and quiet thoughts of the departed.

His father took it hard. He'd been resolute through the whole ordeal, but post-funeral he went downhill. Grief imposed an inversion of routine: he drinks long into the night, and sleeps long into the day. Despondency is absolute. But a long-established image of hardened self-reliance rules out the notion of seeking help.

Hale is young, but prevailing common sense indicates that if his father isn't working, income is nil. At some point the jar of change in the kitchen will need replenishing. At some point the generosity of his father's sister will dwindle, and groceries will stop arriving unbidden. The burden of those economic logistics keeps him sleepless and frightened for every minute his father walls himself away, in steadfast pursuit of an empty bottle.

Visitors are rare, but one day a tray-back ute pulls in off the road and winds its way up the driveway towards the house. Hale watches from a window as the car pulls into the turning bay out front. There are three men in the cab, two big black and tan huntaways tethered in the back. Ears pricked and leashes stretched taut. Bright-eyed and slick-tongued. The engine quits. A weak thread of diesel smoke drifts and disperses. The truck's doors are grimed with road dust, deep tyre tread traced whitely by lime powder.

Suspension shakes as the men alight. They're big guys: wide necks sloping broadly to heavy shoulders, flannel shirtsleeves rolled back over thick cable-tight forearms. Large hands, red and thick-callused.

Hale steps outside. Beyond the truck, the drive follows a slight slope before it meets the road. Beyond that, the gentle undulations of pastureland, gilt-topped by late sun. To the right, a belt of pine trees serves as shelter from wind off the neighbouring paddocks. To the left, his father's Land Rover and a rusted-out tractor shelter inside an arched metal shed.

The air bears that verdant manure and silage odour. The dogs are giddy on it, barking and yelping to be let loose.

The three guys fan out in the yard, shadows cast gangly and hose-like ahead of them. The two passengers have crowbars. One guy is using his to rehearse a golf swing. The second guy has his gripped at each end, braced across his shoulders. His shirt below the bottom button is parted over a fat gut thatched with black hair.

The driver says, 'Heya, matey.'

Hale says, 'Hello.'

'Is Daddy home?'

Daddy. The term is patronising. It rankles. Hale says, 'No, he's not.'

The driver glances at the barn. 'Are you sure? His car's here.'

Hale pauses. Golf swing guy sinks a couple of putts. Hale says, 'What do you want?'

The driver laughs. 'So he is home. Great.'

'He's in bed.'

Golf man makes a visor with his hand and checks the height of the sun. 'Should be up and about, this time of day. Lazy bastard.'

Hale says, 'He isn't feeling well. You should come back another time.'

The driver shakes his head. 'No, if he's in, we definitely need to see him.'

'What for?'

'He owes us some money.'

'No, he doesn't. He doesn't owe anybody any money.'

The guy with the gut laughs. He takes the crowbar off his shoulders and makes a fake baseball swing. Aggressive, head-high. He says, 'Kid's a fuckin' classic.'

A low laugh rolls back and forth between the three of them.

'How old are you, matey?' *the driver says.*

'I'm not your mate.'

'Suit yourself. How old are you?'

'Twelve,' *Hale says.*

'Twelve. Jesus. Thought you were older.' *He smiles.* 'He sends his twelve-year-old kid out to warn us off. Holy shit.'

They all laugh. The guy with the gut kicks a stone skittering towards the shed.

Hale stands and looks at them. 'How much does he owe you?' *he says.*

The driver smiles. 'Yeah, see, now he's not so sure of himself. How much does he owe?' *He scratches his head.* 'We'll call it an even hundred.'

One hundred dollars. One hundred dollars is a lot of money. Much more than what is stashed in the jar in the kitchen.

'Dad doesn't have money like that at home.'

The driver shrugs. 'Well, tough shit, bucko.'

Hale doesn't answer.

The driver says, 'Okay, look. I'm going to run the clock for you.' *He raises his watch, inspects the dial.* 'We'll say five minutes. Either you can bring the money yourself, or your dad can, or he can come outside and have a chat with us. If not, we're going to let the dogs off the chain, and maybe start putting the crowbars to good use. Maybe break a leg or something. Okay?'

Hale doesn't answer. He goes back inside. The door to his father's room is closed. He pushes it open and steps into the room. The air is stagnant, hot and liquor-laced. A faint chemical smell from the heap of clothes he wears to work.

His father is beneath the covers, foetal and immobile. Hale shakes him gently.

'Dad.'

'I can't, John. I can't.'

'There're people here. They want money.'

'I can't, John.'

He doesn't know whether his father is fully conscious or not. Lucidity is intermittent. He panics at the thought he is going to have to deal with the men himself.

A shout from outside: 'That's one minute!'

Hale runs back through to the front of the house. The door is closed. He moves through to the kitchen and tips a chair back on two legs and drags it juddering to the entry hall. Careful not to nudge a doorframe. The shotgun case is stored high, roof-level above the little writing desk that holds the telephone.

'Run, run, little piggies. The Big Bad Wolf's on the way!'

He hears something break. Maybe one of the rear lights on the Land Rover, shattered by a boot, or a practice golf swing. A bout of hard, wild laughter. He braces the backrest of the chair against the edge of the little desk and stands up on the seat. Tiptoed, he can just reach the twin catches securing the lid on the case. He stretches one-handed and grimaces and pops one side, and then the other. The gun itself is recessed slightly: he has to put one foot up on the desk in order to reach it. He gets an awkward grip on the barrel and lowers it carefully, the thing dense and unwieldy, see-sawing gently against his wrist. He lays it on the floor. A thin sheen of oil residue along the barrels, whorls of his sweat standing up against the lacquer on the stock. He breaks the breech quietly and sights through both barrels and sees fresh air at the other end. A burnt aroma of scorched powder and oil touches his nostrils. Hale stands back up on the chair and finds the box of Winchester 10-gauge shells. He removes two and sits down cross-legged on the floor and feeds the shotgun one per barrel.

'Three minutes!'

The key to the shotgun's trigger lock is with the keys to the Land Rover. He hurries through to the kitchen, but they aren't on their normal peg. He checks the bench top. He looks in the fruit bowl. Nothing.

Back to his father's bedroom. No motion from the quilted lump as he approaches the bed.

'Dad, where's the car keys?'

His father doesn't reply. Hale shakes him. 'Dad, Dad, Dad. Where're the car keys?'

'I don't know, John. I don't know.'

He hears another smash. Maybe Land Rover brake light number two. The dogs are barking. Hale tries to stay calm.

There has to be a second key somewhere. He's never known something to have just one set.

He checks the top drawer of his father's dresser: loose change, some Polaroids of his mother, letters from a bank.

'Four minutes!'

He starts to panic. Breath grows light, shallow pants keeping shy of his lungs. He wants to vomit. He checks the dresser, top to bottom. Nothing. Fingers clumsy with shakes. He crouches and checks the shoe boxes his father keeps beneath the bed. No keys.

'All righty, we're coming in!'

Something smashes against the front door. He pictures the lock splitting, the wood along the jamb splintering free.

'Dad, help. Help. They're going to come inside.'

His father doesn't reply. He hears a sudden, dry crack, like the door had split lengthways. He sees the pile of clothing on the floor and kicks it.

Something tinkles — something metal?

He scrabbles, hands and knees, checking pockets, checking folds.

He finds them: the Land Rover keys, and attached: the trigger lock release. The shotgun is on the floor in the entry hall, the breech still open. He runs for it; slams and crashes from the front door. He reaches the gun just as the door gives and Golf Swing man appears in its absence.

Hale snaps the breech closed. He sights on the guy's stomach. Low angle with one hand cupped around the trigger guard, it isn't evident the lock is still in place.

The guy says, 'Whoa, shit. Easy.'

He backs off a few steps, hand raised. The other two move closer for a view through the door, retreat when they see the gun. Hale waits for them to give him some distance, and then he uses the key off the Land Rover's ring to release the trigger lock. Shakes and sweaty fingers, it's third time lucky with the insert. But the gun is now free to fire.

He gets to his feet and steps past the broken door into the yard. A breeze has the trees lolling frond-like. He raises the gun to his shoulder and draws down on the driver.

'Get in your car and drive away,' he says. 'Or I'll blow your head off.'

There's a waver in his voice that the driver catches. 'That's a double-barrelled shotgun. You've only got two shells.'

Hale falls quiet a moment. He tries to keep the gun still. 'So you've got a one-in-three chance of living,' he says.

The driver laughs. 'Maybe we could let the dogs off.'

Hale closes one eye. He hikes the muzzle a fraction and finds the guy's chin. The gun is too heavy to keep static: the sight traces a loose ellipse.

'If you let your dogs off, I'm going to shoot you in the head.'

'You shouldn't promise Christmas presents you can't deliver.'

Hale looks at him and says nothing. He understands the implication: he has to prove he can follow through. A twelve-year-old with a wavering shotgun and a shaky voice lacks credibility. So he swings the gun left and triggers one barrel and puts a 10-gauge load of number four buckshot through the front windscreen of the truck. The recoil thumps the butt against his shoulder. A kiss of gun smoke plumes radially. Glass explodes in a winking arc.

The roar of the shot rolls out over the paddocks, returns as faint thunder off the hillsides, a far-off promise of rain. The three guys duck reflexively and fan out, aghast. Hale keeps the gun raised. He realises afterwards there was a reasonable chance of hitting one of the dogs, but he didn't.

The shot had left a ringing in his ears. The truck windscreen looks like some raw wound, ragged hard-edged shards lining the perimeter. Pieces are still falling free and tinkling inside the cab. Because of the angle, the driver's side window has caught maybe a half-load.

Hale says, 'Drive away.'

'We can come back,' the driver says.

'I don't care. I've got a whole box of ammo.'

They stand staring at him, anchored by the fact he still has one chambered shell left. The dogs are skittish from the shot, hackles raised and prowling back and forth in the tray. The guy with the gut has dropped his crowbar.

Hale keeps the gun up and trained on the driver as the three of them get back into the cab. Glass shards crack beneath the tyres. He watches them until they reach the road and disappear, and then he lowers the gun and goes back inside.

The Haines/Allen residence was two minutes past the liquor store. Double-storey weatherboard, an empty carport annexe to the left. A narrow frill of deck along two sides of the upper level.

Hale left the Escort around the corner and walked back. No car, no sign of indoor activity. He cupped his face to a downstairs window. A parted curtain revealed a kitchen and living area, free of furniture. Maybe a downstairs flat, awaiting tenancy.

Timber stairs accessed the upstairs deck. He went up and knocked on the kitchen door. Nothing. He stood back against the adjacent wall and waited. The neighbouring house on the corner was only single-level. It left the deck exposed to street views on both sides. It was quiet, but he didn't want to hang around. He gave it another minute, and then he picked the lock and went in.

He'd half-expected long abandonment, but the air smelled fresh. The newspaper on the table was a day old. He stood and listened. Summer heat had the fridge on a steady hum. No creaks of cautious feet, but he did a quick walk-through to confirm vacancy. Everywhere the signs of recent use: toothpaste scum in the bathroom sink, a damp shower curtain, a battery-powered radio, still running. *Where are you, Dougie?* It had been a quick trip from the store, but at a stretch the woman could have called in time for him to drop everything and leave.

A fake name and a history of violence. It felt like progress.

He went back to the kitchen and hunted for a cash-stash. The cupboards held flatware only. He circuited the living room. Nothing in the furniture. The television was LCD, slim construction precluded concealment. The medicine cabinet content was lawful. Nothing under the mattress in the bedroom. He checked beneath the bedframe: a shoebox worth of receipts, a plastic container of nine mil hollow points, a box of 10-gauge shells.

He nudged a curtain aside and risked a glance out. Still all clear. The radio's news bulletin predicted drawn-out balminess. He browsed the receipts. Nothing eyebrow-raising. He delved on: a manual for a '98 Toyota Hilux pickup, an envelope with a passport in the name Douglas Allen. *Now we're getting somewhere.* Doug looked late thirties, short dark hair and a sparse goatee. An earnest clench-jawed stare, like he was trying to melt the camera lens.

He returned everything to beneath the bed and checked for a gun safe. Nothing in the closet, nothing above the cupboards in any of the other rooms. It wasn't great news. He didn't want to hang around if the guy was packing something chambered for 10-gauge ammunition.

He headed back to the living room. A false name, an assault record, evidence of gun ownership. The robbery connection had to be more than just idle chance.

It *must* be progress.

He used his cellphone and tried Devereaux's desk line again. No answer. He sat down in front of the television. A photograph on the wall behind depicted a Doug/Leanne headshot. It could have been a wedding snap. Doug was beardless, their smiles bore a 'til-death-do-us-part glow. He wondered how long it had taken to lose the gleam of optimism.

A car pulled up further down the street. He headed down the hall and checked the bedroom window view: one '98 Toyota Hilux parked kerbside, twenty metres up the street. Unobtrusive, but for an off-tune turbo diesel.

Hale stayed at the window. He watched Douglas Allen slide out of the cab and walk towards the house. He had what might have been a Remington 10-gauge shotgun held along one leg.

Shit. Leanne must have tipped him off.

Hale left the window and walked back to the rear of the house. His pulse ramped up. Internal access to the lower floor was boarded off: entry would be via either the kitchen door or the living room ranch slider. The deck was too exposed for him to take the guy as he came up the stairs. He sifted cutlery drawers: forks and non-serrated butter knives only.

Shit.

Footsteps ascending — make a decision. Hale stepped back into the corridor just as Douglas's head crested the stairs. He led with the shotgun, closed in on the kitchen door. Mistake one: Hale hadn't relocked it. Mistake two: Hale's cellphone was still turned on.

You fucking amateur.

Douglas propped the shotgun one-handed and popped the

kitchen door off the latch. It squeaked and yawed a half-metre. Not quite enough to sidle in. But Doug was patient: he stayed on the threshold, gun up. Quiet settled, blanket-soft. The radio commentary was still running, distant and static-laden. The fridge stood at ease, blind to the tension.

A crisp tap of muzzle on glass, and the door swung open. Footsteps on lino: tentative, predatory. Hale pictured him standing there, a squint along a cocked barrel. He backed up, glacier-slow. Fingertips to the wall, toe–heel steps. Sweat beaded his hairline, he willed it not to drip and leave a trail. Tactics were still undecided: part of him advised rushing the guy while he still had run-up space. Part of him cautioned that head-on versus a Remington offered poor odds.

Footsteps resumed. Hale moved left, caught a glimpse of matt-black shotgun barrel. He sidestepped into the bathroom. Toilet opposite, a combined bath and shower stall right of the door. A thick odour of stale steam. The mirrored cabinet bore the ghost of it. He reached the bath. Two tiptoed strides, an agonising held breath. The curtain was partly drawn. He slipped around it into the stall.

Quiet again. He braced for a shot through the curtain. The radio in the bedroom switched off. He backed up closer to the wall, taps and the showerhead nudging him hard. A squeal of floor joist as Douglas came back down the corridor. His search scheme wasn't logical: he was retracing covered ground.

He entered the bathroom. Hale heard his breathing as he passed the door. A lump of shadow against the mildew-sprayed partition. He hoped he wasn't backlit from this side. The drain at his feet gurgled hollowly.

The muzzle nudged the curtain end. A tar-black two-inch stub. It tracked slowly towards him, material bunching against it. A sodden green concertina. The support rings chimed faintly.

The gun paused. Hale waited, pulse raging. Contorted against the stall end, glued awkwardly in situ.

Seconds of ear-bleeding quiet. And then his phone rang.

Hale lunged.

He got a hand on the barrel, just as the gun swung towards him. He pushed it away, dived sideways through the curtain. The sound of the shot was massive, deafening in the bathroom confines. Pellets spewed wide and blitzed the enamel. The spent shell arcing and rattling against the walls of the bath. A skein of burnt powder smoke spreading.

He struck the guy with his shoulder. The impact sheared the curtain pole off the wall. They tumbled in a mess of lime-draped limbs. Hale still had a hand on the barrel. He twisted hard. A scream and a clean crack, like a finger caught in a trigger guard.

Don't hang around.

He clawed hands and knees for the hallway, made the kitchen door at a sprint. He was bleeding — Jesus. Abdomen, left side, above the hip. He pulled the kitchen door, vaulted the deck railing one-handed, hit the carport roof. A jarring drop to the ground, a limping dash across the neighbour's back yard. Damage assessment: his shirt was scarlet, armpit to waist.

He reached the street, glanced back at the house. No sign of Douglas. He was probably still fighting the curtain. Hale's hand shook as he keyed the Escort's lock. He fell in and tore away northbound.

■ TWENTY-NINE

WEDNESDAY, 15 FEBRUARY, 1.32 P.M.

Devereaux stayed at his desk and processed paperwork. Progress and interview reports for week-old minor enquiries, a watered-down recountal of his visit to Pit with The Don. Bare-bone facts, no allusion to witness intimidation. No insinuation of improper conduct. It knocked an inch off his in-tray, and let him keep a low profile. He didn't want to run the risk of bumping into Bowen or Thomas Rhys, couldn't be bothered with the requisite snide exchange should he meet Frank Briar.

He couldn't remember feeling so tired. He ascribed it to massive stress: Monday's shooting, Bowen's debriefings, his run-in with McCarthy. Maybe bad events conspired to coincide.

He was working hard to suppress a migraine. Stress had triggered it. Two cigarettes and a walk up and down Vincent Street hadn't helped. Two painkillers had eventually tamed the pulsing. Much longer, and his eyeballs would have shot blood geysers. Escaping home was out of the question. Absence would contradict the notion he had nothing to hide. There was a big difference between staying low and going AWOL.

The phone was off the hook to eliminate distractions. He checked his messages at two p.m: two missed calls from John Hale. Devereaux called the office down on High Street and got no answer. He tried his mobile, hung up when the phones in the robbery incident room all rang in unison.

He rolled closer on his chair, glimpsed a harried Frank Briar grab a desk line. It was a quick conversation: maybe fifteen seconds, all incoming traffic. Briar finger-combed a mussed hairdo and headed out of the room.

Something urgent. Something *big*.

Devereaux caught him at the door.

'What's happening?'

Briar ignored him. He brushed past and headed for Bowen's office. Devereaux stepped into the incident room. Summer office climate: whirring desk fans, flushed faces, sticky shirt backs. No one offered acknowledgement. Briar had shunned him. Even eye contact would constitute collusion with the enemy.

He picked up Briar's phone, checked the history. One incoming call, thirty seconds prior: Northcom police dispatch. He redialled and identified himself to the operator, asked for a repeat of the message that had just come through.

'Sergeant, we've had a one-one-one report of a possible firearms offence; we were told to notify this number of any activity on that location.'

Devereaux said, 'What's the address?'

The operator told him. It meant nothing. But it had to be robbery-related, otherwise why dial this line?

Devereaux said, 'What was the call?'

'I can play it back to you.'

'No, just give me the gist of it.'

'Neighbour reports what she thought was a single shotgun blast from indoors.'

'Okay. When did this come in?'

'Seventeen minutes ago now.'

He heard his own phone ringing.

'I'll let you go; I've got another call coming.'

He ran back to his desk and answered. John Hale said, 'I tried to reach you earlier. Twice.'

'What's happening?'

'I got walked in on during a house search.'

'We just got a report of shots fired at a place down in Otara.'

'That was me. It was the Haines house.'

Haines. Devereaux drew a momentary blank and then clicked on the name: the fight club robbery, January third. Haines was the caravan man, taking cash.

Maybe bad events conspired to coincide.

'Shit. What were you doing in there?'

'I got a tip-off he was using a fake name. I checked out his house, and he walked in on me with a shotgun.'

'Are you all right?'

'He got off one round.'

Devereaux sat down. His shirt neck breathed a stale odour. 'Yes. But are you all right?'

'I've got some minor pellet damage.'

'Are you bleeding?'

'A bit.'

'Did you leave any in the house?'

'Probably in the bath.'

'Christ. What were you doing in there?'

'Hiding.' He paused. 'At the least I can go down for unlawful entry. If they read it wrong, they could implicate me as part of the robbery team.'

'Are you badly hurt?'

'I think it's minor.'

'You think.'

No answer. Devereaux checked his watch. Almost five minutes since the initial call. He didn't want to give Briar too big a head start. 'What did you touch?' he said.

'No prints; I had gloves. It's the blood I'm worried about.'

'How much is there?'

'I don't know. My shirt caught most of it.'

'So what happened?'

'He knew I was in the house. He came home with a shotgun and searched the place. We scuffled, he got off one round.'

'Where are you now?'

'In the car, on the way home.'

'And where is he?'

'I'm not sure. I know he left the house. He tried to follow me, but I lost him.'

'Can he identify you?'

'Probably not. I don't think he got a good look at me. But a witness I spoke to will confirm I was asking for his address about thirty minutes before everything happened.'

Devereaux cupped the back of his neck. His palm came away damp. 'Ah, shit.'

'Yeah. But things will be a hell of a lot easier to ride out if there's no evidence putting me inside the actual house.'

Devereaux didn't answer. His temples throbbed: the painkillers hadn't yet trounced the migraine. *This cannot be happening.* He said, 'Okay. They've got people moving on this now; I've got to head down there and cool this out. All right?'

'All right.'

'I'll drop by later. For God's sake keep your head down.'

Hale hung up. Devereaux swung his suit coat off his chair back and shrugged inside it. He passed Bowen's office on the way to the stairs. No Bowen or Briar. Maybe they were both heading out. He reached the exit and swore and ran back to his desk. Migraine throb matched him step for step. He dialled Northcom. The same operator answered.

'Who've you got responding to the Haines callout?'

An agonising stretch of keyboard patter. 'Sir, we've got three local patrol units on site. Otara CIB has detective teams inbound, plus an Armed Offenders Squad unit.'

Too many. Last thing he needed was a packed venue.

'Cancel the CIB and the AOS.'

'Sir?'

'The suspect is no longer on the premises, so cancel AOS. And tell the local units that we'll handle everything from this end. We don't need the backup. Keep the patrol teams on the perimeter, but pull CIB out. We don't want anyone going in.'

'Sir, I—'

'Is that clear?'

'Yeah, but—'

Devereaux hung up. He took the stairs three at a time, was on the road a minute later. He figured Briar had maybe a seven- or eight-minute head start. He drove lights and siren. Southbound motorway traffic was light enough to weave. Long vacant stretches let him nudge the car up to one-thirty. He was down there by two thirty-five. Tired housing watched him pass, frail and desperate for attention. The Haines place was one site back from a side street that ended in a cul-de-sac. A patrol car occupied the kerb out front. Two more patrol cars and an unmarked blocked each intersection leg.

Devereaux parked up beside the unmarked. The house was drab and run-down: grey curtains and grimed windows. Movement upstairs: uniformed officers, a suit that could have been Frank Briar. Devereaux locked the car and walked over, badged past a trio of armed officers at the kerb. The guns cued a flashback to Monday. He walked up timber stairs to the first-floor deck, came face to face with Frank Briar stepping out a ranch slider. The harsh outdoor light made him squint. He raised a forearm to shade his eyes. A clown wig of chest hair peeped through a popped shirt button. He looked genuinely disgusted.

'Ah, Jesus. It's you.' He stopped and blocked the door. Behind him, another four uniformed patrol officers.

'What's happening?'

Briar laughed. Overlapping radio chirrups filtered from indoors. 'You dipshit. What does it look like? I'm responding to a call. You shouldn't be down here. Nobody sent you.'

'I know, but we can get to the bottom of that later.'

'Fuck you. You don't need to check up on me.'

'Maybe I do. You've got four guys trooping back and forth inside before the scene examination's even done.'

'Ah, Christ.' Briar waved him off and stepped past. He walked to the deck railing and put a cigarette in his mouth, but didn't light it. The patrol officers saw Devereaux standing there and filed out, heads bent like they'd heard the scorn. Devereaux went in. He caught gun smoke odour. Delicate roses of blood on the carpet. Impossible to remove without Briar noticing.

Sorry, John.

He walked down a short corridor. Cordite tang strengthened. More blood on the carpet. Hale must have lost more than he thought. He stepped into the bathroom. The shower curtain on the ground, the L-shaped curtain pole clinging desperately by one end. A thin drool of water beneath the tap in the bath. A spent shotgun shell lolling in a puddle at the opposite end. A wide spray of pellet scars against the enamel. A black powder coat of soot against one wall, a smear of blood beneath it. He could bleach the blood in the bath, but there was no way to get the stains in the carpet without burning the place. And Briar would have seen everything on his walk-through. If he rigged the scene now, it would be obvious what had happened.

Shit. Hale's blood was on file. Forensics would analyse the samples, and tie him unequivocally to the house.

Devereaux stepped to the door. He was new to crime scene tampering. It had never crossed his mind. He didn't like the fact he'd even paid it serious thought. Anything that seemed to fit the Don McCarthy playbook felt off. A snippet of phone call flashback: *Head down there and cool this off.* He'd implied he could fix things. That paradigm of greater evils again: failing a friend versus breaking the law.

He checked out the house, front to back. The bedroom was in reasonable order. A quilt corner was peeled back from wrinkled sheets. An open dresser drawer showed a full complement of folded clothes. He surveyed the bathroom again, saw the toothpaste residue in the sink. In the kitchen he toed the fridge open. A cool breath touched his midriff. Milk, beer. A limp piece of pizza draped across a plate, out cold.

He walked back outside. Briar turned and looked at him, the unlit cigarette jumping as he chewed the filter. 'Everything up to scratch?' he said.

'Have you spoken to the neighbour who made the call?'

Briar didn't answer right away. He said, 'Why did you cancel the AOS callout?'

'Who says it was me?'

'Process of elimination. I know it wasn't me.'

'Comms said local units were responding, including AOS. I told them we didn't need the backup.'

'And who put you in charge?'

'I don't see anyone here who outranks me.'

'How did you know the suspect wasn't still armed and on site when you cancelled our armed backup?'

'Same way you knew it was safe to stroll in here, I guess.'

Briar smirked and shook his head. He folded his arms and stood by the ranch slider and looked in at the living room. His faint reflection hung just beyond the threshold.

'Don't pretend I need to get permission for anything from you, Frank. You're not my boss.'

Briar turned and faced him. He stepped close. The cigarette in his mouth almost bridged the gap. 'I just find it funny you were so fucking desperate to get down here.' He smiled. 'I just got one of those tingly feelings you get when you sense something else is going on. You know?'

Devereaux didn't answer. *Odeur de Frank* was near caustic.

'Light that cigarette before it wilts,' Devereaux said.

Briar gave him the finger and turned away. Devereaux went back down the stairs. He moved around the front of the house and glanced inside through a parted curtain. Darkened rooms, empty of furniture: a small lino-floored kitchen adjoining a living area. An empty light fixture hanging from electrical cord beneath a flaking plaster ceiling. He circuited the house. A shattered window on the rear side was backed by plywood.

He walked back around the front. A patrol sergeant was stationed on the footpath.

'Know of any other callouts to this address?' Devereaux asked.

The guy stepped off the kerb to drop his eye line. South Auckland liked its cops on the tall side. 'Like what?'

'Anything.'

'The location's flagged. If there'd been anything, you would have heard about it.'

'If your guys talk to the neighbours, ask whether anyone knows about the broken window around the back.'

He gave the guy a card and walked back to his car. The interior was starting to bake. He got in and dropped his window and sat quietly and thought about things. The dash emitted a weak heat haze. Briar saw him from the deck and blew a kiss. Devereaux ignored him. He waited five minutes, and then he started the engine and drove away.

■ THIRTY

WEDNESDAY, 15 FEBRUARY, 2.45 P.M.

It wasn't Hale's first shooting. The downside: repeat experience didn't make things any easier.

The injury made him feel vulnerable. He locked the front door, secured the full bolt and chain quota. His shotgun was in the bedroom, still loaded. Hale brought it through to the kitchen, propped it against the table. A sudden nauseous throb as he bent. He took a foil blister pack of painkillers and a glass from a cupboard, set them on the table with a can of Heineken from the fridge. Bloodied hands stained the frost. He cracked three tablets into the glass, tried to prise the pull-tab on the beer. Slick and shaky fingers struggled for purchase. A thumb nail gained leverage, and he tore the thing open, doused the tablets with beer. He finger-stirred the brew, downed it fast. The remaining Heineken served as a chaser. Alcohol plus painkillers: guaranteed to numb *something*.

He took the shotgun with him when he walked through to the bathroom. He laid it beside the tub and ran the tap. The bloodstain was still growing, but gaining ground less rapidly. He unbuttoned the shirt and let it fall to the floor. Blood rimed his torso. It was drying the colour of rust powder, coppery stink of it thick in the small room. He kicked free of his shoes, peeled off his socks, dropped his trousers and underwear. He shut off the tap and stepped into the bath. Ankle deep: he didn't want to faint and drown. He lowered himself gingerly. Closed eyes aimed skywards, neck corded below a taut grimace. Grip white against the tub rim.

Blood wisps smoked and curled free as he hit the water. Delicate red strings floated from his fingertips. He cleaned the wound area. No visual inspection yet. He was dreading the potential discovery. Hospitals were obliged to report gunshot injuries, ergo bullet lodgement would necessitate self-surgery, minus Lidocaine.

A cautious fingertip made the initial appraisal: a raw entry wound, then a swollen hump terminating at a hard, raised nodule.

No exit wound. The pellet was still inside him.

Douglas, you bastard.

Hale probed delicately. It was small, maybe eight or nine mils in diameter. Maybe double- or triple-aught buckshot. It had stayed skin-deep, ripped an entry wound and torn back through soft tissue. It hadn't gone far. It was subcutaneous. It had probably only travelled thirty mils.

You can do this.

He took a breath. He braced his feet against the end of the bath, turned his head sideways and pressed his cheek against the cool wall behind him. He placed an index finger behind the pellet and tried to dislodge it back the way it had arrived. The wound throbbed dully, spewed a fresh wave of red. He gasped and hunched into the pain. But the pellet didn't move. Gooey, swollen tissue swaddled it unyieldingly.

You can do this.

He waited for pain to abate. Bit of luck, the Heineken/codeine potion was just kicking in. The water was stained a uniform muddy brown. He rolled over, squeaks and groans of skin on wet laminate, raised himself knees and knuckles. Dirtied water sluiced in rivulets off his back. He limped naked to the kitchen and took needle-nose pliers from a tool drawer. He flicked the kettle on and sat and waited. A myriad of bloodied drips on the floor about him. The kettle clicked. He stood and doused the plier tips under a jug-worth of boiling water. It wasn't ER-grade sanitation, but it would have to do. Back to the bathroom. He removed a hand towel from a stack and shook out the folds, twisted it firmly into a thick helix. Then he lowered himself back into the water. He held the twisted towel at each end and placed it across his open mouth, bit down to hold it in place. Impending anguish had his pulse racing.

Hale raised the pliers. He tested his grip, rehearsed the open-close motion. He rolled sideways, exposing the injury. The plier nose hovered close. He spread the grips a fraction, splayed the mouth of the wound.

Instant agony.

He arched and kicked against the end of the tub, screamed inside the towel. The pliers fell free and splashed and clunked beside him. Hale rolled onto his back and waited for the pain to subside. The towel in his mouth had leached his tongue dry. He swallowed and coughed loose cotton strings, felt blindly for the pliers.

Round two.

Second time lucky.

The cyclic throbbing slowly waned. Hale rolled onto his hip to jack the injury out of the water. The embedded pellet sat proud of the surrounding skin, eager for removal. He braced a thumb on its leeward side: a backstop against shaky hands trying to force it deeper.

He bit down on the towel. Massive clench force induced molar aches. Quivering pliers floated close, arms spread. A subtle grip change and the wound entry was forced apart. He roared and tensed his calves against the end of the tub. But he didn't pull back. Deeper, deeper. The pain trembled his vision, his hands. Hurricane shakes as he eased the backstop thumb forward, pushing the round back towards the plier nose.

Closer.

Hale opened the grips a fraction further, panting crazily. The wound stretched like sodden linen. He pictured raw and bloodied fibres tearing. He screamed against the twisted rag, every muscle in his legs and torso braced and wavering with the strain. Heels and head crushed against the end walls. The bath flexing against the massive pressure. Like the birth of some strange beast from its glassine shell.

Closer—

The pliers closed around the pellet. He withdrew. Bloodied pincers, a scarlet ball bearing pinched tight. He couldn't drop the pliers quick enough: they fell with a dense thunk at his side, shocked from his grip. He sighed against the sodden wad and spat it free and curled towards the ache, both hands clutched to his side. Lips peeled back from locked teeth, eyes lost inside a tortured wince.

The water was scarlet. He lay there with his cheek against the wall of the bath. Eyes closed, water rippling with each relieved breath.

Hale soaked the wound site in disinfectant. The bleeding had subsided, reduced to a claggy scarlet mess. He cut a square of gauze and secured it with Band-Aids and duct tape. Another painkiller for luck.

The kitchen took some cleaning: blood on the table and cupboards, a trail of puddles courtesy of his visit from the bathroom. It didn't bother him. Gunshot surgery lent domestic chores fresh appeal. Mopping lino felt comfortingly routine.

Devereaux arrived at three forty-five. He knocked, and Hale released the locks and opened the door. Devereaux shambled in. Beaten and worn out. He looked like a garage sale.

'You normally take the stairs two at a time,' Hale said.

Devereaux didn't answer. He draped his jacket over a kitchen chair and sat down. A sweat crucifix marred his shirt back. He unbuttoned his cuffs and pushed his sleeves to his elbows. The shotgun was lying across the table. He nudged the barrel so it pointed away from him. 'You left blood on your stairs,' he said.

'Yeah. I had a shotgun pellet stuck in my gut.'

'Did you get it out?'

'Uh-huh. With pliers.'

Devereaux sat there blankly. He was sideways in his chair, elbows on thighs. Hands limp between his knees. 'You left blood on the carpet at the house,' he said. 'There was nothing I could do.'

The mop was leaning against the bench. Hale stood beside it and mimicked the pose, folded his arms. 'It's okay,' he said.

'They have your DNA on file,' Devereaux said. 'They can use the blood to prove you were in the house.'

Hale didn't answer. He snagged a thumb in a belt loop.

Devereaux said, 'This will play out easier if you tell them it was you in the house.'

'It won't. I broke in. I broke the law.'

'You'll get found out eventually. Things'll be easier if you just front up now.'

Hale was quiet. His tongue passed behind his top lip. 'How long does it take to analyse blood samples?'

Devereaux stretched out and emptied his pockets. He arranged a neat stack on the table beside him: wallet, phone, keys. 'Few weeks,' he said.

'If I tell them I was in the house, I'll have to tell them I broke in. If I do that, they'll take my PI licence. But with another couple of days, maybe we can close this thing.'

'It's been going since October.'

'And now there's good progress. There's a guy loose with a gun.'

Devereaux didn't answer. Chin on chest, eyes to floor. Hale said, 'You look stuffed.'

'I am.'

'You want something to eat?'

Devereaux looked up. The hunch stretched his throat taut. 'What have you got?'

'I made some scones yesterday.'

'What flavour?'

'Scone flavour. With dates.'

Devereaux massaged chin bristles, thumb and index finger. 'Yeah, I do quite fancy a scone actually.'

Hale took a Tupperware container from a cupboard, popped the lid at one corner. Devereaux eased upright and took a scone.

'Got any cream?'

'No. We're sans cream, I'm afraid.'

Hale took one for himself, left the cache on the table, beside the gun.

Devereaux sat down. He propped his elbow on the table. He said, 'How did you find him?'

'Who? Douglas?'

Devereaux nodded. He took a bite and chewed.

'I wanted to ask him about the fight club robbery. I background-checked Doug Haines, but it came back blank. I questioned his ex-wife; she told me his real name's Doug Allen.'

'She gave you the address as well?'

Hale nodded.

'And then he walked in on you in the middle of your B and E.'

'I think the old missus tipped him off,' Hale said.

'So why did he feel he had to take you on with a shotgun?'

'I got a bit short with his ex. He might have thought I was getting somewhere.'

'Are you getting somewhere?'

He shrugged. 'Why else would he shoot me?'

They chewed for a while. The mop dozed off and fell over with a crack.

'So then, what's the theory?' Devereaux said.

Hale got a toe under the mop and helped it to its feet. He said, 'I think the January robbery was an inside job. Doug and his ex had cash access; they could have faked a heist.'

'The woman can't have been complicit. She made a fuss. It would have been a clean in and out if she hadn't done anything.'

'Maybe they didn't want it too neat. They didn't want it looking like straight staff theft, so they added some drama.'

Devereaux mused, mid-scone. 'I think it's more likely Douglas set it all up, and kept the woman out of the loop.'

Hale didn't answer.

Devereaux's cellphone started ringing. He put a hand on it to stop it disrupting the pile. He said, 'It doesn't look like he packed when he left the house. It looks like he just got in the car and went, like he knew he had to be able to just drop everything and go.'

'No cash either.'

The phone stopped ringing. Devereaux drew his hand back. 'Probably all in the car,' he said. 'He's that edgy, he's probably got everything stashed under the front seats.'

Hale finished his scone and took another. 'Why is it that nobody checked out old Douglas before now?'

'I don't know.'

'It's been almost two months. Presumably someone should have run his name before I did.'

'Presumably.'

'So why nothing until now?'

'I don't know.'

Hale sat down at the table, the movement cautious, slowed by injury.

'You don't need stitches?' Devereaux said.

'Probably not.'

'You removed it with pliers?'

Hale nodded. 'It took me two goes.'

Devereaux put a hand on the shotgun. 'Why are you carrying this around?'

'In case Douglas tries to find me.'

Devereaux smiled. 'You're not normally this paranoid.'

'I botched a simple search. Maybe I should be.'

'If you'd botched it, you'd be dead.'

'Maybe next time I will be.'

Devereaux said nothing.

Hale's lips parted on a thought, but it took a while to surface. He said, 'Do you think one day you'll just wake up and know you're no longer any good at what you do?'

'Yeah. But it's a long way off. *Carpe diem.*'

Hale rocked his head side to side, face blank.

'You morbid old fart,' Devereaux said.

Hale didn't reply.

Devereaux laughed. 'You can't retire. You're not even fifty, for God's sake.'

Hale didn't answer.

Devereaux said, 'You owe it to all of us to get on with what you're good at.'

'Who said that?'

'WH Auden.'

Hale nodded and looked out a window. 'That's a good one to write on the fridge.' He picked a nail. 'Maybe it's better to drop something early than lose your grip on it without wanting to.'

'I think you've got a long stretch ahead of you.'

'Yeah, maybe.'

Devereaux didn't answer. He reached behind him to his jacket and took a cigarette, then went outside to light it.

Night shift, November '98. Twenty-year-old Sean Devereaux, a freshly minted police constable, lets John Hale take the call.

It's their fourth night partnered together. Patrol division staff rotations mean pairings are varied. This wouldn't have been Devereaux's first choice. Hale has a unilateral approach to law enforcement: he drives, he works the radio, he puts the cuffs on. Devereaux feels somewhat redundant. He's voiced his feelings to his sergeant. Sympathy was limited: 'He's got to be partnered with someone, and tonight you're it. And, sometimes, that's just the way it is, sunshine.'

The call is a request for a police check at a nearby address. Details are light: a young woman has dialled 111 and asked for the police. She's given an address, and then hung up. The Comms operator writes it off as a kid having a laugh, but Hale tells the guy they'll check it out. He's leaning back in his seat, handset coil stretched tight from across the dash. He clicks off and U-turns the car and flat-foots it back the way they came. Lights but no siren, engine tone straining and falling with each successive gear change. They're west of central city, Henderson suburbs. The cabin's lit cyclically as they pass beneath streetlamps.

'You are allowed to consult with me,' Devereaux says.

Hale glances at him. A long second, and then back to the road. He conducts himself with a kind of blank confidence. Devereaux doesn't know whether it's meticulous theatre or genuine nonchalance.

'Why would I do that?' Hale says.

'We just diverted from a suspected burglary to a call with no details given. Maybe we could have discussed which was more urgent.'

'This is more urgent.'

'Because …?'

'Because I recognised the address. I've had domestic abuse complaints there. The husband's a shitbag; I think he's got the wife convinced not to push charges.'

'You think she made the call?'

'We'll see. There's a little girl in there too.'

Hale turns and looks at him. Two seconds of eye contact. 'Do you agree that it's more important we roll on this?'

Devereaux nods.

Hale smiles. His side window frames a procession of small dwellings on barren sections. 'I thought that might be the case.'

The address is nearby, only a three-minute drive. The house is a prefab structure jacked knee-high on pillars of crisscrossed timber. A small square of decking ringed by long grass lies below the front door. A lonely mailbox stands slouched by the footpath, a deep tuft of weeds at its feet.

Hale swerves to a hard stop, takes their seatbelts by surprise. He leaves the car facing the wrong way, engine and lights running. Devereaux has to trot to keep up. Hale reaches the door first. He has his torch raised to shoulder height, the beam skittering across a wide arc. He knocks hard and gives the handle a shake.

'Police. Open up.'

Nobody answers. The two front windows either side of the door are both lit.

Hale gives the handle another shake and raps the door again. The torch beam constricts to a tight moon against the timber. A door slams. Footsteps, and then a man's voice from inside: 'Yo. What is it?'

Hale says, 'Police, Jamie. Open the door.'

A long pause. Something catches in the guy's throat, and then he says, 'Nah, everything's good, man. We're all good in here. It's fine, but thanks anyway.'

Hale maintains his knocking. 'I need to check Alice and the girl are okay, Jamie. So they can either pop out and see me, or I'm coming in.'

'Bro, I promise, we're cool—'

'Jamie, open the door now. I won't ask again.'

Bleeps and radio static reach them from the patrol car. Jamie says, 'Hey, is that John Hale out there?'

'Jamie, open the door now.'

'John, I swear everything's good as gold; don't even know why you're here.'

'Jamie. Open the door now.'

The guy reads something final in Hale's tone: 'Dude, chill out, I'm opening, I'm opening.'

Light along three sides as the door eases back. Hale helps it with a big palm, and a security chain snaps tight.

'Bro, you gotta give me some slack here, or I can't get the chain off the thingie. You know?'

Hale backs off, and a finger flicks the chain free. As soon

as it's swinging, Hale pushes the door fully open and steps in. Jamie gets the torch beam full in the face. He turns away, slack-mouthed and blinking, trying to rid the orb from his vision. He tries to stand his ground, fending Hale with raised palms.

'Hey, whoa, whoa, whoa. Take it easy, you don't need to just roll in.'

'Jamie. Step back, or I'm going to spray you.'

'John. Bro. Just be cool.' He sees Devereaux across Hale's shoulder. He flicks his eyebrows. 'Hey, man. How's it hanging?'

Devereaux doesn't answer. The entry is warm, a heavy smell of alcohol prevailing. Hale puts a hand on the guy's chest and pushes gently. Jamie moves back like he's on rollers.

'Who else is in the house?' Hale says.

'Just me and Susie. My little girl.'

'Where's Alice?'

'I dunno. Out somewhere.'

'Somewhere.'

'Bro, get the fuck off my case already.'

The guy reeks of booze, but an admission of drinking could imply Jamie's judgment is impaired by alcohol. Hale doesn't want that on record. He says, 'Put your hands on your head and sit down against the wall.'

'John, I gotta say, I think you're taking things way, way too far.'

'Jamie, do you want to get sprayed again?'

'No.'

'Then put your hands on your head, and sit down against the wall.'

Jamie complies. His shirt is pushed up as he slides his back down the wallpaper. A pale midriff creased by fat rolls is exposed. Behind him, down a narrow corridor, a little girl about six or seven stands in an open doorway. A miniature fist pushed against her mouth, free hand trailing a pink-clad plastic doll.

Jamie says, 'You see, man, embarrassing me in front of my little girl. It's disgusting.'

Hale looks down at him. He's yet to raise his voice. 'So make it easy on yourself and comply with what I tell you to do.'

He walks over to the little girl and drops to his haunches. He smiles.

'Hello, sweetheart.'

She doesn't answer. Jamie says, 'Don't worry, poppet. They'll be gone in a minute.'

The girl's eyes slide to him, and then back to Hale. She takes the fist from her mouth. The knuckles are slick with spit, dented with tooth marks.

Hale ignores Jamie and nods at the doll. 'Who's this?'

The girl shies behind the doorframe, holds him with one eye. 'Sally,' she says.

'Sally. What a lovely name.'

The girl smiles shyly.

'Do you know where Mummy is?' Hale says.

The girl doesn't reply. The smile falters and then dies, like a blown candle. She glances down the hallway at Jamie, and then looks at her feet. Hale's still watching her, calm and patient, the smile easy, alert for signs of subtext. He's sure the girl made the triple-one, but he doesn't want to mention it while her father's in earshot.

He gives her a wink. 'Why don't you be a good girl and pop back into bed?'

The girl risks a glance up at him. She nods once and turns back into the room, and Hale reaches up and pulls the door gently behind her. He rises to his feet.

Jamie gestures wide, hikes his shoulders. 'Bro, this is not like midnight open home or some shit.'

Hale turns around. 'If you take your hands off your head again, I'm putting the cuffs on.'

'Bro, I'm just saying.' But he puts his hands back on his head.

Hale walks away and checks the back of the house. Used dishes clutter a kitchen bench top. A muted television projects a weak flicker across the adjoining living room. An almost empty beer bottle waits beside a worn armchair, three empties in a loose trio nearby. A chair from the kitchen table has been dragged over to beneath a wall-mounted telephone, a loose wave in a rug betraying the move.

He walks back down the corridor and opens another door — a bathroom — and there, on the floor, pulped and bloodied, is a woman. She's on her side, knees drawn up, arms outstretched, upturned fingers curled gently like old paper. Her lips are slack and shiny with blood, a red drip line feeding a small pool on the tile. Her hair is scattered across her face, like cracks in a dropped vase. One eye hooded and aimed wayward.

Hale sees it all, and there's a brief nauseous pause as he stands in the door considering whether the little girl has seen it all, too. And, if not, how much of it she's heard. But it's only a fraction of a thought, before he's into the room, dodging blood spatter on the tile, radioing for an ambulance, crouching beside the woman.

She registers his arrival, and the undamaged eye tracks his progress to her. There's a glimmer of movement in one hand as she tries to reach up for him, but he crouches beside her and pats her arm gently and eases the hair out of her face with a delicate finger and whispers that everything's going to be okay. Not the first time he's used that easy little lie.

The room darkens suddenly as Devereaux shadows the hallway light. And there's the slightest, terrible idle silence before it occurs to Hale that if Devereaux is at the bathroom door, nobody is watching over Jamie. But Devereaux's frozen there, looking in at the woman on the floor, his face pale, everything about him leaden and inert.

Hale surges out of the crouch and pushes Devereaux back, hard enough to slam him against the opposite wall, but Jamie has already reached his bedroom, the door shut and bolted. Hale weaves inside the narrow confines of the hallway, and dips and thrusts his shoulder against the lock. The tongue cracks clean, no match for momentum and the sheer weight of human panic, and the door whips back like a cloth in high wind. Across the bed he sees Jamie kneeling, scrabbling for something hidden. Two steps and a lunge and Hale's across the room, and he wraps Jamie in a tackle and crushes him to the floor, the guy wailing and fighting him, even once the cuffs are on.

Later, they find a 24/7 McDonald's on Great South Road. Devereaux's choice: he'd found cholesterol an effective adrenaline counteragent.

The place is quiet, and the staff are pleased for patronage: no better customers at five a.m. on Great South Road in an empty restaurant than a pair of cops. They order burgers and fries and sit facing each other in a corner booth near the rear. Silence as they begin eating. Lack of conversation isn't an issue: they've had four nights' practice sitting in a patrol car.

Hale says, 'I didn't mean to piss you off.'

Devereaux glances up at him, says nothing. He can sense there're things Hale wants to get off his chest, but he's still irritated enough to make him work for it.

Hale says, 'I've had blow-ups at that address before, so I knew it was going to be a priority. It's not that I don't care about your input.'

'Cheers. I appreciate it.'

Hale slouches lower, drapes an arm along the top of the seat. 'You looked a bit off-colour in there.'

'Don't tell me that's genuine concern.'

'Concern for me, not you. I don't want to carry you if you keel over.'

The delivery's deadpan, it's not until he cracks a smile that Devereaux sees he's kidding.

'You've got a sense of humour too.' Devereaux drops his eyelids and shakes his head. 'Thank heavens.'

Hale shrugs, but he doesn't look put out. 'Whatever. I'd like the record to show that I tried to be civil.'

'No, you're right. I'm jerking your chain.' Devereaux falls quiet, considers appropriate phrasing. He says, 'It brought up bad memories.'

'What part?'

'All of it.'

'What happened?'

'Can't we save Q and A for another night?'

'I'm not trying to be rude. I'm just interested.'

Devereaux chews and swallows. He looks at him a long time. He says, 'I don't really want to talk about it. I appreciate the concern.'

Hale chews a chip, looks away. A plastic sandwich board warning of a wet floor stands above its own milky reflection.

Devereaux says, 'How long have you been a cop?'

'Four years.'

'What did you do before?'

The front door pushes open and two people enter. Hale tracks them eyes only, looks back at Devereaux. 'Military police,' he says.

'Why did you quit?'

He makes a face. 'Wanted to do something other than background-check new recruits all day. What about you?'

'What about me what?'

'What did you do before this?'

'Before this I was in university.'

'Doing what?'

'Studying English.'

Hale nods slowly. 'Read any Steinbeck?'

'Some.'

'Enjoy it?'

'Uh-huh.'

'Good. I like a man who likes his Steinbeck.'

Metallic clatters and the smell of hot oil from the kitchen. 'What will happen to the little girl?' Devereaux says.

'I don't know. I haven't thought about it.'

Devereaux looks at him. Hale makes a little gesture with the hand propped on the seat. He says, 'You see people like that every day; can't worry about all of them. At some point it brims over.'

Devereaux says nothing. The two people take their order and sit down in a booth. They're having trouble maintaining balance. Maybe they'd envisioned a burger-fuelled detox session.

Hale balls his burger wrapper. He checks his hands carefully for sauce traces. 'You want to stay on beat and patrol, or you want to specialise?'

'I'm going to be a detective.'

'Good luck with that.'

'You being facetious?'

'No. I mean, good luck with that. I think there're a lot of shitty people around, so I'm pleased you're trying to balance things out.'

Devereaux nods. 'I'm sorry I froze up on you in there. If he'd managed to get the rifle, we would have been in trouble.'

'Yes. We would have been.' Hale looks across the room, out the front window into the dark, where the cars slip back and forth behind ploughs of white glow. 'All that secret human misery,' he says.

His tone makes Devereaux think there's more to come, but he just sits there quietly and watches Devereaux finish his burger.

Hale stands up and rolls his shoulders. 'You're getting your colour back,' he says. He drops the keys on the table. They ring heavily in the quiet room. 'You can drive,' he says. 'I'm stuffed.'

■ THIRTY-ONE

WEDNESDAY, 15 FEBRUARY, 4.29 P.M.

Ellen called just as Devereaux was leaving. He sat in the car with his door open, one foot on the ground outside.

'You keep missing my calls,' she said when he answered.

'Sorry. Stuff's flat out.'

'You haven't forgotten about tonight?'

He pushed the heel of his hand in one eye. *What the hell is tonight?* 'What's tonight?'

'Drinks at my parents' place. I can't believe you've forgotten.'

Memory kicked in. 'Oh. Yeah. I remembered that. I thought there might have been something else. I don't know.'

'Right. So you'll be coming then.'

The cigarette on his lip was dwindling: he chained a fresh one, tip to tip. He didn't want to go. During the week he'd been forced to kill a man, he could justify non-attendance. But he said, 'Uh-huh. After what time are guests welcome?'

'Well, six. But why don't you come a wee bit earlier, and then you can have a chat to Mum and Dad before everyone else starts showing up.'

He thought: *Jesus Christ.* He voiced it differently: 'Okay, great.'

But it was another hour before he was even home. Afternoon traffic was ill-suited to pressing engagements. His living room smelled like an attic. The ash-heaped saucer sat unmoved since Monday night.

He browsed a heap of mail on the table, like something might have been added covertly. Mortgage to pay. Thank God crime was rampant.

He showered and shaved and searched for fresh attire. His wardrobe was limited on the casual dress front. He unearthed a clean shirt. Presentable jeans were a bigger challenge: he found a pair, belt still threaded. A trio of stretched buckle holes tracked a growing waistline. He went to the bathroom, checked his image. He was a two-tone of blues, but it would have to suffice. He leaned on the sink and gave himself a stare. How long before that gradually retracting hairline was classed as a widow's peak? Was that jowl-droop taking hold?

Thirty-four years old, but he was a ringer for forty. A six-year margin between his true and apparent ages. He wondered if that difference would hold constant, or gradually increase. Probably the latter: he couldn't recall looking thirty when he was twenty-four.

It wasn't until after six that he reached the house in Herne Bay. Guest cars made parking scarce: he left the Commodore up the street and walked back. Tall walls and tightly coiffed hedges protected some of the city's most exclusive real estate. He felt fraudulent, strolling amid such wealth.

Ellen was in the entry hall when he reached the house. Smile in place, trading niceties with exquisitely composed new arrivals. She saw him and threaded deftly through pastel-coloured dawdlers. She leaned on one tiptoed foot and kissed his cheek.

'I thought you were coming early.'
'I was. Nobody told the traffic.'
She smiled and made no reply.

'You look nice,' he said.

'Thanks.' She flicked her head. 'Come and say hi to Dad.'

She led him through the dining area, past the table they'd sat at, to the living room. It reeked of exclusivity: he heard politicians name-dropped, mention of yachts and the Royal Auckland Golf Club. Her father was ensconced by a group of small, balding men. They parted when they saw Ellen.

'Dad. Sean's here.'

A hand on the small of his back, nudging him onward, and then she was gone.

Her father smiled. 'Sean. Hi.'

'Hello, Russell.'

'Please. It's Russ. Everybody, this is Ellen's friend, Sean.'

A wave of raised wine glasses circuited the gathering. He sent a smile round.

'Sean's a police detective,' Russell said.

Mild approval rumbled.

'How was the trip?' Devereaux said.

Russell closed his eyes and nodded. He was a short, heavy man in his early sixties. He'd lost weight while overseas: empty skin hung below his jaw like a sheaf of old leather. 'The Czech Republic was just sublime. Just sublime. Have you ever been?'

'No, I haven't.'

'Oh, it was great.'

Devereaux stood and waited for further enlightenment. He was left wanting.

Russell said, 'Peter, how was the golf?'

A man in tan corduroys and boat shoes said, 'Oh, good. Greens are swift this time of year.' He frowned and looked at his feet. 'Lot of Koreans, though. Even busier than usual.'

Russell said, 'Ah, yes.' He licked his lips, and a smile flickered. 'The ah, Koddians, luff dere goff.'

A nervous laugh flitted back and forth. Devereaux stood there blankly. Idle chat drifted round the circle. Devereaux watched it from side to side, like waiting to cross through light traffic. Members of the group began to peel off as more guests arrived. Eventually, only he and Russell remained.

Russell stepped close. A frown put parallel score marks above his nose. 'Now,' he said. A whisper. 'What's this business I hear about you being involved with a shooting this week?'

'I shot someone on Monday.'

'Yes, Ellen said. Has there been much media attention?'

'A bit. It's been okay.'

Russell nodded. He swilled his wine glass, two fingers. 'What happened?'

'Guy was a golfer. He was shirking his green fees.'

Russell laughed. 'Really?'

'No. He was a robbery suspect.'

'So how's Ellen taking it? She seemed a wee bit concerned.'

'I think she'll pull through.'

'Okay, good. And what about the man that was shot?'

'He caught the train.'

'Excuse me?'

'He's dead.'

'Oh, gosh. That's a shame.'

'Yeah. It's a shame.'

'Well. Maybe just stick to the pepper spray next time.'

Devereaux didn't reply. He couldn't be bothered. He drifted away, weaved through the well-dressed throng. The dining table held a precise arrangement of wines and cheeses. He lingered and worked through some wedges of Brie.

'Try to look happy.'

He turned and saw Ellen.

'I am happy. This is my normal face.'

'Oh. Good.'

'You didn't have to just leave me for your dad to snack on.'

She bit down a smile. 'He's not that bad.'

He waited for people to move out of earshot. 'I feel a bit inadequate.'

'Why?'

'The only times I've handled a golf club is when it was someone's murder weapon.'

She snared some cheese. 'Maybe that's a good thing.'

'Why?'

She smiled and poked him in the ribs. 'You'd be so shit at golf. I can see it now.'

'Thanks. Where's your mother?'

'Gone out to get something.' She checked her watch. 'You've got at least another ten minutes before you'll have to talk to her.'

'Thank goodness. When's dinner?'

'Not until after nine probably.' She gave him another poke. 'Although you're feeling a bit spongy; maybe you should give it a miss.'

'Not only was that unfunny, it was also quite rude.'

She laughed. 'You're going to stay, aren't you? You're not going to try to escape early.'

'No. I'll stay for dinner.' He smiled, and dropped his voice: 'If you're really lucky, I might even talk to your mum.'

'Right. Was that meant to be Bogart?'

'No. That was just me being suave.'

'Right. Well, you can either stay here and work your way through the cheese or I can take you round and introduce you to people. Which would you prefer?'

'Can I eat some cheese first?'

'Okay. I'll come back for you. You want some wine?'

'No. I'll get a beer in a minute.'

He walked outside onto the back deck. Fine-stemmed glasses with half-payloads stood balanced atop the rail. A palm slapped his shoulder blade with a clean snap. He turned around.

'Sean, how're things?'

Ellen's brother, Ryan. He was in his thirties. Russell's stature, but easier on the eyes. Devereaux suspected both children's genes were biased towards their mother's.

'Good, Ryan. How are you?'

He shrugged and smiled. 'You know how it is. Struggling by.' He fingered a moustache that had been absent last time they met. He turned to a young woman in a cocktail dress riding his elbow. 'This is Melissa, by the way. Don't think you've met.'

They shook. Wine glass moisture or nerves had left her hand damp.

Ryan said, 'Hey, I was sorry to hear about what happened on Monday. I hope that all gets sorted out okay.'

Devereaux smiled. 'Yeah. I hope so too.'

A pause settled and bloomed into an aching silence. They looked out at the harbour.

Ryan said, 'Listen, you should come for a beer sometime. The office is just up on Pitt Street, so you could shoot up sometime or I could come down. I don't know.'

'Yeah, that sounds good. Although things have been pretty flat out.' He caught an errant hand raking his hair, dropped his arm at his side. 'Hopefully, in a couple of weeks everything will have cooled down a bit, and we can sort something out.'

'Yeah. Cool. That'd be good.'

Devereaux thought the quiet was going to flare again, but Ryan caught it. 'Hey, I'll leave you be; we're still doing the rounds, but I'll get you to meet some people later. My nephew heard you're a cop and he's absolutely dying to grill you about it, so I'll come and hunt you out later.'

Devereaux's cellphone started ringing. Ryan heard it. A blink of relief in his face at being handed an exit cue. He backed away, a finger aimed at Devereaux's chest. 'Good to see you, Sean. Go grab some wine or something.'

Melissa waved some fingers at him. Devereaux smiled and gave them a nod as he freed his phone. He palmed his free ear and ducked his head and answered.

'Devereaux. Frank Briar speaking.'

'Frankie. What a nice surprise.'

Briar paused. 'You've been summoned,' he said.

'I'm busy.'

'Whatever you're doing, put it on hold.'

'If you've got something to tell me, do it quickly. Cellphones give you brain cancer.'

Briar recited an address. 'Sound familiar?' he said.

It did sound familiar. He couldn't think why, and then it hit. 'Leroy Turner.'

'Yeah, old Leroy.'

'What's happened?'

'Come and have a look.'

Devereaux glanced around, held his voice at a whisper. 'Fuck you, Briar. Spit it out.'

Briar didn't answer.

'Is he dead?' Devereaux said.

Briar ignored the question. 'Get down here now. I hope you haven't eaten yet.'

Briar hung up. Devereaux swore and hit the handrail with his palm. People nearby shot cautious glances. Hurried sips when he returned the looks.

He pocketed the phone and shouldered back inside through static doorway traffic. He couldn't see Ellen. He found a clean wine glass on the table and levelled it up from a random bottle.

Moët. It was beginning to lose its chill. Devereaux downed the glass in two swallows. The feat drew some stares. He left the room, bumped into Ryan again in the entry hall.

'You're heading out?'

'Yeah. Something's come up with work.'

'That's a shame.'

'Yeah … Hey, I don't know where Ellen is, but can you tell her I've got something urgent and I have to dash.' She'd be angry, but there was nothing he could do about it.

'Sure. Is everything okay.'

'Hopefully. Thanks, Ryan.'

Ellen's mother was just arriving as he was stepping out. She saw him and smiled.

'Hello,' she said.

The hesitation before she spoke told him she'd forgotten his name. He smiled back and raised an index finger. 'One minute,' he said. 'Back soon.'

It was a lie, pure and uncut as they come. Maybe he was a sociopath. He walked to his car and drove away, his thoughts already with Leroy Turner.

■ THIRTY-TWO

WEDNESDAY, 15 FEBRUARY, 7.02 P.M.

A jolt of déjà vu on the way in: the same homeless guy on the same bench, the same funereal pose. Bad omen? Maybe a superstitious man would have been more shaken.

The kerb outside Turner's house was already busy: a Scene of Crimes van, two marked patrol cars, two detective's rides, a '69 Chevy Camaro in light grey. Maybe Lloyd Bowen and Frank Briar in the unmarked vehicles, The Don in the Camaro. Vintage muscle sheathed in gunmetal screamed McCarthy.

His heartbeat started to patter. It was the Scene of Crimes van that did it. Something about it implied bloodshed. Neighbours had caught the same vibe: knots of concerned bystanders occupied the opposite kerb. An old woman watched from a doorway across the street.

Please don't be dead, Leroy.

He parked two doors down and walked back. He kept his head down, lest he be asked to comment. His phone was in the glove box: he wanted some distance on it in case of party-related backlash.

The front yard was cordoned off. An old red Commodore sat nose-in behind the carport. A patrol cop recognised him and raised the tape.

'Front's blocked off, there's a kitchen door round the back.'

Devereaux thanked him and headed down the side of the house. A train was passing on the tracks behind the property, roar and diesel waft of the sluggish hulk. He felt the jittering of the ground beneath his feet. A tent and plastic ground sheet were set up at the kitchen door. He donned paper overshoes proffered by a Scene of Crimes officer, and went in.

It was busier than last time he'd visited: technicians in overalls scrutinised the fridge door, print-dusted the table. Nothing packs out a venue quite like murder. He stepped into the corridor.

Frank Briar blocked his path. 'Good of you to make time,' he said.

Devereaux ignored him and brushed past.

Please don't be dead—

On the hallway floor: two bodies, shrouded by sheets. Behind them, Don McCarthy and Lloyd Bowen in murmured conversation, arms folded and chins to chest. Bowen's back was turned, but McCarthy saw him. His expression showed no change, but he breathed something clipped and inaudible. Bowen turned.

McCarthy nodded at him. 'Bit casual.'

Devereaux didn't answer. He dropped to his haunches. The larger body was closer to the door. The smaller victim — probably Leroy — was further into the corridor. Both appeared to be outstretched on their stomachs. A head-to-head arrangement, maybe a metre between them.

Devereaux said, 'What happened?' Adrenaline made his voice catch.

'Blunt force trauma head injuries to both of them,' Bowen said.

Devereaux pinched a sheet edge and raised it. Leroy Turner's cheek was to the floor, his gaze lidded and distant, as if in some narcotic stupor. His nose and forehead had been caved in. His mouth was open, teeth cracked to scarlet stumps, the lower jaw bashed askew. Devereaux checked the second body. The big guy had his nose to the carpet, a single, wide trench stamped in the rear of his skull.

Devereaux replaced the sheet. 'Shit,' he said. He passed a sleeve across his mouth. His temples swelled and ached as he looked at the carpet.

You weren't innocent, Leroy, but you didn't deserve this.

He took a breath. The floor creaked as McCarthy took a measured step sideways. 'Have we got an ID on the second victim?' Devereaux said.

Blood had stained the carpet black. Circular seepage patterns overlapped, linking the two dead men. Like some morbid Venn diagram. Bowen waved off a blowfly.

McCarthy said, 'The big guy's a private investigator named Mitchell Duvall.'

Devereaux looked up. 'You checked his wallet?'

'No. I've dealt with him before.'

'You made a visual ID?'

McCarthy nodded. Bowen's cell rang. He stepped into an adjoining room to take the call. Quiet, and then a hushed tone: 'If it's ready in forty minutes, that'll be fine.'

'Any signs of forced entry?' Devereaux said.

'No.'

Devereaux looked down. He thought of the absconded Doug Allen: a shotgun stock seemed a likely candidate for the head injuries. But Leroy had claimed he knew nothing of the bank heist activity. So had he lied? Not unlikely. Or maybe this was something entirely unrelated.

He massaged his temples. Maybe he should have had more Moët.

He waited for something logical to cohere, but all he got was fog. What was the PI's reason for being here?

I've dealt with him before. Maybe McCarthy was holding something back. Not unlikely either.

Devereaux looked up. Bowen stepped back into the room and said, 'What are you thinking?'

'I'm thinking this doesn't make a lot of sense.'

Quiet for a moment. Technicians passed back and forth. Occasional camera flares startled shadows.

Bowen still had his phone out, spinning it absently between thumb and index finger. He said, 'We thought that given you'd visited recently, you might be able to shed some light on what happened.'

Devereaux looked at him, tried to see between the lines. There was a hidden weight to the statement. Bowen knew he'd visited on Tuesday, hence the hurry to get him down here. Which meant Bowen suspected him of having information he was reluctant to part with. The suspicion was almost circular: Devereaux knew McCarthy was holding something back from him. Question was whether he was holding back on Bowen, too.

I've dealt with him before.

Bowen wasn't an idiot. He'd heard the same comment, and would have made the same logic leap. But his expression was unchanged. Meaning that whatever McCarthy was privy to about this second victim, Bowen probably knew too. Except McCarthy clearly didn't trust Bowen enough to tell him about the gun incident in Pit, or Devereaux would have been out of a job already.

Devereaux held the crouch. 'Whose is the car out front?' he said.

'Commodore comes back to Duvall,' McCarthy said.

'When were they found?'

'About ninety minutes ago. There's a cellphone in Turner's hand. He managed to punch one-one-one before he went.'

'No dialogue?'

'No dialogue. Comms sent a patrol car to do a cruise-past, and they recognised the address from having run parole checks, figured they'd better see what was going on.'

Devereaux stood up, felt his knees crack. The room tilted slightly as he rose. Bowen was watching him carefully, the phone still spinning. McCarthy had his trademark even stare levelled at him. He felt pinned down from all angles. Devereaux said, 'How did the officers get in?'

'They broke the front door,' McCarthy said. 'They could see through the living room window there was someone in the corridor.'

'And there was no pre-existing damage to the door?'

'No. Apparently, Leroy likes to keep the chain on as well, so whoever nailed them was most probably let in.'

Devereaux nodded slowly. He looked to the end of the corridor. The evidence technicians were still examining the table. He wondered whether they'd recovered any of his prints yet.

'Did any of the neighbours see anything?' he said.

McCarthy said, 'We don't know yet.'

Bowen put his phone away, kept his hand in his pocket. He spoke carefully, as if adhering to some rehearsed statement. 'Sergeant, there're a few details that would be good to iron out. What would be good at this stage is to just sit down and run through some questions.'

'What, here?'

He shook his head. 'Back at the station.'

It was probably a twenty-minute trip back to town. He

recalled Bowen's phone conversation: *If it's ready in forty minutes, that'll be fine.*

Devereaux smiled. 'Fine. Who's going to run things at this end?'

'Detective Sergeant Briar is more than capable of supervising progress.'

Devereaux didn't answer. Bowen took a hand from a pocket and made a lead-the-way gesture. Devereaux took a last glance at Leroy, and walked back down to the kitchen, heard McCarthy and Bowen following. A quiet little procession as they walked around the front of the house. Down the street, Pollard was pulling up in an unmarked.

Devereaux turned to Bowen, held up a peace sign. 'Two minutes,' he said.

He walked away unbidden. Pollard saw him coming and dropped his window. Devereaux put his hands on the sill and leaned down.

'You look like shit,' Pollard said.

'You look like a yard of pump water.'

'I'm touched.'

'Likewise. I just saw two dead guys. Do me a favour; I'm light on info, but I've got to leave right now. One of the vics is a private investigator named Mitchell Duvall—'

'I heard.'

'Yeah, see if you can find out what the hell he was doing down here.'

Pollard nodded, watched McCarthy slide into the Camaro. 'Why do you have to take off so fast?'

'They're bringing me in for a chat. They think I'm holding back.'

'Who's they?'

'Bowen and old Clint Eastwood.'

Pollard's eyes flicked up. 'Are you holding back?'

'Yeah. But a lot less than they think.'

Pollard paused. 'You don't look quite right. What's going on?'

'I don't really know.'

Pollard's mouth hooked. 'They think you did it?'

Devereaux ignored the question. 'Look, if you could give me a call that would be great. It'll probably only take twenty minutes to get back to town, but anything you can scrape together would be better than nothing.'

'You owe me a six-pack.'

'Find me something worthwhile, I'll make it a dozen.'

They took separate cars. McCarthy drove lead, Bowen brought up the rear. Calm air had let a light smog linger: a jaundiced pallor above the central district.

They paralleled the railway line and went northeast along New North Road. Heavy traffic through Mount Albert stalled them. Old two-storey façades stood behind heaved bitumen footpaths, veranda shades straining against rusted tie rods. The grimed and jigsawed rooflines, walls lined by downpipes. Windows crammed with air-con units, the grille-ended stubs leaking vapour.

Devereaux watched the lurid brake-light stream arc ahead. God, the hunger. Even a double bludgeoning hadn't quelled his appetite. He watched a Chinese food vendor jiggle a steaming wok above a flame. The deprivation was torture. He turned back to the road, saw McCarthy place a call on his cell. Seconds later, and his mirror framed Lloyd Bowen, phone to ear.

What are you talking about, fellas?

They crawled onwards. He kept his attention split: one eye on Bowen in his rear view. They hung up in unison, two minutes later. Bowen's finger was keeping a beat on the top of the wheel.

Devereaux stretched across and took his phone from the glove box. Two missed messages: one from Ellen's mobile, one from the house in Herne Bay. He thought about calling her back, but opted out. He was in the wrong frame of mind to be explaining himself. It wouldn't end well.

They reached the intersection at Saint Lukes Road. Devereaux raised the phone and faked a call. He kept it simple: a nod, some silent mouthed nonsense, a hang-up. On cue: Bowen put his phone to his ear, and one car in front, McCarthy answered. They didn't last long either. Thirty seconds, and then they clicked off.

Further north, and The Don led them onto Dominion Road. Less than ten minutes from the station. Devereaux glanced at his phone.

Come on, Pollard.

Down past K' Road, through low-rise commercial and apartments on Upper Queen Street. Past Myers Park, left into Mayoral Drive. Pedestrians long-shadowed in the late light.

The cellphone rang. Caller ID: Pollard.

'You're leaving it late,' Devereaux said.

'And you're an ungrateful bastard.'

'What have you got? We're nearly there.'

'Not much. The PI's name is Mitchell Duvall, but I think you knew that.'

They turned into the garage, under bright electric light. Strictly speaking, it was police vehicles only: The Don's lofty status meant the Camaro was welcome.

Pollard said, 'I spoke to that guy Frank Briar. He said Bowen put a message out with Comms that this Douglas Allen guy is wanted in relation to the Turner-Duvall homicide. I don't know whether he had some sort of info, or whether he just made a good guess. But by the sounds of it he put out the alert before he'd even seen the scene. So I don't know.'

'Okay, good. What else?'

He found his slot and ripped the brake.

'There's a folder in Duvall's car, he'd built up his own info on the robbery investigation. He's got clippings on the October job, the fight club job in January, and the shootings earlier this month.'

'So why was he talking to Leroy?'

'I don't know. If I find something, I'll pass it on.'

'Okay, cheers. Look, you might have to text it through; I'm not going to be able to take calls.'

'Yeah, sure.'

'Have you found anything that indicates this guy Doug was definitely at the scene?'

'Not yet. There're some tyre tracks in the lawn they're checking out, and I'll get patrol to do a house-to-house, so we'll see what turns up. Keep your phone on.'

An interview room was ready and waiting: door ajar, a two-versus-one chair arrangement across the obligatory square table.

Devereaux sat down. His allocated position was obvious. McCarthy rounded the table and drew a seat out and turned it sideways. He sat down and folded his legs. Bowen closed the door slowly, a solemn little click as the tongue caught. He slipped his suit coat off and draped it over the back of the third chair. A protracted pause as he unbuttoned his cuffs and rolled them neatly to his elbows. Forearms raised, like surgery preparation. It seemed like he relished the build-up. He seated himself and rested his arms on the table. Nice contrast: Bowen hunched forward, brow gently furrowed, McCarthy resting easy, elbow on the backrest, head propped by two fingers.

Bowen said, 'Tea? Coffee?'

'No thank you. I'm fine.'

'You look a little preoccupied there, sergeant.'

Devereaux shrugged. 'Vicious double homicide,' he said. 'Sitting here doing nothing doesn't seem that productive.'

Neither of them replied. Bowen looked down and watched his fingers knit tightly. At length McCarthy said, 'Don't you think the sergeant's aged recently?'

Bowen didn't answer. He said, 'Is there anything at all you wish to disclose at this stage?'

'I don't know.'

Bowen shook his head gently. His lips dipped at the corners. 'I can't see that the question could have been much clearer.'

Devereaux shrugged. 'It's the sort of question that implies you're anticipating something specific. I'm not quite sure what you're expecting to hear.'

Bowen didn't answer. McCarthy just looked at him.

Devereaux said, 'What exactly is the purpose of this meeting?'

Bowen said, 'This afternoon you attended a crime scene in Otara.'

'You're referring to the home of Doug Allen?'

'I am.'

Devereaux nodded. 'I did.'

'You weren't informed of the call. I'm just curious as to how you knew to attend.'

'I saw Frank Briar receive a message that looked urgent. I called Comms and asked what was happening.'

'You seemed very eager to get down there.'

'I was. It's my job.'

McCarthy shifted in his seat, laid an ankle across one knee.

'Sergeant,' Bowen said. 'Don't get short with me.'

'I'm sorry. I'll endeavour to use longer sentences.'

Bowen didn't flicker. McCarthy smiled, but it looked more like contempt than humour.

Devereaux said, 'I think the biggest mystery is why nobody alerted me to the fact something had happened.'

Bowen smiled thinly, like a slice of moon. He stretched his arm in front of him and rolled his shoulder, checked his cuff roll. He said, 'Sergeant, as you can imagine, the purpose of this little get-together is to discuss the fact that less than forty-eight hours after you paid a visit to Leroy Turner, he ends up dead.'

'The tone you use makes it seem so much less innocent than happy chance.'

Bowen's eyebrows hiked. 'Happy chance?'

'Poor choice of words. Pure coincidence.'

Bowen didn't reply. The lighting cut out, blinked itself awake after a short lapse.

Devereaux said, 'If you want to talk alibis, I'm rock-solid.'

Bowen shook his head. 'I don't think you killed anyone. I just think there's information you're not giving me.'

Devereaux's heart skipped a beat. He hoped they didn't sense it break stride. 'What gives you that impression?'

'You visited Turner's address on Tuesday morning for no apparent reason.' He pouted gently; knitted fingers rose and then fell. 'You'll have to forgive me for thinking it seems a little strange.'

'I object to the "no apparent reason" part.'

Bowen spread his hands. 'So go ahead and justify.'

'I got Turner's name from Howard Ford. You had him in custody Monday night.'

'I seem to recall instructing you not to speak to him.'

'I'd dealt with Ford previously. I knew he'd been associated with Turner, and that Turner had been involved in robberies from time to time.'

'Okay. And you felt the need to visit him at one a.m. on a Tuesday morning?'

'I'm a light sleeper.'

Bowen cracked a grin, razor-edge cool. Devereaux remembered Hale's description from Monday: sharp as a paper cut, and just as unpleasant. 'So what did you talk about?'

Devereaux's phone sounded. He braced for a long lament before the voicemail kicked in, but the tone was short-lived. He rolled sideways on his chair and the phone slid from pocket to cupped palm. He checked the display. Text hogged the screen: *Duvall's file note says: Informed by Const. Charles Easton that Leroy Turner assaulted by Det Frank Briar during Q&A.*

So Leroy hadn't lied. He had third-party corroboration of his assault tale.

Devereaux laid the phone on the table, face down. Bowen and McCarthy glanced at it in unison. The sudden reflexive tug of curiosity.

Devereaux said, 'I spoke to Turner, but it was a waste of time.'

Bowen looked up from the phone. He clenched his teeth. Jaw muscle swelled and faded. 'Why?' he said.

'I questioned him about the Savings and Loan robbery on October eight; he told me he'd been in prison at the time, and knew nothing about it.'

Bowen was quiet a long time. His gaze was steady, but Devereaux could see something battling to leave the cage. It looked like excitement. It looked like the thrill of entrapment. McCarthy had tipped his chair up on two legs. The sense of something waiting to drop.

'Did you push him?' Bowen said.

Devereaux shook his head. 'Not my style.' He looked at McCarthy. 'I leave the arm-bending to others.'

McCarthy didn't budge. Not even a dent.

Devereaux said, 'He was apprehensive of me. I think even if he did have useful information, I would have struggled to get him to divulge it.'

Bowen nodded and looked down at the little triangle of table corralled by his forearms, as if consulting notes. 'Your description of events to Inspector McCarthy on Tuesday when he found you at the address was that you'd found the house empty. Is that correct?'

'That's what I told him, yes.'

'So in fact you lied to him?'

'Yes.'

McCarthy let his chair down soundlessly. Devereaux didn't look at him.

Bowen said, 'You realise the gravity of that admission?'

Devereaux nodded. 'It was necessary, based on what Turner had told me.'

Bowen's eyes went back and forth a couple of times, clock-like. 'Elaborate for me.'

'Turner told me he had been questioned in relation to robberies dating back to October. He claimed he was assaulted by one of the officers interviewing him.'

'I struggle to see how that entitled you to provide a false verbal report to a senior officer.'

'If you could indulge me a few moments longer, I'm hoping I can alleviate your confusion.'

The thin smile again. Bowen spread upturned palms: please continue.

Devereaux said, 'Turner couldn't name the officer who assaulted him. The description he gave was vague. We were seated in his kitchen, and heard a car pull in off the street. Obviously, it was a police vehicle. Turner saw it and panicked, told me not to let anyone inside.'

'Which is what you did.'

'Which is what I did.'

'Okay. So your contention is that Turner was so traumatised after being interviewed, he couldn't face further contact with the police?'

'It wasn't the interview that bothered him. It was the physical assault that came with it.'

'And knowing you're a police detective, why was he prepared to talk to you?'

'I told him I knew Howard Ford.'

'And he believed that?'

'He recognised my name. Ford had told him about me.'

Bowen smirked. 'So you came highly recommended.'

'I think he described me as an "okay dude".'

Bowen's face didn't change: not even an eyebrow waver. 'Sergeant, I'll be honest with you. This all sounds like total bullshit.'

Devereaux didn't answer.

Bowen said, 'What? And because the guy's dead, I'm meant to say, "Well, there's no way to find out now so I guess we'll have to take your word for it."'

'The postmortem might confirm whether he was recently assaulted.'

'Yeah. Keep your fingers and toes crossed.'

Devereaux didn't reply. He flipped his cellphone over, slid it across the table to Bowen with a flick.

Bowen looked down. He smiled. 'I think it's meant to be you that's offered the phone call.'

'Read my last received text.'

Bowen's eyes took a long time to drop. He looked down and picked up the phone. Dampened keypad clicks seemed amplified in the quiet. He paused. He read.

Devereaux pictured it: *Duvall's file note says: Informed by Const. Charles Easton that Leroy Turner assaulted by Det Frank Briar during Q&A.*

Bowen licked his lips and slid the phone left, to McCarthy. The Don leaned forward, skimmed the message, leaned back.

Bowen folded his arms. He looked at the table and ran a thumb down a sideburn. 'Did Turner mention the name Charles Easton when you spoke to him?'

'Here I was expecting an apology.'

Bowen didn't reply.

Devereaux said, 'No, he didn't mention the name.'

The room was quiet. McCarthy's face had lost a little blood. Bowen cocked a loose fist and checked his nails. 'What did you do when you saw the unmarked car arrive?' he said.

'I went outside to meet it.'

'Why did you not stay indoors with Turner and get him to confirm whether or not the officer who had arrived had been involved in this alleged assault?'

'He was panicked. Whoever it was, he didn't want anything to do with them, irrespective of whether or not they'd attacked him.'

'Right. So after Inspector McCarthy left, why did you not go back inside to confirm whether he had been involved in the assault?'

Devereaux smiled. 'I didn't even consider that Inspector McCarthy could have been responsible. Clearly, you know him a little better than I do.'

'Glibness won't win you points, sergeant.'

'Turner wouldn't let me back inside, so I left.'

The pair of them shared a glance. Bowen turned back and laid on a minatory stare. A pause strained, long and tight. 'We're done,' he said.

■ THIRTY-THREE

WEDNESDAY, 15 FEBRUARY, 8.13 P.M.

His phone rang again as he left the room — the Herne Bay number. Devereaux didn't answer. He called Pollard, but it went through to voicemail. He left a message: 'I'm out of the interview, call me back ASAP.' He hoped he didn't sound too curt.

A mug on his desk held a finger of cold coffee. He downed it and found pad and pen, sketched the Turner address in plan.

What happened, Leroy?

Something made him feel pushed for time. His heart held a high tempo, urged on by some illusory deadline. He checked his phone again and re-read Pollard's message.

Whoever Charles Easton was, Duvall had obviously felt compelled to verify the claim. But the chronology lacked clarity: had the killer walked in on Duvall and Turner, or had he arrived first and struck when Duvall arrived?

One thing was almost certain: Turner knew the assailant. The house showed no signs of forced entry. Plus Turner had been paranoid. He wouldn't risk admitting strangers if he could avoid it. Which raised the question of how Duvall had gained admission. Maybe proof of PI status had been sufficient. Or maybe he confessed knowledge of Turner's interview session with Frank Briar. *I know who beat you up, sonny. Now let me in.*

He realised he was still standing, hunched there above the desk as if conducting some furtive search. He hooked his chair in and sat down, dropped his face into waiting hands.

If Pollard was right, Bowen had already pegged Douglas Allen for the deaths. The timing seemed compatible: he could have fled to Turner's address following his run-in with John Hale. Turner lets him in. Doug's wired on adrenaline. He spills his story in a breathless panic:

There's some private investigator after me.
He ambushed me in my own house.
I took a shot at him.
I'm in deep shit.

Douglas would have stayed on edge. The shakes take a long time to fade. A knock at the door would have re-twisted tortured nerves. Devereaux pictured it. Hale hadn't thought Douglas got a good look at him; if someone showed up claiming they were a PI, Doug's survival instinct would have snapped the leash.

Mitchell Duvall, mistaken for John Hale.

Devereaux looked at the floor sketch and saw theories crystallising. He pictured Douglas poised in the living room entry as Turner opened the front door. Duvall entering. Douglas Allen smashing the back of the guy's head in with the butt of a shotgun. Turner awestruck, Turner screaming. Douglas silencing him with a blow to the face.

His desk line rang. He forgot to check the ID screen to vet the number, and picked up without thinking. It was Ellen.

'Sean, where are you?'

A strange question: she'd had to dial his desk to reach him. 'I got a call,' he said.

'What? And just up and left? You said you were going to stay for dinner. You didn't even say goodbye to anyone.'

He strained for background noise: was that guest chatter, or just a bad connection?

'I'm sorry,' he said. 'It was urgent.'

'You can't just vanish.'

The line went quiet. He couldn't pick whether she was fuming or just sad. He sensed crying on the horizon.

'Look,' she said. 'Dinner's at nine, like I told you. I would really, really love you to make it. Everyone would. So can you?'

I can't do this right now.

'Ellen. Look.'

She cut him off: 'No, come on.' She paused, and he could hear her breathing. 'It's eight-thirty. If you leave now, you can get here and not be late.'

He had his eyes closed, one hand buried in tufts of hair, both elbows on the desk.

'Ellen.' It sounded weak and contrite. He was oddly conscious of his own voice, like a quiet bystander to his own private moments.

'Please, Sean. It's just one dinner. It's just one goddamned dinner. Please just come. It'll only be an hour. Nobody's going to keep you late.'

'Ellen.' He grimaced as he said it. 'I really can't.'

'You really can't.' A heavy waver: here comes the crying. He gnashed his molars, braced for some shouting. But she just said, 'Well, I'll see you then, Sean.'

She ended the call. It felt a little more final than he would have preferred. The farewell a little too firm, the hang-up a little too gentle. But she'd probably call back. He sat with his elbows on the desk and the dial tone in his ear a moment, then placed the handset in the cradle.

He leaned back in his chair and turned on the desk light. Interesting how things deteriorate: his evening had slipped from wine and sunshine to thoughts of murdered men. Was there something tragic in the fact it didn't bother him? Maybe it was a symptom of something. Preferring the dead to the living.

You have no life.

No, that wasn't right: he had a life, he just liked work better.

The phone rang again.

Second time round he was more prudent: a caller ID check showed Don McCarthy's office. Tempting just to let it ring through, but that wouldn't stop McCarthy visiting in person. Devereaux picked up.

McCarthy said, 'Come through. We need to talk.'

'Now's a bad time.'

'Don't give me cheek, boyo. I want to see you.'

Devereaux hung up. He gave it a minute, and then walked through to The Don's office. McCarthy was standing in front of the desk, back to the door. Ceiling lights splayed his shadow in weak triplicate. A bottle of Jack Daniel's Black Label stood beside the computer monitor, an inch of whisky in a tumbler hanging in one hand.

'Close the door,' McCarthy said. He tipped his wrist back and forth. The whisky rolled side to side.

Devereaux closed the door to the hallway. The tongue gave that clean little click, reminiscent of his interview.

McCarthy nodded at the Jack. 'I'm off the clock so don't say anything sanctimonious.'

'I was hoping not to say anything at all.'

McCarthy didn't answer.

Devereaux said, 'What do you want?'

'Who was that you were on the phone to?'

'It's none of your business.'

McCarthy's mouth downturned, and he shrugged. 'I didn't mean anything by it. Just wondering.'

'My apologies. I thought it was just casual intrusion.'

McCarthy showed no response, like he'd been deaf to the jibe. He said, 'My wife left me, I think it was almost the phone calls I missed the most. Those little domestic intrusions, you know?'

He saw something in Devereaux's face and laughed, humourless, scraped off the back of the throat. 'Don't worry; I wasn't listening in.' He paused for a moment. 'I see a hunched, elbows-on-the-desk phone conversation, I know it's probably wife trouble. Or something similar. Anyway.' He winked. 'I hope it all works out hunky-dory.'

'What do you want?'

He took a small sip and smiled on the swallow. He set the glass on the desk and topped it up with the bottle, head sideways to gauge the level. 'What makes you think you can walk in here and use that tone with me?'

'It's probably a respect thing.'

The photographs on the desk presided over a mess of paper: arrest sheets, photocopied handwritten notes. McCarthy took another hit off the whisky, set the tumbler down again. Creamy ellipses where his fingers had imprinted the glass. He turned around and stepped close. Near enough they could have waltzed.

'I don't give a shit what you say to Bowen,' he said. 'I know there're things you keep to yourself.'

A long spell of cold quiet. For once he actually looked worn out: eyes bagged and half-lidded, crowning hairs swirled. Devereaux said, 'Is there anything else?'

McCarthy smiled. 'I just get the feeling that when all of this is wrapped up, we're going to find you knew more about certain things than you let on.' He sucked his top lip gently, waved the fingers of one hand, watched their far-off trajectories.

'I see little personal motives flitting about, but God knows what they mean.'

Devereaux kept his face empty. He said, 'Have you spoken to Frank Briar about why he's been accused of assaulting a suspect?'

McCarthy's mouth curved upwards at one edge. 'Someone will chat to him in due course,' he said. 'But that's not for you to concern yourself with.'

'Chat sounds a little informal. I think the seriousness of the allegation would merit a pointed discussion.'

McCarthy didn't answer. He stepped back to the desk and knocked back the tumbler contents. He sucked a hissing breath and set the glass down beside the bottle, appraised the framed accolades as if taking the measure of his own life.

'Don't ever lie to me again,' he said. 'You have no idea how much it pisses me off.'

He stepped to the door and disappeared into the corridor, leaving Devereaux alone in the office.

■ THIRTY-FOUR

WEDNESDAY, 15 FEBRUARY, 9.28 P.M.

The bleeding didn't stop.
Hale relented and visited an Accident and Emergency. The nurse joked it looked like he'd been shot. Hale told her he'd fallen against something. He tried to look abashed. Prayed it seemed plausible.

A brisk and over-taxed doctor applied sutures and admonished him to avoid heavy lifting. Hale left and drove home, one shoulder hunched to alleviate stitch strain.

A Fiat Punto hatch was parked at the top of his driveway when he got back to the house on Scenic Drive. He pulled in beside it. The driver waved at him through the glass, then slid out. He smiled back and climbed out, motion rendered awkward by bandaging.

'Hello, Ellen.'

'How you doing, John?'

He read it immediately: boyfriend trouble. Give me some Sean Devereaux insight. He wondered how long she'd been out here. A chance visit from his friend Douglas would not have played well.

'Moderate,' he said. 'You want to come in?'

'You want to stand out here in the cold?'

She said it with a grin, and he smiled again. He retrieved the shotgun from the back of the car, and she followed him up the stairs to the front door. Locks undisturbed: he stood aside and let her enter first. She found the light switch by trial and error: third swipe lucky. The entry hall and kitchen blinked awake in weary succession.

'You want a drink?' he said.

'What have we got on offer?'

'Tea, coffee. Maybe even something a little firmer.'

'Maybe just tea. I've got to drive.'

They went through to the kitchen. Hale leaned the gun beside the fridge and set the jug going. Ellen scraped a chair back from the table and sat down.

'You carry that thing round with you all the time?'

'Only when things are a little edgier than normal.'

'What DEFCON level are we on at the moment?'

He laughed. 'I just like to be cautious.'

'So is my car going to be safe out front?'

'Should be. My aim from the front deck is normally pretty good.'

He checked the fridge. Beer predominated by an order of magnitude. He took the milk bottle from its slot in the door and set it on the bench.

'Is that blood?'

She pointed out a lone scarlet speck on the table top.

'Probably.'

'There was some on the stairs outside, too.'

'Yeah. I injured myself.'

Headlights strafed the window, whorls of grime sharply white and then invisible as the car passed. His breath caught until dark returned.

'How?' she said.

He made a face. 'Being careless.' He indicated his newly

repaired torso. 'I got stitches, though.'

She didn't push him further. She folded her legs and smoothed her skirt and leaned forward onto folded arms. Steam from the kettle plumed and beaded against the window.

'I thought Sean would be here,' she said.

He settled himself in the crook where the bench turned a corner. 'No. Just me.'

'It smells like cigarettes.'

'Yeah. He was here this afternoon.'

Her nails clicked a shy rhythm on the table top.

'Do you ever worry about him?' she said.

'Sean?'

She nodded.

He shook his head. 'No, I don't.'

She waited for further exposition.

He said, 'I never have. I've known him a long time. It's just the way he is.'

'What way is that?'

He shrugged, and the stitches made him regret it. 'I don't know. Whatever way that's concerning you enough to ask if I worry about him.'

She passed a hand through her hair. Surprised strands sat up loosely and then eased back into place. 'Well. The current concern is that he's got no peripheral vision.'

'In what sense?'

She turned and placed both hands knife edge on the table, palms parallel. 'He's got a narrow focus. He can see work. And that's it.'

'I don't know whether it's narrow focus or an addictive personality.'

'Hence the smoking?'

'Yeah … I suppose.'

'You ever try to get him to quit?'

'No.'

'You don't worry about him getting lung cancer?'

'He's intelligent enough to have balanced the risk of early death against whatever satisfaction he gets from working through a pack of Marlboros every day.'

'Nice way of looking at it.'

He shrugged, good side only. 'He's reconciled the decision quite happily; I'm not going to be able to undermine whatever rationale he's gone with.' He paused and considered it. 'Telling him to quit would be selfish because ultimately I'd miss him if it killed him. Also, it's none of my business.'

She didn't answer. The jug clicked. Hale added tea bags and boiling water to two mugs, levelled them up with milk.

'I've got scones as well,' he said. 'If you're that way inclined.'

Her eyebrows rose approvingly. 'You cook scones?'

He smiled. 'I've never had an offer of food met with such incredulity.'

'No. I just can't picture you as a baker.'

'Trick is to pop in a bit of lemonade. Helps aerate the mixture.'

She shook her head. 'Jesus. No, I think the tea will do me. But thanks.'

He nodded towards the door. 'Come sit in the living room. More comfortable.'

She followed him through, eyes on the wavering liquid line in the mug. She sat down slowly on the low couch, mug cantilevered awkwardly in cupped hands. Hale took an armchair opposite.

'He was meant to come to this thing tonight at my parents' place,' she said.

'Yeah. He told me.'

'He only managed to stay for about twenty minutes.'

Hale didn't answer. Another car passed. He tensed until the light through the ranch slider had vanished.

'It was just one dinner,' she said.

Hale nodded. 'He doesn't like dinners very much.'

'He never answers my calls.'

'He never answers mine either. Trick is to not answer his.'

'He doesn't tend to ring me in the first place.'

Hale tried to stretch his legs. The stitches wouldn't comply. He settled for a hunch. She nodded at his vinyl music collection, arranged neatly on a bookshelf.

'You can get those on cassette tapes now,' she said. 'In fact the really progressive folk buy what're called CDs.'

He feigned offence. 'That's a terrible thing to say.'

She laughed: a flash of even teeth. 'No, you're right. I've got a box of old LPs buried somewhere in the garage. Somehow I managed to keep the music and give away the record player.'

'Well. If you're polite, and don't condescend to my scones, you can borrow mine and relive your distant youth.'

She took a sip, smiled eyes only across the top of the mug.

Hale said, 'Were you hoping for advice on Mr Devereaux, or were you wanting to intercept him?'

'I thought I might get both. With a bit of luck.'

'Why did you think he'd be here?'

'I called him earlier and he was at the station. I thought he'd probably guess that I might try to reach him at home, and come here first. So I just gambled and came straight to your place.'

Hale laughed. 'I think you give his little brain too much credit.'

She smiled weakly, and they were quiet for a spell. She said, 'Do you think he'll lose his job for killing that guy?'

'No. I don't think he will.'

'Honest opinion, or are you just being reassuring?'

'Honest opinion.'

She nodded slowly. Hale considered bringing the shotgun through from the kitchen. He chose not to, in the interests of living room etiquette.

'You think he's all right at the moment?' she said.

The tea was substandard: too milky. He hoped she found hers acceptable. He said, 'I suspect he's probably feeling a little stretched. But he's used to that. It comes with the territory.'

'Is he stretched because of actual workload, or because he's obsessed?'

'Sort of question you'd need to ask him.'

'You think he's obsessive?'

Hale nodded. 'I guess. Probably his best and worst quality, depending on perspective.'

'You consider it a virtue?'

He nodded. 'Then again, I'm not his girlfriend.'

They sipped some tea.

She said, 'Every time a car goes past, your hackles go up.'

He smiled wearily. 'I'm a little stretched too.'

'Are you in trouble?'

'If not now, then eventually.'

'What happened?'

He looked at the window while he thought about what to censor. Beyond the reflected room, trees swayed under the weight of darkness. He said, 'I was searching a house, and the owner found me.'

She didn't show any surprise. She reached and set the mug down on a table beside the couch. 'And you're carting the gun round in case he manages to find you again?'

'Yeah. Essentially.'

'Is that how you got hurt?'

He nodded. 'He had a shotgun with him. I got a pellet lodged in my side.'

Something doubtful about his frankness: 'Really?'

'Really.'

'Are you okay?'

'Yeah. I took it out. And I got stitches.'

'Does Sean know?'

'He doesn't know about the stitches.'

'Does he know you got shot?'

'Yeah, I told him. I haven't told anyone else yet. Except you.'

She didn't answer. Another car passed. He tried to maintain indifference.

At length she said, 'So was this a work-related break-in, or purely recreational?'

'Work-related.' He smiled. 'Although I do enjoy a good house prowl.'

'Are you allowed to tell me the details, or is it covered by investigator-client privilege?'

He laughed. 'Can you keep a secret?'

She zipped her lips, mimed a locking motion, flicked away the key.

He said, 'You remember the fight club robbery back in early January?'

She nodded.

'My client's daughter was injured. He wants me to find who did it.'

'Are the police still working on it?'

He nodded. 'They haven't had much luck.'

'And what about you?'

'I've been shot. So I must be getting somewhere.'

She tried to laugh, but it didn't really make it off the mark.

'What happened to the daughter?' she said.

'She got hurt during the getaway. The money was in a caravan towards the rear of the site. A crowd formed around it during the robbery.'

'So they had to beat their way out.'

'Yeah. More or less.'

'Is she okay?'

'She wasn't at the time. Multiple head injuries.'

She drew her legs up beside her on the cushion, rested her cheek against a fist. 'How many is multiple?'

'Three.'

She was quiet a while. 'Have you got a file or something?'

'It's at the office. You want to see the pictures?'

'Not really. I'm just thinking.'

He didn't reply.

She said, 'They had to fight through a crowd to get to the road.'

He nodded. 'They had a car waiting.'

'So it's frantic. They want to leave in a hurry. Why'd they take the time to hit her three times?'

The question hadn't occurred to him before. 'I don't know,' he said.

She said, 'I would have thought if you wanted to get away in a hurry, you wouldn't stop to hit someone more than once.'

'Bit of a half-hearted escape, you think?'

She made a face, shrugged as if dismissing the idea. 'I think the psychology seems a bit off. You want someone out of your way, you hit them once. I don't know. Hitting someone two or three times implies a greater level of aggression.'

It made sense. He saw theories ease out of the shade. That cool internal rush that heralded progress.

'Earth to John.'

He looked back at her. 'You could work in forensics,' he said.

She laughed and stood up. 'Thanks for the tea.'

'You don't want to stay and see if he shows up?'

'No.' She arched her back, spoke through a yawn: 'The Boyfriend Game gets old quite quickly.'

Hale stood up. 'I'd better walk you out.'

'Yeah. Go and get your gun.'

Progress. Devereaux felt poised to announce 'case closed'. *A bit longer and you might actually crack this.*

He background-checked Douglas Allen. A troubled history unfurled. Adolescent drug possession flourished into more serious offending: Douglas had done time for fraud, and injuring with intent. As such, his January third robbery attendance served as strong cause for suspicion.

If only it had been picked up.

He ran some checks on the fictional Douglas Haines. Nothing: police, driver-licence and credit-rating databases returned zero hits. Land Information indicated nobody by the name Doug or Douglas Haines owned Auckland property. A Securities Register check came back empty. To be anticipated, when hunting someone non-existent.

So why did nobody click that this was the case?

He trawled incident room filing cabinets and accrued some fight club robbery paperwork. Attending officers' reports, follow-up documents from CIB, witness lists and statements. It took him three trips to get everything back to his desk.

He scanned the witness lists first. Doug Haines had made page one. An address was noted, but no driver's licence number. Devereaux wondered how he'd picked the name: he'd encountered a few pseudonymous Smiths, but this was his first Haines. He flipped through another folder: crime scene photographs, additional shots that established wider physical context. Twenty minutes in: an image of a neighbouring property showed a Haines Haulage truck, backed into a driveway. Dougie was clearly quite blasé with regards to fake name selection.

He progressed to the next ream of paper: CIB progress reports. The witness lists would have been checked for prior offending. He wanted to know who'd signed off on them.

There were about five separate copies of the actual list, eighty names total. Extra sheets were appended, further information on those with a criminal history. Douglas Haines/Allen was not included. Devereaux re-read the lists. No indication of who'd performed the vetting. He appraised the stacks of paperwork. He could read ceaselessly all night and achieve nothing but blindness.

His desk phone rang. He answered and mumbled a greeting.

'You sound like you need a beer,' Pollard said.

Devereaux laughed and closed his eyes. He put an arm on the desk and sat head in hand. 'Too many Nurofen. It wouldn't be a good mix.'

'You asked me to call you back?'

'Oh, yeah. Thanks. Have I missed much?'

Pollard said, 'They found tyre tracks in the lawn at the Turner address. We matched them to a tread pattern they found at the Haines or Allen place or whatever the hell his name is.'

Devereaux switched off his desk lamp. The dark behind his eyelids lost its bloody tint. 'So it was definitely Douglas who did Turner and the PI.'

'It's stacking up that way.'

'And we haven't found him yet?'

'No. We haven't.'

'You're slurring a wee bit.'

'I'm not surprised. I'm three gins in to a long night.'

Devereaux didn't answer. Around the room, lonely telephones rang in ragged symphony.

Pollard hissed breath through his teeth, easing the quiet aside. 'Look, if there's nothing else, I'll let you go.'

Fatigue left comprehension lagging: auditory input took a second or two to decrypt. Devereaux said, 'Yeah, sure.' He opened his eyes. The mess around him recrystallised, and he remembered why he was here. 'Oh, hang on, wait.' He stirred random papers, trying to keep his brain out of bed. It wasn't even that late. *Get a grip, for God's sake.* 'Are you there?'

'Uh-huh.'

'Do you know who did the backgrounding for the fight club thing?'

'What are you talking about?'

'The fight club robbery in January. Who ran the background checks on the witness lists?'

'It was meant to be Otara CIB. But Don McCarthy had it moved up to Central.'

'Yeah, I know. But do you know who ran the checks?'

'On the witnesses?'

'Yes. On the witnesses.'

Pollard thought about it. A glass-on-glass chime preceded a gentle glugging. 'It was Carl Grayson,' he said.

'Are you sure?'

'Well, yeah. He volunteered for it. I can't think why he wouldn't do it if he asked for it.'

■ THIRTY-FIVE

WEDNESDAY, 15 FEBRUARY, 10.27 P.M.

Devereaux sat at his desk and felt implications drawing clearer. His last conversation with Leroy Turner was getting some good mental air time:

Because cops did it. Because cops robbed that bank. Because cops robbed that fight club thing.

He'd dismissed it at the time. The conspiracy aspect reeked too heavily of urban myth. Plus the gospel according to Leroy had to be taken with a pinch of salt. But maybe he'd been closer to the mark than anticipated. The Douglas Allen angle raised fresh queries. Namely, was Dougie's prior offending covered up, or was it genuinely overlooked? Maybe Douglas had official assistance in keeping his name out of the suspect pool.

As a law-breaking scheme, it probably had potential: a badge-toting inside man. Divert attention should the wrong people come under the law enforcement lens. Eliminate suspects before they were nominated as potentially dubious. Ensure the likes of Doug Allen garnered no official attention.

He rubbed his eyes and saw swimming phosphorescence. It was Grayson who distracted Lloyd Bowen long enough for Devereaux to secure a cellblock visit to Howard Ford. Maybe he'd been aware of the connection between Ford and the late Leroy Turner. Then again, he'd used Grayson's computer to access Turner's details after Ford had revealed the name. Maybe Grayson thought Turner was privy to more than he was. Maybe Grayson cupped Doug Allen's ear and whispered 'Kill him'.

He sat there for another minute, just thinking. Then he found his car keys amid the disorder and headed downstairs. He drew some worried looks — *is that guy fit to drive?* He couldn't help but wonder the same thing.

It was fifteen minutes from the city to Grayson's place off Gillies Ave. He parked in the short driveway beside the house, headlamp reflection gliding orb-like across the windows.

Grayson met him at the front door. One arm propped a sleeping daughter, his neck encircled in tender embrace.

'Hi, Sean.' He sounded tired, not welcoming.

'Can I come in?'

A short pause settled. Devereaux sensed the silent yearning to decline entry.

But in the end Grayson just nodded and said, 'Yeah. Give me a second.' He tilted his head towards the stairs, stepped away to jettison his passenger.

Devereaux took a pace inside and closed the door gently. A light clicked on upstairs. A female voice, and then Grayson's muted tone. He heard Grayson say, 'Sean Devereaux,' and then, 'I don't know.'

Devereaux stayed in the entry hall and waited. A warm domestic odour prevailed: curried chicken, a floral aroma from a bouquet of roses on a small table. Inside the door, two miniature pairs of pink trainers were arranged neatly beside a pair of leather men's shoes. A moment later Grayson came back downstairs, flexing pins and needles out of one arm. His hair on one side was perked, as if mussed from sleep.

Grayson smiled, 'Not more printing, I hope.'

'No. Just a bit of a chat.'

'Good.' Clipped, a hint of impatience. He finger-combed his hair to restore order, gestured down the hallway. 'We'll talk in the office.'

Devereaux led the way through, flicked the light. The shelves rose up, packed to topple. Grayson closed the door.

'We'd better keep this brief, man. It's getting round to eleven.'

'Yeah. We'll keep it brief.'

Grayson read something in the tone. He leaned back against the door and folded his arms. 'What's up?'

A chair was tucked in beneath the computer table. Devereaux would have killed to sit down. He compromised and rested a hand on the back support.

He said, 'You did the background work on the witness lists for the fight club job.'

Grayson's chin dipped to his chest, he passed a palm across his forehead. Bloodshot eyes settled on the window. 'Yeah. Rings a bell.'

'You did check them?'

'Yeah.' He looked worried, tried a smiled. 'What's with the frown?'

Devereaux shook his head. 'How did you stuff it up so badly?'

Grayson's expression slackened. He wiped his mouth with his wrist. Stubble scratched. 'What? What are you talking about?'

'How did you stuff it up so bad? Have you heard what's been happening?'

'Yeah. Of course. The Haines/Allen shit.'

Devereaux nodded. 'And we would have been on to him a month ago if the background work had been done properly.'

'Sean—'

'No, Carl.'

'Jesus, don't shout. You'll fucking wake—' He closed his eyes, exhaled through his nose, opened his eyes. 'You'll wake her up again.'

'Yeah, well. It'll be the least of your worries.'

Grayson spread upturned palms. 'What? This is bullshit. I don't even know what you're—'

'Okay, look. Shut up and listen. I'll lay it out for you—'

'Yeah. Lay it out for me.'

'Essentially, you failed to properly background-check a witness to the fight club robbery back in January. If you'd done your job, that witness would have been a suspect—'

'We're talking about the Doug Allen guy?'

'Yeah. We're talking about the Doug Allen guy.'

'And he gave a fake name, and I checked it out, and it came back clean—'

'Too clean. Way too clean.'

'Yeah, but how am I supposed to know he'd given made-up details?'

'Because it's so goddamn obvious, Carl. That name comes back with no credit rating, no driver's licence, no land holdings. When you hit something like that, there should be a little bell in your head that goes ding-ding-ding, I'm on to something here. So why didn't it?'

Wide-eyed and emphatic: 'Because I ran him through our system and it came back clean-slate.'

Devereaux shook his head. 'Carl. The guy supposedly witnessed a major robbery. You must have realised you needed to check him out with a bit of care.'

'Dude—'

'Dude? Since when do you say *dude*?'

Grayson shook his head. 'Don't heap this all on me.' His

knees dipped and he slipped slightly, against the door. He looked slack and worn out. 'Don't put this on me. I made a mistake. But I can't deal with this now.'

'It doesn't look like a mistake. It looks like more than a mistake.'

'Look, I've lost you. I don't know what you're on.'

'You don't have to squint too hard at things to make it look like you covered for this guy.'

'Jesus, are you mad?'

'One way to justify a fuck-up is to say, well, maybe it wasn't a fuck-up at all. Maybe you covered for this guy. Maybe you knew his background was going to pick up some interest, and you made sure it stayed out of sight.'

'I— Shit. I can't believe you.'

'Why did you volunteer to run the background checks?'

'Please just keep your voice down.'

'Why did you—'

'Get off my case. For God's sake.'

'Carl, I'm pulling rank here. Answer the question. Why—'

'Okay, okay, okay. Look.' Grayson's hands came up. He scrubbed madly at his face. His lips were slack and ajar. 'I've just been so, so stressed out. I don't know.' He smiled weakly. 'I put my hand up for something I thought I couldn't stuff up.'

He shrugged one shoulder, a tip of the hat to the irony of it all. He looked at the floor.

'I'm sorry, okay? I just—, I don't know whether it's the hours, or the pressure of it all, but I stuffed up. I stuffed up. And I promise that's all it was. Jesus. I'm not watching anyone's back.'

Devereaux watched and listened, and said nothing.

Grayson said, 'I heard this afternoon those two guys are dead. You think I'd want anything to do with that? You think I'd want to hold myself accountable for that for the rest of my life? God.

I can't believe you'd even think that.'

He looked at the ceiling and passed a tongue behind locked lips.

Devereaux didn't answer. He saw the guy was telling the truth. He could read human behaviour: gut instinct of innocence trumped all other factors.

He said, 'I'm sorry.'

Grayson moved away from the door and leaned sideways against the wall, held there by one shoulder. He said, 'You keep pulling crazy bullshit like this, people really will think you've lost the plot.'

Devereaux didn't answer. In his pocket his phone purred with an incoming call, but he couldn't feel it.

'Get some sleep or take a pill, or something,' Grayson said. 'But just get out of here, I mean it.'

Devereaux swallowed and opened his mouth to say something. Grayson waved him off. 'Get lost. Just get lost.'

Devereaux opened the door and stepped into the hallway. He didn't see Grayson's wife standing there. He shoulder-knocked her on the way past. In the brief glimpse as he turned to apologise he saw the confusion and fear in her expression. But he didn't break stride. He couldn't. The voice behind him high and rushed: 'What's going on, Carl? Are you okay?'

A breeze sucked the door closed on his heels. Muscle memory got him to the car. He was mentally void. He backed out onto the street and drove up towards Gillies Ave. A red light halted non-existent traffic. Devereaux sat there alone and waited for green.

He drove home. He tried to stay empty-headed. He didn't want regret gaining too strong a handhold. The night was clear and quiet. An ivory moon hung high and fat behind torn-cloth cloud. The harbour immense and sullen as he wound along the waterfront.

It was eleven-thirty by the time he got home. The security light had blown its bulb. He stood on the doorstep in thick gloom, keys spreadeagled in his palm, hunting touch-only. He let himself in and locked the door again, put the kettle on in the kitchen. Hallway lights stayed off, like he didn't want to wake the house. He made himself some instant coffee. Kettle roar and the gentle chime of spoon on glass. The familiar quiet nocturne. It made him wonder what other lonely beverages were at that instant being prepared.

Two mouthfuls of tap water cleansed the taste of a long day. He took cigarettes and matches from a drawer, lit himself a smoke. Winged elbows and chin to chest as he coaxed the tip alight. A grey zigzag tendril as he shook the match out. He held the cigarette in his front teeth and tilted his head back and plumed a long smoke geyser. The kettle clicked. Devereaux ignored it. He stood with palms braced against the edge of the sink and watched his reflection in the kitchen window. When the cigarette was done, he smoked another, dribbled the tap to douse the butts.

He removed his phone from his pocket and laid it on the table. Ellen had rung just before eleven p.m. He remembered the missed call in Grayson's office. He drank his coffee slowly and tried to think what to say to her. Nothing volunteered itself. His brain was verging burn-out, but he couldn't bring himself to stop. He didn't want to break train of thought and squander a chance of closing the whole thing. The downside being that at some point commitment tipped into obsession. Maybe he'd already got there.

Devereaux finished the coffee and rinsed the mug slowly under the tap. He sat back down and the chair creaked, like a wince at what might ensue. The phone waited patiently. He leaned forward on his elbows, blank-faced and still. Then he picked up the phone and dialled. It was fifteen minutes to midnight.

He raised the phone to his ear, caught the final muted purr before she picked up. She said, 'Let's not do this now.'

Like she knew what he was going to say better than he did.

His voice caught, low down. He cleared his throat gently and said, 'I'm sorry. I only just got in.'

'I've been trying to get you all evening. But I can't do this now. I'll ring you in the morning.'

'I might not be around.'

'You'll have to make an exception. For once in your life you can make an exception. All you have to do is answer your phone.'

'Please just give me a minute.'

She didn't answer.

He said, 'I'm sorry I didn't stay. Two people were murdered. I had to go.'

'You didn't tell me.'

'I asked Ryan to tell you I'd left.'

'You could have told me in person. It would have taken you two minutes.'

'I'm sorry.'

'I know. I know you are. But you've got to start doing things differently. Otherwise it's not going to be good for either of us.'

'I know.'

'I don't want to just be some sort of — I don't know — the hanger-on who just talks to you on the phone sometimes.'

'I know.'

'You keep saying that, but I just keep on thinking that you're missing bits of the picture.'

He didn't answer.

'I went to John's this evening,' she said.

'Why?'

'I thought you might show up there. I wanted to see you.'

'I was still at work.'

'Yeah. I figured that.'

He didn't reply.

The phone stayed quiet a long time. 'I worry about you,' she said.

'Don't say that. I worry about you worrying about me.'

'Don't kid yourself. You don't worry about me.'

'Ellen.' He could feel the heat of the phone against his cheek.

'Sean, you're a nice guy. You're a really nice guy. But you've got to stop doing this.'

'What's *this*?'

'It's almost twelve. We'll talk tomorrow.'

She hung up on him.

He swore and thumped a fist on the table.

He redialled. The call connected. He heard her voice, and there was a glorious beat of warm naïve certainty that he could rectify everything. Then the pre-recorded greeting told him to leave a message. Devereaux said, 'Please call me back.'

The phone was hot and slick in his hand. Devereaux slid it across the table, out of reach. He pictured her lying in bed, on her back, debating whether to call back. She probably wouldn't. He crossed his fingers for an uncharacteristic lapse in principle.

No luck.

He exhaled and netted his hands behind his head. A familiar quiet came in and sat down with him. He watched the window like his own hindsight was projected against it: everything he should have done, and everything he should not.

■ THIRTY-SIX

Thursday, 16 February, 12.01 a.m.

Sleep eluded him.

Hale tried to rest, but suture ache kept him edgy. He couldn't shake a heavy feeling of *what if?*

What if the girl's injuries were more than just unusual?

What if he'd been bullshitted?

He endured inaction until quarter past midnight. Then he rose and dressed and took the shotgun with him down to the car. The world dim beneath that pale lunar half-light. He drove east and was at the office by fifteen minutes to one in the morning. High Street was quiet. Balled litter tripped and tottered in the lonely thoroughfare. The façades sheer and deep-shadowed. An almost Gothic backdrop, in the absence of normal hustle.

He let himself into the office, locked the door behind him. Rowe's file sat amid clear desk space, as if expecting company. Hale sat down and brought the lamp in close.

Page one: the pulped and bloodied Charlotte Rowe. The massive facial injuries: the broken jaw, the broken teeth, the broken eye socket. The flesh a swollen palette of reds and purples. The hair knotted and claggy with blood, shaved in places to expose the full extent of the injuries.

Hale browsed. He found the attending police officers'

reports. Photocopied handwritten notes described a 'young female' with injuries consistent with those photographed. No explicit mention of a Charlotte Rowe.

He got up and went to the cabinet opposite the desk. The grog cache had dwindled to a bottle of Cointreau, and some Langs Supreme Scotch whisky. He put a finger of the Scotch in a tumbler and sat back down, behind the desk. He checked drawers and found a phone book, located a number and dialled.

Early morning, staffing was light. It took him a long time to come off hold. He made a polite enquiry, regarding Charlotte Rowe. He gave his name as Detective Sergeant Sean Devereaux. Even claims of official standing won him few favours: divulging information over the phone contravened approved protocol. He said he was just trying to chase down minor details; that is, dates only. He was told the system held no records corresponding to the name Charlotte Rowe.

He tried two more numbers. More hold music, and then a null result in both instances.

The clock hit one-fifteen. He tried another number. He spieled his introduction for the fourth time, made his request.

He was put on hold. Hale waited, pulse in his ear leaping heavy.

'You still there, detective?'

Hale said, 'Yes.'

'I think I've got it.'

'Let's have it.'

Hale listened to the reply, and clicked off. Then he said, 'Well.' He held the glass in his lap and leaned back in his chair and thought about what to do next.

Devereaux didn't make it to bed. He fell asleep on the couch: arm across his eyes, The Smiths on the stereo — the same CD he'd mused to Monday night, post-shooting.

He kept the phone close at hand. He couldn't help but hope that maybe she'd ring back.

The call came at one-thirty. He caught it just before the voicemail was due, and didn't check the screen. From the pause after he answered, he could tell it wasn't Ellen.

Don McCarthy said, 'Hello, sergeant.'

McCarthy. Shit. His wish for a call-back couldn't have gone more awry.

Devereaux said, 'What do you want?'

'We're going to have to work on your basic etiquette, aren't we?'

'Nobody's polite at this time of night.'

McCarthy laughed drily. 'If you go and open your front door, you'll find a large, middle-aged police detective sheltering beneath the eave. Do yourself a favour and let him in.'

Devereaux ended the call. He dropped the phone on the floor beside him, didn't move from the couch. After a minute there was a hammering at his front door.

'Jesus. All right. I'm coming.'

He rolled sideways and found his feet. The hammering continued until he reached the door. He opened up, and Don McCarthy stood looking in at him. Typical wolfish attire: a grey suit, neatly buttoned over grey tie and white shirt. His hair bore a faint Brylcreem gleam.

'Hello, Sonny Jim.'

'Now's not a good time, Don.'

McCarthy ignored him. He stepped inside. 'I think your security light's busted. Shit, it's dim in here.' He found the switch by guesswork, lit up the hallway. 'We need to have a bit of a talk. Where's your living room?'

He didn't wait for a reply. Devereaux closed the door, went

back to the kitchen for his cigarettes and lighter. He went through to the living room. McCarthy was perched on the edge of the chair facing the couch, fingers meshed gently. The ash-heaped saucer still adorned an armrest.

'Smoking gives you cancer,' McCarthy said.

Devereaux lit a cigarette. The flame bestowed ghoulish face shadows. 'I'll risk it.'

McCarthy smiled thinly. Devereaux sat down opposite him, mirrored his pose. A metre or so separation. Devereaux moved the cigarette to the corner of his mouth, secured it with molar pressure. He spoke through clenched teeth. 'What do you want?'

'I've been doing some reading.'

'I'm pleased to hear it.' Devereaux stretched and tapped ash into a coffee cup.

McCarthy's eyes followed the movement. 'A neighbour reported seeing a black Ford Escort leaving Douglas Allen's street shortly after a shot was heard this afternoon.'

Devereaux didn't answer.

McCarthy grinned broadly. He tightened his grip. Knuckles cracked in neat sequence. 'You've got a great poker face,' he said.

Devereaux shrugged. 'I don't know what we're talking about.'

'Well, how's this: your old friend John Hale drives a black Ford Escort. Are we almost on the same page now?'

Devereaux didn't answer.

McCarthy said, 'I thought it was funny you were so eager to get down there. But what could explain it?' He smiled and narrowed his eyes, tipped his head back and forth in mock thought. 'Maybe because Mr Hale called you in a panic and told you what had happened? Am I getting slightly warmer here?'

Devereaux held the cigarette two-fingered, watched the ember crawl nearer as he drew in.

McCarthy stood up suddenly, crossed the room in one step. Devereaux worked hard to suppress a flinch. McCarthy leaned and picked up the cigarette box. He rattled it gently: a kid testing a wrapped gift. 'May I?'

'Please do.'

McCarthy popped the top, inspected the contents carefully. He selected a cigarette and placed it in his mouth. It took him three flicks to get the lighter to flame.

He blew twin smoke trails out his nostrils, set the cigarettes and lighter back on the shelf. He raised an open palm, waggled the thumb. 'Ageing joints,' he said. 'I guess arthritic smokers have to use matches.'

McCarthy sat down again. He held the cigarette delicately between thumb and index finger. He looked at it with deep interest. 'My first one in more than twenty years,' he said. His eyes came up, shined and malevolent. 'You just bore witness to a milestone event, sergeant.'

'Don't drop any ash.'

'I had your phone records checked,' McCarthy said. He returned the cigarette to his mouth, smiled around it. 'You took a call from John Hale at two this afternoon. I trust I'm making sense here.'

He was making sense. Devereaux hoped it didn't show. 'Not really,' he said. 'Talk slowly.'

McCarthy hollowed his cheeks with a long drag. 'Drop the bullshit. I know Hale was in the house. He called you afterwards and told you he was.' He jabbed the cigarette for emphasis. 'The big question here is why you kept it quiet.'

Devereaux didn't answer. He could feel the poker face slipping.

McCarthy said, 'There's blood in the house, he probably left other evidence, too.' He spread his hands, shrugged. 'I don't know, maybe I've lost the plot. Here I was thinking maybe he'd called you down to try to clean up after him.' A smile inched through one cheek. 'Do you see what I'm getting at?'

'Speculation doesn't carry a lot of weight.'

'I'm just tossing some theories around, see where they lead us.'

'Frank Briar was with me. I think if I'd tidied the scene he would have noticed.'

McCarthy laughed. 'You indicated in our meeting this afternoon that Frank Briar isn't such a trustworthy character. But now you're telling me he's reliable enough to corroborate your innocence?'

'I didn't mention anything about trustworthiness. I said he assaulted a suspect.'

McCarthy smoked some cigarette. 'Irrespective of what you did or didn't do, you took the call, and you went down there thinking you should help him out. I know you did, and you sure as hell know you did, too.'

McCarthy leaned back, blew a near-perfect smoke ring ceiling-bound. 'Anyway, bottom line is: I know there's stuff you're not telling me.'

Devereaux didn't reply. It was going on two a.m.

McCarthy said, 'If I have to step out your front door with no more information than I came in with, I'm not going to be a happy chappie. At which point things'll get unpleasant for you and Mr Hale.'

'How many people have you told about assaulting Shane Stanton?'

McCarthy smiled, shook his head. 'Don't act like you've

got chips to bargain with. You pulled a gun on me. Nothing trumps that.'

'How about the fact it's two in the morning, and it's my house?'

McCarthy laughed. 'What are you going to do when they analyse the blood in the house, and find it's John Hale's, and you told no one?'

'I don't think that's going to happen.'

'Stoic. I can almost respect that.'

Devereaux didn't answer.

McCarthy said, 'Look. I don't give a fuck about your little indiscretions. If Hale was in the house, I don't really give a shit. All I want to know is why he was there, and how he knew to turn up. And if I know that, maybe I know enough to be able to find old Douglas. You see what I'm getting at?'

Devereaux watched him. 'You're sweet on this guy Doug Allen.'

McCarthy shook his head. 'Sweet on him doesn't even come close.'

'You think he killed Turner and that investigator?'

'Yeah. And I think he's complicit in robberies dating back to last October.' He fell quiet and smoked a bit. 'Sure as God in heaven.'

'You a religious man?'

'No. I just wanted to say something that would help convey the certainty of my convictions.'

He stood up, slipped his hands in his pockets. The cigarette sat restless on his lip. A light fog lingered at the ceiling. 'I'll grant you full amnesty,' he said. 'Anything confessed within the safety of these four walls will be kept in confidence.'

'Generosity. I can almost respect that.'

McCarthy smiled. 'Touché.' He sized up the bookcase, top

to bottom. He smoothed his tie. 'Perdition catch my soul,' he said. 'You've even got some Shakespeare.'

Devereaux said, 'I wish I could trust you.'

'You can't afford not to. If I walk out that door disappointed, you're going to reflect on this moment sometime soon and wish you'd played things a little differently.'

Devereaux leaned back and crossed his legs. The Don watched him closely, like he could see behind the curtain.

McCarthy said, 'Five seconds, then I'm gone. Be smart about this.'

They fell quiet. Morrissey sang 'Last Night I Dreamt that Somebody Loved Me'.

McCarthy turned on his heel and stepped to the door.

Devereaux said, 'Wait.'

The Don paused.

Devereaux said, 'Hale checked the name Douglas Haines and found it was fake.'

'Why did he feel the need to check it out at all?'

'He was hired to investigate the fight club robbery.'

McCarthy placed the cigarette on the saucer on the chair. He smiled as if something revelatory had just hit. He said, 'So he found the name was a fake. Who gave him the real story?'

'Nobody. He checked out the house and got walked in on.'

McCarthy thought about it. His eyes did a few laps of the bookshelf. 'Bullshit. You're lying.'

Devereaux made no reply. He sucked the cigarette down to the final straight.

McCarthy said, 'Allen ambushed him with a shotgun. He knew someone was in the house; someone tipped him off. So I'm guessing Hale ran some interviews and got a bit of background info before he ran his break-in. Don't tell me I'm wrong.'

Devereaux looked up at him. A stern and chilly focus gazed back. He was too tired to slip a lie past it. He said, 'He spoke to Allen's ex-wife.'

McCarthy smiled and looked away, like past guesses were proving close to the mark. 'The Blair woman,' he said.

He stepped to the door.

Devereaux stood up. 'Hold on.'

McCarthy looked back, across his shoulder. He looked eager. He looked set to kill something. *At some point commitment tipped into obsession.* This was not normal police work. *What's your angle, Don?*

Devereaux stabbed out his cigarette. 'I'm coming with you,' he said.

McCarthy winked. He swung his keys on a hooked finger. 'Glad to hear it, sonny. There's a nice moon out.'

■ THIRTY-SEVEN

Thursday, 16 February, 2.00 a.m.

They took McCarthy's car — the grey Camaro. Left-hand drive, black leather upholstery, a massive three-spoke steering wheel. Seat squabs gave a tight groan as Devereaux climbed in. He caught a hard whiff of cleaning fluid.

McCarthy reached for a laptop on the back seat and set it in his lap. 'Got to be royalty to sit up front in this car,' he said. 'Consider yourself privileged.'

'I'll try not to touch anything.'

McCarthy put the key in the ignition and started the engine. The old V8 settled into a throaty rumble. He squinted and pecked at the keyboard, index fingers only.

'We've got a Leanne Blair down Otara way,' he said. 'That'll be her, won't it?'

Devereaux made no reply.

McCarthy clapped the computer shut and laid it on the back bench. He tapped the pedal and belted up. 'I guess this is what they call an uneasy alliance,' he said.

'Don't hurt her.'

The Don put the car in gear. 'Is that a request or an instruction?'

Devereaux looked across at him. 'You had trouble making that distinction last time around. And I think you came off second best.'

They pulled into the street. 'Don't try to convince yourself you've come along to keep me in line. You just want to see it through to the final credits.'

'I want to see it through to the final credits without you breaking the law.'

McCarthy laughed. 'Your slate's not exactly squeaky-clean, so don't go giving me that bullshit.' He lapsed into quiet. They made it down to Tamaki Drive. McCarthy turned west. The lamp-lit switchback of the road ahead, starkly yellow beneath that immense lid of darkness.

'Here's a case study for you,' McCarthy said. 'Twelve, fifteen years ago I went to question this guy about a rape. No hard evidence on him, but he had sexual violence priors going back maybe ten years. Anyway. This girl, she was seventeen, she'd been raped in a park nearby, and a woman had spotted this guy — my suspect — in the area round the time of the attack. So he looked pretty good for it. But you know how it goes, I went to question this guy, and he refused to come in for an interview, so I talked to him there in the house. And he denied, denied, denied, denied. We've all seen it before. But then towards the end, he suddenly got a funny look in his face and said to me, "I've seen pictures of the girl. Whoever did her must have had an absolutely amazing time." Verbatim, I promise. And while in a legal sense it was nowhere near a confession, it was still the sort of thing that made me want to cut the guy's throat, bone-deep. Bit extreme, so I broke his nose, and six teeth. He never reoffended. So then you ask, well, which is worse: me sidestepping judicial procedure and dealing to the guy, or lack of evidence meaning charges couldn't be laid?'

'Unilateral decision-making seems a little undemocratic.'

'Yeah. But so is rape. People only see black and white. Judicial equality; one system of punishment applied to everybody, all that carry-on. Whereas my experience has taught me that violence is necessary, and appropriate, and effective. And I don't give a shit about whether the current academic consensus is that punching people in the face is not right. Because unless you've actually experienced things at arm's length, I'm not interested in any moral absolutism bullshit that says beating up sex offenders is wrong.'

'Knock around all the rapists you like. Just don't hurt anyone tonight.'

McCarthy shook his head. 'Here's the thing, sonny. Even bleeding heart liberals can be persuaded to admit they don't mind the thought of rapists having it handed to them. But in most people there's an ethical cut-off line that says, "Below this point physical violence as punishment is unwarranted." I've got one, you've got one. And unless you're some crack-head moralist who believes that violence is unacceptable irrespective of context, then I find it pretty fucking arrogant when people, who have not the slightest inkling of the tragedy I've seen, claim that their own datum for right and wrong is somehow more "correct" than mine.'

Devereaux didn't reply. McCarthy clicked his tongue. 'Anyway,' he said. 'That's just my view.'

Devereaux was quiet a long time. At length he said, 'If you find that tonight your particular ethical cut-off line sanctions assault, I might have to help you recalibrate it.'

McCarthy smiled. He reached across and clapped Devereaux on the knee. 'Good luck,' he said.

Hale waited until two-fifteen, then dialled Alan Rowe's home number. It rang through to voicemail. The machine invited him to leave a message. He redialled instead. A woman answered, and Hale asked for Mr Rowe.

'He's still out,' she said.

'Where is he?'

'Sorry, who's this?'

'John Hale.'

'Oh. Hi. Yes, it's Yvette speaking. You watched us play tennis the other day.'

'That's right.'

'God,' she said. 'It's late. Or early actually.'

Hale didn't answer.

Yvette said, 'Well, anyway, he's not back yet, and I'm not entirely sure where he is.'

'Have you got a mobile number?'

'For Alan?'

'Yes. For Alan.'

'Well, it's only for emergencies really.'

'This is an emergency.'

'Well. Okay then.'

She found him the number. Hale thanked her and hung up. He sat in the quiet a moment, and then he dialled again. He had to call twice more before Rowe finally picked up.

'Fuck's sake. What is it?'

'It's John Hale.'

'How'd you get this number?'

'I guessed it. It's taken me all night to finally get you.'

'Right. Here I was thinking you'd gone and disappeared on me.'

'I need to see you.'

'What, now? It's half past two in the morning.'

'Where are you?'

'In town.'

'You'll need to be more specific than that.'

'You actually want to see me now?'

'Yes. I actually want to see you now.'

'So you've got a name then?'

'Uh-huh.'

Rowe gave him an address. 'It's down by the Customs Street-Queen Street corner. You know the building?'

'Uh-huh.'

'We're in the penthouse apartment, up the top. But I'll send one of the boys down to meet you at the street.'

'Give me ten minutes.'

'Oh, okay, shit. You're quite close.'

'Yes,' Hale said. 'I'm quite close.'

A penthouse appointment necessitated a good look. He had his fitted Yves Saint Laurent suit on standby for such an occasion. Navy virgin wool, two buttons. He wore a pale blue shirt beneath it, no tie. Polished black brogues completed the effect. He appraised his mirrored self in the window: professional, self-confident, a pervading sense of *je ne sais quoi*.

High Street to Customs was a three-minute walk. The address was an old heritage building, near the Queen Street intersection. Rowe's minder Wayne Beck met him outside, at the Customs Street entrance.

He looked up from a text message, pocketed his phone. 'Looking sharp.'

Hale didn't answer.

Beck swipe-keyed them through a private access. Two abreast up a broad staircase, the handrail in wide, ornate timber, darkly polished. The penthouse was up on the eighth floor. Beck pulled the door and let him enter first. Hale smelled the liquor on him. Through a short hallway and he emerged into open-plan kitchen and living. To the north, windows framed by concrete pilasters faced towards Customs Street. The back of the Mercure Hotel blocked a harbour view. An empty wine glass stood alone atop a long balcony, as if contemplating a dive.

The living room furniture was low and leather. Five guys in suits reclined in easy chairs. Collars splayed and ties loose, beer bottles perched on armrests. In the kitchen two men leaned against a countertop, loud and slurred conversation attended by a spread of empty wine bottles.

The guys in the kitchen ignored Hale's arrival, but heads turned in the living room. Alan Rowe rose unsteadily from a cream leather armchair. He weaved slightly as he crossed the room, like his balance needed a bit of polish. A half-full tumbler in one hand chimed with lolling ice.

They shook hands. At the far end of the room, a telescope sighted on a Mercure window stood atop a tripod.

Rowe said, 'It's not the best time, but what the fuck.'

He turned to one of the guys still seated. 'James. We use the office?'

James acceded with a limp wave. Rowe paused mid-step to take a small hit off the tumbler, then led the way. The office was behind the kitchen. A window opposite the door looked west towards Queen Street. Below it, two chairs faced each other across a timber desk. A keyboard and computer monitor had been slid aside, short cocaine lines neatly arrayed in their place. A man was hunched over the set-up, a rolled banknote touched to one nostril.

He glanced up as they entered. Rowe spread his arms. 'Casey. Jesus. Place has a bathroom.'

The guy didn't answer. He vacuumed left to right: four lines, five seconds, shivering hard with the influx.

Beck entered the room behind Hale, left the door ajar. 'Stuff's the good shit, eh, Case?'

'God, yeah.'

Rowe rounded the desk and fell in the chair. 'Take it easy with that. Shit gives me nose bleeds like you've got no idea.'

'Just a bit of blow. I've been up since six. You need the office?'

'Yeah. If that's all right.'

'Give me a shout when you're done.'

He walked out and pulled the door to behind him.

Rowe arched his head back and downed his drink, set the tumbler on the desk. The ice had diminished to little rounded buds. He gestured across the desk. 'Take a seat.'

Hale stepped forward and leaned on the chair's backrest. He wasn't going to sit down. 'Nice digs,' he said.

Rowe shrugged, palmed coke residue off the desk.

'Not mine; we just come along for a bit of a piss-up.' He smiled to himself, shook his head. 'No matter how well you think you hold your liquor, there's always a lawyer out there who can hold it a little better. Holy shit.'

Hale didn't answer. He sensed Beck lean back against the door.

Rowe clapped his hands. 'Now,' he said.

Hale gazed back pleasantly. A framed and glassed print of Picasso's *Femme en pleurs* adorned the right-hand wall.

Rowe laid folded arms on the desk, leaned forward. 'I can feel the last eight hours of wine and food coming through, so we'll try to keep this brief.'

Hale didn't answer.

Rowe said, 'You told me you had a name.'

'To be honest, I only said that to get me in the door.'

A silence settled gently.

Rowe said, 'What, you thought I was going to slap my knee and have a good old giggle? Don't waste my time.'

Hale said, 'I've hit a bit of a discrepancy.'

'In relation to what?'

'You told me your daughter was injured during the fight club robbery on January third. But hospital records show she was admitted for emergency treatment on November twenty-seventh last year.'

Rowe shrugged. He raised the tumbler and drank a trickle of melt water. 'I don't see what the issue is.'

'The issue is that I was hired on the basis your daughter had been hurt in the course of a robbery, and you wanted to know who was responsible. And given that that isn't true, I've got two questions: firstly, why you hired me to investigate a crime you have nothing to do with; and, secondly, what actually happened to your daughter?'

Rowe smiled. He was calm, no agitation. 'I appreciate your help,' he said. 'Beck will show you out. Don't forget to bill me.'

Hale smiled. 'I don't really want to drop this just yet.'

'You're obligated to; I don't need you any more.'

'As an upstanding citizen, I feel a pressing civic responsibility to pursue it a little longer.'

Beck put a hand on his shoulder. Hale shrugged it off, but didn't turn around. He said, 'Don't touch me again.'

Rowe leaned back in his chair, crossed his legs. He held his glass with two fingers, rocked it up on its edge. A jiggling foot betrayed impromptu scheming. He said, 'Let's do this somewhere more private.'

Hale smiled and saw his parenthesised logic: *Let's keep this quiet. Let's do this somewhere clear of witnesses.*

Hale nodded and popped both suit jacket buttons. 'Okay,' he said. 'Let's go.'

▪ THIRTY-EIGHT

THURSDAY, 16 FEBRUARY, 2.42 A.M.

McCarthy knew the streets. He was a dab hand at South Auckland navigation. They pulled up three houses shy of the Blair address.

McCarthy winked. 'What do you want: good cop, or bad cop?'

'I'll be good. You can do whatever you want, long as it's legal.'

McCarthy thought about it. 'Legal. Doesn't sound quite as fun as outright fucking badass.'

Devereaux said, 'Let me take the lead.'

McCarthy laughed. 'No way.' He opened his door, put one foot on the road. He looked back across his shoulder. 'Think of this as a complimentary tour. Keep your hands to yourself, and don't interrupt the guide.'

Devereaux didn't answer. They got out of the car and walked towards the house. Ahead of them a stray dog slipped lean and low-headed along darkened frontages. A single window in the Blair house was lit, like a one-eyed doze. A security light clung to an eave, but it stayed blank as they reached the front door.

McCarthy balled a fist, knocked three times. 'Police. Open up. Open up.'

The house stayed quiet. McCarthy didn't relent: he

maintained a high-tempo hammering. Devereaux heard feet scurrying, a faint voice crying, *Mum, Mum.*

'She's got kids in there, take it easy.'

McCarthy paused, fist cocked. He said, 'Fuck off. My issue isn't with the kids.'

He hit the door again. Something gave a brittle crack.

'Police. Open the door.'

From inside: 'Okay, okay. Just give me a sec.'

Steel bolts sliding free, and then the door pulled back a fraction. A classic McCarthy entry: a one-hand shove, a sudden surge inside. Devereaux followed. Straight into the living room: a decaying couch, plastic lawn chairs, curled carpeting, smell of alcohol. Like walking into a hangover.

Leanne Blair back-pedalled, trying to keep The Don at arm's length. 'Who are you? What the—'

'Police. Sit down and shut up.'

She tripped and fell back against the couch. She was wearing grey sweatpants and a faded red T-shirt, the neck stretched to accommodate neck and shoulder. Hair bird-nested by sleep. In a doorway, two boys perhaps eight or ten years old peeped around the frame. Wide-eyed and teary as Devereaux approached.

'Don't you do anything to my kids. I swear to God. You leave them alone.'

Devereaux squatted and smiled. 'Hey, why don't you fellas pop back to bed?'

Quiet suddenly in the room. He felt McCarthy's eyes on his back.

The elder boy said, 'He can't do that to our mum.' Delivered on a wobbling lip.

'He's not doing anything. He's just going to have a chat.'

'About what?'

'He's just going to ask her some questions.'

'What's your name?'

'My name's Sean. What's your name?'

He stood up and took the kid gently by the upper arm.

'Isaac.'

'What's your brother's name?'

'Storm.'

'Well, bring Storm, and we'll get you back to bed.'

Their room was narrow; a thin cartoon print curtain across the window, two foam mattresses pushed side by side on the floor. One wall was a collage of skateboarding posters, a magazine fold pattern crisply inlaid.

'You two just stay here for a little while, okay? We're not going to be here for long.'

'Don't let him hurt Mum.'

Devereaux looked down. The kid met his eyes beseechingly: a bruised and desperate stickman.

'Nobody's going to hurt her. But you have to stay in here. All right?'

Through the wall he heard McCarthy's voice on high volume: *Are you Leanne Blair? Is your name Leanne Blair?*

'Are you a policeman?' the kid said.

'Yes.'

'Is he a policeman too?'

'Yes. He's a policeman too.'

He felt sick as he left the room.

Back in the lounge, and McCarthy was standing waiting for him. He said, 'Thanks for that, Mary Poppins.'

Leanne Blair drew her legs up, hugged her knees. 'What do you want? It's, like, three friggin' a.m.'

McCarthy half-turned and folded his arms. He looked down at her along the aim of an elbow. 'See if you can guess.'

'Already tried that.' She shrugged. 'Just came up with nothing.'

McCarthy put a foot up on the seat beside her. The cushion pinched with a squeal. 'Where's Douglas, Leanne?'

'I don't know.'

'I know you're lying, don't dick me about.'

'I ain't dicking you. Jeez. You haven't even showed me ID or nuffing.'

'Where is he?'

'I don't know. No idea.'

McCarthy watched her closely, switched tack. 'Tell us about yesterday afternoon.'

'What bit?' She looked genuinely confused.

'I'm not the first person to ask about Douglas, am I?'

'No. A dude asked me yesterday.'

'Specifics, Leanne. Who's the dude?'

'The PI or whatever. The John Hale guy.'

'What did he want?'

'He was asking about Doug and I told him and then he left.'

'And then what did you do?'

'I dunno.'

'Yes, you do.'

'Man. Leave me—'

McCarthy bent forward from the waist, close in for a holler: 'Yes, you goddamn do!'

She flinched, raised an arm in reflex. 'Okay. I called him. I said there was a guy asking for him.'

McCarthy eased upright. 'Right, there we are.'

A telephone console was fixed to the wall beside the couch. He ripped it free one-handed without shifting stance and dumped it in her lap. She hunched into the impact. The handset lolled free and hit the floor, tethered by the spiralled cord.

'Man. It's fixed to the wall. It's meant to stay on the wall. The landlord's going to flip.'

'I'm crying inside, Leanne. Ring Douglas now. And don't tell me you don't know the number, because you just told me you called him yesterday.'

McCarthy spun as Devereaux grabbed his shoulder. He almost looked surprised. Devereaux kept his tone even: 'Don't shout at her, don't rip things off the wall.'

McCarthy pushed him back: a big hand hard on his chest, like pushing through the front door. 'Piss off,' he said. 'I told you to stay out of the way.'

'We haven't even been here two minutes; you're already frothing.'

McCarthy smirked. 'Wait fifteen years, get a bit of clout, and then tell me what to do.'

He turned away. Blair looked up at him. 'Ring him why?' she said. Like she'd had the question on hold the whole time.

McCarthy said, 'Because I said so. Because I want to know where he is.'

She looked up at him, sealed shaky lips. She sucked some air through her nose, stoking the bravery. 'How about yous both just piss off?'

McCarthy backhanded her casually. She caught it across the mouth, snapped sideways with the force of it. A rope of spit waved pendulously. She cried out and shied away from him. Her mouth was bleeding. She spat a blood-basted tooth chip.

McCarthy flipped his coat-tail back, freed a holstered Glock, levelled it at Devereaux. 'I saw that look in your eye. Don't go doing anything silly.'

'Don't hurt her.'

'She's trash; don't sweat it.' He nodded at the gun. 'And I guess we're even now.'

He laughed, dropped the Glock to his side. The woman stared up at him, wide-eyed and ashen. The exchange with Devereaux seemed to shock her more than the slap. Violence hinted at a mean streak, threatening a colleague implied outright psychopathy.

She leaned forward. A shaky hand found the fallen phone.

'What'm I supposed to say?' she said.

'Oh, you'll think of something. Just don't forget about the gun in my hand.'

'Please don't hurt me.' She dribbled some blood down her front.

'Then do as I say. Obedience is a virtue, if you want to avoid getting shot in the head.'

Devereaux inventoried the room: the television would do some damage. A plastic chair wielded correctly could cause injury. Or he could just take The Don on without a weapon. Two steps and he'd be across the room. That torturous dilemma: take McCarthy down now while his back was turned, or wait and see if the woman could be coaxed to divulge something useful. The risk with the latter was he could end up complicit in Male Assaults Female. Or homicide.

McCarthy turned around and looked at him. 'Don't move, boyo. Don't say a word. In fact, hold your breath, if you can manage.'

Leanne whimpered, looked up imploringly. 'I don't know what to say.'

McCarthy glanced down. 'How's this: ring his number, tell him it's you, ask him where he is. All right?'

'And he's going to say, "Why you ringing at three in the morning?"'

'And you can tell him that you've been wanting to call, but the police have only just got out of your hair.'

She glanced between them, looked at Devereaux. He tried to smile. 'Just do as he says. It'll be fine.'

'Yeah,' McCarthy said. 'It'll be fine.'

'He mightn't believe me.'

McCarthy said, 'Make him believe you. I don't really give a shit what you say, I just want to know where he is, okay? If you can manage that, I'm going to disappear, and you'll never have to see me again.'

'I don't think I can remember his number, just off my head.'

'Well, why don't we just push redial, and see who picks up, eh?'

'Okay.'

'That thing got a speakerphone?'

'I think so.'

'Good. Turn it on, and then hit redial.'

She did as instructed. A short pause, and then Doug Allen's ring tone sounded: an obliviously mirthful rendition of the *Friends* theme song.

The tune stopped. Static prevailed. A male voice said, 'Hello?'

McCarthy wheeled an index finger: *Say something*.

Leanne said, 'Doug?'

'Ah, shit. Leanne.' He sounded relieved. 'I think I'm in trouble.'

McCarthy dipped his knees. He pointed at his lips, mouthed: Where are you?

Leanne's voice shook. It took a couple of false starts to get the words out. 'Where are you?' she said.

'At a motel.'

'What motel?' She paused, glanced up at McCarthy. 'What motel? I can come see you.'

A long crackle-hiss on the phone.

'Doug? Are you all right?'

'I don't know. I think I've been better.'

'Where you at?'

'I told you. Motel.'

'I want to see you.'

'Ah, shit, Leanne. Is that a good idea?'

McCarthy nodded furiously.

Leanne said, 'What's the place called, Doug?'

'Paradise Inn, I think. Haven't seen much paradise yet.'

McCarthy nodded, signalled a cut-off motion. The woman looked at him, the phone to her ear, lips shined and bleeding from where he'd hit her.

She smiled and said, 'Sweetie, get—'

McCarthy was fast. He bent and slammed a palm against her mouth, muted her instantly. Her hands went to his wrist. McCarthy grabbed the console, swung it high and ripped the jack out of the socket. The cord snapped taut and then leapt free. He wound the phone back like a softball pitch and threw it at the woman's face. It cracked off a raised forearm, and she shrieked. Devereaux heard movement behind him and turned just as the kid Isaac raced free of the door. Devereaux knelt and scooped the boy wailing and pulled him close. He rushed him back to the bedroom, the boy kicking and thrashing against his grip. The second kid huddled and catatonic in the corner.

Screaming in his ear: 'He's going to kill her. He's going to kill her.' So loud he had to tip his head away to stop his eardrum busting.

Devereaux dropped the child back down on the mattress. Urine smell: the blankets on the neighbouring bed were soaked in a ragged ellipse.

'He's going to kill her—'

'No, he isn't. She'll be okay.' Back to the door. He had to hurry. 'I'm going to pay him back. I promise I'll pay him back.'

He tried to help the woman, but she wouldn't let him. Tear-streaked, hysterical. She screamed at him to get out. He left the house and sprinted back to the car. McCarthy was waiting for him.

Devereaux said, 'I should have shot you when I had the chance.'

He sidestepped around the hood. McCarthy moved with him. He grabbed Devereaux's collar, a two-hand choke grip, spun and slammed him against the passenger door. Breath hot with adrenaline.

'Here's my catch twenty-two, sergeant: I don't like you very much, but I need you to help me take this guy down. See the problem? If he's packing a shotgun, I'd rather have you than thin air backing me up.'

Devereaux didn't respond. The edge of the roof bit hard across his shoulder blades. The Don's fingers were savage: Devereaux felt temple-throb set in. He went up on his toes as McCarthy pushed him back further.

McCarthy said, 'I loved that look on your face in there: distressed, but with a little hint of wanting to make some progress. Most people can't go that far. Most people are pussies. Most people forget we've got people dead, and violent robberies dating back months, and approach it all "Yes, ma'am, no, ma'am." Unbelievable.'

He cinched up his grip. Devereaux gagged and grimaced. McCarthy said, 'I don't think he's been tipped off, but if he has, he's long gone. So listen carefully: you can either get in line, and we'll go pick this guy up, or I'm dumping you here.'

Devereaux raised his hands: *I give up.*

McCarthy loosened his grip. Devereaux grabbed The Don's ears and head-butted him in the face. McCarthy's nose cracked. He scythed a knee up, missed Devereaux's groin, hit him in the top of the leg. Devereaux sagged, slid down against the car. He launched forwards and wrapped McCarthy in a waist-tackle, picked him up and slammed him on the road. The Don's breath punched out of him. Blood erupted from his nostrils. Devereaux balled up and attacked his midriff: hard, short punches until McCarthy was a foetal wheezing mess. Devereaux tried to roll free, but The Don fought dirty: he felt hands in his hair, a wet tearing as clumps were ripped free. Devereaux pushed to his feet, stomped on McCarthy's arms, his head, kicked him in the ribs.

McCarthy rolled back on his side and spat blood. Devereaux knelt and removed the holstered gun from his belt, took the keys to the Camaro from his pocket. McCarthy tried to swat him off, to no avail. He clutched his side, pinned him with one eye. 'You piece of shit.'

Devereaux stayed on his haunches. He checked left and right. No bystanders. Dark and dreary housing looked on forlornly. The dog he'd seen earlier slunk in silhouette across the road ahead. He patted McCarthy on the shoulder. 'Don't tell me you weren't warned.'

McCarthy spat blood. 'The gun's not loaded.'

'Doesn't make a difference to the person you're pointing it at.'

He stood and looked around. Blood spray against the road markings. This dismal little scene. He wondered what other squalid conflict had come and gone in that same moment, under that same moon.

He removed his cellphone and called Comms. Paradise Inn: one Auckland listing, a nearby address. Devereaux considered requesting an ambulance, but decided not to. Let him bleed. He thanked the operator and ended the call.

McCarthy had crawled to the footpath. He was sitting on the edge of the kerb, head tilted back, pinching the bridge of his nose. Knots of Devereaux's hair weaved through his fingers. Twin crimson trails ran out along his cheeks, like some garish moustache. Devereaux stood and watched him a moment. A winking aircraft light slid high across the nightscape, a slow and distant arc.

Devereaux looked at the Blair house. All the windows were lit. He heard children crying. He got into the car and drove away.

■ THIRTY-NINE

Thursday, 16 February, 3.00 a.m.

'Let's all take a drive and have a chat.'

Rowe's suggestion. The destination was unspecified, but Hale didn't push it. 'Chat' seemed euphemistic: he sensed strong-arm cease-and-desist tactics were probably intended.

The car was a silver Chrysler 300C sedan, parked down on Fort Street. Beck normally drove, but Hale's presence shook up the status quo: Rowe took the wheel, Beck sat in the back with Hale.

Rowe drove them out onto Queen Street and turned left, uptown. The Chrysler's reflection tracked them ghostlike, a grey distortion leaping big then small, one window to the next.

Hale said, 'You can start explaining now.'

Rowe tipped his head back, firmed up his tie knot against his throat. 'Watch your manners in my car.'

Beck laughed.

Rowe said, 'I've acted for some really shitty people, and not all of them were in a position to pay.' He found Hale's eyes in the mirror. 'So bear in mind I'm owed favours from some pretty unsavoury individuals.'

They stopped at a red light, all alone on that quiet street. To the left, Vulcan Lane fed through to High Street. He thought of the Escort parked there, the shotgun concealed in the back seat. He almost smiled at the stupidity of it.

Rowe propped an elbow on the sill, picked a thumbnail. 'Your ethics are a little concerning,' he said.

Hale didn't reply.

Rowe said, 'I would've thought a cornerstone of professionalism is that you investigate a job only when asked. I didn't think — how did you put it? Civic responsibility — would factor into it.'

'I'm quite progressive.'

Rowe laughed. He looked at Hale in the mirror. 'Your services are no longer required. I get the feeling you're going to take a bit of persuading to agree to that.'

'What happened to your daughter?'

'You're wasting breath.'

'You wasted my time. Three days' worth.'

The light went green. They eased onward. Beck sucked a tooth, watched shop fronts film-reel past.

Rowe said, 'And I offered to pay you. I'm struggling to see the issue.'

'Pull over up here. I'm done with this.'

'No, you're not.'

'Is this a kidnap, is it?'

'No. You got in the car voluntarily.'

'Problem lies in the fact I can't get out again.'

Rowe shrugged. 'It's No Parking all along this stretch.'

'I'll pay the fine.'

'Bad luck, sunshine.'

'Then I'm sorry.'

Rowe's crinkled eyes in the mirror. 'Why's that?'

'If I'm abducted, I'm pretty well licensed to do anything short of murder.'

Beck didn't see it coming. Hale dealt him a low, left-hand jab, struck him in the side of the gut. Beck crumpled into it, dropped his arms in reflex. Hale came over the top with a big right and punched him twice in the face: mouth, then nose. He felt stitches rip, pulled back in agony.

Rowe said, 'Jesus, Beck. Don't just take it.'

The head-hits left Beck stunned and bleeding. He aimed a straight-right for Hale's nose. It was a poor blow. The seat cramped him. His belt held him back. The shock wasn't helping. Hale locked the guy's wrist and held on. Rowe swung them to the roadside: a graunch as the high kerb chewed polished wheel rims, a hard lurch as he ripped the brake. Hale kept his grip on Beck's arm. He popped his seatbelt and landed another punch. Beck caught it on the ear and slumped against the window.

Hale's door opened behind him. He felt hands on his shoulders, around his neck. Rowe dragged him out onto the road. He watched his own splayed legs slide backwards across the seat, dropped and thumped against the pavement. A bleaching dazzle of headlights, a panicked horn blare as a car chicaned past. Instinct made him keep his face protected: he took two punches on raised forearms, then spun and kicked out. He made shin contact. Rowe backed away and took off up Queen Street. Hale rolled over and found his feet.

Beck was out of the car. His nose was bleeding: both nostrils gushing full on. He came in hard. Boxing tactics: arms raised to parry headshots. It left his lower torso and legs exposed. Hale kicked him in the groin. Beck retched and dry-heaved, then folded forwards, one arm raised weakly. Hale tracked around him, a crab-stepped quarter-circle. The injury slowed Beck down: he couldn't match the move. Hale stepped high, kicked him hard in the cheek with his heel. Beck's head boomed and bounced off the sheet metal. He spat a loose arc of blood and hit the road.

Hale said, 'You wouldn't have been much work for Sugar Ray.'

He walked around the back of the car, a man-shaped shroud

across one brake light and then the other. He popped a collar button and checked inside his shirt. Dougie's bullet wound had bled through the bandaging. He should have considered seepage before donning the suit.

The hazard lights were blinking patiently amber. Somehow Rowe had thought to flick the switch.

Hale looked left, saw Rowe southbound on Queen. Hale pursued. The stitches pegged his sprint back to a limping jog.

Rowe turned and saw him coming. 'Jesus.' He raised an open palm, trying to ward him off. Hale swung a wide kick mid-step and swept Rowe's ankles from under him. Rowe tripped and went down. He crashed on outstretched arms.

'Christ. Don't hurt me.' He rolled over.

'I got shot yesterday; still took you guys two-on-one. Stay on the ground.'

He checked his shirt. It was showing evidence of scarlet ooze. He rebuttoned the suit jacket. Down the street the car stared at him, headlights a fierce white, road in vivid relief. Beck was up on one knee, leaning against the bonnet.

Hale said, 'What happened?'

'I don't know what you're talking about.'

Hale put a foot on his throat. He applied gentle pressure. Rowe bucked and gagged, clawed at his ankle. 'Jesus. Don't.'

'Answer the question. If you sit up, I'm going to kick your teeth in.'

A car passed by on Queen. Alone there on the pavement they were unmistakable, but it didn't slow down. Rowe watched with sick longing as it diminished. He said, 'People owe me favours. You've got no idea how much shit you're in.'

'I'll sleep with one eye open.' He trod hard across Rowe's fingers.

'Fuck. That's my tennis hand.'

'Start talking.'

Rowe snatched his hand back, brought the arm close to his chest, like comforting something feeble. 'Beck had a thing for her.'

'Your bodyguard had the hots for your daughter?'

'Yeah. She's a looker; he's only human.'

'Keep going.'

'Look, it's no big deal. He made a move on her, she wasn't interested. He got kind of wound up, roughed her up a little bit.'

'Roughed-up is a bit of an understatement.'

'Well. She's okay now.'

'Where is she?'

'She doesn't live with me. It's fine; I send her money. It's all totally, totally fine.'

'You kept the bodyguard and got rid of the daughter.'

'He's good at what he does.'

'I know; I saw the pictures.'

'So he's wound a little tight.' He shrugged. 'I took it as a good sign.'

'There's nobody around, maybe I should kill you.'

'Don't kid yourself.'

'I'll tell them you tripped and broke your neck.'

'No, don't. Please don't.'

'What should I tell them then?'

'Don't hurt me.'

'Why did you have me looking into the robberies?'

'Just money.'

'You thought I'd find the loot and give it to you? You've got to be joking.'

'No, there's a contract out.'

'How much?'

A car had pulled up alongside the Chrysler. Hale saw a

woman climb out of the passenger seat.

Rowe said, 'I could call out.'

Hale shrugged. 'It'll take them a while to walk over here. Longer than it would take me to break your arm.'

Rowe shut up.

Hale said, 'How much was the contract?'

'Half a million.'

'Why didn't you just tell me that to start with?'

'Well. It's kind of unofficial.'

'Who posted it?'

Rowe told him.

The dilemma: call for backup and hit the motel with armed support, or satiate the urge to finish things himself.

Devereaux called for backup.

The same Comms operator answered. Devereaux explained the situation. The operator told him to wait. Devereaux said the suspect had been potentially tipped off about an arrest, and he had to move now. He didn't wait for a reply.

The Paradise Inn was north of the Blair address, a ten-minute drive up Great South Road. It was a long single-level building paralleling the road, set back behind low metal fencing and a tarsealed stretch of parking. Devereaux drove past and stopped the car on the opposite side of the road, fifty metres out. McCarthy hadn't lied: the gun wasn't loaded. He found a box of nine-mil hollow points under the passenger seat, fed the magazine with damp and jerky hands.

Come on. Get it together.

His own advice kept seesawing. On the one hand: be patient and wait for some help. On the other: you've lost a lot of sleep over this. You've earned your starring role.

He got out of the car, and just stood a moment watching the

motel. A drape behind an open window waved at him limply. He crossed the street, shirt untucked to disguise the gun in his belt. There were half a dozen cars in the lot, no Toyota Hilux. Maybe Doug had dumped it. Or maybe he'd already fled.

There was a double-level admin annexe at one end. He figured reception at ground level, a live-in manager up top. The door to reception was locked. He put a hand-visored gaze to the glass, saw a counter protected by drop-down security mesh. A laminated sign above a magazine rack displayed an after-hours emergency number.

Devereaux rounded the corner of the building, out of sight of the attached units, dialled on his cellphone. A woman answered.

'You realise this is the emergency number, not general bookings.'

'I'm a police officer, I need you downstairs immediately. Don't turn on any lights.'

'What's going on?'

'Please just come downstairs.'

He moved back around to the door, watched the long row of rooms as he waited. After a minute a woman in her early sixties appeared behind the desk, obscured by the security grille. Glow from an adjoining room backlit her gently. He didn't have his badge. She must have decided he looked like a cop. She came through a side door beside the counter and unlocked the main entry. Devereaux stepped inside.

'I told you not to turn on any lights.'

'If I tripped and fell down the stairs, you'd have a proper emergency, I tell you.'

Devereaux pulled the door gently. She sized him up.

'Heavens. You've got a gun and everything.'

'You had any new check-ins today?'

'Two actually.'

'Guy in a Toyota ute?'

'That like a pickup sort of thing?'

'Yeah.'

She nodded. 'Yes, we did.'

'Is he still here?'

'Well, I guess so. Though I wouldn't know if he's left during the night.'

'What room is he?'

'Is he in a lot of trouble?'

Devereaux nodded. 'Fuck-loads.'

'There's no need to talk like that.'

'It's been a long day. What room is he?'

She thought about it. 'I put him in twelve. Only one we had free.'

'You got a master key?'

'You just going straight in?'

'Yeah. We'll see what happens.'

She moved back around the counter, removed a key from a drawer.

'Any of the rooms have a chain on the door?' he said.

'Some of them do.'

'Does number twelve?'

'I can't remember.' She handed him the key. 'Do you want me to do anything?'

'No. Just stay here. There'll be more police coming soon.'

'Will you be okay by yourself?'

'If not, it'll be a sign of something.'

She didn't understand what he meant. He thanked her and walked out. His pulse ran in double time to his step. The cold darkness and the weight of the gun in his hand. The concrete underfoot, the long row of doors, it reminded him of his cellblock visits. Maybe this was what it was like to approach the electric chair. The last dark walk before the end. He made it along to number twelve and just stood there facing the door. The neat brass numerals staring back.

He waited and listened, square on to the door. Like summoning the guts to knock for a first date. Swap that gun for a nice bouquet. A car passed on the road and strobed him weakly. The Glock grips slick in his hand. His shirt clinging. Heart racing at blow-out tempo.

Suicide. You should wait for backup.

He put the key in the lock. The slightest metallic grating. He turned the key and the knob at the same time and stepped inside, gun up.

The room was small. A breakfast bar separated a kitchen in the back from the main living area. A man was seated on the near side of the bar, a shotgun laid across a table beside him, muzzle aimed at the entry. A reading lamp on the wall above his head was switched on. The yellow glow diminished radially into a leaden darkness.

Devereaux said, 'Put your hands on your head and lie down slowly on the floor.'

'I thought you'd be coming.'

'Put your hands up.'

He shook his head. 'No. And don't come closer. Just stay there. Just stay in the door.'

He looked scared, and stressed. Devereaux tried to sound calm. 'I just need you to move away from the gun, Douglas.'

'I can't.'

'Yes, you can. Of course you can.'

'Don't come closer. Just stay in the door.'

'Okay. I'm staying in the door. Just keep your hands steady. I don't want to shoot you.'

'Suicide-by-cop, right? That's what they call it.'

'Yeah. But we're not going to do things that way.'

'You were lit coming to the door,' the guy said. 'I saw where your feet made a shadow. I could have shot you through the door.'

'But you didn't because you want it to end.'

'I never thought that things would go this bad.'

'I know you didn't. But they have.'

'You're a police officer?'

'That's right. Why don't you just come away from the table?'

'I can't. I'm so scared.'

'Nothing's going to happen. You just need to move away from the gun.'

'I saw the shooting.'

'What shooting?'

'In January. In the morning. I saw from the car. They were just meant to be getting the money back, but they killed everyone. I saw them shoot those policemen in the front yard. I didn't want it to go that way. I didn't.'

'Where are they now, Douglas?'

'Who?'

'The men who did the shooting in January.'

'They're dead. I didn't want it to go this way. They were just meant to go in the house and get the money. The money was meant to be in the house, but they didn't find it. It was just a waste of time. They'd killed all those people, and it was worth nothing. I thought it could fix everything. But it hasn't. It just makes it worse. I killed Leroy and that other guy this afternoon. Don't come closer.'

'I'm not. I'm still in the door.' Sirens so far off they could be coming or going.

Douglas said, 'I never believed people could get to the point where they hate themselves. They can. I already do.'

'Just come away from the table. It'll be all right.'

'I don't want to go to jail. I've done time; I don't want to go back.' Siren noise ramping up.

'It's all right.'

Devereaux wouldn't have picked it: offering comfort at the end.

The parking lot entry and exit were at separate ends, like a drive-through. Patrol cars converged from either direction. Everything swamped by siren wail.

'Keep them back. Don't let anyone come in here. I swear I'll make you shoot me.'

'Okay. They're staying back. I don't want to shoot you.'

Huge blue and red tint patterns across the ceiling. 'Your gun's shaking.'

'Why don't you just come outside?'

'I've got the truck parked against the back door, so don't let them think they can come in through there.'

'I know. Just relax.'

Douglas swiped sweat off his brow. 'I'm only thirty-eight, man. I'm young.'

Devereaux heard radio chatter: *Backup units be advised we have an officer on scene—*

'I know. Just relax. It'll all be okay.' Questions forming despite the mayhem: 'Tell me who you're working with.'

'What?'

'Who are you working with, Douglas?'

'It doesn't matter. They're all dead. Everyone's dead. I shot them after we drove away.'

'Where are they, Douglas?'

He got no answer. Doug had tuned out. He grabbed fistfuls of hair, squeezed shut his eyes. 'I didn't want it to go this way.

I promise this is not what I wanted.'

Armed Offenders Squad is ETA two minutes; can we have an updated situation report?

Devereaux took two steps closer. Douglas's lids blinked wide. 'Don't. Stop. Either I kill you or you kill me. That's how it is. Get back to the door.'

'Okay. I'm backing up.'

'No, you're not. You haven't moved.'

'No, look. I'm backing up.' Devereaux braced his shoulder against the doorframe. He looked outside. Two police cars, two officers from each, ducked behind open doors. Coiled handset cables pulled taut.

'How long will I go to prison for? Will I be able to get out? How long will I be locked up?'

'I don't know, Douglas.'

Sweat trails on an anxious face. A methodical dripping off his lower jaw. 'I don't want to die in prison. Please. I promise I didn't want it to go this bad. I promise I didn't.'

AOS be advised on-scene officers report suspect is likely outside taser range, over.

'I can't even pick the point at which it all went bad. God.'

'Douglas, just be sensible here.'

'I'm scared of prison; I don't want to go in. Please, we can work something out.'

'Not here we can't. But you can come outside and tell me everything.'

He shook his head. 'No, I can't.'

He reached for the gun.

Devereaux shot him.

One round to the shoulder to immobilise the hand nearest the trigger. Douglas screamed. He reached across himself with his free arm and scrabbled for the shotgun. Devereaux shot him again. And then again, a third time. Brief flashes in tight sequence. The room in sharp orange relief. Doug took both rounds in the torso, a neat grouping below the armpit. He collapsed against the table.

Devereaux lowered the gun, uniformed officers surging past into the room, securing the gun, checking for a pulse. Devereaux turned and walked outside. That horrid cocktail: ears ringing, the smell of gun smoke, the tense thundering in his chest. A now familiar feeling. He sat down on the bonnet of a patrol car. McCarthy's keys tight in his pocket, McCarthy's gun in his hand, McCarthy's blood on his knuckles, McCarthy's bidding on his conscience.

Someone said, 'Sergeant, why don't you let me take that.'

Déjà vu: it sounded like Monday's script. He handed over the gun wordlessly. Doors were opening up and down the length of the building, gown-clad guests venturing outdoors. One guy was panning a cellphone camera: this'll look great online. Nothing beats YouTube fame.

He went back into the room. Cops clustered around the table. This strange little motel requiem. The shotgun had been relocated to the floor. A thin sheen of blood glossed the table. One arm hung slack, curled fingers grazing the floor. A small tattoo down one forearm read *Mistaken for Strangers*. Devereaux recognised it as a song by The National. He wondered if he'd be able to listen to that track ever again.

He walked out, leaned against a car.

From inside: 'Christ, we've got a pulse. Get the first-aid shit in here.'

Devereaux put his head in his hands. It was Monday evening, redux. He almost wished the guy was dead. One dosage of victim-on-life-support anxiety had been more than enough. He didn't want a second go-round.

People were asking him if he was okay, but he made no response. The moon was still there, high and pale, but down here in this moment everything was red and blue.

O'Dwyer didn't come back to the car for him.

A female officer transferred him to another marked vehicle and drove him to a police station. He didn't recognise the route. Night homogenised the view to a meaningless light show. Someone had traced the word PIGS with a finger against the glass. He sat and watched the letters appear and disappear, phased to passing streetlamps. Once or twice he saw the driver looking at him in the rear-view mirror, but she didn't speak to him, and Sean pretended he didn't notice her watching.

Now he's sitting in a room with a grey-haired woman named Lynette, who has told him she's a lawyer and that she has a little girl Sean's age. Lynette repeats a lot of the questions O'Dwyer has already asked, and it takes a long time because she has to write everything down. When she's finished she lays her pen on her paper and leaves the room briefly and when she returns she sits down and doesn't say anything. She has a smile on her face though, and everything she does is very quiet and unrushed. It doesn't feel uncomfortable being there with her.

The room is very plain. He and Lynette are next to each other at a circular table. The chair is too tall for him, and his feet don't reach the floor. The carpet is hard and grey, like in a classroom. On the wall is a poster showing a mother hand-in-hand with two children. A policeman is crouched, talking to one of the children. Everyone is smiling. Sean thinks that most people who need to talk to the police wouldn't look that happy.

The door has a little window with wire mesh in the glass, and he gets a glimpse of O'Dwyer, outside in the corridor. The top of the window only reaches his shoulder, and he has to stoop for a peep. Lynette gets up, still smiling, and steps outside to talk to him. She leaves the door ajar. O'Dwyer's voice is deep, and he can hear a faint murmur when he speaks, like a sleep-talker in the next bedroom.

Then the door opens and they both walk in. Lynette sits down beside him and aims the smile at him for a short spell. O'Dwyer's carrying a pad of paper, and also a cassette recorder. His jacket's off and his shirtsleeves are rolled up. The sleeves are rolled neatly, but a wide tongue of shirt hem has escaped his pants, and his hair is still a mess.

He puts everything on the table and sits down. The pad slips off the top of the recorder and lands neatly in front of him.

'How we doing, bud?' *he says.*

'Good.'

'You sure you don't need anything to eat? We can get you something to eat if you want. Or a Coke?'

'I'm not really hungry.'

'OK. That's fine. Now, I've got a recorder thing here, so we can tape what we talk about. All right?'

'Why do you need to tape it?'

O'Dwyer leans forward on folded arms. 'When you get to be as old as I am, the things you put in your brain don't tend to stay there too well.' *He winks, pats the recorder.* 'Pays to have a backup copy.'

Sean nods but doesn't say anything. O'Dwyer turns the thing on and says 'Testing ...', *then winds the tape back and hits play. When he hears his own voice he rewinds a second time and presses Record. It looks like something he's done many times, and Sean thinks this whole thing isn't very exciting for him. He thinks it strange that someone's idea of what's normal could be shifted so greatly.*

O'Dwyer states everyone's names, then the date and time. He states the time to within a minute without looking at his watch. Then he reads aloud some things he's written down on his pad.

O'Dwyer looks up. There's a smile in place, but the man underneath looks tired. He looks like he's had enough of today. He says, 'I'm going to run through some questions with you, but before we get into that, is there anything at all you want to tell me, or ask me?'

The recorder makes a quiet rhythmic click as the tape spools reel-to-reel. Sean watches it and says, 'Derren killed her.'

He knows it isn't true. He knows the wife killed herself. But Derren needs to pay.

O'Dwyer's face doesn't change, but he runs a hand through his hair. Grey strands flatten, then spring to attention. Sean thinks O'Dwyer's holding back a bigger reaction: he looks at Lynette, but they don't say anything. Lynette's notes are on a pad of lined paper, and she raises the first sheet and reads something on the second. She does this very quietly so the recorder won't register the crackle. Sean wonders if the right sort of news would make her smile go away.

He says it again: 'He killed her.'

It feels good. The thought that his actions have the power to influence Derren's future. Instead of the other way around. He doesn't think about hindsight, or about the weight of future guilt that could be ascribed to that simple claim. He just sits there, swinging his legs gently, hands jammed under his thighs, as O'Dwyer starts to ask his questions.

■ FORTY

THURSDAY, 16 FEBRUARY, 4.01 A.M.

Lloyd Bowen was never far out of the loop: fifteen minutes post-bloodshed and Devereaux took a call from him on his cell.

Bowen said, 'Christ, twice in one week.'

'I'm not happy about it either.'

'Yeah, I'm sure.'

Devereaux didn't answer.

Bowen said, 'Stay there. I'm about twenty minutes away.'

Devereaux hung up on him. Instructions to stay put only made departure more compelling. He had McCarthy's keys in his pocket. He walked across the road to the Camaro and got in. The creak of leather, some brass shells rolling loose in the passenger footwell. The spirit of the bastard alive and well. Devereaux started the car and drove away northbound, a dozen thoughts fighting for front and centre.

Empty streets: he barely had to lift his foot off the pedal all the way back to town. The city stark and regal ahead of him, neatly bejewelled by window lights. He wondered who else with blood on their hands passed unseen at that moment.

He drove the Camaro into the basement garage and left it in The Don's slot. The night watch was still coming off shift. The lift was full of tired uniformed cops with thoughts of home.

He merited some nods, but no hellos. He walked through to CIB. More empty coffee cups than people. He sorted through McCarthy's keys until he found one that fitted his office door, and let himself in.

He flicked the light. Still and airless, like he'd taken the place by surprise. McCarthy must have visited since Devereaux had last been by: the room was scrupulously neat. No desk mess, just the computer, and the photographs.

He swung out the chair from behind the desk and sat down. The filing cabinet key was present in the bunch. The small size made it an easy find. He freed the lock and removed the file on the January thirty shooting. Quicker than a bent paperclip.

He sat at the desk and read. Fatigue fuzzed out the print. He could smell the gun smoke on his hands. More importantly: he could smell closure.

So close.

Endorphins kept him going. This is what he lived for: the rush of the final straight. That brief elation as he broke the tape.

McCarthy's landline trilled at his elbow. He ignored it. At five a.m. he felt his own phone ring in his pocket. Don McCarthy's name lit up the screen. He kept him waiting a half-dozen rings, and then he answered.

McCarthy said, 'I don't know what I'm going to do with you.'

He didn't sound agitated. He sounded like the gears were meshing.

'Did you call yourself an ambulance?'

'No. I'm tougher than that.'

A long stretch of quiet on the line. McCarthy read something in it. 'Oh, God,' he said. It sounded almost gleeful. 'Don't tell me you killed him.'

A voice in his head piped up: *we'll see.*

Devereaux said, 'I won't miss you.'

McCarthy didn't answer.

Devereaux closed the file. He dropped it back in the cabinet and rolled shut the drawer. 'You recognise that sound?' he said.

McCarthy hung up on him. Devereaux stood in the middle of the room with his hands in his pockets, looking at the desk. After a moment he walked out and closed the door behind him.

He dozed at his desk. Far from comfortable, but he'd done it before. He was tired enough he could have slept standing. The cellphone woke him. He came awake like he'd been dropped, checked the time as he answered: six a.m.

John Hale said, 'I've been arrested.'

'What for?'

'I beat up a client.'

'Rowe?'

'Yes. Him.'

Devereaux wanted to tell him about the shooting. He wanted to admit he'd almost killed another man, and that he feared he'd never forget it. He wanted to hear John Hale declare it a righteous deed, and say *Don't worry about it*.

Hale said, 'You still there?'

'Yeah. Where are you?'

'Auckland Central lock-up. You're my phone call.'

'I'm still in the building. I'll come down.'

'No, just stay on the line. I've got some stuff for you. You got a pen?'

'Just talk.'

It was six-thirty when he left for McCarthy's house. Daylight had arrived, but rush-hour traffic hadn't. It took Devereaux less than fifteen minutes to get down there. The narrow streets;

the houses high and hard-edged. The gleaming sedans nosing cautiously into the world.

He parked the Camaro on the street outside The Don's house. He placed a quick call on his cellphone, then got out and knocked on the door. Footsteps on the internal staircase, and then McCarthy opened the door. He'd changed to a fresh suit. A long cut marred his forehead. Tissue paper plugged one nostril. His hair was shower-fresh. He stood there calmly and didn't move aside.

'Bit soon for round two, isn't it?'

'I wanted to bring the car back.'

'All that hoo-ha about not hurting people and you go and shoot a man. Great irony.'

Devereaux tossed him the keys. They hit him in the chest and dropped, and he caught them one-handed without looking down.

Devereaux said, 'I know what you did.'

■ FORTY-ONE

Thursday, 16 February, 6.58 a.m.

McCarthy took him upstairs. They went out onto the deck, rooftops and early sun dead ahead of them.

I know what you did. McCarthy hadn't replied, and Devereaux didn't push it. He waited to see what would happen.

McCarthy leaned and put his arms on the rail. 'I don't know why I'm so civil with you,' he said. He took a peek over the edge. 'Part of me wants to just toss you on the road.'

Devereaux didn't reply. He wouldn't have put it past him. He had his hip against the rail, arms folded, watching The Don in profile.

McCarthy said, 'How does it feel to take someone's life?' A cruel smile. 'Twice.'

'He isn't dead yet.'

'He's getting there; I round to whole numbers.'

He sounded like he knew the story. Bowen probably kept him apprised of salient bloodshed.

Devereaux said, 'I had to do it.'

McCarthy shrugged. 'Either way, people are hurt and dead, and it's your fault. Hell of a sensation; you're not ever going to forget it. You'll dream about it for years. You'll relive it incessantly and convince yourself you couldn't have done any different, when in fact all you had to do was not pull the trigger.'

'I had to do it.'

'And I'm sure people will back you up. Then again, you can guarantee there's some jaded son of a bitch out there who thinks you just outright wanted to kill people. And you'd better hope he's not the one deciding whether or not you get to keep your job.'

Devereaux checked the time. He'd been in the house three minutes. 'I'm not going to lose my job.'

McCarthy laughed. 'Well. I hope you don't. I think we've got the same blood in our veins.'

'I'm nothing like you.'

McCarthy smiled. 'Cling to that thought.'

Devereaux said, 'I read the file work for the January shooting.'

McCarthy held him in the corner of an eye. 'You can find out all kinds of things when you've got my keys on your side.'

Devereaux didn't answer.

McCarthy said, 'You could have just asked. I might have saved you some effort.'

'What happened to confidentiality?'

McCarthy knuckled his nose plug. 'It's pointless now. It's over.'

'So talk.'

McCarthy was quiet a long time. He palmed something off the rail, dusted his hand on his shoulder. A car passed slowly on the street below them, white exhaust scurrying to keep pace. He said, 'The shooting in January was tied in with the robberies. Long story short, one of the heist guys got cold feet and called for police protection. His colleagues got wind of it and killed everyone.'

A flashback to his stolen file, taken from McCarthy's office: William Rankin, convicted armed robber, dead by shotgun. Police officers Ian Riley and Kyle Miller, granted the same hard farewell.

Devereaux said, 'Who set up the protection?'

'It was unofficial. The guy being watched was already a suspect in the robberies. He got in touch with a police contact and said he needed help.'

'William Rankin.'

'Yeah, Rankin. We pulled his phone records. January twenty-ninth, evening before the shooting, he placed a call to this guy Kyle Miller, who'd interviewed him back in October about the Savings and Loan robbery. Rankin called him, said he had information about the robberies, and that he needed protection. Miller obviously called this guy Riley and roped him in.' He looked out across the street. Morning wearily climbing the stairs. 'And then by sun-up they were all dead.'

Loose ends resolving: Doug Allen's smashed downstairs window. Maybe Rankin had broken in, stolen Doug's robbery takings, then demanded police backup. Doug gets wind of it, masterminds a retaliatory dawn raid.

Devereaux said, 'Douglas confessed before I shot him.'

The Don's eyebrows came up. 'Dying breath?'

'He's still alive.'

'He's in limbo. I think his last words have probably been spoken.'

Devereaux didn't answer.

McCarthy said, 'What would yours be?'

'Excuse me?'

'What would your last words be? If you could choose.'

'I don't know. I think other people's words are the ones that count.'

McCarthy was quiet a moment. He said, 'What did Douglas tell you?'

'He said he drove the getaway car on the morning of the shootings. I asked him who else was involved, and he said it didn't matter because they're all dead.'

'He killed his own teammates?'

'Apparently. I think he drove them somewhere and killed them.'

'So where are they?'

'I don't know.'

'You didn't ask him.'

'He didn't tell me. But I'd guess somewhere along the line we're going to find a burned-out car.'

'With two very crisp passengers.'

'Yeah. Something like that.'

McCarthy glanced at him. 'Did he apologise?'

Devereaux paused. He didn't want to divulge those last shared seconds in the motel. He didn't know why. He couldn't have explained why a good as dead criminal warranted discretion. 'Does it make a difference?'

McCarthy shrugged. 'I always wonder whether these people feel remorse.'

'I think he feared imprisonment. Or death.'

McCarthy shook his head. 'People fear the transition, not death itself.'

'Well, whatever. I think he regretted what he'd done.'

McCarthy nodded slowly. 'That's nice.'

Devereaux didn't reply.

McCarthy said, 'I know you've got a gun on your right hip.'

'Don't forget about it.'

McCarthy stretched one leg behind him, like easing out cramp. 'I might have opened the door and kicked you in the balls if you weren't carrying.' He kept his elbows on the rail. 'But now we're a metre apart, you couldn't clear belt before I broke your nose.'

'Let's test the theory.'

The Don laughed. 'You'd kill a respected policeman on his own deck? Jesus.' He smiled to himself. 'Three shootings in four days. It would have to be some sort of record.'

Devereaux fought the urge to back off. He said, 'They didn't recover any money from the house after the shooting.'

'On the thirtieth?' McCarthy nodded. 'You're quite correct.'

'The file said you were first on scene.'

'You're two-for-two.'

'The money from the bank jobs was in the house. You took it.'

McCarthy didn't move. 'I'd be careful about the claims you make.'

'There was money in the house. The money was the whole point of the raid: Douglas wanted his cash back. He didn't get it. He told me they couldn't find it.'

'We'll never know for sure. He's going to die.'

'I think he was telling the truth.'

McCarthy shook his head. 'Nobody trusts you. You're shit. Your testimony's worth nothing.'

Devereaux stepped things up: the trump card. He said, 'I know you put out a contract. I know you asked Alan Rowe to investigate the fight club robbery.'

McCarthy didn't reply.

Devereaux said, 'Normally, this is the point people start denying.'

'No law been broken; I'm not going to waste energy on a defence.'

'You used stolen heist money to finance an unofficial investigation.'

McCarthy turned away from him, faced the street. Devereaux checked his watch again. Eight minutes inside. McCarthy said, 'Every little piece of your life accrued to bring you to this moment. All you needed was a single different decision out of decades' worth of choices and you could be somewhere else at this instant. But you're not.'

'So?'

'Maybe there's something malevolent nudging you towards a bad ending.'

'I've dodged bad endings all week. I'd say something's trying to nudge me towards a good one.'

McCarthy laughed drily. 'Get out of here. I'm done with you.'

Devereaux didn't move. 'I've got proof. They're going to send you to prison.' He wanted to clap him on the shoulder: befittingly McCarthyish for a parting jibe.

McCarthy said, 'Get out.'

Devereaux swallowed: copper, like blood or bullets on the tongue. He said, 'Why don't you come in and answer some questions?' The first time he'd laid that line on a policeman.

The Don said, 'I used to love saying that.'

Devereaux didn't answer. McCarthy said, 'I'm not going with you. Get out of my house.'

Devereaux held his ground. McCarthy flipped his jacket hem back — fast. He slipped something off his belt. Fist-sized, metallic: that mythic .380. He kept it waist-high, muzzle on Devereaux's gut.

Devereaux said, 'What will the neighbours think?'

'Go back inside.'

'This isn't very smart.'

'Go back inside.'

Devereaux felt behind him for the edge of the slider, stepped indoors. He nearly tripped on the runner. McCarthy followed, pulled the door to behind him. Devereaux looked around. The room wasn't worried: a copy of *Time* magazine lay splayed on an armchair, a mug sat almost empty atop a coaster. A reading lamp's glow had been bleached out by morning sun.

McCarthy raised the gun. Devereaux visualised the trajectory. He pictured a sucking chest wound.

'Hollow point ammo,' McCarthy said. 'Shit's going to get ruptured.'

Devereaux didn't answer.

McCarthy said, 'And to think you could have walked out of here under your own steam.'

'You don't want to shoot me in your living room.'

'I could. I can dress this up anyway I like. You turned up here with a gun. You've already killed two people this week, maybe you decided to make me snuff number three. Top the antagonising boss.'

'Have you killed anyone before?'

McCarthy didn't answer.

Devereaux said, 'You're in for some sleepless nights.'

McCarthy smiled. 'You're in for some lifeless nights.'

'They're going to search the house and find where you've put the money.'

No reaction.

Devereaux felt sweat in his hair. He came across braver than he felt: 'We don't have to wrap things up like this.'

'Use two fingers and take the gun off your hip and place it on the floor.'

'I'm pretty keen to keep it.'

McCarthy laughed. 'Let me know if you're going to get uncooperative, and I'll get that dealt to.'

'Deal away.'

Too glib: McCarthy stepped forward. He swung low, hit Devereaux in the stomach with the muzzle of the .380. The blow folded him. Devereaux hit the ground. McCarthy dealt another big swing. Devereaux took it on the ear. His head bounced off the floor. He saw blue and red light: a motel flashback still very raw. He felt McCarthy's hands at his belt, stripping his gun. Devereaux crawled away, knocked a half-closed door fully open. A quick, blurred glimpse: a ragged loose-leaf collage of paper on corkboards, crime scene shots from the Savings and Loan robbery, close-up snaps of dead men hand-dated thirty January. The Don's home office-cum-brooding pen. A cream leather chair stood behind a desk loaded high with binders. Edward Hopper's 'Queensborough Bridge' hung framed behind. Post-its bearing hand scribbles scattered here and there. He got a good gut feeling. It was The Don's inner sanctum. It was prime territory for a stolen cash cache—

A hand on his collar, and he lost the thought. McCarthy dragged him out of the room. He watched his own clawed fingers raking backwards through carpet. He heard McCarthy nudge another door, and then they were through into a different room. Cool white tile greeted him. His blood so red and perfect against it. McCarthy dumped him against a bath edge. A light clicked on. The brightness seared. Devereaux raised an arm. He didn't even see the punches coming: a quick one-two, cheek then mouth. He felt bottom-row dentistry break. He spat teeth. McCarthy was panting. He sounded crazy. Devereaux pictured him leering and frenzied. Hellbent on a good killing. Payback for all that pent-up resentment.

Devereaux spat blood on the floor. He was better at verbal conflict. Something told him to keep talking. He said, 'It was a lot of risk for not a lot of money.'

It came out wet and gurgled. He lowered his arm. Panic bestowed shocking hyper-clarity: blood droplets were a rich and vivid scarlet, Warhol-garish. A high-tensile buzzing underpinned aural input. He saw McCarthy run a sleeve across his mouth. Maybe he was calming down. He licked his lips, shook his head. 'No. Big risk, big money.'

There it was: admission. Albeit nonplussed and anticlimactic. Devereaux said, 'How much?'

'Two hundred grand-plus.'

The Don tucked the gun in his belt, at the small of his back. 'All you had to do was hold your tongue and you could have walked out of here with all your faculties. Including your life. I gave you the option; you could have left unscathed.'

Devereaux tried not to think about it. He wiped blood off his mouth. He said, 'How was it so much?'

McCarthy's eyes half-lidded. 'What do you mean?'

'The bank and the armoured van were only sixty grand, tops.'

McCarthy listened to the street a moment, face distant. Devereaux felt his phone ringing. There was blood all over his chin. McCarthy tuned back in. He pinched his jacket, two-fingered by the lapels, slipped it off carefully. He draped it over a towel rack and said, 'You remember our talk with Shane?'

He wouldn't ever forget it: the Q and A session with Stanton, that bathroom in Pit.

McCarthy said, 'He told us he had a dealer chasing him.'

'The Leonard guy.'

'Yeah. The Leonard guy.' McCarthy sat down on the edge of the tub. He leaned forward, elbows to knees, took Devereaux's chin in two fingers. He said, 'I'm thinking Douglas had run some thefts we weren't aware of.' He grinned. Spit gleamed on his teeth. 'You're not looking your best.'

Devereaux said, 'He supplemented bank funds with stolen drug money.' His mouth felt fat and loose. Supplemented came out shupplemented.

'Yeah. Or the other way around.' He pushed Devereaux away.

'You thought you could take me one on one,' he said.

'I managed it once.'

McCarthy smiled. 'You're pretty lucid. We'll see how long that lasts, eh?' He leaned and pulled open a drawer.

Devereaux heard metal things. Scissors, tweezers, razors. Jesus. He was panicking. Survival instincts were at odds: fight him, versus keep him talking. He said, 'Tell me how you took the money.'

McCarthy shrugged. 'I got called out on January thirtieth, after the shooting. I searched the house and found two hundred grand in a duffel bag under the floor in a bedroom.'

'And you took it.'

'There are worse things in life.'

'That moral relativism again.'

McCarthy ignored the comment. He was quiet a long time. Eventually, he said, 'Life's such a big crazy place; it's amazing you can get locked into just one thing.'

Devereaux stayed silent.

McCarthy shook his head. His eyes narrowed: that gaze could raise blisters. He bent in close. Devereaux felt his breath. McCarthy said, 'Honestly. You don't know what obsession or addiction is until you've had your nose to it. Honestly. You just cannot understand.'

Devereaux didn't answer. The room smelled of blood and steam. Cheek to the floor, the grid-mesh tile grouting seemed to stretch forever.

McCarthy rolled shut the drawer. A pair of nail clippers in each hand. He worked them idly. 'I just wanted to know who hurt the girl. Just that. Just that one simple thing. You're not going to scream, are you?'

Devereaux didn't reply. His mouth was full of blood. He wasn't sure he could have screamed if he wanted to. McCarthy looked calm. Docile, even on the brink of bloodshed. He said, 'Listen to me a moment.'

Devereaux spat his mouthful. 'I'm listening.'

McCarthy said, 'I wanted daughters. I wanted three girls.'

Devereaux said nothing.

McCarthy's face was empty. He gestured with the clippers. 'People who take people's lives. It's like a giant fuck you to all those others who want children more than anything else in the world. All I wanted to do was find who hurt that girl. Can you understand that? Does that make any kind of sense to you?'

'You're going to kill me.'

'Yeah, but you're different. You accepted the inherent risk in fucking with me.' He shook his head. 'I'm talking about the innocent.' He thought for a moment. 'People shouldn't have to put up their lives as collateral against a normal routine. Do you know what I mean?'

Devereaux didn't answer.

McCarthy said, 'Edgar Allan Poe said something along the lines of man's happiness being derived from the idea something better is just around the corner. There isn't anything better around the corner. This is the peak of the hill. I hope you take some comfort from that. You would have struggled on in this vein for the rest of your life and never made a difference to anything.'

He dropped one pair of scissors, grabbed Devereaux's jaw in one hand.

The bathroom door opened.

Pollard stepped in. Devereaux heard his breath catch. He pictured the view from the threshold: blood everywhere, he himself rag-doll and beaten, McCarthy in his shirtsleeves, poised to take life.

Pollard was shouting: 'Jesus, Don. Let me see your hands. Real slow. Let me see your hands.'

McCarthy glanced over. He didn't look surprised. He looked as if everything was unfolding as per the grand plan. He released Devereaux and drew the gun from his belt, slow.

Pollard said, 'Jesus Christ. Don't. Don't make me shoot you.' Knees and muzzle both wavering.

McCarthy ignored him. He reversed his grip on the pistol, slipped his thumb through the trigger guard. He put the muzzle in his mouth.

Devereaux kept his face blank. A tough look-away-or-keep-watching dichotomy. He didn't want to indulge the guy's desire to evoke shock. Maybe a last sick wish, unfulfilled.

Pollard said, 'Oh, shit. Don't. Don, don't.'

McCarthy smiled, tombstone teeth light on the barrel, like holding a fat cigar. 'I'll be seeing you, sonny,' he said. 'Rest easy. Only the dead know your bad side.'

And then he pulled the trigger.

The shot blew out the back of his head. Skull and brain matter sprayed the tiles behind him. The bath caught a big gore arc. Pollard ducked in reflex.

McCarthy's head tipped forward, chin to chest. A slack arm released the pistol. It hit the floor with a thud. The muzzle leaked a careful, gentle plume. Devereaux crawled away, tried to stay clear of the blood.

Backup arrived shortly afterwards. They were separated for questioning. Pollard was interviewed downstairs, Devereaux stayed in the living room. A uniformed sergeant took his statement while a paramedic patched him up. Devereaux kept details lean. He said he'd arrived at the house and McCarthy had assaulted him. He said The Don shot himself when confronted by Pollard. He didn't explain why he was in the house. He omitted details of the conversation that preceded the attack. They pushed him for specifics. Devereaux said he'd discuss the matter with Lloyd Bowen.

Bowen showed at seven forty-five. Devereaux was outside on the deck. The inspector walked to the door of the bathroom and stood there a moment. He and The Don went back years. The suicide news must have left him numb: a crime scene tech's question bounced straight off. He ran a hand down his tie and turned and came outside onto the deck. He was keeping it together well: a good blank face was on display. *A hard edge of a man.*

Devereaux was propped on the rail, facing the window.

Bowen stood beside him and looked out over the street. He removed silvered aviator shades from a jacket pocket without looking down. Two neat clicks as he unfolded them. 'I told you not to leave the motel.'

'I needed to come here.'

'So you could drive him to suicide?'

Bowen donned the glasses and looked at him. Devereaux saw his own reflection: a distorted miniature in each curved lens. He said, 'I didn't drive him to anything.'

'You don't look like you should be standing.'

He didn't feel like he should be standing either. His head was throbbing. His mouth felt raw. But he didn't want to take a stretcher and risk having Bowen bedside. The idea of being talked down to didn't thrill him.

'What are you doing here, sergeant? And don't fuck me about. I haven't had my coffee.'

Devereaux told him. Bowen listened blankly: calm verging on boredom. 'You think he was in possession of stolen money?'

'Yes.'

'A senior police officer complicit in theft?'

'I've heard of stranger things.'

'But that's your contention?'

Devereaux nodded. 'I think he was complicit in all kinds of stuff.'

Bowen eyed him humourlessly. 'Who needs respect for the dead, eh?'

Devereaux turned and put his hands on the railing. 'He was going to kill me. The respect might take a little while to surface.'

Across the road he could see kettle steam condensing against a window. A half-height curtain framed toast being buttered. Maybe nobody knew they had a dead neighbour. The buildings all huddled on their narrow streets, the lives within so perfectly separate, devoid of overlap.

Bowen said, 'I don't know whether to hope you're wrong or not.'

'If I'm wrong, he wouldn't have beat the shit out of me.'

Bowen didn't reply.

Devereaux said, 'I told him I knew he'd stolen money from the crime scene after the shooting in January. He denied it and told me to leave. I didn't, so he attacked me.'

'And then shot himself?'

'Pollard walked in on everything. I guess he felt he didn't have many other options.'

'What was Pollard doing here?'

'I called him from the car before I came inside.'

'A cynic might interpret that as some kind of premeditation.'

Devereaux said, 'A cynic might interpret that as a naïve and PR-centric remark.'

'PR-centric?'

'If McCarthy was a crook, you're not going to come out of this looking too good.'

Bowen let the comment slide. He said, 'Why did you feel you needed to call Pollard?'

'I thought there was a good chance of things going bad.'

'But you didn't want to wait for more backup.'

'Bad is relative. I thought things might get uncivilised as opposed to horrific.'

Bowen watched him a while. He said, 'You're keeping it together well.'

'I don't find it all that sad.'

Bowen turned and looked at his reflection in the ranch slider. He folded his arms. 'You think we're going to search the place and find stolen money?'

He wouldn't have bet his life on it. He said, 'I'd bet my life on it.'

Bowen said, 'So what's the motive?'

'Not like you to actually believe something I say, Lloyd.'

'It's inspector, or sir.'

Devereaux didn't answer.

Bowen said, 'What's the motive?'

'He wanted to find who hurt the girl during the fight club robbery in January.'

'That doesn't sound like a motive.'

'He issued a contract to find who was responsible. He had a lawyer named Alan Rowe looking into it. Rowe hired a private investigator to work the case, on the basis it was Rowe's own daughter who'd been hurt.'

Bowen contemplated for a moment. 'And I'm guessing this aforementioned investigator is your old colleague John Hale.'

'You don't miss much.'

Bowen stepped to the ranch slider. 'Wait here. If you leave the scene, I'll have you arrested.'

'I thought you'd want to stay and bargain with me.'

Bowen moved back to the railing, looked down at the street. 'You sound like you're building up to threaten me with something.'

'I was actually going to make a request first.'

'First.'

Devereaux didn't push it.

Bowen said, 'I'm listening.'

Warm toast smell riding a warm breeze. Devereaux said, 'I want to keep my job, and I don't want any charges brought against John Hale.'

'I don't have unilateral control.'

'But you have clout. You can make stuff happen. Or stop it from happening.'

'Why would I want to do that?'

Devereaux directed a nod indoors. 'You've got a senior detective implicated in major crime. You really need to keep a lid on it.'

'You're not going to spread the story.'

'If I'm no longer employed, I'll have no reason not to.'

Bowen didn't answer. The sunglasses obscured inner workings.

Devereaux said, 'Certainly, John Hale isn't obliged to keep his mouth shut.'

Bowen looked at him. 'You seem very confident.'

And yet he wasn't feeling it. Devereaux said, 'You don't seem all that shocked he's dead.'

'Neither do you. And it's your reaction that's most important.'

'Because?'

'No reason. You normally carry a gun around with you?'

'Only when accusing people of theft.'

'You know how he sustained those head injuries?'

'I don't want to discuss this any further.'

Bowen smiled. 'The number of guilty men I've heard say that.'

Devereaux didn't answer.

Bowen moved back to the slider. 'You'll know by the end of the day,' he said.

'About what?'

'If we find cash on the premises, you're off the hook. Otherwise, I need to book you in for a talk.' He paused on the threshold. 'You'd better pray to God Doug Allen doesn't die.'

He stayed on the deck a long time. Nobody joined him. People knew his place in the scheme of things: *he was here when it happened. He saw Don McCarthy shoot himself in the head.*

Frank Briar showed up. He checked out the bathroom, but he didn't hang around. He saw Devereaux through the glass and came outside to join him.

'You prick. You killed him.'

'If only.'

'What's that supposed to mean?'

Devereaux didn't answer. Briar came close. Devereaux smelled alcohol: maybe a swig of something before he left home, to take the hard edge off the news.

Briar said, 'People know you didn't like him. People know you were scared of him. You'll go down for this. You are going to fucking burn.'

Devereaux didn't move. Briar was bigger than him: one nudge would send him backwards onto concrete. Devereaux said, 'I know what you did to Leroy Turner. I know what that pig Blake did to Howard Ford. I only hope you have the decency to do what McCarthy did, before I have to do it myself.'

Last straw: Briar grabbed him by the throat and shoved him

hard, screaming something wild, arching him back over the rail, his torso hanging in fresh air. He clung to the rail, eyes clenched, until the slider opened and the officers from inside pulled Briar away from him.

He went outside and found a patrol car and shut himself in the back. That sudden lovely quiet. He called custody at Auckland Central Police and asked for Hale.

'This isn't reception at the fucking Hilton.'
'Put John Hale on.'
He waited out a spell of complaining.
Hale came on the line. He said, 'What happened?'
'McCarthy's dead.'
'You killed him?'
'No, he shot himself in the head.'
'So it's over.'
'Yeah. It's done.'
'Tell me what happened.'

Devereaux walked him through the morning. When he'd finished talking Hale said, 'I'm going to get a dog.'
'Why?'
'Because I want one. I met one called Gerry the other day.'
'Who does he belong to?'
'Hopefully, nobody yet. I'm going to go and get him from the SPCA.'
'You haven't had a dog in ages.'
'I know. I had an epiphany in jail. I need a dog.'
'Okay.'
'When you visit we can walk it.'

Devereaux watched cops and ambulance men exit McCarthy's front door. A latex symphony as gloves were torn free. He saw an empty stretcher carried out. He could smell his own blood on the hand holding the phone. He said, 'All right, good. We'll do that.'

The call came through that afternoon: gold Nissan Maxima found abandoned south of Auckland, two men KIA in the back. Devereaux had taken the afternoon off, but Comms dialled him direct. He decided to check it out. He wasn't dire: a doctor had diagnosed mild concussion. He'd been given painkillers and a dental referral. A drive wouldn't be fatal.

The car had been left on the verge of a small country road, not far off the main highway. It had probably been sitting there since January thirtieth. Passing traffic was meagre: two weeks before someone twigged the Nissan was more than just your standard breakdown.

Devereaux got down there just before two. He was calm. McCarthy's death hadn't rattled him. It was relief more than shock. He'd made it to the end credits, and he couldn't help but feel good about it.

Highway cops had taped off the street. A couple of patrol cars and an unmarked were queued up behind the cordon edge. Pine trees lined one side of the road: Devereaux parked in close to try to catch some shade. He got out and badged his way past the uniforms at the tape. Facial bruising drew some stares. He went and checked out the car.

It was missing both back windows. The rear windscreen had been blown out. Buckshot damage pockmarked the roof. Two bodies occupied the back seat. They'd been shotgunned, head and chest. The nearest passenger was missing the left half of its skull. The right half was still intact, edged roughly by torn flesh. The entire rear of the cabin had been spattered bloody. The whole thing rancid and heaving with flies.

He put a cigarette in his mouth, but didn't light it. He walked a wide loop of the car. No glass underfoot, no bloodstains extant. He checked the front of the car. The plates had been switched: the bumper tags didn't match the registration sticker in the windscreen. Devereaux called Comms on his cell and requested a vehicle check: the bumper plates came back to one Avis Crocker, of Greenlane, Auckland. The registration sticker came back to a Glyn Giles. He recalled Don McCarthy's questioning of Shane Stanton on Tuesday night: *Someone said the name Glyn Giles. That's all I heard, I swear. Giles.*

Devereaux thanked the operator and ended the call. He ducked under the tape and walked back up the road. Frank Briar was seated in the driver's seat of the unmarked, cell to his ear. Devereaux waited for the call to wrap up, then headed over. Briar buzzed his window down. His temper seemed to have downgraded since that morning: he looked pissed off rather than livid.

'Don't light that thing while you're standing on a crime scene.'

Devereaux leaned on the roof. 'He pulled over ten minutes north up the road and shot them.'

'That's very precise.'

'He didn't kill them here. And he wouldn't have wanted to drive very far with the car in that state. Ten minutes, maximum.'

Briar said, 'I don't know what I'd do without you.'

'You look a bit off. Do you miss Don?'

'Fuck you.'

'They uncovered a hundred and sixty-five grand in stolen cash from his home this morning.'

'Great. What has that got to do with anything?'

Devereaux thrummed his fingers on the roof. 'All told, there should be over two hundred. Either he spent some, or someone else has the rest.'

'Good maths. Why the fuck are you telling me?'

'You look mighty confused.'

Briar didn't answer.

Devereaux said, 'McCarthy found the money in the house after the January thirtieth shooting. More than two hundred grand, and he stole it. Except that's a lot of money to move off a crime scene unnoticed, unless you pay someone to turn a blind eye.'

'You sound like you're about to accuse me of something.'

Devereaux stepped away from the car. Briar looked like he might be about to climb out, but he stayed seated.

Devereaux said, 'Someone else knew about the theft, and McCarthy paid them to keep quiet. I know you were on scene after the January thirtieth shootings, and I know you showed up not long after Don did.'

Briar didn't answer.

Devereaux said, 'Most of it was stolen drug money. It belonged to this guy Leonard I asked you about the other day. Apparently, he wants it back so if you've got it hidden somewhere, you might want to at least find out what he looks like.'

Briar said, 'Take your bullshit elsewhere.' The window went up.

Devereaux stepped in close. He said, 'McCarthy paid someone off. Whoever it was, I'm going to find them, and take them down so hard they won't feel themselves hit the ground.'

The glass made him shout. He drew some bemused looks from over by the tape. Devereaux walked away. He lit the cigarette and got back into his car, then drove back to the highway.

■ FORTY-TWO

THURSDAY, 23 FEBRUARY, 10.59 A.M.

She had hints of old injuries: scarring around the mouth, around the brow where she'd been struck. Her nose hadn't been set straight.

Hale stayed in the hallway as she opened the door. He kept his licence up and open. 'Charlotte Rowe?'

She nodded. He knew she was twenty-three, but she could have passed for younger. 'Can I help you?'

'My name's John Hale. I'm a private investigator.'

'I see that.'

She hadn't been joking, but he smiled. 'You mind if I come inside a moment?'

'What's this about?'

'I just wanted to talk to you about your father.'

'What's happened to him?'

'Nothing. He's fine.' A white lie: Rowe was recovering well.

She moved away and didn't reply. Disappointed maybe. He entered and closed the door behind him. The address was a two-room studio apartment on Albert Street. The building itself was just a bland matrix of tiny units, like a wall of post office boxes — pigeonhole accommodation. The living room had space for a table and two chairs and little else. The window overlooked a left-right flurry of traffic. Across the street an alleyway stretched away, grey and derelict, walls scaled by paste-on bills like a pelt of wet feathers.

'I'd offer you tea, but I'm fresh out.' Polite. The antithesis of Rowe senior.

'It's fine. I won't stay long.'

There were open textbooks and papers covering the table. She swept them together deftly in a neat stack and dropped them on the floor.

'Don't shift anything on my account.'

She shrugged, but didn't reply.

He said, 'What are you studying?'

She pretended she hadn't heard. It was a pointless question anyway. He knew the answer, just like he knew everything else: he knew her mother had been dead twenty years, he knew she'd been in here three months, he knew her meagre bank balance was bolstered by regular payments courtesy of Rowe senior.

Most importantly: *he knew what had happened.*

He watched her eyes and spoke carefully, so there'd be no misunderstanding. That heavy little sentence: 'I know what happened.'

She leaned against the window and folded her arms, the table between them. 'Sorry?'

He read it as faked confusion: maybe some residual denial. 'I know your father's bodyguard hurt you.'

The ruse withdrew. She looked at him calmly. 'Congratulations.'

'I'm not trying to offend you.'

She shook her head, smiled slightly. She was tall and lean. Nothing like Rowe senior. 'No, I'm sorry. I know you're not.'

'Your father hired me to investigate a series of robberies. A girl about your age was injured during a theft earlier this year. He told me it was you.'

'God, what? No, it definitely wasn't me.'

'I'm aware of that.'

'I can't believe it. He pretended I'd been hurt in a robbery?'

'Yes.'

She said, 'What happened to the girl who was hurt?'

'She was hit in the skull with a hammer. She's severely brain-damaged.'

'When was this?'

'Earlier this year.'

'Oh, God. Was this that thing back in January?'

'Yes.'

'What happened?'

Hale gave a rundown of the fight club robbery. He gave what he hoped was a tamer version of events. He wasn't sure how much she'd read or already knew.

'Will she be okay?'

'I don't know. I think she'll need a lot of help.'

She leaned against the window. Her reflection stood back to back. 'And my father saw her as a great opportunity.'

Hale didn't answer. She looked embarrassed, waved the comment off. 'Sorry. That's a horrible thing to say.'

'Well, I think he did see her as an opportunity.'

She said, 'I'm sorry. I'm sorry he wasted your time.'

'Don't apologise. You had nothing to do with it.'

She kept her eyes on the street. 'I haven't spoken to him in three months.'

'It's probably a good thing.'

She didn't answer. He kicked himself for being so offhand. He said, 'There was reward money. He wanted it.'

'How much?'

'Six figures' worth.'

She shook her head. 'Nothing if not greedy.'

Hale waited for more. She asked him how he'd discovered what happened to her, and Hale told her. He omitted violent particulars: no mention of what he'd done to Beck, no mention of Mr Rowe's flustered footpath confession.

She listened quietly to his distilled recountal, then said, 'He's a disgrace, I hate him.' She turned from the window. 'I'm sorry he wasted your time.'

I hate him. It seemed considered. It seemed like the product of protracted musing. There was vehemence in it.

'Don't apologise. I'm glad he hired me.'

She didn't answer.

Hale said, 'You never told anyone.'

'Sorry?'

'You were assaulted, but the police have no record of it.'

She shrugged. 'He gives me money. I need him for the money. I need him to pay for this place. There's like an implicit agreement. I keep my mouth shut, my father coughs up for the rent.'

He reached forward and placed an envelope on the table. 'Don't open it now.'

She frowned, untrusting. She reached forward quickly and grabbed it off the table, removed the cheque from inside. A thumb in the fold made it yaw gently.

'Holy shit. Nine hundred thousand dollars. Are you kidding? Shit. Is this a joke?'

He shook his head. 'It's good. I promise.'

'I can't accept this. God. I've only just met you.'

She was shaking. She pulled a chair back and sat down at the table.

Hale said, 'It's not my money.'

She looked up. 'What, you stole it?'

'No. I did a job and got paid on commission. But it's too much. I don't want it.'

'What sort of job pays this kind of commission?' She waved the cheque for emphasis. He glimpsed his signature. Point nine of a million, bequeathed with a Bic and a flourish.

'I recovered ninety million dollars.'

'And took one per cent?'

He nodded.

She said, 'Not many people would have second thoughts about that sort of arrangement.'

'I think you need it much more than I do.'

'I don't know whether to be grateful or offended.'

'I don't really give a shit. Please just take it.'

She looked shocked; he raised a placating hand. 'I'm kidding. But please just take it.'

She held the cheque in two hands, folded it open and then closed. She smiled slightly. 'You look like the sort of guy who'd say: "Hale, John Hale."'

He laughed. 'I save that for the evening appointments.'

'Look, I don't know what to say.'

'Just say thanks and put it in your pocket.'

'Wow. This is unbelievable. I didn't think people did this in real life.'

He said, 'I don't make a habit of it. But I like the idea of good fortune trumping misfortune. It's a better feeling than having nine hundred thousand dollars sitting in the bank.'

'Really?'

'For now at least.'

She slipped the cheque back in the envelope. 'I'm studying biology. I'm in my final year.'

'Do a PhD. You can afford it.'

He saw tears welling. 'God. I don't know what to say. I'm just ... Thank you very, very much. I can't believe this.'

He left her in a daze at the table.

▪ FORTY-THREE

Thursday, 23 February, 11.41 a.m.

He didn't think he'd be so nervous: sweats and a thumping heart. Who knew going back would be so hard.

Devereaux stood on the porch and knocked on the door, knuckles versus cracked paint. A dreadful quiet before it opened. Derren stood there in its absence, blank-eyed and unsurprised. Two decades of non-contact, and the visit still seemed expected. He smiled and said, 'Thank God you finally grew.'

The first words he'd heard from him in more than twenty years.

Devereaux shrugged. 'A couple more inches wouldn't have gone amiss.'

He thought of all the dark evenings spent drafting what he'd one day get to say. That long-rehearsed indictment, squandered. First words only come once.

Derren turned, tilted his head towards the house behind him. 'You want a cup of tea?'

Devereaux nodded. 'Yeah. Why not?'

They went in. He took a glance back outside as he crossed the threshold. He remembered himself as a ten-year-old, sitting in an unmarked at that very kerb. The back seat with O'Dwyer. The shy, dry crackle as he unwrapped his gum. Everything he'd told him and everything he hadn't.

The kitchen had been modernised: lino for timber, stainless steel for granite. Derren flicked on the jug. Twenty years hadn't served him too badly. He'd gained wrinkles and a paunch, but bench press time had kept him big through the shoulders. A body well cast for its role: military man, verging on retirement.

An awkward period of floor-gazing as they waited for the tea. Their last shared experience long ago and best forgotten.

They had the tea on the back deck. A veranda cast a wide band of shade. Side by side on plastic chairs, a wobbling metal table between them.

Derren took a cautious sip, made a cautious comment. 'I heard you became a policeman.'

'I did. I still am.'

'I thought about it a while, but then it didn't really take much thinking. Seemed like a natural choice. Person like you.'

Devereaux didn't answer. He sampled the tea: too milky, too sweet.

Derren said, 'So what's on your mind?'

Devereaux set his mug on the table. He popped his cuff buttons and slid his sleeves to his elbows. He lit a cigarette. 'What do you mean?'

Derren said, 'First visit in twenty years; I thought you'd either tell me something or ask me something.'

Devereaux watched fumes unravel. He made a shape with his mouth, a sort of facial shrug. 'I always thought I'd have some things to say if I saw you again. Now I'm here, I don't.'

Derren nodded. He watched the rear fence. It had been reinstated in fresh timber. Devereaux remembered kicking a ball against its predecessor. He remembered dislodging a board and paying for it in fevered lashes. The bench press and shed were still present, all these years later, grass still tufted at their feet. Derren said, 'Always made me sad you never called or anything. I would have liked a visit.'

'You could have called me. Or visited.'

'Always figured if you wanted to see me, you'd come. Figured with you being a policeman you could find me right quick.' He smiled. 'Although I'm in the same house so it wouldn't have been too hard.'

'I used to be terrified of you. For a long time I was adamant I never wanted to see you again.'

'But here you are. Maybe you've hardened up.'

'Maybe.'

'Are you married?'

'No.'

'So no kids?'

'No kids.'

'Girlfriend?'

'Kind of.'

'What does that mean?'

'It means things could be better.'

'You like her?'

'Uh-huh.'

'Does she like you?'

'Most of me. But there's a reasonable portion she doesn't like.'

No answer.

Devereaux said, 'So how have you been?'

'Do you really care?'

Devereaux thought about it. 'Yes, I really care.'

Derren cleared his throat. He swallowed. 'I got cancer. I don't have all that long.'

'Where is it?'

'Throat. Oesophagus.'

'Well. I'm sorry about that.'

'Look. I know I did some bad things a long time ago. I know I shouldn't have treated you the way that I did. But it was a long time ago and I hope we're not going to end up with bad blood between us while we've both got sun on our skin.'

Devereaux blew smoke into the yard. 'How long have you got?'

'Months. Maybe a year or so. They say throat cancer's hard to catch. Normally, by the time they pick it up it's spread, or, what's the word?'

'Metastasised.'

'Yeah. Metastasised. Which is what mine's done. It's in my lymph nodes. Doctor could feel it.'

'I'm very sorry to hear that.'

'You'll be next, if you don't give them things up.'

'It doesn't really bother me.'

'Why?'

'I have very little to live for.'

'It's the things you don't have that make life worthwhile.'

'Because you've got something to work towards?'

Derren shrugged. 'I don't know. It was my father's saying. But I guess that's what he meant.' He sucked a tooth gently. 'It's funny. Reminds me of being a kid and starting a new school. You think you're going to cope with it. But then it's the day and you turn up at the gates and suddenly it's a whole different kettle of fish. You wonder how all the time you had leading up to that moment managed to slip past you.'

'Apparently, we don't fear death, we fear the transition.'

'Who told you that?'

'Another cop. He shot himself in the head.'

'Well, I guess that's all well and good. With throat cancer there's supposed to be a good chance of drowning in your own chuck. Whether that's fearing death or the transition, I don't really care. But I'm mighty worried about it. It's strange, though. I get tired, but I don't feel that off-colour. Healthiest dead man I ever heard of.'

'How old are you?'

'Not old enough.'

Devereaux got up and tapped ash on the lawn, sat back down again. He said, 'You remember the night it happened?'

It. The bathtub and the blood.

'Like I'd forget or something?'

'The police interviewed me. There was a guy called O'Dwyer.'

'I remember.'

'He asked me what happened, and I lied to him. I said I'd seen you use the mirror to cut her. But I hadn't. I hadn't seen any of it.'

Derren thought about that a long time. He sipped some tea. 'There's no point carrying guilt around for this long. It gets to the point where you've grown into a different person. And I can't see the wisdom in carting round someone else's regret. I did my time and got out. Even if I didn't kill her, I deserved some sort of punishment.'

Devereaux finished his tea. He tapped ash in his mug. 'I've lost sleep over it for a long time. And I didn't want to die without confessing or apologising for it.'

'Can't see you've got anything to apologise for. But I guess that's just a tick in your favour, if you can be that critical of yourself. I don't know. Any case, I thought you were a good little kid, and I still do. A good person, I mean. I don't hold anything against you.'

Devereaux looked away, working carefully on his cigarette. Small drag after small drag. The smoke in cyclic eddied plumes.

'You want to stay for lunch?'

'I can't. I'm sorry.'

'Work?'

Devereaux nodded. They sat there in almost comfortable quiet.

'Will you come to my funeral?'

He turned to him and thought about it. This man he'd feared. This man he'd hated. The long years of wishing to face him eye to eye and speak his mind. He said, 'Yes, of course.'

He drove up to Duvall's place. A short trip beneath searing heat. The sad contrast of grim errands in balmy climes. He turned in off the street and rolled through the low-rise apartment complex towards Duvall's unit. Two kids on bikes cut gentle swerves in his slow wake.

He stopped nose-in to the door and got out. The unit sheer and narrow before him, neighboured wall to wall on either side. He used the key and let himself in. The air all hot and languid as he entered. The barren living room, with its single lamp. No man is an island? Get a load of this.

He checked the spare bedroom. The file work was gone: it had arrived at CIB that Monday. Pages of witness testimony, reams of typed case research. Devereaux had spread it all on the floor in his cubicle. His desk couldn't accommodate the spread. The collected paperwork exceeded his own case notes by a factor of two. It was extensive. It looked meticulous. It looked like unbridled obsession.

He'd run a background check. Duvall was ex-police. He'd signed up in 'eighty-one, resigned in 'ninety-seven. Unmarried, no dependants. His parents were dead. He had no criminal record. Ministry of Justice had him on file as a licensed private investigator. Devereaux checked out his finances. He'd had no substantial income for the past eighteen months. He'd cashed a few lightweight cheques the previous year. He'd re-mortgaged a property in March. The loan seemed to have kept him above the breadline. But nobody had made any payments to him since October. Meaning he hadn't been chasing robbery leads at the request of a client. He'd delved on his own volition. For some reason he'd felt he had to.

Devereaux toured the flat. Boxes of clothes still remained, cartons of canned food. The walls were bare. There were no shelves. There was no phone. It wasn't home. It was man-sized storage at best. He tried to conceive of the focus it would take to live in such a manner. The devotion and the loneliness. It read like self-enforced penance. It had a vibe to it that seemed guilt-driven: maybe he'd wanted to negate shitty karma. He'd probably succeeded: getting killed had to count for something. Murder must have cleared his debt, wholesale.

He walked across the living room and opened the door to the small deck. The main road lay behind a shelter belt of trees. He stood there with his back to the rail and smoked a cigarette. The room looked back at him, expressionless. This strange and empty testament to a strange and failed aim. He hoped his own home would never trigger that same thought to somebody else.

Noise from adjoining units reached him weakly. He looked in at the barren room with its single lamp and thought: How does a man appoint the sole function of his life?

He called her that night.

She was in a good mood. She said she was glad he'd rung. He asked her if she'd like dinner. She declined, politely. She said maybe Saturday.

But he was happy. He still had her. She was not yet lost.

He called Carl Grayson and got no answer. He'd had no

answer from him for two weeks. He was less confident he could win him over.

He ate by himself in the living room. Plate on his knees, The Doors on the stereo. McCarthy's funeral had been the previous week. Devereaux attended. He didn't really have a choice: his absence would have been obvious. Non-attendance would have fuelled conspiracy. But it was a way overblown affair: friends, relatives, colleagues in full blue regalia, all in one overwhelming hit. Lloyd Bowen pulled him aside afterwards. Five words only: 'You're off the hook, sergeant.' He'd gone home and found mail waiting patiently: written confirmation of Bowen's curt message, beneath an official police letterhead. A second letter from Thomas Rhys, declaring that the Independent Police Conduct Authority would not be bringing charges. He'd returned the letters to their envelopes once he'd read them and put them on the kitchen table. They were still there: tangible evidence he was in the right. Certainly, the thought was worth keeping.

The CD finished, but he didn't replace it. He sat there in the dark a long time. When he slept he dreamed he walked a moonlit street with a parade of innocent dead.